T0209073

Broken Eagle

The Adventures of Germanus the Gaul

VOLUME 1

Sacred Blood of Prythain:
Struggling for Britannia and the Roman Empire

David Baker

authorHOUSE

AuthorHouse™ UK
1663 Liberty Drive
Bloomington, IN 47403 USA
www.authorhouse.co.uk
Phone: UK TFN: 0800 0148641 (Toll Free inside the UK)
UK Local: (02) 0369 56322 (+44 20 3695 6322 from outside the UK)

This is a work of fiction. All of the characters, names, incidents, organizations, and dialogue in this novel are either the products of the author's imagination or are used fictitiously.

Published by AuthorHouse 11/04/2021

ISBN: 978-1-6655-9423-3 (sc)
ISBN: 978-1-6655-9424-0 (hc)
ISBN: 978-1-6655-9422-6 (e)

Print information available on the last page.

This book is printed on acid-free paper.

CONTENTS

Dramatis Personae..ix

Main latin terms used xi

Chapter 1   Germanus and Lupus leave for Roma.........................1

Chapter 2   Germanus and Lupus have an audience with
             the Pontifex Maximus..6

Chapter 3   A broken home and a broken man 16

Chapter 4   A queen with ginger hair appears............................27

Chapter 5   Germanus and Aureliana fight to win; Lupus
             becomes a man 36

Chapter 6   Iacta alea est: Germanus consults his oracle 46

Chapter 7   Germanus, Lupus and Aureliana sail across the
             channel...52

Chapter 8   Germanus wins an important game; then on to
             Viroconium where the intrigues begin 56

Chapter 9   A spy's identity is revealed; Germanus meets
             his new high command; Severianus considers
             his options 63

Chapter 10   Lupus rages, Coelestinus is perplexed,
             Germanus baptises..72

Chapter 11   Aureliana communes; a Saxon arrives;
             Germanus falls from grace 81

Chapter 12   Germanus travels to Londinium; Ambrosius
              knows his enemy; the Vortigern plots and plans........87
Chapter 13   An ally is captured; a rescue mission is launched.......99
Chapter 14   Drustans is unchained; Memor saves the day;
              Germanus fights on 106
Chapter 15   Germanus lives; the Vortigern holds a triumph 116
Chapter 16   Germanus brings forth a new Patricius and
              gains an ally.......................................123
Chapter 17   Newborn, new bond, new sign...........................133
Chapter 18   Severianus waits; Germanus deals 141
Chapter 19   Aureliana seduces; Lupus is lost 148
Chapter 20   Lupus is saved; Coelestinus shares a secret...........154
Chapter 21   Lupus restored; Severianus appeased; Visinius
              silenced 161
Chapter 22   Barita reports back.................................. 171
Chapter 23   Germanus learns of Eustachia and appoints a
              chaplain 174
Chapter 24   Coelestinus finds secret papers; Germanus sees
              a ghost; Severianus receives a letter.................182
Chapter 25   Germanus gains a daughter.............................188
Chapter 26   Viroconium is attacked; Severianus watches
              and waits 191
Chapter 27   Germanus conquers in that sign........................ 200
Chapter 28   Severianus gloats; Germanus triumphs, then falls ...203
Chapter 29   Severianus advances; Germanus dreams;
              Ambrosius triumphs 207
Chapter 30   Coelestinus thinks quickly; Germanus
              investigates; Severianus arrives 210
Chapter 31   The Vortigern's plan; Germanus and Aureliana
              are one, for now 213
Chapter 32   Agricola plans revenge; Lupus greets his destiny......217

Chapter 33	Nulla dies sine linea: Coelestinus resolves to keep going	222
Chapter 34	Germanus and the Vortigern make far-reaching decisions	225
Chapter 35	Two bishops consider their options	229
Chapter 36	The march to Londinium begins; the Vortigern counterattacks	232
Chapter 37	Memor and Coelestinus reflect on the battle to come	236
Chapter 38	Hengest ponders; Germanus dreams	240
Chapter 39	The troops advance; the strategy is formed; Lupus takes sides	244
Chapter 40	Drustans is fearful	248
Chapter 41	The battle ebbs and flows; dream turns into nightmare	250
Chapter 42	Two enemies assess their positions; Germanus receives an invitation	255
Chapter 43	Memor pleads in vain; Germanus and Agricola meet	260
Chapter 44	Memor, Coelestinus, Germanus, and Drustans become unlikely partners	265
Chapter 45	Nil desperandum: all but one live to fight another day	269
Chapter 46	Coelestinus has an unwelcome guest; a visitor to Britannia arrives	273
Chapter 47	Constantius says a last goodbye; Aetius waits for his host	278
Chapter 48	Germanus and Coelestinus wonder if anyone can be trusted	283
Chapter 49	Lupus and the Vortigern: two minds made up	287
Chapter 50	Old rivalries surface as the battle for Britannia begins	291

Chapter 51   Lupus is in trouble; Aetius must decide; a
              traitor is outed 294
Chapter 52   Constantius meets his fate; new alliances are
              forged; Lupus promises 299
Chapter 53   Renewal on every front 303
Chapter 54   All roads lead to Verulamium 306
Chapter 55   Battle lines are drawn; Lupus is shocked; Aetius
              and Severianus ally 309
Chapter 56   The fight to end all fights, for two men at least.......313
Chapter 57   Elafius makes a surprise discovery...........................316
Chapter 58   One man's fight ends; another's begins...................319
Chapter 59   Comrades reunited: but can anyone be trusted? 322
Chapter 60   Albanus is the goal; Lupus descends into oblivion...326
Chapter 61   Surprises all round 329
Chapter 62   The Vortigern's final attack is launched 332
Chapter 63   A wanderer returns 336
Chapter 64   A disappearance and an appearance 339

DRAMATIS PERSONAE

Aedesia: a slave of the Vortigern

Aello: Patricius's dog

Aenor: guard at the pope's mansion in Rome

Aetius: General and sometime Leader of the Western Imperial Army

Agricola: head of the British army; senior member of the Vortigern's High council and his *magister militum*

Albanus: reputedly the first British Christian martyr; a possible name for an ancient British cult, adopted and adapted by later Christian missionaries and others

Amator: late Bishop of Armorica

Ambrosius: Aureliana's younger brother and husband

Augustus: former *equite*; a spy for Germanus in Severianus's congregation at Eboracum and elsewhere

Aureliana: Queen of the West Britons; sister of Ambrosius and Aurelianus

Aurelianus: (deceased) King of the West Britons; brother of Ambrosius and Aurelianus

Barita: an orphan girl

Boudicca: erstwhile Queen of the Iceni

Coelestinus: *Pontifex Maximus* (pope)

Constantius: *rationalis* (high-ranking fiscal officer); the Vortigern's treasurer

Drustans: Aureliana's *magister militum*

Elafius: a young Christian priest in Viroconium; Restitutus, his father, converted Eustachia, wife of Germanus, to Christianity

Eustachia: wife of Germanus; mother to Patricius and adopted mother to Lupus

Ferox: one of the Pontifex's servants

Galla Placidia: Dowager Empress; mother of Placidus Valentinianus

Germanus: Governor of Armorica; Archbishop of Britannia; former high-ranking General in the Imperial Army

Hengest: King of the *Saxoni*

Litorius: General Aetius's second-in-command

Lucius: a servant of Germanus and a former member of a group of *bagaudae*

Lupus: Germanus's adopted son

Memor: *haruspex* (a soothsayer); Segovax's father

Nectovilius: one of Aureliana's agents, based in Londinium

Nigra: wife of Visinius, leader of a small Christian community

Nonus: a servant of Germanus and a former member of a group of *bagaudae*

Oeric: Hengest's son

Palladius: priest, the pope's personal private secretary (and son)

Patricius: Germanus's biological son

Pelagius: Christian high priest (heretic) in Britannia; senior member of the Vortigern's High council

Placidus Valentinianus: Emperor in the West; a minor

Restitutus: priest; father of Elafius

Samianta: one of Germanus's servants

Segovax: Germanus's estate manager

Severianus: Bishop of Eboracum; ruler of the North and Deputy Leader of Britannia; Agricola's father

Sevira: daughter of the rebel/usurper Emperor Magnus Maximus

Sulpicia: wife of Constantius

Titus: one of Aureliana's agents, based in Londinium

Visinius: leader of a small Christian community near Lindum

Vortigern: ruler of Britannia

MAIN LATIN TERMS USED

accubitus – couch

amphora, amphorae – container, containers, typically used for storing and transporting commodities such as olive oil and wine

ampulla – small vessel, usually made of glass

ancula – maid

arca – chest

archiepiscopus - archbishop

auxilia - auxiliary

bagauda, bagaudae – robber(s)

ballista, ballistae – bolt thrower(s)

balteus - belt

barbarus, barbari – barbarian(s)

barritus – war cry

basilica – hall or church

bellator - warrior

birrus Britannicus – hood of a cloak

bucellarii – escort troops used by high-ranking military personnel

calix – drinking vessel

caminus - furnace

cardo – north/south street

carnifex - butcher

carruca - cart

castrum - camp

celeres - bodyguards

cenula – street urchin

cistula – small chest

clerici - clergy

clibanarii – heavily-armed cavalry

cohors equitata – a standard Roman cohort, typically of 480 soldiers

colonia - colony

consilium - advice

contubernium, contubernia – squad(s) of soldiers sharing a single tent

cornu - horn

cubiculum - bedroom

cultellus - knife

cunnus - cunt

cupona – lodging house

curiosi - spies

dapis - feast

decumanus – east/west street

dictator - dictator

druida - druids

duritiam

dux - duke, leader

equite, equites – cavalryman/men

evocatus, evocati – re-enlisted soldier(s)

exploratorem – explorer, spy

ferrarius - blacksmith

fiducia - trust

focale - scarf

foculus/foculi – brazier(s)

focus - hearth

foederatus, foederati – ally/ies, confederate(s)

follis - fool

foris - gate

galea - helmet

gladius, gladii – sword(s)

harena - arena

haruspex - soothsayer

horreum – grain store

imperator - emperor

imperatrix - empress

insomnium - insomnia

instans - instantly

iudices - gentlemen

jentaculum - breakfast

juscellum - soup

lararium – house shrine

lectulo - eating couch

lectus – bed, couch

limitanei – frontier soldiers

lodix - blanket

lorica - body armour

macellum - slaughterhouse

magister militum – master of the soldiers, a Roman equivalent of 'field marshal'

manuballista, manuballistae – crossbow(s)

Mare Britannicum – English Channel

Mare Hibernicum – Irish Sea

mensa – table

miles, milites – soldier(s)

momentum – importance

mulier - woman

munifex – serviceman, foot soldier

navicularius – ship owner

necessaries - necessary

numerus, numeri – infantry unit(s)

nuntius – messenger

nutrix - nurse

optio – executive officer

orba - orphan

pax Romana - Roman peace

pedes, pedites – infantryman/men

pes - foot

Picti – Picts

pilum - javelin

poculum, poculi – drinking cup(s)

pontifex maximus – greatest priest

portitor - boatman

praetorium – general's quarters

processio – procession

proditor - traitor

pugio - dagger

rationalis - treasure

rex - king

Rhenus - Rhine

Romanitas – Roman-ness

rostra – speaker's podium

rustici - peasants

sacculus - sack

sacramentum militare – oath of loyalty

Saxoni - Saxons

Scotti - Gaels

scriba - scribe

scrinium – chest for books

scutum - shield

secundae mensae - dessert

sella - saddle

senex – old man

senex mulier – old woman

serva – servant girl
stabulatio - stable
stilus – writing implement
stola – female equivalent of a toga
stratum – bed cover, blanket
tablinum - study
Tamesis - Thames
templum - temple
testudines – shelters formed from solders' shields
tisana vel sucus – barley soup
tribunus – tribune – high Roman rank
triumphus - triumph
tuba - trumpet
tympana - drums
urgens - urgent
uricia - urchin
velamentum - covering or curtain
vestium – garment or robe
vexillum - unit
vicus – ditch defences
vinariam - vineyard

ROMAN BRITANNIA about 410

■ **Roman army camps**   *Iceni* **Native Briton tribes**

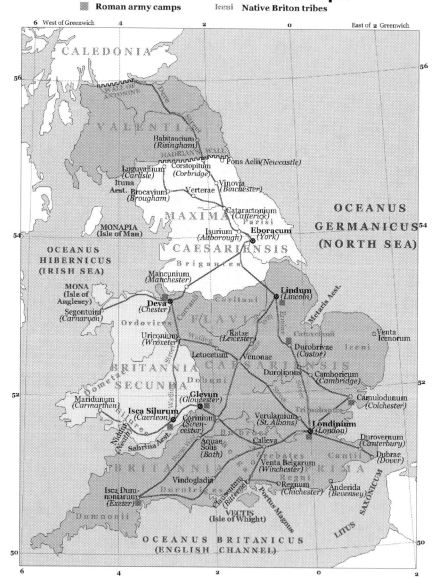

West of Greenwich 6   4   2   0   East of 2 Greenwich

CALEDONIA

WALL OF ANTONINE

VALENTIA

Habitancium
(Risingham)

HADRIAN'S WALL

Luguvallium
(Carlisle)   Corstopitum
(Corbridge)   Pons Aelii (Newcastle)
Ituna
Aest. Brocavium   Vinovia
(Brougham)   Verterae   (Binchester)

MONAPIA
(Isle of Man)   Isurium   Cataractonium
(Altborough)   (Catterick)
MAXIMA   Parisi
Eboracum
(York)

OCEANUS
GERMANICUS

(NORTH SEA)

CAESARIENSIS

OCEANUS
HIBERNICUS
(IRISH SEA)   Brigantes

MONA
(Isle of
Anglesey)   Mancunium
(Manchester)

Segontium
(Carnarvon)   Deva   Lindum
(Chester)   (Lincoln)

Ordovices   FLAVIA

Uriconium   Ratae   Venta
(Wroxeter)   (Leicester)   Icenorum

Letocetum   Venonae   Durobrivae
(Castor)   Iceni

CAESARIENSIS

Durolipons   Camboricum
(Cambridge)

BRITANNIA
SECUNDA   Dobuni   Trinobantes   Camulodunum
(Colchester)
Maridunum   Glevun
(Carmarthen)   (Gloucester)

Isca Silurum   Corinium   Verulamium   Londinium
(Caerleon)   (Siren-   (St. Albans)   (London)
cester)   Durovernum
Aquae   (Canterbury)
Solis   Calleva
(Bath)   Dubrae
BRITANNIA   Venta Belgarum   (Dover)
(Winchester)
Regni
Vindogladia   Regnum   Anderida
Portus Magnus (Chichester)   (Bevensey)
Isca Dum-   Clausentum
noniarum   Bitterne
(Exeter)
VECTIS
Dumnonii   (Isle of Wight)

OCEANUS BRITANNICUS
(ENGLISH CHANNEL)

CHAPTER 1

Germanus and Lupus leave for Roma

Germanus stopped his horse suddenly, dismounted and climbed to the top of a small hill. Lupus saw the glint in his master's eyes as he looked down on two *bagaudae*, who spoke in broken Latin; one wore a legionary's sword and buckler; the other was examining his spoils, the coins, plate, and various kinds of silver goods already hacked into pieces for ease of trade. A fire burned in their makeshift camp.

Divesting himself of his cloak, Germanus crouched down and tiptoed towards the robbers, circling round by the blind side of their camp. Lupus could only look on; there was no sound or movement. Then, as if from nowhere, Germanus sprang out, shouting a loud, fearful *barritus,* and engaged them. Surprise gave him the upper hand and he drew first blood. The one with the legionary's weapon was the more threatening of the two, as if he had some basic training in one-to-one combat, but Germanus was too cunning for him; the other fool just stood there gawping. The 'fighter' lunged too far and Germanus disarmed him with a combination of sword and arm-hold.

The *bagaudae* stood motionless as Lupus tied them up to a nearby tree, and Germanus relieved them of their booty. They were only too willing to talk: the fighter was a deserter from the Roman Army; his younger brother told of the death of the rest of their family at the hands of some *barbari.*

'Is this what you have come to? Stealing from your own?'

'What other choice do we have, my Lord?' The two thieves spoke in tandem.

'There is always a better choice.'

Germanus turned away from his pathetic prisoners, walked over to Lupus, raised his eyebrow, and waited for a response. Having received one, he turned back to the *bagaudae,* nodded slowly, and spoke to them.

'You are working for me now. Step out of line once – just once – and you are dead. Understood?'

⁂　　⁂　　⁂

The Vortigern looked across the sea. Wisps of snow drained across the weak January sky. He closed the window, drew a purple fur-trimmed cloak around his upper body and returned to the throne at the head of the council table. He surveyed the men seated around him and then motioned a servant to add coals to the brazier. The fire quickly devoured the black rocks, spitting and snarling. Two dogs yelped awake as sparks flew across the room and hit their rumps.

The door to the chamber opened and in strode a tall man in full military uniform. He gave his sword to one of the servants standing at the entrance, walked into the middle of the room, bowed his head curtly, and straightened himself up before speaking.

'Germanus is dead, my lord.'

The Vortigern looked the arrival up and down. Agricola was wet from the rain that had pursued his party all the way back from Gallia to Dubris. He took off his helmet and laid it on the edge of the round table where sat the men who governed Britannia.

The Vortigern shivered but remained silent. He motioned for more coals on the foculus; the servant threw fuel onto the fire. The floorboards creaked as Agricola shifted his weight from one leg to the other, waiting for his master to react.

'You fool! I told you to recruit him to our cause, not murder him.' The Vortigern stood up and threw off his cloak. His tall figure was clad all in black, a decorated belt tied tightly around his thin waist. His gold chain of office gleamed in the firelight.

'He was already dead when we arrived. Someone had beaten us to it.' Agricola clenched his fists together and sighed, shaking his head gently.

'What do you mean someone had beaten you to it?' The Vortigern looked up at Agricola, now more sympathetic to his magister militum.

'I mean that Germanus's head had been severed from his body and placed on a pilum in the middle of the central courtyard at the general's villa. The whole place had been ravaged. You could see the smoke for miles around. We were at least a day too late.'

'How do you know that it was the general's head, Agricola?'

It was Pelagius, the high priest. He got up from his place to the left of the Vortigern's throne, beyond the light of the fire. He rose to his full height as he crossed the room and went so close to Agricola that the two men were breathing in each other's face. Agricola tolerated the heavily ringed hand on his shoulder for a few seconds, then pushed it away in disgust.

'Because one of the few survivors said so, and the headdress and hair were clearly those of a high-born man', Agricola replied, turned away from Pelagius and looked back at the Vortigern in the corner of the room. The high priest had now moved across to the fire and was playing with the golden chain around his neck, fingering the large cross that hung from it.

'How can you be so sure that this "survivor" tells the truth?' continued Pelagius.

'I don't answer to you', Agricola replied. 'I take orders from the Vortigern, or father my Bishop Severianus as his second-in-command.

You are a disgrace to the Roman way, Pelagius, with your rings and your crosses and your new Mithras.'

'You will answer to me as Bishop Pelagius one day, Agricola, and you will believe my words, either by your will or my force, so take care.'

'Be that as it may, Pelagius, but we are where we are now, and as far as I am concerned you are but a mere priest, and even worse a Christian one.'

'Just like Severianus', Pelagius growled.

'My father may be a cross worshipper, for as long as it suits him, but I care not for all this theology, even though I am supposed to be his son.' Agricola shook his head.

'Bishop Severianus may be a Christian, but he is the wrong kind, Agricola. I preach the true faith.' Pelagius made the sign of the cross as he spoke.

Agricola snorted. 'You and your bloody faith. Give me the old gods any day.'

'Agricola, Pelagius – enough. Sit down, the both of you. You are supposed to be senior members of the high council. Try to act as if you are. The Vortigern cares not for talk of religion. And neither do I.' It was Constantius, the Vortigern's *rationalis*, with his softly spoken voice and educated accent. His finely woven striped linen tunic was immaculately laundered. The other members of the high council had remained silent until now, mainly because they were waiting to judge the Vortigern's mood before daring to express an opinion, nodded and grunted in agreement. One even knocked his clenched fist on the table in approval.

The Vortigern spat into the *foculus*, as if to rid himself of a bad taste.

'I simply cannot believe that Germanus would have given in so easily. When I knew him, he would have killed all his attackers single handed, with no need of an army. There must be some other explanation.'

The Vortigern looked across to Agricola, now seated at his place at the high council.

'And what of Germanus's wife and child?' he queried.

Agricola hesitated, then looked at the Vortigern. 'The woman was raped and killed.'

'Her name was Eustachia,' interjected the Vortigern. 'The most beautiful woman in all Gallia, allegedly.'

Pelagius looked at Agricola quizzically. Agricola responded by shaking his head. Constantius cleared his throat, trying to move the conversation forward so as not to dwell on the unasked question about the Vortigern's knowledge of Germanus and his family.

'There was no sign of any children. Who were we looking for? Boy, girl, both?' Agricola asked.

'Boy,' the Vortigern replied, stroking his chin. He nodded to the servant to put food on the table and offer it first to Agricola. 'There was only one son, as I recall. Strange that there was no sign of any child.'

'Does it matter that Germanus is dead, my lord? Why was he so important to you?'

'Yes. Pelagius, it does. He would have been the ideal person to be my commander-in-chief.'

'I thought I was in charge!' Agricola stood up, knocking his food and drink off the table.

'Calm yourself Agricola. You are. But I need someone to take command of the *joint* forces. When Hengest and his troops arrive, our men will be outnumbered three to one. Only someone like Germanus could command the respect of the Angles and the Saxons and the Jutes as well as my own forces. You have much prowess Agricola, and you will be in charge one day, but I needed Germanus!'

CHAPTER 2

Germanus and Lupus have an audience with the Pontifex Maximus

'I thought never to be in Roma again, Lupus. And not in these sad times. Look at this place. I remember how it used to be. You are too young to know of the eternal city in its glory days.'

Germanus halted his horse and leant forward to reward the stallion with a pat.

'Do you wish to stop here, master?'

'No Lupus, but I want our two *bagaudae* to go ahead and find out where the Pontifex's house is'.

The two *bagaudae* had made good servants, Germanus decided, looking at them as they disappeared towards the city gates in search of the pope's palace. Lucius was obviously the brighter of the two and proposed that, once the address had been located, he would send his younger brother Nonus back to lead Germanus and Lupus through the city.

Germanus looked across at Lupus and smiled. The young man had seen so little of the world. But he had welcomed his adopted son's companionship on the journey from Antissiodorum to Rome. Germanus had been impressed by how well Lupus had stood up to the hardships of travel across the disintegrating empire. He thought back to the day when Eustachia and he had first met Lupus, had taken him in as their own, had made him a full part of their family.

'I know that it is a diminished city master; even I who have never visited can see that.' Lupus said.

'The only time that I was in Roma before today was as a victor. Our great Emperor Theodosius had brought the empire back together, but only too briefly. Much has happened to me and our country since then. We are overrun with *barbari*: men who can barely write their name; who live in squalor and filth with their hordes of uncouth followers. These are difficult times, Lupus.' Germanus looked wistfully ahead at the city walls, now in serious disrepair.

Lupus nodded. He thought how difficult it was to call Germanus 'father', even though he was now finally and formally adopted. He remembered the day two years before. Germanus had been his real father's former army commander, and the obvious choice to look after Lupus after he had become an orphan, thanks to the barbarian attacks in Dacia. Germanus had willingly agreed to look after Lupus as a second son alongside Patricius, his own flesh and blood.

Lupus looked across Germanus. His master and father was remarkably short for a soldier and completely bald, apart from a little white hair around the sides of his head. He was like a small bull, with muscular arms and legs and a particular way of standing, as if to say 'come on, try and get the better of me, but I warn you, you will fail, for I am tougher than any other.'

Now, as Germanus and Lupus entered the city walls of Rome, followed by Lucius and Nonus, they were greeted by beggars: men, women, children: thin, diseased, blind. They wanted food, not money; coins were worthless in a world where trade and commerce were increasingly things of the past, Germanus observed. They came across many narrow buildings with external colonnades that had accommodated shops, offices, and other amenities. Most of the fronts were boarded up; a few places were still selling basic goods, but there was no sign of the fine outlets where one could buy clothes or silver ware that provincial visitors would once have frequented. Some taverns remained open for business, and as the two riders passed, the occupants took time out from their drinking to stare and wonder. Many of the rich houses were empty; those that were occupied were heavily guarded by the retinues of the lord who owned them. Lupus's horse stumbled on the ill-repaired street pavement. Germanus pointed out where some of the famous fountains had been as they approached the city centre; they were now dry because of damage to the aqueducts by the waves of invaders.

Germanus dismounted at the gates of the pontifical mansion. Lupus did likewise. Both men looked up to where heavily armed guards occupied the watchtowers. Lucius and Nonus held the horses.

'Who goes there?' one of the soldiers shouted, pointing a spear over the battlements.

'Germanus Patricius Magnus, governor of Armorica.'

'And his aide, Lupus, here to see the Pontifex.'

'Who says so?' The soldier up above spat out his *mastiha*. Lupus lurched back to avoid it landing on his head.

'His holiness says so, insolent *babulus*! Call yourself a *miles*? Stand to attention and speak to me as you should to a general in the Imperial Army. Go on, do it!' Germanus took a scroll from his saddle pocket, opened it and waved it up at the watchtower.

'Yes sir. Sorry sir! I will be down right away sir.'

The guard wiped his mouth nervously, brushed down his uniform, stood to attention then scuttled off, while his compatriots stood to attention, eyes straight ahead, heads up, not wishing to see General Germanus at his angriest.

The horses pawed at the cobbles in front of the gatehouse, impatient to be led in, unsaddled, fed, and watered. One of the mounts dolloped where it stood, as if to let its irritation at being kept waiting known. Sounds of scuttling could be heard behind the thick wooden gates. A lock turned, a bolt slid, then an armoured head peeped out.

'Welcome sir, sorry sir, can't be too careful these days. Pontifex's orders. I have to see your pass sir, sorry sir.'

'You'll be careful when you are in my service, if I ever see fit to have you under my command.' Germanus barked. Lupus shuddered. Even now he could not relax in his master's presence. But that was how it should be, he thought. You didn't get to be a general, a governor and master of all Armorica by being nice to people.

'What is your name, soldier?'

'My name? Er, my name is, is, er… Aenor, sir.'

'See Lupus, not even a Roman. He is a German, I suppose, judging by the name. Are you German? Are there no real men to guard the palace?'

'Yes, I am sir, but very loyal to Roma sir, I swear it. Sorry sir. Come this way sir.' Aenor took the two horses and led them through the portal. As Germanus and Lupus walked into the courtyard that lay beyond, they were greeted by a young man in white robes and long blonde hair.

'Have we reached Heaven Lupus? Or have the angels come to earth already?' Germanus laughed.

'I do not know, master; this is not what I expected to find, but then I am no Christian. Give me the old gods anytime.' Lupus thought about asking Germanus which gods he sacrificed to, but, seeing the grimace on his master's face, decided against it. The angel came up to Germanus and Lupus and bowed its head.

'Greetings. You must be Germanus and Lupus. I am Palladius, your brother in Christ and the Pontifex's personal private secretary.'

Germanus declined the angel's proffered hand, raising a scornful eyebrow instead; Lupus decided to cover the secretary's embarrassment and shake the limp wrist.

'Now take us to your pope so that I can hear what business he has for me; then we shall be on our way home.' Germanus took off his helmet, then his gloves, which he threw inside the headgear, before handing it all to Palladius. Lupus followed suit, but the angel dropped the headdress, obviously too heavy for him, so he handed everything to Aenor. Germanus and Lupus followed the private secretary as he guided them through another portal. Lucius and Nonus took the horses away for stabling.

Inside was the largest courtyard that even the well-travelled Germanus had ever seen. It stretched what must have been a quarter of a mile to the far side. Majestic pillars held up the slated roof all the way around, while in the centre were well-tended gardens whose centrepiece was an ornate fountain with three levels; water cascaded from one to the other and then out into a large pond. Two priests were sitting on a stone bench by the side of the water; a further three people tended the gardens.

Palladius led the two visitors around the side of the courtyard and into a large reception room. At the entrance were rich drapes, in front of which stood two guards. Along the two side walls were statues and busts; the two visitors initially took them to be of former emperors, but then Germanus pointed out that one was of Jupiter, another of Mars, and a third, surprisingly, of Venus. Palladius motioned Germanus and Lupus to move forward halfway into the room, where they were told to stop and wait until further notice. At the far end, the floor was raised in a kind of dais, at the right-hand side of which were three steps that led up to a large seat painted in gold and covered with rich cloth. Above it was a large canopy, also made of the same cloth, with the arms of St Peter in the middle of the front part. On either side of the dais stood a guard, holding a long staff; both were armed with a *gladius* at their belt. In one corner of the reception hall was a long table, at which sat a scribe poised to note down any discussions that might take place. In the other was a pair of doors. Germanus wondered if this was the place where emperors once sat to receive member of the senate and high-ranking officials on state business.

'See how the poor Christian leaders live, eh, Lupus?'

Germanus nudged Lupus playfully as the double doors opened.

First came more guards, dressed in the same uniform as all the other military types in the building. Then came two priests, dressed in floor-length cloaks with long hoods that went down their backs almost to their waists. Finally, the *Pontifex Maximus* appeared. The rings were those of a nobleman; the one on the left index finger was large and held a precious jewel that glinted as he clasped the large pectoral cross. His shoes were red, with gold lining. Between the top of his ankles and the bottom of the robes, the legs were shrivelled brown. His face was wizened and worn: the nose was thin, narrowing to a point so sharp at the end you could have cut bread with it. There was hardly enough skin left to stretch over the bone and muscle. Wisps of white hair curled down from underneath the front of the Pontifex's crown.

'I had not expected him to be so, well, so old', Lupus whispered.

'His eyes aren't old.' Germanus motioned Lupus to look at the pope's face.

Coelestinus smiled.

'Welcome, Germanus Patricius Magnus. And who is your assistant?'

'Lupus. I am Lupus, the General's aide, your Majesty.'

The pope laughed. 'Do be seated gentlemen. My power is not of this world, Lupus, or at least, it is not supposed to be. You may call me "your holiness".'

'It is as much of this world as mine is as governor of Armorica.' Germanus looked cynically at Lupus as he spoke.

'Ah yes, Germanus the Pagan. Unlike your wife; a staunch follower of the one true faith. What was her name? My memory is not what it was. I remember now: Eustachia!'

'How do you know my wife's name?'

'She is a believer. One of my flock. I know all about her. And you for that matter.'

Germanus stood up, hand on the hilt of his *gladius*.

'I am an old man, Germanus. My 75 years cannot deal with sudden movement.' The pope recoiled.

'You know nothing of me, priest. How dare you mention my wife! I want nothing of you and your Christ. I have not come here to be preached at. Your message told me of a mission to save Rome, not your pathetic religion.'

The Pontifex motioned Germanus to return to his seat. Lupus guided him away from Coelestinus before the old man came to any harm.

'Thank you, Lupus. I can see that your master is quite a handful. But then, I need a man like you, Germanus.'

'For what?' Germanus looked keenly at the Pontifex.

'For the most important mission of your life, Germanus.'

'Not to preach your infernal gospel, please.' Germanus straightened up on his couch. His hand went again to his *gladius*.

'Something far more important than that', the Pontifex snorted. 'The future of Rome and the Empire will depend on you.'

Coelestinus stood up shakily from his throne, took his walking stick in his hand and stepped down from the podium. He limped and wheezed over to Germanus's couch, sat down next to him, and took the general's right hand in his.

'I want you to become Archbishop of Britannia.'

Germanus burst out laughing in response.

'What are you asking me to do? Give up everything I believe in?'

'Quite the contrary, Germanus. You are a loyal Roman citizen. You have fought to keep Gallia in the empire against mounting odds. But I need you to repel a far bigger threat to our future.'

'*Our* future, Coelestinus?'

'No church, no empire, Germanus.'

'Did the emperor put you up to this, your grace?'

'That pimply youth? You must be joking. No – but his mother and I keep in close contact.' Coelestinus's eyes glinted as he spoke.

'The fair Galla Placidia. I remember her well.'

'You know her, master?' Lupus was surprised to learn of Germanus's friendship with the dowager empress.

Germanus smiled, remaining silent.

'Do I have to worship this Jesus Christ?' Germanus looked at his hands as he asked the Pontifex.

'I don't care what you do Germanus. I want you to save the Empire.'

'You keep saying, your grace. But what am I saving it from?'

'Say you will be Archbishop of Britannia, Germanus, and I will tell you.'

'This is ludicrous!' Germanus got up and began to walk to the exit.

'Come back! Listen to me! In due course, when the time is right, if you succeed in this mission, a mission that only you can do, you will be pope **and** emperor. Why shouldn't God's general be an earthly one too? Think of it, the empire at your command, backed by all the resources of my church. There are people out there who will willingly go to their deaths if I, or you, tell them to. I can give you 1,000, 10,000, 100,000 or even more if you like. They would all go to their death for the cross, for Jesus, for their hope of eternity. They are all over the empire, including Britannia.'

Germanus rose and turned his back on the pope. He looked at the door but did not move. The two guards barring his exit would be no match for him, even with their spears crossed to stop anyone from leaving. He looked at Lupus as if asking for his assistant's advice. Lupus merely shrugged his shoulders. Germanus exhaled a sigh.

'You do realise, "your holiness", that this is not the first time that I have been asked to take holy orders?'

Coelestinus looked quizzically at Germanus.

'No, I did not know. When? Who asked you?'

'Ten years ago. Bishop Amator. He was looking for a successor to govern the church as well as the diocese'

'And what was your response?'

'I thought about it', Germanus laughed. 'It would have given me total authority on my patch: church and state combined in me. But I am a man of honour, as you have already implied, Coelestinus, and I did not feel at the time that I could be ordained, despite attempts to force me to take the tonsure. I had a lot more hair in those days, of course.' Germanus smoothed his right hand over his bald pate, as if to emphasise the fact.

'What happened? I knew nothing of this!' Coelestinus looked around at officials but there was no response.

'Ah well, memories are short these days, and I don't suppose any records were kept of the discussions held at the time. The see was left vacant. I have governed for church as well as state, despite my unbelief. Once a pagan, always a pagan. The Christians left me alone as I did them. I think they felt that a strongman in charge would let them get on with whatever it was that they wanted to get on with; saving souls, I suppose.'

'Ah yes, I had forgotten about dear old Amator. That was before my time. Then you can be Bishop of Armorica as well as Archbishop of Britannia.' The Pontifex smirked.

'This is getting ridiculous, Coelestinus. From Mithras-worshipper to Archbishop of all he surveys in one evening. That truly would be one of your Christian miracles!'

'Well, I intend to appoint you to both roles, at least for now. We can talk later about your ultimate promotion. Can we please get on with it? Time is not on our side!' The *Pontifex Maximus* tapped his fingers.

Germanus looked at the pope and then Lupus. He walked over to the entrance doors, inspected the guards (who remained motionless throughout their top-to-toe kit inspection), looked at the Bacchanalian murals – breasts and buttocks everywhere – then fiddled with his *gladius* as he returned to his seat. He bent forward; his fists were clenched between his legs. Then he put his hands on his thighs to push himself erect, pulled down his tunic and spoke slowly and clearly.

'Very well, but I say yes not because I believe in your ridiculous

Christ but because I am a loyal Roman and I will do what is necessary to protect and preserve the Empire, and I will continue to sacrifice to my gods when, where, and how I please.'

Coelestinus smiled. 'You may please yourself, my Lord Archbishop. Come, let me lay my hands on you. Kneel before me. Then I will brief you on your mission.'

CHAPTER 3

A broken home and a broken man

'Is it done?' the man growled.

'Yes, your grace.'

'No survivors?'

'No. Not one. Well…'

Bishop Severianus looked up from his *scrinium*, put down his pen and narrowed his eyes. He calmly adjusted the wooden cross that stood in front of his writing tablet as he prepared his next words.

'I asked if there were any survivors', Severianus said softly, studying the edge of his desk carefully, tracing his finger along the fine carvings.

The assassins looked at each other and then at their master.

'My Lord; we couldn't find the boy.'

Severianus leaned back in his chair, putting his hands together as if in prayer.

'So young Patricius escaped; or at least his father managed to spirit him away.' The voice rose in volume.

'We killed every youngster we found, female as well as male just in case, but none matched the description that you gave us. We could not see anyone with the trappings of a governor's son. I don't see how they could have known about our attack in advance, even if the men of the estate put up a stout defence.'

Severianus pushed the table forward so hard that it fell over onto the feet of the assassins. They dare not howl in pain. Then he stood up and kicked the chair over too for good measure. He pushed back his sleeves and fidgeted with the snake amulets on both his forearms.

'Even in death I wouldn't trust Germanus. There would be some trick or other up his sleeve. Where is the bloody boy?'

'We could go back and try and find him, your grace.'

'Don't be so stupid.' Severianus sighed. 'No, let us not worry about the boy's whereabouts, for now at least. The deed is done and the Vortigern has lost his commander-in-chief. Let us see whether Agricola can rise to the challenge that will be put before him in consequence.'

※   ※   ※

Having blessed the new Archbishop of Britannia, Coelestinus beckoned an acolyte over and whispered in his ear. The young servant went away.

'I have a present for you. I hope you like it.' Coelestinus smiled at Germanus.

Germanus grimaced, presuming he was going to be given some priestly robes or even a cross. He was already having second thoughts about becoming a Christian, even in name only. When he saw what the acolyte had brought, he laughed loudly.

'I thought you would like it. It is yours to keep. Take care of it.' The Pontifex smiled as he spoke.

Germanus took the staff and held it close so that he could inspect the *aquila* on top. He spent a long time looking at the silver eagle.

'These are yours also', added the Pontifex as a second acolyte entered, carrying ornate gilded robes.

'See Lupus; see what I have been given.' Germanus laughed again. 'These are the robes and insignia of a Roman consul. Perhaps being a bishop will not be so bad after all.'

'I am a man of my word, Germanus. And this is a token of what lies ahead if you succeed in your task. From consul to emperor: think of it.'

The Pontifex told the acolyte to pack the honorific robes and then gesticulated to Germanus and Lupus to follow him into an ante room where the three men could talk privately. A small *foculus* gave out heat and light enough for the group to be comfortable. A servant brought food and drink. Once the man had poured wine for them, he closed the curtain.

'Most people think that the main threat to the Empire in the west is the *barbari*.'

Lupus nodded; Germanus swilled the wine in his cup and looked at the fire, remaining silent.

'Well, there is a far greater threat than the hordes, Germanus. Has it ever occurred to you that these attacks on the Empire might be co-ordinated?'

Germanus laughed, then thought better of his response and having thought more seriously about the proposition, began to frown. 'You mean that some great mastermind is controlling all these different tribes and planning their attacks on the western provinces?'

Coelestinus adjusted himself on his chair. Lupus decided that the Pontifex must have piles.

'Even I can tell that these attacks are not coordinated. The *barbari* are not that clever', Lupus snorted.

'But their master is. These are the new tactics. No need for old-style centuries and cohorts and what have you.' Coelestinus waved his arms vaguely as if searching for the correct military terms. 'He has an unending supply of manpower in these tribes. They want what we have, and this man will give it to them. And if you attack from all sides with these *barbari*, however unskilled they may be, then you put the empire under impossible pressure. And what do you have?'

'Which is what we are seeing now: attacks from all sides.' Germanus began to nod in agreement. 'Who is this evil genius, then?'

'The Vortigern, ruler of Britannia, aided and abetted by his high priest, Pelagius.'

'Vortigern - that is not a Roman name, is it?' Lupus queried.

'It is not a name at all', the pope replied.

'It is a title – high king. I remember the word from when I was last in Britannia; even then they wanted to go native and leave the Empire.' Germanus smiled as he spoke.

'I had not realised you had ever been over there, master.'

'Oh yes, I have a past before you.' Germanus laughed.

'That is one of the reasons why I want the archbishop to go over there now. He knows the place, speaks the language, can deal with this threat better than anyone else that I can think of. But this is no insurrection, no unilateral declaration of independence; this is world domination.' The pope shuffled uneasily on his throne once more before continuing. 'I fear that this Vortigern wishes to take the purple for himself, as so many of those Britons have tried to do before. But whereas his predecessors failed because of the might of the empire, we are much weakened now, despite General Aetius's great skill. I fear that the Vortigern may succeed, simply because of the sheer numbers of his men, even though they are *Saxoni,* and if they team up with their brethren on this side of the Mare Britannicum, then they could overpower us without much difficulty.'

'And who is Pelagius?' Germanus was on the edge of his seat, listening intently to the old man. Lupus smiled at the glint in his master's eyes.

'He used to be one of us, Germanus; a Christian, that is. But he is a heretic. His brand of Christianity is not the way forward.'

Germanus snorted, indifferent to the various branches of theology that had already grown up around this Jesus Christ.

'What does he want the Vortigern to do? What's in it for him?' Lupus asked.

Coelestinus had no time to answer; Germanus answered for him.

'If the Vortigern becomes emperor, then Pelagius will be pope.'

Coelestinus pursed his lips and nodded.

'And who knows what will happen then? It will not be the Roma that you and I know and love, Germanus. It will be an empire in the grip of the *barbari*. Think of it: Angles, Saxons, Jutes and many more, not just at the gates of the eternal city, but running the place. There are also still many of the ruling classes here and in other parts of the empire who are pagan, or who only profess Christianity because it suits their purposes. If things were to change and a pagan party were to gain the upper hand, then it could set us back hundreds of years. A pagan offensive launched from Britannia is my real fear, especially if the pagans and the Pelagians were to combine under this Vortigern. There is much in Pelagius's teaching that would allow many to tolerate paganism alongside Christianity.'

'Is there no part of the British nobility that remains loyal to Rome?' Germanus seemed unconvinced.

'We have men and women loyal to the one true faith in Britannia. But they are hounded and persecuted thanks to Pelagius's religious dominance within the Council. The only member of the Vortigern's High council who has any sympathy for the Catholic Church is Bishop Severianus, ruler of the North and Deputy Leader of Britannia. There is no love lost between Severianus and Pelagius. There was once, as I understood it, but Severianus sees no future in the Pelagian heresy if it means that he himself will not come to power across all Britannia. There is an opportunity to exploit that tension, especially as Agricola, Severianus's son, is Head of the Vortigern's forces.'

'This is all very interesting, Coelestinus, but I have still not been told what my mission is meant to be.' Germanus clapped his hands together.

'Simple: you are to overthrow the Vortigern, foil his barbarian plot, get rid of the Pelagian heresy and bring back Britannia into the empire and the true Christian church. You will be supplied with troops from the imperial army. I have asked Aetius to let you have as many of his men as he can spare. He will not let me down, just as you will not let me down.'

'I know that Aetius will not let me down. We were comrades many years ago.' Germanus paused for a moment, then continued. 'And why should I do all this for your Jesus Christ and his church?'

'You will do it for Rome, and yourself. Think of what it will mean if – when – you succeed, you will be *Pontifex Maximus* and *Imperator*. I guarantee it.'

'Iacta alea est'. Germanus smiled imperceptibly.

'The die is cast indeed.' Coelestinus sat back on his throne, exhausted.

⁂   ⁂   ⁂

Germanus knew something was wrong as soon as he and Lupus, followed by Lucius and Nonus, reached the outskirts of the villa complex. Where one would have expected to see estate workers coming to greet him there was silence: a complete lack of activity. Cows and horses still grazed in the fields, but there was no milking, planting, tilling; nothing, no human activity at all. Lupus was first to see smoke rising from the villa: one of the corner towers belched flame; the grain store was well alight. Germanus now realised what must have happened and kicked his horse into action. Lupus rode quickly after him. Lucius and Nonus, despite their recent past as *bagaudae,* followed more warily.

The horses came to a sharp halt by the first corpse. Germanus slid off his mount and jumped over the body, and another, and a third. Lupus went more gingerly, worried that the general might yet be ambushed by the attackers. By the time that he had joined his master in the centre of the villa, Lupus was aware of the full horror of what had happened. Meanwhile, Lucius and Nonus, having encountered the first mutilated and bloodied corpses, propped each other up as they vomited.

The next group of bodies lay in the entrance to the central courtyard.

It was clear by now that the males of the estate had either been killed as they defended the villa or strung up around the courtyard to suffocate to death after they had surrendered. The women and girls had been rounded up, stripped naked, raped, and then had their throats cut. Amongst all this carnage, Germanus and Lupus did not at first notice the bloodied head of Segovax, the estate manager, stuck on the top of the statue of Venus in the fountain that was the centrepiece of the villa's high-status rooms. The torso had been cut into pieces and draped about the plinth. Lupus burst into tears as he recognised the remains of friends and co-workers. Even the slaves had not deserved to die like this. Germanus came over to comfort him. Then the two of them went to the statue of Venus.

Germanus stroked the bloodied cheek of his estate manager. 'Poor Segovax', Germanus lamented. He remembered how his *optio* and he would carouse the night away: drink, and women, then more drink; all to celebrate their victories. What service they had seen together, especially in Britannia in the good old days! 'He must have put up stout resistance. You can tell that from the wounds on his body. I recognise his hands; hands that saved my life more than once. They must have beheaded him on the spot, Lupus, but not before they had tortured him. But he would not have given anything away; not my Segovax.'

'Why is he wearing your clothes master?'

Germanus bowed his head, and then turned back to Lupus, tears in his eyes.

'Is it not obvious, why he is wearing my clothes? He was pretending to be me.' Germanus smiled, palely. Then a look of horror spread over his face. 'Where are Eustachia and Patricius? We must find them.'

Lupus and Germanus, aided by Lucius and Nonus (now they had regained their composure) searched every room in the main villa and then the farm buildings and estate offices. There was no sign of either wife or son. Then Germanus had an idea: Eustachia would have gone to the little chapel at the far end of the formal gardens. As Lupus and he approached they could see a trail of blood. Entering the building, with its *chi-rho* symbol above the portal, Germanus heard a low moan.

'You came!'

'Eustachia!'

'Over here, my love… And you brought Lupus with you. Such a good boy.'

Lupus lit an oil lamp, then a second. Up against the altar lay the half-naked body of Germanus's wife. The remains of her tunic were covered in blood. Germanus cradled Eustachia in his arms.

'Where is Patricius?' Germanus could hardly contain his despair.

'He is safe. An angel came for him.' Eustachia croaked.

Eustachia fell into sleep.

'Stay with me. Where is Patricius?'

'I told you, an angel took him. He is safe. Now hold me close, I feel cold. That's it, hold me! I wanted to see you, for you to take me in your arms one more time.'

'I know. I will. But who did this to you?' Germanus beckoned Lupus to bring water.

Eustachia sipped then coughed. 'I forgive them. You must forgive them also.'

'But how can I forgive the men who did this to you, to all that we have worked for?'

'Forgive them as Jesus would forgive. And I know how you feel Germanus, my love, but I want you to turn to Christ as well. Please – will you do this for me, my dearest husband?'

'Tell me who they were.' Germanus cradled his wife, moving her gently backwards and forwards as if rocking her to sleep.

'I don't know who they were. There were so many of them. But…' Eustachia lost consciousness again.

Lupus gave her more water, brought the oil lamp nearer, stayed close so that he could help Germanus to hear what Eustachia was saying. She opened her eyes again, smiled at Germanus and then turned to Lupus.

'You are a good boy Lupus. You and Patricius must look after your father and master. Now Germanus, say that you forgive them and that you turn to Christ.'

'Was there a leader? Did you see him?' Germanus looked into his wife's eyes as he spoke.

Eustachia nodded. 'He – he wore a snake amulet on his arm.' She motioned to her own arm as she spoke. 'Now have you turned to Christ; will you pray with me, Germanus?'

'More than that. I went to see the pope. Well, he has made me Archbishop of Britannia, and Bishop of Armorica too, like old Amator wanted. That wily old cleric friend of yours got his way in the end, didn't he?'

Eustachia laughed. She raised her hand to Germanus's face, stroked his cheek, then tickled his stubble. 'You will make a great and wonderful archbishop, just as Amator said you would. And I shall always be your *univira*: you have always been, and always will be, the one man in my life. Take care my love, may God go with you.'

Then she pushed herself up with her forearms, gazed adoringly at the silver cross hung from the apse end of the chapel and shouted: 'Alleluia! Alleluia: Christ is risen! He is risen indeed!' Eustachia slumped back into her husband's arms and closed her eyes for the last time.

'No! No! No!' Germanus shook Eustachia, rubbed her, stroked her, kissed her, shook her again. Her smile and her gaze remained fixed on him. Lupus let him grieve on his own for a while and then came forward to restrain hs master from any further attempt to breathe life into the dead body.

Lupus felt strangely detached from the emotion. It was as if their roles had been reversed and he was now acting as the parent to the sobbing child knelt in front of the bloodied corpse. At last, Germanus turned away from Eustachia and towards Lupus.

'She is still the most beautiful woman in the province, and of a family as noble as my own; more so, in fact. We were an unbeatable couple in the old days: the promotions came thick and fast, you know, Lupus. It always paid to have good connections in the army and the senate. I loved her so much. I will find out who did this; I will have my revenge on every one of those murderers. I swear by the gods that my wife will be avenged!' Having made his promise, Germanus took Eustachia's wedding ring from her and placed it on his own ring finger.

'There is still Patricius to find, master.' Lupus had never found the courage to stop calling him master and mean it. He never would. Germanus took notice and put both hands on Lupus's shoulders.

'Yes, you are right. Thank you.' Germanus stammered as he squeezed his adopted son's shoulders. 'But didn't you hear what Eustachia said? "An angel took him". That means he's dead Lupus.'

'So where is his body? I have yet to see it.' Lupus regretted speaking so sharply.

'Go search again. I will join you shortly Lupus. Give me a little time here.'

Germanus lay Eustachia's body on the altar at the eastern end of the chapel. The general moved slowly, looking up at the portraits of the saints on the walls. Was she with them now? If there was a heaven, then Eustachia would have gained easy passage there, given all her good works. Her death would be lamented throughout Armorica by rich and poor alike. If anybody could have persuaded him to be a Christian, it would have been her. But not even the love of his life could make him turn away from the old gods, even if he was now archbishop of all he saw. He smelt her perfume; the sort that she always wore and always had worn.

Germanus kissed Eustachia on the forehead and lips once more and then went to join Lupus. The two men searched every corner of the villa; over and over again, together as well as separately; they made Lucius and Nonus do the same. They tried all the hiding places that had been built into the villa and the outbuildings just in case of emergencies like this; Patricius was nowhere to be seen; the hidey-holes were all empty. They did find more bodies: kitchens, barns, state rooms, workshops, everywhere.

Germanus and Lupus came back together in what had once been the main reception room. Lucius and Nonus served them with drink that they had managed to rescue from the ruins of the kitchens. They supped together; the four of them talking about what might have happened. Lupus thought back to the times when he and Patricius had played together; or rather fought together. It must have been difficult for him, the only son until his father adopted his dead second-in-command's offspring. And Lupus was 18 months older than Patricius. That would really have endeared the blood-linked son and heir to his new, lower-born, adopted kinsman. Lupus sighed to himself as he realised that his now 'younger' brother had taken his demotion rather well. In any case, it was obvious which child the father favoured. Lupus would always be an employee, an assistant, an aide, a worker; not really a son, even if he was now the one to inherit the family fortune. There was he, the cuckoo in the nest, tall, gangly, dark haired, no athlete, and certainly no fighter. Then there was Patricius, the warrior-prince: golden haired, good at everything he did, from running to rhetoric, a young man at ease with himself, assured in command, confident in battle. Already he had served with his father. A fragile voice stirred Lupus from his unfavourable self-comparison with Patricius.

'He was a brave boy. I taught him to be a good soldier. He would have fought well.'

'I am sure he would master. Where would he go if he escaped? Who is this angel that Eustachia spoke about?'

'She was delirious Lupus. It would be her imagination running wild.' Germanus laughed hysterically, shaking his head.

'Maybe, but we have not found him, have we?' Lupus held onto that thought, even though he could not determine how he felt about his step-brother, dead or alive.

CHAPTER 4

A queen with ginger hair appears

In the following days, the bodies of the estate workers, servants, and managers, were buried in the fields near the villa. The fires were put out and what possessions that could be salvaged were reclaimed. Germanus and Lupus were much helped by the return of the Armorican Guard from the eastern front (would that they had been at home when the attack on the villa had taken place) and the arrival of General Aetius's legions. They were fewer than needed, but more than Germanus dared hope for. Thank Jupiter that they had turned up. Given the losses that the western Roman armies had suffered along the Rhenus, it would have been understandable if Aetius had said no men could be spared. Germanus trusted his Armorican Guard, many of whom had been his most loyal troops when he was in the Imperial Army, though there were not enough to mount a full invasion of Britannia. But there were now enough troops to make the 'holy' mission achievable in Germanus's estimation. Aetius had even sent a small detachment of *clibanarii*, useful where heavily armoured mounted fighters were required. Men and women came from all over Armorica to offer their sympathy and their services to the bereaved governor. Many men volunteered to re-join the army if it would help Germanus, such was his standing in the area. Given his concerns about the troops available to him for Britannia, he selected the best and had the less able or experienced trained to defend the province and the home shores while he and his men were away.

In all his military career, Germanus had rarely seen such ferocity in the butchery that had taken place while he and Lupus had been away. He estimated that they could only have missed the marauders by a day or two. There had been guards on duty at the villa and some of the male farm workers were retired soldiers, but they had been no match for the attackers. Germanus cursed his own absence; if only he had been there to take charge, even without his Armorican Guard being available. It was as if the attackers had been setting an example, sending a message, by killing and destroying in the way they had. The marauders had done a very thorough job of destruction. Everything of value had been carried away and, if it was not portable, then it had been vandalised and, in the case of the buildings, set alight. The finest horses had been taken, for later use, no doubt. The rest of the animals had been left alone, apart from a small number of sheep and pigs that had been captured and then killed for food. This was as nothing compared with what had been done to the people. Men had been crucified, dismembered, disembowelled, beheaded; women and children stripped, beaten, raped, speared, knifed. When one of the smouldering barns was opened by Aetius's men, it was clear that some of the estate's inhabitants had been rounded up and locked in the building before it had been set alight. Every means of killing human beings had been brought into play, just for the fun of it.

It was generally agreed that the ruination of Germanus's property was the act of the *barbari;* many of the troops in Aetius's legions commented on how marauders were becoming ever bolder as resistance and retaliation from the empire and its forces was on the wane. It was not the first incursion of raiders from the east, but it was the most extensive and by far the most horrific. News about the event had soon spread throughout Armorica. But who was really behind the attack? Was it, as Pope Coelestinus had suggested, the Vortigern and his troops, now lying in wait over on the other side of the *Mare Britannicum,* ready to launch their invasion? Did it not make sense to stop the counterattack from Gallia before it had even started; taking the fight to the enemy? A bold move, as Germanus himself agreed.

All this time Eustachia had been lying in state in the house chapel. She had persuaded Germanus to build the place for her when she had converted to Christianity. Strangely, the building had escaped destruction and even desecration: no graffiti, nothing. The apostles still looked down from their pillared niches all around the room. What a fuss Eustachia had made about it all! The time, effort, and expense of getting those figures painted on the plastered walls had been considerable. Then there was all the hours that she spent in there praying, for her husband's conversion, amongst other things. It would have been old Amator who would have put her up to it. That and the enforced celibacy as, according to Eustachia, they were not now man and wife as brother and sister in Christ. That had been hard to take, and Germanus had not taken it. But it had never felt the same, lying there afterwards, as it had done in the good old days.

Germanus gazed around the chapel and felt nothing. No voice from heaven; no whisper from the soul of his wife; nothing. Look at those faces up there: how bloody smug they looked! Those outstretched hands had not protected Eustachia, had they? Germanus looked again at the faces of the apostles and smiled to himself. Eustachia had never discovered his little joke (or she had never said anything) about the fact that St Peter bore a striking resemblance to the Governor General of Armorica, her husband. Then for a moment he thought he heard her whispering to him: 'I will make a real saint of you yet, my one true love.'

It was now time for her funeral. Germanus called for the local priests to organise the ceremony. News of Germanus's general's elevation had already travelled round the local church hierarchy, and they deferred to Germanus, much to his frustration and annoyance, in terms of what was to happen.

'You are the bloody Christians: you tell me what to do! I will have the best for my wife, I want what she would have wanted, so see to it! Don't bother me again until you have everything properly arranged!'

One of Amator's senior *clerici* took the service, robed all in white, with a freshly shaved tonsure revealed when he took off his mitre at the beginning of the service. Germanus was surprised by how many of the townspeople of Antissiodorum, not to mention the recently-arrived legionaries, as well as Eustachia's family and friends from across Gallia, not only attended the funeral, but also took an active part in the service. Most of the attendees demonstrated their knowledge of the Christian faith. Germanus was unaware of the detail; he was in his own world thinking about his life with Eustachia and how he would cope without her. He died a little more inside every time a shovelful of earth hit the top of the stone sarcophagus, laid deep in the trench outside the chapel. He remembered the care she had taken with the instructions to the stonemasons and her insistence that the *chi-rho* symbol be the single prominent decoration all the way around the sides. How she had prepared for death. He preferred to live. But life without her…

Germanus was the last to throw soil into the dark void. He stayed long after the others had expressed their condolences to the new widower and gone off for the refreshments organised by Eustachia's sister.

'Enough. I will see you again my love and my life.'

With those words Germanus strode back to the makeshift reception hall that the legionaries had erected to accommodate the funeral guests. He was to meet more people that afternoon than he had done in a single gathering for a long time. Only one of the hundreds of guests was to change his life irrevocably. That person had not actually been invited.

※   ※   ※

Germanus had no appetite for food or company. He drank: to forget everything; to protect himself from the expressions of condolence, genuine or feigned; to erase the images of his beloved wife that were constantly before him; to fill the emptiness inside. The wine was foul, but at least it dulled his senses and took the edge off the overwhelming grief that surrounded him and those of his family and servants who had survived. He was in a place full of other human beings yet felt totally alone. He could have drunk every *amphora* dry and yet, underneath it all, the pain would still have been there, ready to come out and hit him in the stomach when he least expected it. The outpourings of sympathy he could handle; it was the little details that someone or something reminded him of which brought back the unalterable fact that Eustachia and Patricius were dead; and buried in the case of his wife. Yet more extensive searches of the villa, the grounds, the farmlands, the district, by his newly-arrived legions had still unearthed nothing of Patricius: no sightings, no possessions, no trail, nothing. His son had simply vanished. In stranger moments, Germanus laughingly wondered if Patricius had really been taken by an angel, leaving behind no earthly remains; even Christ had left evidence of his resurrection. No, bodies do not just vanish into thin air.

Germanus had always been able to hold his drink and his wife's funeral celebration was no exception. But there came a point when he became unsteady on his feet. Lupus, who had been keeping a distant eye on his adopted father, decided that it was time to give the widower some air.

'Come, master, let's get you outside, you need to breathe.'

'Father! Lupus – I am your father, and you are my only son!' Germanus hit Lupus in the chest with his arm by way of a reproach. Even inebriated, the man had considerable strength. Lupus attempted once more to pull Germanus towards the exit, but he could not move a dead weight as powerful and muscular as this, despite the small frame.

'Let me help you. He's very drunk, isn't he?'

Lupus turned around; he could not believe what he was now seeing.

'Cat got your tongue Lupus?'

'I – what? Who?'

'Don't worry Lupus, I don't bite; well not always.' The girl giggled to herself as she motioned to Lupus to try and move Germanus once more, but this time with her help. They each took an arm and half guided, half dragged the governor-general out of the reception tent. They sat him down in the hope that fresh air would revive him.

The sun was setting and a faint, misty rain was coming down. The girl pulled back the hood of her *birrus Britannicus*. Even by the light of the torches that the troops had set up around the courtyard in which the makeshift dining hall was situated, Lupus could easily determine that she was the most beautiful woman he had ever seen. If this was the face and body of an angel, then the sooner he converted to Christianity and went to Heaven the better. Perhaps there was something in this new religion after all...

'Stop gawping Lupus. We need to get your master sorted out.'

'He is my father, my adopted father, as well'. Lupus blurted out the words, trying to find some way of regaining his composure, as well as his standing in this girl's eyes. 'But he will always be my master above all'

'Well, let's try and get your adopted father or your master, or whatever he is, sobered up, shall we?'

Lupus knelt in front of Germanus, looking up at his drooping head. The girl leaned over the general and stroked his cheek gently.

'My lord, it is time to wake up.'

She continued gently stroking his cheek. Lupus could not help but notice the swell of her breasts. The girl leaned further over the motionless Germanus. As she did so, her body brushed against Lupus. He could have sworn that she let her hand graze his bare forearm deliberately. It felt odd to the young man; the way her fingers touched his skin, making him shiver. She had such dark eyes and the most amazing red hair, long and straight. Did angels have red hair?

The girl looked at Lupus. How did he describe her eyes? How did he? Really, **how did he**? There was no way. Heaven on earth: one look and he was dead to the present misery; to the obligations that he now had to Germanus and the empire; to anything and everybody; to the whole world; to anything but this beauty.

'Are you going to help me get him inside, Lupus?'

Germanus was heavy: heavy with drink. Lupus and the ginger-haired angel manhandled the inebriate into an ante rooms at the far side of the courtyard, well away from the funeral festivities. Without uttering a word, the governor-general's two aides had resolved not to let any of the guests see the great man in this sorry state.

As they reached the doorway, Germanus stirred enough to rush over to the edge of the formal garden and throw up, crying as he did so, remembering that he had watched Eustachia plant most of the bushes and the flowers herself. Having wiped his mouth, he turned back to the doorway, groaned, then half fell, half collapsed into the red angel's arms. Much to Lupus's surprise, the girl-woman could not only stop the drunkard from crushing her but was also able to push him back into an upright position and guide him inside.

'Go fetch some water, Lupus.'

Lupus obeyed her without question. By the time that he returned with a small jug full, she had managed to get Germanus onto an *accubitus*. He lay there, one arm dangling on the floor, the other on his chest to prevent his stomach heaving more contents northwards. He was staring at her without any real recognition of his surroundings. She looked up at Lupus and motioned with her eyes for him to put the jug down on the floor, just beside her feet. She dipped a hand into the jug and, removing it, flicked water onto Germanus's face. After the third spray, he regained consciousness and sat up abruptly.

'Where...what...who are you? Lupus, what is all this about? What is going on?'

Lupus was too slow off the mark in replying; the girl-woman beat him to it.

'Calm yourself my lord. You just had too much to drink. But you are sobering up nicely.'

'I can never have too much to drink.'

'Grief is a strange thing. It alters us in surprising ways. We cease to be the people we once were. I know that now, since my brother was murdered.'

'Who was your brother? Who are you?' Lupus asked, surprised that this goddess, this angelic being, this woman that he already adored, could have human counterparts.

'I am Aureliana, Queen of the West Britons. My brother was Aurelianus, King of the West Britons; until the Vortigern had him murdered.'

'Why?' Germanus was now fully alert as well as upright.

'Because that man wanted the whole of Britannia for himself and his cronies; not that he has any right to it.'

'Who does have a right to it, then?' Lupus asked.

'Now that my poor Auri is dead, I do. I am the rightful Queen of Britannia, and I want my country back. You two will get it back for me!'

'What demand I am in, all to conquer this mysterious Vortigern and a forgotten outpost of our once glorious empire!' Germanus stood up, his composure now regained, before continuing. 'I am already under contract on this one milady; in any case, I don't take orders from a young whipper-snapper like you!'

By now Germanus and Aureliana were eyeball to eyeball. The Queen of the West Britons bade her time then smiled back at Germanus.

'You will if you want to find your son.'

Germanus visibly weakened, shrivelling up outside and inside.

'You what? You know who took him? What happened to him?'

Germanus grew angrier and angrier until he started shaking the girl-woman-angel. Lupus had to restrain his master.

'I will help you find him. I believe that he has been taken by kinsmen of mine, for his own protection.'

'Where? When? Who? I want to know about my son!'

'Win Britannia for me and I will help you find him. Trust me!'

'Why should we trust you?' Lupus decided that he had not only to help his father but also to assert himself in this dialogue. 'How do we know that you are who you say you are?'

'I tell the truth, o ye of little faith.'

Germanus grinned sarcastically as he recognised the biblical quotation.

'So, a fellow Christian, are you?'

'I am about as Christian as you are, general, commander, archbishop. It is all the same to you, isn't it, as long as you are in charge, in control, giving the orders and making people answerable to you? That's all that I want, in my own country. And you can help me, Germanus Patricius Magnus.'

CHAPTER 5

Germanus and Aureliana fight to win; Lupus becomes a man

The moon was full and clear over the ruined villa. Three figures stood at the far edge of the courtyard, their steaming breath intertwining beneath the eaves of the peristyle. The woman opened her cloak, undid the top buttons of her dress, reached inside, and pulled a bejewelled torc from around her neck. Germanus looked intently at Aureliana; Lupus tried to work out what each was thinking and planning. Germanus smiled wryly; Aureliana nodded, then turned away and toward the central lawn. Once there, she waited for Germanus to join her. With her back to the two men, Aureliana drew a *gladius* from under her outer tunic.

'Here!' a voice cried.

Aureliana turned round to see Germanus ready to fight.

'See if you are a match for me, Briton!'

'I am a match for any man, Roman or no.'

Aureliana spat into the dust and cast off her over-robe to reveal muscular shoulders and arms, glistening already with sweat. She breathed heavily in anticipation of the challenge that lay ahead. Germanus moved his sword rapidly from hand to hand.

'Come then.' Germanus beckoned the Queen of the West Britons to begin the combat.

The battle-hardened warrior and the angry young woman circled each other. She moved on tiptoe; he crept like a tiger. Aureliana lunged and stabbed, but Germanus was too quick and too cunning for her: he sidestepped the princess, gripped her forearm, and pulled it behind her back with his left hand, drawing her to him, his right hand putting a *gladius* to her throat. How quickly it was over! Or so Lupus thought. But no, the Briton retaliated, punching him in the stomach with both elbows, putting him off balance with a kick to the shins. The *gladius* withdrawn from her neck, Aureliana regrouped, again facing Germanus. The elbow-punch had taken him by surprise but done no damage. Lupus remembered how he had often seen his master's rock-hard stomach, made tight and firm by many hours of disciplined exercise. It would have taken an iron bar to make real inroads into his torso.

Briton and Roman circled each other more carefully. Germanus thrust his sword; Aureliana responded with a good defence; she counter-attacked; Germanus anticipated her move and, following her sword-stroke, pushed her back and against a courtyard pillar. His greater strength looked as if it would end the contest. Aureliana had more surprises. Germanus did not expect to be kneed in the groin but kneed in the groin he was. After his initial gasp, he laughed:

'I remember now – this is the way Britons fight!'

Whereupon he pointed behind Aureliana as if to warn her of a surreptitious attacker: she was stupidly taken in for an instant; long enough for her guard to be down. Germanus glanced his sword against her arm, fine enough not to draw blood, firm enough to cut away the material to leave her arm and breast exposed. Lupus gasped, unsure whether to laugh, to commiserate, or to avert his gaze. In the end he just stood there, in silence, staring. Unabashed, Aureliana mimicked her opponent's *gladius*-switch, determinedly passing the sword from one hand to the other, eyes glinting as she worked out her opponent's next move. The two thrust and parried, neither gaining the upper hand, both using the whole courtyard as their battle ground. A false step was Aureliana's undoing, forced on her by Germanus. Advancing, he caused her to step backwards too hastily: she tripped and fell. Germanus acted swiftly, coming forward for 'the kill.' As he leaned forward over the princess, now too weary and winded to get up and continue the fight, Germanus threw down his *gladius*, held out his hand to help her up and burst out laughing.

'A worthy opponent. You are a true daughter of the Cornovii. That little skirmish tells me more than any torc could. You could have stolen the jewellery; but only a Briton could have fought like you did back there. Where did you learn to fight like that, Aureliana, Queen of the West Britons?'

'We all have to be ready to fight in Britannia, even women and children. We have been for very many generations now – even before you Romans came to our islands.' Aureliana made no attempt to cover herself; neither Germanus nor Lupus protested about her nakedness, nor made to cover her bare flesh.

'I know', Germanus replied. 'You have always been worthy foemen and', he grinned, 'women.'

It was Aureliana's turn to burst out laughing: 'until next time, my lord.'

'I hope that we are on the same side then. Now cover yourself, woman, and tell me what you want of me.'

'I will, I promise. Think of it: you will get your revenge on the Vortigern for killing your wife and desecrating your property. With your forces and my men, we will conquer from the west. The Vortigern will be no more, and I will be Queen of all Britannia!'

⁂　⁂　⁂

'A letter has arrived for you, your holiness.'

Coelestinus looked up from his *scrinium,* put down his pen and took off his glasses. Despite the heat from the *foculi,* the Pontifex shivered, unable to get warm. He stretched out his bony arms as if to measure the folds of dry, loose skin that hung down from them. Scratching his nose where the glasses had rubbed, he opened the correspondence and read its contents. Tears were in his eyes as he looked up at the deliverer of the news.

'O my! How could this have happened? It was not part of the plan, none of it.'

Coelestinus turned his head to one side and then the other, looking for his walking sticks, trying to ease himself out of his chair. He thought better of it, instead barking out an order to Ferox, his assistant.

'Fetch me a *scriba.*'

The Pontifex bit his fingernails and then inspected the result. After a few moments he began to tap his fingers on the *scrinium* and either tut-tutted or, when the phlegm built up too much, cleared his throat. Eventually the scribe scuttled in and sat down with his portable writing desk, ready to take down his lord and master's every word.

'Are you ready?'

The *scriba* nodded vigorously, dropped his *stilus,* then upset his desk. The Pontifex rolled his eyes in disbelief.

'Will you stop fidgeting and get ready to take dictation!'

The scribe rearranged himself and looked expectantly, if nervously, at the Pontifex, who cleared his throat and began to speak.

'Germanus, my son; my thoughts are with you. You have done well, but you must not waver, despite the news about your wife and your son. Stay loyal to the cause. You are my greatest asset and ally in the upcoming struggle. Your reward will be great if you succeed. Regular reports please, especially when you are over the water. May the gods go with you!'

'Don't you mean God, my Lord?

The Pontifex narrowed his eyes and spoke back at the scribe through gritted teeth.

'What I have written I have written. Now go!'

'Thank you, my Lord. Is that all, my Lord?'

'It is enough, scribe. Now see that it is delivered post haste; the archbishop-general is on his way.'

❈   ❈   ❈

Lupus took off his over garments; kicked off his boots. He fell onto the bed, face down. It had been a long day, a long week, a long month. The only woman that had ever really been a mother to him was dead and buried. Lives, his as much as anybody else's, had been changed irrevocably since that visit to Roma to see the Pontifex. Lupus began to think that he had gone there as a boy and come back as a man; then decided that there had yet to be any real transformation.

'That'll be the day!' he laughed. 'Lupus - the wolf. Will I ever be a real man?'

He hoped for sleep; longed for it. Slumber did not come. His mind would not let him drowse He kept thinking. Going to Britannia with Germanus meant that he could prove himself; become a *bellator* like his father back in Dacia. There was no way he could be like Patricius. Patricius was tall; he was short. Patricius was athletic, he liked reading books. Patricius commanded troops at the age of fourteen; he hadn't even taken charge of a *carruca* pulled by two mules. But where was Patricius? Was he dead? There was no body; no evidence to suggest that he had escaped or been spared. Aureliana had suggested that some of her kinsman had him but had as yet given no further evidence to back up her assertion. Not that it seemed to matter to Germanus. It was as if he had already given up any hope of seeing his son alive. Battling for Britannia was now his only objective, and if Lupus could seize the opportunity to prove himself, then so be it. Patricius had been given all the advantages so far; now they belonged to Lupus. What was it that his father had said to him? His true worth and destiny would be revealed to him when the time was right. He was of noble birth; and he was to be a great leader one day. That was certain, or so he had been led to believe.

Lupus put away those memories. The morning would bring much work. At least he could organise things for Germanus. Lupus told himself that he was good at that if nothing else. And his talents as an administrator seemed to be appreciated. So that was that. Lupus contented himself with being a good aide to a great *magister militum*.

He could have been asleep for only instant or an eternity. But no matter; he was awake. It was still dark. There was no sound, no movement. Yet Lupus knew that he was not alone.

'Salve? Who is there?'

Why was he whispering? If there was no-one there, then he need not speak quietly. And the villa walls were strong and thick. Germanus had seen to that; he had taken great pride in his home.

There was no response to his soft greeting, but Lupus knew he was not alone. He could feel the rise and fall of another life breathing close to him. Germanus had taught him well: as always, his *gladius* was under his bed. He reached down for it.

'I wouldn't do that if I were you Lupus.'

'You! What are you doing in my room?'

'That's the wrong question, Lupus. That's not what you should be asking me. And put that *gladius* down. I am interested in a different kind of weapon.'

'Which weapon? What should I be asking you?' Lupus was now up on his elbows to make out the figure in the shadows.

The shadow laughed.

'You should be asking me what I am going to do to you, once I am in that bed of yours.'

Lupus gulped, trying not to think of what might be about to be done to him.

'I only have a *gladius*. No other weapons. Germanus asks that we have something to defend ourselves with in our rooms, nothing more.'

The shadow snorted.

'There is no defence from me. *Faciam ut mei memineris* – I will make you remember me.'

Lupus shuddered as she placed her hand over his. He tried not to look her in the face, knowing that once he let her see his eyes, she would know how he felt. Her fingers touched his chin, laughing as the stubble tickled and prickled her palm.

'I like a man with hair, especially on his face. Look at me Lupus. Don't be shy Lupus, look at me.'

'I cannot, dare not…'

'But why not?'

'I…'

Lupus felt the blood pounding in his head.

'Look at me Lupus. *Look at me!*'

There was a russle of cloth. Aureliana's over robe landed on the bed.

'Look at me Lupus. *Aut viam inveniam aut faciam;* I will either find a way or make one!'

He resisted once again, looking down at his chest for what seemed a lifetime, but when she gently cupped his chin in her hands, he did as he was told; he lifted up his head. She was naked down to the waist. It felt the most natural thing in the world for him to put his face between her breasts. Aureliana encouraged him by putting her hands behind his head and applying gentle pressure, nudging the young man further into her.

'You have never been with a woman before, have you, Lupus?'

There was no answer.

'Have you Lupus?'

Lupus murmured.

'I thought not; but it doesn't matter. I will show you; teach you.'

Aureliana laughed. She made to put his hand on her breast to cup it and caress the nipple.

'No! I cannot!'

She guided him.

'I must not.'

'Shhh. What are you worried about? Germanus is not going to stop you having sex now that he is an archbishop.'

Aureliana laughed. One breast was now in Lupus's hand as the nipple of the other touched his tongue. He kissed it. Lupus thought to himself that he had now kissed a woman's nipple. He had never even touched a woman before. Aureliana pulled off his night robe. Lupus quivered as she bared his legs, then stroked his upper thighs with her thumbs, pushing her face towards his groin. How large he had become! He looked down to see himself standing almost vertical, pointing upwards towards Aureliana's belly. She bent over and kissed him with her lips, licked him with her tongue, enveloped him with her mouth. Lupus groaned: his mind was nowhere and everywhere at the same time.

'You are ready Lupus, and I am here for you.'

Aureliana rose, pushed down her tunic, let it fall all the way to the floor and stood out of the pile of cloth gathered at her feet. Slowly, she straddled Lupus and lowered herself down. He looked down to see the hair between her legs, her smooth firm belly curving up towards her breasts that once again Lupus nuzzled. He felt her hand searching between his legs; she gripped him like a soldier grips the handle of his spear. She held him sword-iron straight and lowered herself further.

'Look Lupus. Look down and look at us.'

He saw that they were touching. Curly red hair meshed with black. He could feel her moistness; soft flesh touched hardness. She pushed down, sudden, and hard; Lupus gasped. Further, further, further she pushed, until her buttocks were resting on his thighs. Slowly, Aureliana began to move, raising herself, and then lowering her body back onto him. Occasionally, she ground right down, forcing Lupus deep inside. Their breathing quickened. He put his hands either side of the slim, taut, muscular body, looked and lusted at the flesh, nuzzled her, licked her, bit her.

'Ow! Gently! Gently, my Lupus.'

The young man could not restrain himself. He cupped her buttocks, circling them with his palms. She responded by moving backwards and forwards on top of his body. The pleasure was agonising. She gasped, he gasped, they gasped: again, and again; faster and faster still. Then they groaned. Aureliana cried, digging her nails into his shoulders. Instinctively, he pushed deep into her one last time, gritting his teeth in anger and desire simultaneously; then he shot, shot, shot, shot, wanting to force every last drop inside her.

'Aargh! Lupus!' She quivered, then fell silent, collapsing onto him with a final light kiss to his neck. 'Lupus.'

Later, after he had grown slack, Aureliana lay in his arms. She was lightly asleep. He dared not move her; did not want to destroy the intimacy, nor end the moment. His legs were numb, but he did not care. He had done it.

Aureliana awoke. She looked out of the window and saw the darkness.

'I must go, my young wolf. Not a word of this to anyone. You understand?'

'But I love you!'

'No, you don't, you silly boy.' She kissed him on the forehead like a mother kisses her young son goodnight.

'My love!'

'Let me go Lupus! We need to be ready for the journey tomorrow. Not a word of this, though; our secret.'

'But will I; will we...'

'Who knows?' She ran a finger down his nose. 'But not if you can't keep our secret. Now I am going, and you must get some sleep!'

She was dressed and gone in an instant. He knew there was no point in trying to make her stay. But he did love her, whatever she said.

He fell into a deep dream: Germanus was standing in front of him, shaking his head, then raising a finger to point at him. Then Aureliana pushed Germanus aside, looked down at Lupus and laughed.

'*Auribus teneo lupum*', she cried, thrusting a dagger into his stomach. 'I hold a wolf by the ears!'

CHAPTER 6

Iacta alea est: Germanus consults his oracle

A dank mist had settled over the remote valley. The greyness of the sky gradually merged into the whiteness of the ground. Frost covered everything in sight. Germanus shivered, watching himself blow the cold air out of his mouth, just like he did as a boy. He wiped his wet nose on his sleeve, looked around to make sure that no-one was watching, and proceeded towards the cave-house. He thought back to when he had last been here: to seek advice on whether or not to marry Eustachia and how he should prepare for his future. He was back, without the love of his life, and with only a limited prospect of success. A scrawny, bald cat looked down at him from the safety of its ledge by the entrance to the home of the *haruspex*. With its one eye, it looked him over, jumped down at his feet, hissed and spat. Before Germanus had time to kick it away, the horrible creature had run inside the hovel that it shared with its owner.

The smell of wood smoke could not mask the stench of rotting flesh. The bones of various animals lay scattered around the entrance. Germanus walked inside. It seemed empty, at least of people. There were signs of occupancy nevertheless: a fire, more smoke than flame; a cooking pot simmering with foul-smelling *tisana vel sucus*; a growling dog, wary of anyone taking away its bone. Habitation was confirmed when a scratchy voice began to speak.

'I wondered how long it would be before you turned up.'

Germanus turned towards the sound. As his eyes grew accustomed to the smoke and the darkness, he could see the *haruspex*. The hair on the man's head was white, neatly parted in the middle, falling down to the cushions on which he was sitting, cross legged. Just as long and just as white was his beard; round about his chest it forked into two platted halves. The man stared straight ahead, unblinking.

'How did you know that I would come, Memor?' Germanus laughed nervously, bending down to stroke the dog, which rolled over in mock obeisance, keeping a weather eye on its bone all the while.

'You have changed. The death of a loved one always leads to transformation of the bereaved, for better or for worse.'

'Who told you of Eustachia's death?'

'No-one, Germanus. I knew.'

'And I suppose you knew that Segovax was dead?'

'Yes, I knew that he would die pretending to be you. That was his fate, and he was proud to go to his death protecting the great Germanus.'

'Then why did you not warn me what was going to happen? Why did you not warn Segovax? He was your son after all.'

'I can only foretell the future, Germanus, not change it. It was meant to be. My Segovax was destined to die for you, so that you could go on to greater glory.'

Germanus snorted. 'Spare me the fine words Memor. I have no need of greater glory. Not now. I would give away every piece of your so-called glory if I could have Eustachia back.'

'But you have already accepted your orders from the highest authority in the empire and, not only that, from the Queen of the West Britons to boot. There's a dilemma if ever there was one! And that is why you are here. You want to know what to do. Whether or not to go across the water, who to support, and what you will find in Britannia, whoever your leader and paymaster is.' Memor cleared his throat and spat out the contents of his mouth, missing the dog by a whisker. Germanus smoothed his head with his hand, as if trying to remember what it was like to have hair. He walked over to Memor and looked him in the face. Nothing: no gesture, no expression, no glint in the clouded eyes.

'Sit down Germanus, and I will tell you. I am only blind to this world; I can talk to the gods on your behalf. They have already told me what is in store for you in Britannia.'

'Must I go?'

'Yes. You have never passed up on an opportunity like this; your mission's success is crucial to the future of your way of life, one that my son embraced, treasured and eventually died for.'

'Will I succeed?'

'That is up to you. I know that you will be sorely tested beyond endurance, again and again. Eventually, you will have a decision to make, and what you decide will seal the fate of the Empire.'

'Will I succeed?'

'Go to Britannia and find out for yourself.'

'Will I succeed?'

'It depends upon how you define success; but yes, you will succeed.'

'Take this stone, Germanus. When you press it hard to your forehead, I will be there to help you.'

'Is there something else, Memor?'

The *haruspex* rose, held out his hand to the dog, which sniffed and then licked it. Memor then walked towards Germanus, coming right up to him. Their gaze met. For a moment, Germanus thought that the old man's eyes had cleared and that he could see.

'Can you tell me what happened to my son? Where is Patricius?'

Memor hesitated, clearing his throat to give him time to think of what to say.

'I wish I could answer that question, Germanus. He is somewhere very far away; too far away for me to feel anything. I am sorry.'

'Is he alive or dead?' Germanus squeezed Memor's shoulders.

'That I cannot tell you. I feel nothing; there is no aura about him. But that does not mean to say that he is dead, only that he is somewhere very far away.'

Germanus sank back inside himself and sighed as Memor continued.

'There are only two more things that I can say now. Get back to your exercising and stop drinking so much. You are becoming portly in your old age.'

Germanus laughed. 'You are right about that. Yes, I must get fit again. And the other thing?'

'Beware the ginger girl. She will be your undoing, if you are not careful.'

※　　※　　※

'My troops will we be waiting for us at Isca. I have already sent word to Drustans, my *magister militum*, to meet us there. We will then proceed to my capital at Viroconium where the council of war can be convened.'

'Just a moment, high-and-mighty princess. Who is overseeing this campaign? In any case, I answer to a higher authority than you.'

'What? The Lord Jesus Christ?'

'No, someone far more important: Pontifex Maximus Coelestinus.'

Aureliana giggled, staring straight at Lupus, who blushed and turned away to hide his embarrassment. Apart from snorting, Germanus showed no emotion. Rather, he looked down to the floor and thought of Patricius, wondering how Lupus would now shape up as a substitute.

Aureliana reached down inside her tunic and pulled out a ring. She extended her arm out and held it between the thumb and forefinger of her right hand.

'Will this convince you?'

'Let me see that!', said Germanus angrily, rising from his silent, private mourning. He gently took the golden circle from Aureliana and looked at it closely, then nodded. He stared into the queen's eyes.

'Eustachia gave the ring to Patricius on his tenth birthday, did she not?'

'How do you know that?'

'I know a good deal about you.'

Germanus grimaced.

'You have the proof you asked for, my lord.' Aureliana bowed her head slightly as she spoke.

'Proof that you, or someone, has taken his ring from his finger. He could have been dead when it was removed.' Germanus shook his head.

'Having that ring means nothing.' Lupus added.

'I need you to help me defeat the Vortigern; to free Britannia from his tyranny. To return the country to its rightful rulers.' Aureliana raised her voice.

'You mean to Roma?'

'I mean to the Britons, Germanus.'

'But my mission is…'

'I know what your mission is Germanus. But you are working for the Pontifex, not the *Imperator*. You can serve him and me; there is no conflict of interest. We both need you to defeat the Vortigern. And if – when – you do, I will help you get your son back, and more.'

'More?' Germanus stroked his chin.

'Well, you are not stopping just a mini-tyrant if you stop the Vortigern. We all know he has designs on the empire, just like his forebears. You must have heard of Magnus Maximus.' Aureliana held her hands out as she spoke.

'Germanus half laughed and shook his head.

'I have indeed, Aureliana.'

'The usurper?' Lupus asked.

'Some say that he could have been the saviour of the western empire.'

Germanus scratched his head, then ran his hand over the little hair that he had left.

Lupus gasped; Aureliana merely smiled. Germanus raised an eyebrow.

'I will tell you some other time Lupus, but as you already know, I have been to Britannia before.'

'And now you are going again my lord. And your rewards will be great. You will get far more than just your son I can promise you. I have to pay homage to the Vortigern as a client ruler. I have no alternative. He is too powerful. But your troops and mine. Unbeatable. We can rid the world of this horrible man and his Saxon mercenaries.'

Germanus bowed his head, then looked at Aureliana, staring straight into her eyes. His cheek muscles flexed. He turned briefly to Lupus then back to the Queen of the West Britons.

In came Lucius.

'Your troops are ready my lord, your grace. Only say the word and we shall set off for the coast.'

Germanus turned again to Aureliana, then back to Lupus. Aureliana looked at Lupus. Lupus averted his gaze. Germanus said nothing for a very long time, then pulled out his *gladius*.

'Very well. Let it be so.'

Germanus raised his sword and shouted 'Alleluia!'

CHAPTER 7

Germanus, Lupus and Aureliana sail across the channel

The crossing was rough; the roughest that Aureliana had ever known in all the years she had been sailing across the *Mare Britannicum*. Germanus had known it rougher and gave no indication of being scared. Quite the opposite; for most of the voyage he was at the front of the lead boat standing up in the bow, like a figurehead: rock solid, bolt upright, unmoving. Not to be outdone, Aureliana stood behind him, her long red hair blowing like a *vexillum* at the mast. Lupus, Lucius, Nonus and many of the soldiery were too ill to be inspired by this vision. When not throwing up, they were busy thinking about throwing up or even, at the height of the storm, whether they were even going to live. Occasionally, when less ill, Lupus wondered what Aureliana would think of him leaning over the edge of the boat ready to be sick again. As they reached the shores of Dumnonia, the squalls subsided. It was difficult to see the coast through a dense fog; and it was hard to know where the rest of the fleet was. As suddenly as the mists came down, they disappeared, to be replaced by cloudless blue sky and a vista of cliff and beach. The landing craft were rowed to the shore and moored at a half-derelict jetty.

Germanus was the first to step off, followed by Aureliana. As the boats were being moored and their contents unloaded, a small group of armed men marched down to the jetty. These soldiers stood to attention as soon as they saw the Queen of the West Britains. Lupus did not recognise the insignia on their shields or their weaponry. It was obviously not Roman, but it did not look like the kind of armoury or dress that *barbari* wore either. Aureliana spoke to them in British. Germanus stood silent for a few moments and then began to join in the conversation. Lupus smiled at the realisation that his adopted father spoke the local language fluently. Aureliana looked at Germanus half surprised, half angry at the revelation that the new Archbishop of Britannia was a linguist.

Germanus and Lupus were introduced to Drustans, the commander of Aureliana's forces. The local forces were encouraged to become acquainted with the legions of Romano-Gallic troops and Germanus's Armorican Guard once all had disembarked and pitched their tents. With the armies well settled and the initial pleasantries over, Germanus, Lupus, Drustans and Aureliana rode up to their quarters on the cliff tops. The house was a good choice, as Germanus pointed out; it was possible to see down the coast, across the countryside to the north and there was an excellent view of all routes into and out of the port. Aureliana smiled at Germanus in gratitude for the implied compliment to her tactical ability.

Germanus dismounted first, followed by Aureliana and then Lupus. Drustans waited until the Queen of the West Britons turned to him and nodded. Only then did he get down from his mount. The horses were tethered to the wooden railings that still girdled the walkway, though it was difficult to find timbers that were strong enough, for much of the construction was rotten. Aureliana led the way inside. Germanus walked slightly behind her, hand on *gladius*.

Though the villa was in poor condition, it was possible to see what it must have been like when it had been occupied and fully maintained by its owners. There was an entrance room, square and simple in decoration. Beyond were colonnades, with an overhanging roof, or what was left of it, enclosing a small area where the owners would no doubt have sat to admire the views. It was clear that the house had been situated in such a way as to take best advantage of the scenery and especially the hills, woods and valleys that stretched for many miles to Isca Dumnoniorum in the north and the coast towards the south. The roof gutters and drains designed to carry away rainwater to a cistern where it could be used for washing and cooking were still in place. Beyond the colonnaded area was an inner courtyard, from which access was gained to a dining room, with its mosaic floor and rich wall decorations. The outer side of the floor was bordered by leafy decoration, inside which was a circle. Within the circle were several female busts and figures. The central figure, representing Roma, was seated, holding an orb. The other busts and figures were personifications of the different provinces of the Roman Empire. There was Africa, Egypt, Asia, Gallia and so on. Even Britannia was there. On every side of the dining room there were folding doors or windows to ensure light and air. The surrounding scenery penetrated the space as much as possible. Drustans spoke once all four had entered the building.

'This was once part of my father's estate. He often entertained guests from the neighbouring villas, towns and even, at times, Londinium. Slaves would serve food and wine; there would be conversation and music, gossip, and laughter; the latest news from the governor or the eternal city itself would be discussed and debated. But that all seems so long ago now.'

'It was a different world, then, Drustans. Come, your rooms have been prepared. Once you have freshened up, we can eat.' Aureliana replied, untying her hair, shaking her head as she did so. Lupus blushed at the sight. Yes, he truly loved her.

Drustans motioned to the two servants who had been waiting patiently for the party to arrive and for orders to be given. Germanus and Lupus were led to their quarters while Aureliana stayed behind.

Lupus looked at Germanus, querying the wisdom of leaving the Queen of the West Britons with her *magister militum,* but Germanus merely inclined his head slightly then moved off as directed by the servants. To the left of the dining room was the *lararium.* The niches where the guardian deities once stood were empty; one pottery statuette only now remained, smashed into pieces on the floor. To the right of the dining room was a large salon, then a second one of about half the size of the first. Lupus remarked to Germanus that this last room seemed cosier than the other reception rooms and that it had perhaps been designed as a winter retreat. Leading off from the room was a chamber with a bay window, designed to admit sun all day long. Germanus said nothing, which in Lupus's experience, could mean almost anything.

This last room was where Germanus and Lupus were to sleep. Set in the wall of the chamber was a closet. The door to this piece of furniture had been wrenched off at some point and the contents emptied, but Germanus said that it was reasonable to assume that the receptacle had been a place to store books. Linked to this 'library' chamber was a bedroom; there was a central heating system to keep the occupants warm, and the floor decorations included a central, blank, rectangle, where two crudely made single beds now stood. As the room was now much ruined, it was possible to see some of the pipes in the walls and floors that had been used to circulate the hot air round the sleeping space. The only way of being warm in this room now was to stay close to the *foculus* in the far corner.

The servants then showed the two guests the bathhouse. This was only partly usable; one of the pools had been filled in so that the room could be used to thresh grain, but most of the rest was *in situ* and available for use. Germanus asked that the rooms be made ready for them.

'Let us rest a while.' Germanus looked at Lupus and smiled.

CHAPTER 8

Germanus wins an important game; then on to Viroconium where the intrigues begin

Aureliana called it fidchell. She carried the board with her everywhere. It had belonged to her father. It was a British game, she asserted proudly, played by royalty and even the old gods. The four of them, Germanus, Lupus, Drustans and Aureliana, would wile away the evening playing it. Drustans looked indifferent; Lupus apprehensive; Germanus nonchalant; Aureliana enthusiastic. The three males all agreed, nonetheless, to play the game if only to keep the Queen of the West Britons quiet.

Lupus was the first to go, pitted against Aureliana, who set out a wooden board divided up as a grid into seven squares by seven and on which there were two sets of pieces at opposing sides. In the centre of the two sets of wooden 'men' was a 'king', who had to be protected against attack from the opposing army. The king had to do more than just defend himself: he must get through the attackers, with the help of his army, to one of the corner spots on the board in order to achieve victory. Aureliana urged Lupus to make a clear path for his king so that he could get to where he needed to be. He was little match for his new lover, however, and before he knew where he was, the king was surrounded by his attackers, his defenders almost nowhere to be seen; or at least not on the board.

'You need much teaching, my Dacian cousin!' Aureliana laughed at Lupus's ineptitude.

Lupus could not help but be roused by the glint in her eyes and the glorious smile on her face; he managed to resist the temptation to ask for a lesson then and there.

Drustans was next. He knew this game already, stressing to the group that he had often played it. That was clear from the speed with which he, just like Aureliana, moved the pieces round the board. Lupus whispered to Germanus how strange it was to be entranced by pieces of wood being moved by hand! He and Germanus wanted Drustans to beat Aureliana; to teach her a lesson, to see her lose, to have to admit defeat. At first, it seemed as though Aureliana would win easily; but then Drustans got back into the game, and Aureliana's king was in grave danger. Was she fooling Drustans? At the point where the Dumnonian thought, and Lupus and Germanus believed, that victory was his, she pounced, finding a way through for her royal charge to the corner of the board. Drustans grunted grudging congratulations. This left only Germanus.

'Are you aware of the import of this game, Germanus? Are you willing to play with me?' Aureliana turned to him. Germanus smiled wryly and nodded. 'It is just a game to pass the time', she continued.

Lupus turned to Drustans, hoping for an explanation, but the Queen's *magister militum* put a finger to his lips and shook his head. The two combatants sat squat and square opposite each other, hunched forward to focus on the game. The light was fading, but Lupus and Drustans could see the tension on Aureliana's face. The fire in the corner threw their bodies into relief, casting shadows on the painted dining room wall: two black shapes framed against the classical decoration of pillars and curtains and Greek gods.

Aureliana made the first move. It took her a long time to decide where to place her attacking piece, and she held onto it long after selecting the square. Then her fingers let go and she leaned back to await a response. Germanus's hand hovered over the board, as if selecting fruit from a market stall. He touched several pieces, feeling their weight, before selecting one to move, just as a good general would have chosen his best men on the eve of battle. Drustans sighed, whispering to Lupus that Germanus was leaving his king dangerously exposed to attack from the side. Aureliana's next move seemed to confirm the vulnerability. Lupus decided to concentrate not on the board but on the combatants' faces, for, though no tactician, even he realised that this game would be won, or lost, in the mind.

Aureliana's lower lip was curled up and under the upper, her top teeth biting hard into the flesh of her chin. Her gaze was fixed on every one of the 49 squares. Outwardly relaxed, Germanus rested his head on his left hand, cheek pushed up towards eye as a result. From time to time he raised his right eyebrow as he studied not only the board but his beautiful opponent. Germanus's next move saved his king from capture, but Drustans and Lupus looked at each other as if to agree that it was only a matter of time before the Briton took the Gallo-Roman captive. Then, almost imperceptibly, Aureliana seemed to lose ground after her initial gains, with a series of moves that became ever less sure: eyes moved quickly round the board, identifying, assessing, summing up options; lips pursing, fingers tapping, then a move. Germanus countered quickly; Aureliana had not anticipated well enough. She thought long and hard before her next assault. Another move from Germanus saw Aureliana become more disturbed; the king was near his throne and the enemy was no longer at the gate. She made one last ditch attempt to achieve victory through attack. But Germanus was ready for her; it was soon all over as he moved the king to his throne, out of danger of his enemies. The new Archbishop of Britannia could not quite contain his satisfaction. Lupus recognised the slight upward curl of the corners of the mouth, the most that would ever be detected of the pleasure of triumph. Germanus brushed his hand over his head as Aureliana sighed all the air out of her body. Her shoulders sank.

'Your tactics were masterly: the way you lured me to my defeat. I am glad that you are on my side, Germanus.'

'I am not on "your side", Aureliana. You know why I am here.'

'But it is an omen: an omen that you will conquer, that you will rule. Let this be a sign to you, Germanus.' The Queen of the West Britons looked adoringly at her new *magister militum*. Lupus began to worry as a result.

❋   ❋   ❋

Crowds rushed to the city gates as Aureliana led the combined forces into her capital. Many came from the fields outside the walls where they had been tending crops. They stood by the ditches that formed the first line of defence against the Vortigern. Others lined the main street leading to the forum. There were cheers as people realised who was arriving home. Children ran alongside the foot soldiers, mimicking the marching. Men and women followed the royal party, carrying wood, food, small livestock, *amphorae,* and other kinds of storage container.

'Welcome to my home; welcome to Viroconium Cornoviorum.'

Germanus nodded in acknowledgement of Aureliana's greeting while Lupus took in the sight before them. There was a busy market operating in the centre, with shops, a bakery and various merchants' establishment all doing a brisk trade. There was no sign of a church, but there were several temples and many shrines to the old gods. Aureliana explained how the original central buildings had been refurbished as much as possible, but that some of the repairs had been done badly: a lack of the proper materials and, even more of a problem, skilled workmen. Germanus remarked to Lupus how Viroconium was not like Antissiodorum, where *Romanitas* still held sway. Here, most of the civic structures made of stone and brick had been pulled down at least to their foundations and replaced with equivalents made of wood.

Aureliana kept trying to impress on her guests how Roman ways were still followed. Nowhere, she argued, was this more evident than in her own palace, whose wooden frame rested on the foundations of the old basilica at the place where it joined what remained of the public baths, now home to an open-air market. Eventually, Aureliana realised that her guests were less than interested.

'My apologies, my Lord Germanus, comrade Lupus. You must be tired. You will be taken to your rooms. I have already arranged for you to have private access to our baths. We still have proper plumbing here; we are civilised people.'

※   ※   ※

Lupus looked out of the window of his room in the palace: lots of hustle and bustle; shouts and smells of people buying and selling; a woman breast-feeding her baby at the edge of the *macellum*; a one-legged beggar imploring passers-by to give him some scraps; a take-away food stall where a man cooked meat over a *focus* while people queued all the way around the corner of the palace in anticipation. Beyond this scene were shops and businesses, houses, and offices; a *ferrarius* was beating a sword into shape; a potter tried to show his apprentice how to form an *amphora*: men at a *cupona* whistled and flirted at the girl who was serving them. There were two temples: one to Jupiter and one to Mithras. But there was no sign of a Christian church of any sort. To both north and south lay open spaces where crops were cultivated within the safety and security of the city walls. In the far distance, by the northern-most city gate, were the remains of the *castrum*. Lupus saw the men of the combined forces pitching their tents there and then receiving a first round of rations. There must have been at least 2,000 soldiers having their evening meal in that compound. Most surprising of all was what lay in the further distance: an aqueduct, still working, according to Aureliana, who had already invited Lupus to refresh himself at the town baths. So much for the collapse of *Romanitas* in Britannia. A steam, a shave and a massage were more than he had been able to get in the eternal city.

'So then, Lupus, here we are in Britannia.'

'I did not hear you enter, master.'

'The element of surprise, that is what we must hope is our advantage over the Vortigern.' Germanus clasped his hands as he spoke.

'But do you not think he will know of our arrival in Britannia by now? After all, Aureliana is a *foederata*; she only rules here with his consent.' Lupus looked at Germanus, keen to get his views.

'I know, Lupus.'

Lupus looked at his master. For the first time since the destruction and murder back in Armorica he thought that Germanus was tired; old even. His eyes were grey and sore. But then he changed; became a different man. Germanus looked up and motioned Lupus to keep talking, then stood without a sound, though only a *pes* separated the two of them. Lupus realised what was happening: Germanus must believe there was someone on the other side of the bedroom wall. Once in place, Germanus whisked up the latch, threw back the *foris* and overcame the spy; all in less than a *momentum*.

'Who on earth are you?'

※   ※   ※

'So Germanus and his troops are in Viroconium?'

'They are, Agricola. I am more impressed by the man than I thought I would be. He knows much of warfare and is well in command of the troops. Aureliana's forces will respect him; he will have no difficulty commanding them.'

'And you will give him his orders?'

'Nobody gives Germanus orders. He is his own man. Have another grape and stop asking questions.'

'If you say so, but I…'

'But I nothing. Soon we can overthrow the Vortigern, claim the riches that Coelestinus has promised me and rule, as is my right, over all of Britannia, just as my forbears did. No more usurpers, no more Vortigern and his Saxons, no more Romans, and no more Christianity: back to the old ways, once and for all!'

'The whole of Prithain – and you, its ruler!'

'My family, my race, my religion: all will be avenged!'

'And does Germanus know what you plan to do to him to make this happen?'

'No.'

'You are sure he has no inkling of the "sacrifice" he will have to make?'

'He can have no idea of what is in store for him. He knows nothing of our ways; of what has to happen to ensure that all will be well.'

Agricola flung the *lodix* off the bed. His thumb and first finger rubbed a nipple until it swelled erect; the hand then traced its way down the body; it circled the navel, then continued to the top of the thighs; fingers grasped the hair, teased it, stroked it, arranged it; then parted it to ease the way in.

'Not again Agricola. There is no time. I must meet my high council and hear from Germanus about his plans. You need to get back to Londinium and your master before you are missed.'

'We will make time. Germanus and the Vortigern must wait…'

Agricola helped himself onto the bed then down over the naked body beneath him.

'No. There is no time…'

'There is always time. *Audentes fortuna iuvat*, Aureliana. Fortune favours the brave!'

CHAPTER 9

A spy's identity is revealed; Germanus meets his new high command; Severianus considers his options

'So, my friend, who are you and what were you doing listening at the door?'

No response.

'Staying silent will not get you anywhere with me. We can sit here for as long as you like; you will not leave this room until I know what you are up to and who sent you.',

Still no response.

'Would you like something to eat?'

Germanus looked over to the apples on the table by Lupus's bed.

'No? Well, I am going to have one. I'm hungry. Lupus – throw me an apple and help yourself to one too.'

Germanus took an enormous bite from the fruit.

'Mmmm – excellent. It's a long time since I tasted an apple this good – almost as good as those in my orchards. What say you, Lupus?'

Lupus pursed his lips, took and munched a second apple, then scrunched his face in agreement, wiping the excess juice from his stubble as he did so.

'Are you sure you don't want anything to eat?' Germanus pressed the intruder.

This time there was a stubborn shake of the head.

'Here, take the rest of mine. I haven't poisoned it.'

Lupus watched Germanus give the little spy the rest of his apple. The spy took it. Not much of a secret intelligence service if they send a child to listen in, he thought. Or perhaps it was a cunning move; a waif like this one now greedily devouring the rest of the apple would largely go unnoticed, especially when they looked like the son, or daughter (the *exploratorem* seemed sexless), of a slave family. But then Aureliana had boasted on the journey up from Isca that there were no slaves in Viroconium; she had abolished slavery when she ascended the throne. The Queen of the West Britons might have done away with slaves, but she had certainly not eradicated poverty if this poor creature was anything to go by. It had no shoes on; looked as though it had not had a wash in weeks; wore the filthiest tunic that Lupus had ever seen. Then there was the smell.

'Would you like another one?' Germanus looked kindlier at the surprise visitor this time.

The waif looked up, thought for a moment, then nodded. Germanus selected what looked like the best apple still in the bowl.

'You can have this on one condition: you have to tell me your name, and who sent you.'

The apple was proffered. The waif lunged forward; Germanus whisked the fruit away. Another futile lunge; and another; then the creature finally spoke.

'Barita. My name is Barita.'

At first Lupus could hardly make out what was being said, but he had at least been in the country long enough to recognise that this was how a Briton spoke Latin: very badly and with a thick accent. The interrogation continued. Germanus switched to British.

The waif-spy could not stop talking, in between gorging on the apple, now that Germanus spoke in her own tongue. It was she, Germanus explained to Lupus, an orphan; parents killed in the war between the Vortigern's troops and the West Britons two years previously. Eventually Barita burped, then held out her hand for something else to eat.

'No more until you have told me why you were listening at the door.' Germanus shook his head. Lupus tutted in agreement. Barita pouted. Germanus could not help but smile to himself at the waif's *duritiam*. But he persisted.

'Barita, look at me. Why were you listening at the door? Who told you to do it?'

The proffered apple was accepted.

'Ambrosius.'

'Ambrosius? Who is Ambrosius?' Germanus demanded.

'He is the Queen's younger brother,' Barita replied.

'But I thought her brother was dead?' Lupus was getting confused.

'That was Aurelianus. He was our king until he died. Barita looked sad as she explained.

'So why is Ambrosius not king in his place?' Lupus remained confused.

'The Britons have different ways Lupus,' Germanus interjected. 'If Aureliana was the second born after Aurelianus, which I assume she was, then she would inherit the throne, even though she is a woman. If she dies before Ambrosius, then he will become king.'

'Thank you for the explanation, master. What strange ways the Britons follow!'

Germanus and Lupus looked at each other.

'He's the man who kills people', Barita whispered

'Who is? Ambrosius?' Germanus and Lupus spoke in unison.

Barita nodded.

'Who does he kill Barita? People you know?'

Barita nodded stiffly. Tears ran down her cheeks. No reply. No movement. No emotion except the moisture on her face.

'What did Ambrosius ask you to do, Barita?'

The girl looked up at Germanus. She had the biggest brown eyes that Germanus had ever seen. Even Lupus felt a paternal pang as the waif replied.

'Ambrosius said that I should watch your every move. That I should listen out for what you said, what you were planning, who you talked to, and report back every day when the sun went down.'

'Did he now? And what have you told him so far?' Germanus looked at Lupus as he spoke.

'Nothing. There is nothing to tell.' Barita looked down at her feet as she replied.

Germanus turned away from Barita and raised an eyebrow at Lupus. Lupus knew what that look meant; something was being planned. Germanus rummaged in his pocket and pulled out a gold coin. Barita's eyes lit up. Germanus held the money between his thumb and forefinger and then stretched out his arm in front of the waif's face. Lupus remembered the times when he had seen his master play with Patricius, asking his son to guess which of his hands was clutching the coin that would be given as a prize if Patricius guessed correctly.

'Barita, how would you like to work for me? But it will have to be our secret. You must tell no-one.'

Barita reached out to take the coin. Germanus withdrew his hand as she tried to grasp the money.

'Will you work for me, but pretend that you are still working for Ambrosius as well? Our secret?'

The coin was again proffered. And an apple; the whole bowl, in fact. Barita nodded. Germanus looked at her; looked into her eyes. He smiled gently at the waif; stretched his hand out.

'Our secret?'

The girl nodded. Germanus did not move. She looked up at him, questioning. Then she realised what he was waiting for.

'I promise, by the gods', she stated firmly, in her best Latin.

She snatched the money and the fruit as soon as it had been held out to her.

'Very well. Now this is what you will tell Ambrosius; what you heard Lupus and me talking about. And…'

Germanus flicked another coin into his hand and held it directly before Barita's eyes. Barita waited patiently for her new master to issue his further instructions.

'And…you will watch his and Queen Aureliana's every move, every word. Then you will come and tell me what happened, what was said, what was planned. You understand?'

The girl nodded and smiled. As she accepted the money, she thought how much this man Germanus looked like the father she had always wanted.

※　　※　　※

'I have heard a good deal about you, my Lord Germanus. And this must be Lupus. I am Ambrosius, *tribunus*. You already know Drustans'.

Ambrosius stood up slowly and saluted as Germanus and Lupus entered the council chamber through a door at the top of a narrow wooden staircase on the outside of the building. The rest of the high council followed them. The outer door was closed, and the curtains drawn. A servant had to bolt the window tight shut as the cold January wind blew outside. The councillors turned and bowed, each in turn, as Ambrosius introduced them. Here were the men who ruled what Drustans explained had been the old sub-province of *Britannia Secunda*.

Drustans was the final one to bid the strangers welcome. Lupus could not help but notice the fine bleached togas over silk tunics, the rings, the bracelets. Each of the eight men of the city council had a servant behind them, ready to do their bidding. Germanus said nothing as he walked towards the far end of the room. Lupus followed him to the two seats placed either side of the throne, set apart on its raised dais.

'Queen Aureliana will be here soon. Then we can begin.' Drustans cleared his throat as he spoke. His speech was almost as stiff as his *focale*, thought Lupus. As if in response, Drustans loosened the scarf from around his neck.

Germanus raised an eyebrow, nothing more, with the suspicion that he was being kept waiting. The men gossiped to each other in British. Lupus grinned at the shocked faces when Germanus joined in the conversations, demonstrating his command of the language, even down to the slang that some of the councillors were using. The wait for Aureliana was a short one. Drustans was about to apologise to Germanus when in walked the Queen of the West Britons. Lupus gasped when he saw her. He had thought her beautiful before when he first met her the night after Eustachia's funeral; now, there were no words to describe her radiance. This was the woman for him. Her red hair was tightly pulled back from her forehead and tied off with braids at neck level. The headdress glinted with jewels. She wore a long purple *stola,* above which was draped a cloak wrap with a gold trim. On her right forearm, she wore a snake amulet. If this had been Eustachia, thought Lupus, she would also be carrying a fan or a mirror; instead, Queen Aureliana had her left hand on a *gladius* sheathed at her waist. A true queen and a real warrior; but then he and Germanus already knew that. They were to sit down at a council of war, but not before Lupus had raised himself slightly to get a good view of her cleavage.

'Please be seated. My Lord Germanus, next to me if you will. Lupus, on my other side next to my husband.'

Lupus gasped. He started to speak but no words came. 'Husband?' he thought. 'How can she be married, and to this man?' He looked at Aureliana, hoping that she would give him an explanation, becoming indignant when she ignored him. Or did she? Was there a slight shake of the head in her eyes. Germanus squeezed Lupus's arm. The young man steadied himself. He would talk with her later. In the meantime, Lupus now took a close interest in Viroconium's *tribunus,* given his relationship with the Queen of the West Britons. Ambrosius was the tallest man in the room by far; long, straggly, unkempt black hair, the bronzed, muscle-bound arms and legs pushing out from under his short tunic. His thick hair covered much of his face, but there was no way it could ever conceal the deep scar that ran down from his forehead to his left cheek via the socket where his eye had once been.

'My Council knows all about you, and your new bishopric, my Lord Germanus. They have already been briefed; including about your recent losses – for which they – for which we - are sorry. But enough; we must go straight into talk of strategy against the Vortigern.'

Aureliana bade the two visitors sit, as already instructed to do so. She nodded to a servant standing patiently by the entrance. He came and cleared the table of its glasses and plates and then retrieved a large, rolled map from a cupboard by the window.

'This is a map of...'

'Of Britannia.' Germanus cut the Queen of the West Britons short.

Lupus watched one and then the other, keen to observe more of this new formality between general and young monarch; it was not like the banter he had witnessed when Germanus and Aureliana had first met. Lupus was not the only one; Ambrosius watched intently as the talk of tactics began; but Aureliana's husband said nothing. Drustans did all the talking for the West Britons, and in Latin; they all spoke Latin when Germanus was present from now on.

※   ※   ※

It had snowed heavily in Eboracum. Traffic and trade from and to the south had slowed almost to a halt. Severianus thought back to when he was *dux* of the garrisons on the wall. Those were the days. When he was in charge and there was something to be in charge of; and he would be again, as Vortigern, Pontifex and Imperator. Severianus took his Bible, opened it at the place that he had marked, ready for the service that he was now about to take. One of the Jew's parables.

'Render unto Caesar', he muttered. 'What a load of rubbish!'

The Bishop of Eboracum looked at his Druid insignia, carefully hidden under his cloak.

'That's what I render unto; always and forever!'

It was cold in the church, but the place was full. Severianus looked round his congregation. His flock represented every sort in northern Britannia. Young, old; rich, poor; Roman, Briton; soldier, civilian. There were even a couple of his old unit members waiting there for him to preach. This last group included old Augustus, or so he called himself; a deluded and delirious old man who went around all the time with an old cavalry banner. There cannot have been a single person left in Eboracum who had not grown tired of his stories of daring and adventure when he was in the cavalry. But not one of the old guard rembered ever seeing him in uniform of any description.

Severianus began his sermon. Speaking quietly at first, he gradually increased the volume, periodically pointed at the cross and individual members of his flock. He knew them all by name; knew their backgrounds, their histories, their hopes, their fears. Made each one personally responsible to him; not Jesus Christ, but him, Severianus; that was how he ruled. He could see into their hearts; all the more easily since they, and he, had embraced Christianity. And that was what would see him to the Papacy.

Severianus finished by warning the congregration against following false prophets, and especially those who came from across the *Mare Britannicum*. They would bring nothing but misery, like their forbears. Only Severianus, as God's servant here on earth, that is, could deliver better times. No more rule from Londinium, no *Saxoni*. Just like the good old days, but with Jesus as the Saviour. The congregation cheered. Another triumph.

'What a two-faced bugger I am!' smiled Severianus to himself.

'Praise the Lord', they all shouted.

'Alleluia, He is risen!', the Bishop of Eboracum replied.

'He is risen indeed', came the response.

Augustus hurried out of the church without leaving a donation. He limped agitatedly back to his apartment by the city walls, making sure that no one was following him, scuttling, and shuffling through the side streets as he hurried home. Once inside his little home, he sat down to write his latest report to Germanus. There was much to tell his old commander...

CHAPTER 10

Lupus rages, Coelestinus is perplexed, Germanus baptises

'How could you? How could you make me think that – that there could be something between us?'

'But there is something between us, my little wolf.' Aureliana giggled and shook her head, letting her hair cascade down her shoulders.

'You are married! You announced Ambrosius as your husband! And I thought that I meant something to you!' Lupus banged his fist on the table that separated him from his love.

'You do. But you should not be in my private chambers, you, and me, alone, again.' Aureliana wagged a finger at Lupus.

'Why did you not say anything? About being married!'

The Queen of the West Britons came over to Lupus, put her hand up to his face and stroked his cheek. 'Why should I? What does it matter?' She put her hand behind his head, ruffled his hair, pulled her towards him.

They kissed. Lupus tried not to respond to her advances, but he could not help himself. He eventually pushed Aureliana away, looking down at his feet to avoid her eyes. 'I should go. Like you said, I should not be here. I am sorry to have disturbed you, your Majesty.'

Aureliana laughed. 'My dear sweet boy. Ambrosius and I are brother and sister. We only married to protect our bloodline after Aurelianus was killed. It is our tradition; nothing more. There was no love involved; other than the love that you share for your family.'

'But you share his bed!' Lupus dare not look at her as he spoke.

'As brother and sister, yes. But not like I do with you, my Lupus.'

'I do not believe you. Brother – sister – husband – wife. I don't understand. You confuse me – you are just toying with me, laughing at me. Why did you seduce me? Why did you make me want you?' Lupus buried his head in his hands; began to cry.

'Because I wanted you Lupus. I was attracted to you. I still am.' Aureliana cupped the young man's face in her hands. 'Look at me Lupus.'

Lupus shook his head. Aureliana opened her tunic, forcing his face in between her breasts. He resisted, tried to pull away. Aureliana countered; made him stay in his special resting place. The place where he wanted to be. She stroked his hair, kissed his head, giggled.

'Come, my little prince. Let me lie with you. I will make everything all right again, I promise. And I want you to promise to keep our little secret. Yes?'

Lupus looked up at Aureliana's face, framed between her breasts. A nipple was pushed into his mouth. He licked and sucked. Then he nodded.

'Now tell me all about your master and what he is up to. When you have finished doing what you are doing now, that is…'

※　　※　　※

Coelestinus waited for the sun to rise. Even with every candle lit, he could not read the words properly. At least he had found the relevant document. The Pontifex unrolled the dusty scroll. He sneezed, loudly, then turned to make sure that nobody had heard. Even in the pontifical palace there were dangers: rivals for the papacy everywhere; pagans ready to go back to the old ways; *barbari* too present in all walks of life, or what was left of it.

'Germanus will save the day, I know it!' Coelestinus drew the candle on the library desk nearer to the scroll, put on his glasses and began to read. He murmured to himself as he traced his finger down through the text. The Pontifex shook his head, tut-tutted, leaned back, and sighed. He was tired; there had been little sleep since he had met Germanus and given him his orders. And he had promised the Queen of the West Britons a share of the empire; it was written in the agreement between them. He needed Aureliana; needed her to keep Germanus focussed on his task; needed her to report back to him.

※   ※   ※

The amphitheatre was one of the most impressive Germanus had ever seen. Bigger than the one in Antissiodorum where, as governor, he had presided over games and other celebrations. Its size and robust brick construction surprised him, given all the other ruined public buildings that he had observed since landing back in Britannia. The gates opened in front of their horses. Germanus and Lupus rode through and dismounted. Lupus knew that something was wrong as soon as he and Germanus entered. This was not the inspection and drilling of Aureliana's troops that had been requested. Yes, there were men waiting inside, but not standing to attention in neatly ordered ranks; the centre ground was empty, the stalls full of people, many of them women, waiting as if for a gladiatorial contest. Ambrosius stepped out from behind the gates, clapping his hands together to signal their closure.

'Is this how you obey my commands?' Germanus turned to face Ambrosius, angry at the Briton's duplicity.

'You are a Roman, Germanus. I don't trust Romans after what I have been through. I am British. If you are to command me and my men, then you must prove yourself worthy of your generalship. And in this country, there is only one way to do that.' Ambrosius stuck his *pilum* into the ground and walked towards the centre of the amphitheatre.

'Does your queen know of this? I answer to her and the Pontifex in Rome, not you.' Germanus shouted after him

'I am her *tribunus*. Aureliana relies on me to help her govern.'

'And what about you Drustans? You are *magister militum*. Do you not answer to Queen Aureliana? Has she not ordered you to obey my commands?'

Drustans said nothing and averted his gaze. Lupus could see the twitch in his cheek muscles. Perhaps at least one of the Britons was a man of principle.

'So just the two of us, Ambrosius?'

'That's right, General. If you beat me in open combat, witnessed by my men, my people, then you will deserve to command them – and me.'

There was silence all around the amphitheatre.

'But not your queen?'

'Aureliana has gone to visit the northern part of her kingdom. She will return before long.'

Germanus sighed, then turned to Lupus and gestured for him to take his cloak and find a *scutum* from the pile that he had noticed as they arrived at the amphitheatre. There was plenty of choice. Lupus brought two back. Both were of standard wooden construction, with bronze bosses. One had an old-style Roman design on the front: wings and a thunderbolt. Germanus smiled as he remembered bearing such a shield when he was a young *protector*. Lupus had wondered about bringing the other shield for Germanus to look at and possibly choose. His master was now a Christian Bishop: the *chi-rho* symbol should be at least offered, even if only as a joke to lighten the mood. Much to Lupus's surprise, that was the *scutum* Germanus chose. He was already wearing his *lorica*. He now put the ceremonial *galea* back on his head and checked his *gladius*. He gripped the shield handle, arm straight in classic combatant pose, and waited for his opponent to make the first move.

'So, you are ready to take me on, old man?' Ambrosius laughed.

'I am ready. You do not frighten me, young Briton. You are no match for me.' Germanus spat on the ground.

'Even with one eye, I am twice the man you are, Germanus.'

The crowd began to chant. Men beat their spears into the ground to drum up a rhythm. Germanus took out his *gladius*, hoisted his *scutum* in front of his torso and waited for his opponent to ready himself. Ambrosius motioned for a *scutum* and a *gladius*. Once equipped, he looked up to where the crowds waited silently, wondering what would happen next. Amrbosius stared back at Germanus and waited pursing his lip and looking around the crowd.

Germanus pushed his shield boss into Ambrosius and knocked him off balance. The crowd laughed and jeered. Ambrosius gasped and rolled over to avoid Germanus's follow-up sword thrust, then pushed himself up onto his knees with the aid of his *scutum*. Turning to face Germanus, he went on the attack, cutting, slashing, and lunging with his *gladius*. The crowd was in awe of Germanus's footwork. Ambrosius could not get close enough to land a serious blow on his opponent.

'Is this your best effort, Briton?'

'I am not finished with you yet, Roman!'

Germanus laughed, taunting Ambrosius by dancing round him, scarring his arm and cheek with slices of his blade. The Briton wiped the blood away and advanced once more. The battle continued. Lupus noticed that Germanus used the whole of the central space in the amphitheatre; at first moving towards his opponent, next withdrawing and moving away and then attacking again. Germanus also took full advantage of Ambrosius's missing eye and blind-sided him at every opportunity.

Then the one-eyed man began to fight back. Was Germanus tiring? The movement was less agile, the response less rapid. Lupus estimated that Ambrosius must have been 15 or 20 years' younger than his master. The Briton sensed the weariness also. Before long, Germanus was backed into a corner of the amphitheatre, right by the entrance doors. He took a false step, aided by Ambrosius's right leg. Germanus fell backwards. Ambrosius leaned over, ready to push his *gladius* through the older man's heart. But it was a trick. Germanus was not weary at all, for as Ambrosius moved in and down for the kill, the archbishop-general leapt towards his opponent, gripped his wrist, forced the sword from his hand, tripped him up and had him on his back. Within seconds the position had been reversed. Ambrosius's own *gladius* was about to be thrust into his neck.

Germanus laughed manically, looking around at the crowd to see what they wished: complete silence. He pushed the *gladius* further into Ambrosius's neck. For a second Lupus thought that he was going to kill the loser; the victor's eyes were so full of anger. Then the fury dissipated; a calm came over him; his body relaxed; he slackened and stood up. Ambrosius coughed and spluttered and turned his head away. Lupus was wondering what would happen next when the amphitheatre gates burst open. It was Aureliana. Never had he seen a woman so angry.

'What have you been doing? 'Stop this at once!'

All eyes turned to the gates, now reopened. The crowd rose; the soldiers stood to attention.

'Aureliana! I thought you were…'

'I was, but once I knew what you were planning…'

'How did you know?' Ambrosius looked sick with worry and remorse.

'I am the Queen. I know everything! Now stop it at once! We have more important battles to fight!' She dismounted, shouting at Ambrosius and Drustans as she did so.

'No Aureliana, I will not! Germanus has beaten me; he has the right to choose whether I live or die.' Ambrosius kneeled down, ready to accept his fate.

'You will do as you are told, Ambrosius!'

'This man had to prove himself. Drustans and I should be leading the troops. Not him!'

'Germanus is the chosen one. And now he has proved it. He has triumphed in battle against the fool Ambrosius. You should be getting ready to fight the *Saxoni* – not our leader.' Aureliana slapped hard on the cheek.

'Let him be, your Majesty. I have been slaying men like him for years.' Germanus had finally spoken. He took the *gladius* away from Ambrosius's throat and stood up. Then he looked all around the amphitheatre, slowly, as if weighing up every man, woman, and child. He called the British soldiers out of their seats and to attention in the middle of the ring. Germanus then made them repeat his words, the words of the old Roman *sacramentum militare*, albeit carefully adjusted to swear loyalty to the Queen of the West Britons and the Archbishop of Britannia as her new supreme commander.

'You had no need to do this, Germanus. To indulge in our petty squabbles.' Aureliana rode over to Germanus as he ordered the troops back into neat lines.

'I had every reason to do it, Aureliana. And you know that as well as I do.'

Lupus looked at Germanus then watched Aureliana react to his words to her. Then it dawned on him. His master, his adopted father, was his rival for the queen's affections; not Ambrosius. Should he laugh or cry? He wondered what Germanus was whispering to Aureliana. It must have been a question, and one that she was taking a good deal of time to answer. She seemed to be writhing inside as she decided what to do; Germanus said nothing, merely stared at her waiting for an answer. Eventually she nodded almost imperceptibly. Aureliana clapped her hands; four servants came running. She issued orders to them in British and they scurried off to do her bidding. Drustans and Ambrosius looked at each other, obviously shocked by what the servants had been asked to do.

Germanus went to the far end of the amphitheatre and stepped up into the royal box. Aureliana, Drustans and Ambrosius followed. Unsure what to do, Lupus waited until Germanus beckoned him to join the platform party. From their stand, the group was able to see all around the packed theatre. Germanus motioned everyone to sit down, then addressed the crowd.

'I have been asked by your Queen Aureliana to command her forces. I come with my own troops and those of General Aetius, commander of the western imperial armies. You will have seen my men stationed just outside the city walls. Together with your forces, we can beat the Vortigern and bring civilization back to this island. Look around you. Look at how it used to be; look at how it is now and think how it could be again. You could have it all: more than enough food and water for everyone; education, trade, prosperity. Freedom from outside attack; a place where you and your children can grow up and grow old without fear: no violence, only peace; no hate, only calm. Think about it. This is what you had; this is what you could have again.'

By now Germanus had everybody's attention. He waited until any further murmuring had stopped and then continued. He inched to the edge of the platform as if to bring his audience closer to him.

'But that means we must work as one force, whatever our differences, whatever our prejudices, whatever our private desires. Without one common goal then there is nothing; nothing but squabbling, infighting, anarchy.'

Lupus looked across at the others sitting behind Germanus. Aureliana straightened her dress across her lap, over and over, clasping and unclasping her hands. Ambrosius pursed his lips, then stroked his chin, then pursed his lips again. Drustans looked down at his feet, crossing and uncrossing his legs.

'I do not care about your petty squabbling or your tribal loyalties.

Not for now, anyway. You can deal with that later, peacefully, through discussion, compromise, and agreement. You cannot fight a power like the Vortigern in your present disorganised state. It weakens you, and I need to know that you are strong.'

Germanus paused. Was it to work out what he was to say next? Was he gauging his audience? Was he wondering how they were reacting; how they would react to what he wanted them to do? He turned to look at Lupus for a brief moment and smiled. Germanus must have had an idea and it began to dawn on Lupus what was going to occur.

'That is why I am going to baptise you all: my soldiers, your soldiers; husbands, wives, children, grandparents, grandchildren; families and friends, locals and visitors. Anybody and everybody who wants me to command them, to lead them to victory, must swear allegiance. Germanus paused again. He looked at the others behind his master on the platform party and smiled. Aureliana, Ambrosius, and Drustans looked horrified.

'Very clever', Lupus nodded and whispered to himself.' Very clever indeed. He is a crafty old bugger.'

CHAPTER 11

Aureliana communes; a Saxon arrives; Germanus falls from grace

Despite the bitterness of the February wind, she did not feel the cold against her naked body; rather she relished the way in which the air made her nipples rise and her skin dimple. The moon was full and clear; the thousand thousand stars dotted across the blue-black sky gave her all the warmth that she needed. Beyond the city walls, deep into the northwest, lay Mona. She pictured the road, first Roman, then British, then secret ways hidden from all but the Knowing Ones: the side roads, the tracks, the paths, the waterways. Finally, there was the temple; the place where she had been initiated, where she had become high priestess. The last of her kind, she had been called. But she would be the first of a new line now that she had coupled with Lupus. Once the gods had been appeased; been given the ultimate offering; then she would triumph.

Her fellow priests and priestesses would be there, all in their robes, all waiting for her to plunge a dagger into the offering's heart and to pull it out and hold it high, up to the gods. They would watch as the smoke from the burning body rose to feed the stars, the same stars that watched over her now. Yes, the gods would be pleased with her; they would favour her beyond measure when she brought them Germanus, especially now, when he had committed the worst possible sin against them. She had watched him baptise all the people of Viroconium in the sacred Hafren. Even she had agreed to be doused but, unlike the others, she had kept her clothes on, and Drustans and Ambrosius had only stripped to the waist and left it at that. They had done it though; sworn allegiance to this Jesus Christ; had the water poured over them; had the sign of the cross made on their foreheads. As a result, Germanus had gained sway over all of them; chosen the one thing that could bind them together as a fighting force: he had made this Jesus sound like a person that anyone could be loyal to without sacrificing custom or tribe or the old gods; like someone who would bring peace and prosperity to all, like it used to be, like her father had told her how it was in the old days. Or so it seemed.

'Very clever, Germanus, very clever…

They were now Christian: not Roman, not the Vortigern's, not Saxon slaves, not of the Pontifex. All of them; at least for now. Her people would not be so easily fooled in the longer term. Germanus's own people might do whatever he told them, but not Prithains like her and her tribe. The gods understood. They knew that she had to pretend to accept this one ridiculous, unworthy god. But they would reward her with victory over all once she had given them the ultimate prize: Germanus.

Aureliana laughed, knowing that she carried Lupus's child. This was her destiny – his destiny – their destiny: the ultimate victory over her enemies and the perfect revenge for her family and her tribe. Suddenly she felt cold. She turned away from the window, closed the shutters, put on her night robe, and went back to bed.

The Queen of the West Britons slept soundly that night.

✼   ✼   ✼

'Welcome!'

The Vortigern was in all his finery: best armour, rich robes, and overcoat; royal rings on his fingers. His honoured guest was less well attired: beneath a thick, fur-lined cloak, the new arrival wore a cloak fastened at the shoulder by a golden brooch; underneath was a simple tunic with a girdle round the middle, below which were trousers and then leggings from knees to toes. On the man's feet were rough leather shoes secured with straps. As if to emphasis his origins in a cold country, the visitor was still wearing hat and gloves.

'Come, my Lord Hengest. Take off your cloak. Wine and food after your journey?'

Hengest looked around the room. He nodded acknowledgment to Agricola, standing by the fire in the far corner of the room. The Saxon scowled at Pelagius as soon as he saw the pectoral cross hanging from the priest's neck. Hengest took the wine that was proffered to him and downed it in one go. He belched and wiped his mouth with his hand.

'Where is Germanus? I thought he was supposed to be here.'

'He should have been, but one of our enemies got to him first.' The Vortigern stood up and came over to Hengest. He gestured to the Saxon to sit down at the table and eat.

'What do you mean?'

'He was assassinated. Him and his family.'

'You. You are Agricola, right?'

'Yes, my Lord Hengest.'

'And this one. The Christian?' Hengest sneered.

'I am Pelagius. You will answer to our Lord Jesus Christ one day, I promise you.'

Hengest roared, looking the priest up and down. 'I will be with Woden and Frigga and all my gods before I turn to your Christ!' The Saxon paused, bowed his head. 'But I am sorry about Germanus. I was looking forward to fighting with him again.'

'We all were, Hengest.' The Vortigern looked over at Agricola as he said these words. Agricola avoided eye contact. 'But I have full confidence in you, and Agricola, of course.'

'Look what I have brought you my Lord Vortigern.' Hengest

motioned to the Vortigern to come over to the window. He nodded to a servant to open the shutters. Hengest smiled as he pointed outside.

The Vortigern thought that the parade of men would never end. Hundreds, thousands, tens of thousands.

'How many men?' The Vortigern smiled at Hengest, put his hand on the Saxon king's forearm.

Enough, your Majesty. More than enough, in fact.'

※   ※   ※

'Don't be too hard on him, my Lord.' Aureliana put her hand on Germanus's forearm. 'Germanus? Please?'

He grunted, only partially persuaded by the Queen of the West Britons.

'Why did you marry him?'

'What on earth makes you ask me that?' Aureliana laughed.

Germanus turned to look her straight in the eyes.

'I would have thought you would have chosen a stronger man than Ambrosius. He seems to be a flawed individual.'

'He was my only choice; family duty and family loyalty. He is my younger brother. It was our custom, in the circumstances. There is no sex though.'

Germanus raised an eyebrow in the way only he could do. 'I knew of your old British practices, but I thought they had died out when we took over.'

Now it was Aureliana's turn to grunt.

'Not all civilization emanates from Rome. Not now, not ever!'

Germanus was surprised by the venom in Aureliana's voice.

'How do you think my brother lost an eye?'

'In battle?'

'Two years ago, Ambrosius was on his way back from meeting with none other than your General Aetius. Yes, the great man himself. I can see that you are surprised. Ambrosius had gone, despite my advice that it was futile, to try and persuade your commander of the armies of the west to help the Cornovii defend ourselves against the Vortigern's attacks and retake the whole of Britannia. But Aetius refused, saying that he could not spare any troops. We did not have Germanus doing the asking then, of course.' Aureliana laughed as she paused. Germanus thought that there was now a tear in her eye but decided it was the candle flicker. 'On the way back from meeting with Aetius, Ambrosius was captured and tortured by the Vortigern in Londinium.'

'How was he captured?'

'He was betrayed by someone in my camp. We never found out who.'

'And in any case, Aetius was not to be moved; he said that his senior tactical advisor for Britannia was totally opposed to it.'

'So that was the end of it?'

'That was the end of it.'

'And who was this senior tactical advisor?'

'We were never told. Would you happen to know who he might have been?'

Germanus shrugged his shoulders.

'I thought not. No matter.'

'What happened then, Aureliana?' Germanus gripped his chin with his hand.

'Ambrosius was used as a bargaining chip, to coerce me into being the Vortigern's *foederata.*'

'And the eye?'

'Well, I didn't give in straight away. The eye was gouged out and sent back to me as an incentive to do as I was told. More followed, notably what used to lie between his legs. But we don't talk about that.'

'Talking of bargaining chips, where and how is my son? Where is Patricius?'

Aureliana came close to Germanus; looked up at him, stroked his arm with her hand.

'All will be well with your son, I know it. I swear to you on the graves of my ancestors that I will help you find him once the Vortigern has been overthrown. I make no excuses for Ambrosius's behaviour, but perhaps his anger is understandable. And his jealousy.'

'His jealousy? Who is he jealous of?'

'Why you of course.'

An eyebrow was raised.

'I cannot tolerate this kind of emotion when it comes to the battlefield and my command.'

'I was thinking more of your bed, Germanus.'

She put her arms around his neck and kissed him. He did not stop her, not then; nor when she kissed him again.

CHAPTER 12

Germanus travels to Londinium;
Ambrosius knows his enemy;
the Vortigern plots and plans

The road to Londinium was well preserved and the first part of the journey from Viroconium was easy. Beyond the boundaries of Cornovian territory, however, caution was needed. The Vortigern might be ruler of all Britannia, but that did not prevent the appearance of *bagaudae*, former slaves and farm workers who had lost their livelihoods as the Roman elites had left or been removed from their positions during the purges of previous generations. The Vortigern had not been much better; power and wealth had been centralised and concentrated in the capital and estates turned over to senior troops loyal to the new regime. It was safe in the towns, but not outside them. Drustans explained the ever-present danger on the open roads. That was why, whenever possible, he led them along old tracks that had been there long before the Romans ever arrived in Britannia.

Lupus wondered why he was part of the group. He would have been more use back in Viroconium, keeping an eye on Ambrosius. But Germanus had briefed Barita on who and what needed to be observed and, in the case of a real emergency, she was to get a message to them via one of the horsemen he had appointed to run his personal post service. Lupus still smarted at the thought of being cuckolded by Aureliana, and now that he had plenty of time to observe the Queen of the West Britons and his master at close quarters, he wondered who else was a rival for the Queen's affections. Yes, periodically she smiled at him in the special way that made him quiver, just like he had done that fateful night when he had lost his virginity to her, but those moments paled into insignificance compared to the amount of time that Aureliana spent laughing and joking with Germanus. He even saw her stroke the archbishop's arm at one point. Germanus flickered a smile, or so Lupus thought.

From a safe house near Londinium (where the four of them spent the night), it was only a short ride to the capital. It was deemed safe enough for them to go back to using the main road. The remainder of the journey was uneventful. Occasionally, the group passed small clusters of huts set back from the main road and, if the smoke emanating from the centre of the pointed roofs was anything to go by, still in use. There were few other travellers on the road, which was in such bad repair in places that the horses had to be guided onto the banks either side of the highway so that they did not stumble. The mileposts still allowed travellers to judge their rate of progress, and by the time that the sun was at its height, Germanus and his inner cabinet were within sight of the city. It was a clear, still day, and smoke drifted straight up into the blue-white sky from buildings within the walls. Properties that lay just outside the defences were all deserted and derelict, though there were men and women in the surrounding fields cultivating food. It was undoubtedly meant for the people inside the walls, as there would be little point in transporting provisions further afield when the amount that could be yielded from these few acres would more than feed everyone inside. Once close to the capital's defensive walls, it was possible to gauge the size of the city. Lupus commented that it must have been as big as some of the large towns of Italia or Gallia. Germanus gave a knowing nod. By the bridge across into the city gates, ships were moored, on both river banks. Goods of various kinds were being loaded off onto specially designed piers. *Amphorae* filled with what these storage vessels are usually filled with-oil, wine, perfumes-were in abundance on the quayside. At the head of the bridge were two soldiers, in Roman uniform. Germanus slowed his horse down to a walk, as did the others, and brought the beast to a halt immediately in front of these guards. The men had been leaning lazily by the bridge gateposts, talking to a woman carrying a basket with vegetables in it. They stood to attention once Germanus approached. He spoke to them in Latin, as if he were their commanding officer. Old habits must have died hard, and while their uniforms looked shabby and less-than-well-maintained, the guards rapidly snapped back into Roman soldier mode when greeted by someone they took to be a senior officer.

Lupus, Aureliana and Drustans looked at each other. This hardly seemed the best way of entering Londinium unnoticed, but, whatever Germanus said, he was believed and the four went on their way across the bridge. One of the soldiers warned the riders to watch their step; some of the timbers were starting to rot and needed replacing, and while this had been promised (according to the guards), nothing had yet been done about it. Germanus motioned the others to follow him in single file. There was silence just in case someone said something inappropriate. Lupus could not help wondering why Aureliana acceded to Germanus. Yes, he was her commander-in-chief, but she was still the Queen of the West Britons, in all her fiery, red-haired glory. For now, at least, it was obvious that Germanus was in charge. They moved slowly across the bridge, again passing men and women carrying wood, food, small livestock, *amphorae,* and other kinds of storage container.

The gates on the north side of the river were open; guards were there ready to close them in the event of attack. There would be plenty of time to do so, given the clear view that they had not only of the south bank of the river, but also the roads and countryside beyond, all of which had been cleared of trees for several miles. These guards ignored Germanus and his colleagues, given that the group had been vetted by those at the entrance to the bridge. The four passed under the strongly built gatehouse and into Londinium. The city reminded Lupus of Antissiodorum, though it must have been at least twice the size of his adopted hometown. There were the customary beggars and urchins who walked, ran, or hobbled, depending on their level of decrepitude, and the occasional tradesman or shopkeeper shouted appeals to try their produce or their workmanship.

Germanus whispered that the standardisation of the street plan meant that the forum would be easy to find. It was bound to be in the normal place at the centre of the city, where the two main roads crossed, north-south, east-west. The four were riding along the *cardo*, the north-south road, towards the centre of economic and political life of the city. Two small boys speaking in broken Latin ran alongside asking who the riders were and where they were from. One asked to hold the reins of Germanus's horse and lead it, but he shooed the lad away, as did the others when they were also approached. The urchins gave up the chase as the four riders crossed a stream by a sturdy stone bridge; then a second, this time less sturdy, and made of wood. Because of the potential danger, Germanus led the way and ordered the others to go one-by-one across this structure so as not to place too much weight on it. Soon they were in the forum, or what should have been the forum, for there was little that was left of what had once been a fine structure. Only a few stumps of pillars showed where the centre of the city had been. Similarly, the basilica had been demolished long ago. The only building of any significance left standing was a temple that lay just through and beyond the remains of the basilica.

Drustans pointed to a house near the centre of the city. Lupus and Aureliana looked at Germanus to see if he was going to react. Nobody spoke. This brazen entrance right into the Vortigern's capital was not going to work. Surely, they would be discovered at some point, arrested, questioned, tortured, killed; but it was as if Germanus knew something that the others did not; had some secret protection. Lupus even wondered if his master was beginning to believe in all this Christianity stuff. His suspicions were further aroused when Germanus stopped to talk to some children begging for food. He threw them a few coins which they fought over in the mud under the horses' hooves. The four riders dismounted and guided their rides through the uneven surfaces that had once been the forum. The neatly arranged pillar bases made for an odd contrast with the untidy way in which material from the buildings they had supported had been left in disorganised piles: bricks, posts, tiles, all mixed up together. It did not look as though any of this was to be used for a new edifice any time soon.

'It seems such a waste, does it not, Lupus? All this fine building turned into rubble, just because the Vortigern wanted to demonstrate that his power lay elsewhere.'

'How do you mean Drustans?'

'This was once the centre of Roman Britannia. Governors of the province, or at least the southern part of it, had this as their headquarters. This was the hub of political and economic activity. Until, that is, the Vortigern took over. He wanted to centralise his power away from the civic leaders. He rarely comes to the city now. But when he does, he stays over there.'

Lupus, followed by Germanus and Aureliana, looked over to what must have been the southeast of the city. The four of them were now straddling the *decumanus,* the main west-east road, as it intersected with the *cardo.*

'That is his fortress. He does not trust the populace to support him, so those to whom he takes a dislike end up in one of the cells inside there, as many, notably Ambrosius, can testify; and his little fortress is far easier to defend than the city walls. It would take a whole legion to man these ramparts properly. I should know, for it is where my father lived briefly after he was proclaimed Emperor.'

Germanus turned to Drustans, surprised by this revelation. Aureliana smiled, knowingly.

'Yes, he even took the purple there.' Drustans nodded, smiling sadly as he did so.

'Constantinus? The last British Emperor?' Germanus queried, almost incredulous that the man had any surviving relatives. He nearly blurted out that he had been present at the usurper's execution but then thought better of it.

All around the citadel were preparations for war. Soldiers exercising, being drilled, in mock-combat with each other, checking weapons and armoury. Germanus was tempted to look more closely but Aureliana took him by the arm.

'Let us go inside now', she said, wearily. 'I have a house in one of the side streets in the north of the city. We will be safe there; we will be among friends.'

The sun was beginning to go down as Aureliana knocked on the door, three times. Once inside, it was almost impossible to see. A few oil lamps were burning on a table in the centre of the entrance hall, while off to one side a *foculus* glowed with hot coals. Lupus shivered nevertheless; such a small brazier could never give any real heat. Aureliana could see he was cold; she smiled at him and for a brief second brushed her arm against his.

The Londinium contingent was already assembled, waiting to greet Aureliana and her new commander-in-chief. Lupus was surprised at their dress: instead of the lordly attire that he had expected, the men sitting round the dining table were shabby, even by British standards; workers not overseers; peasants and servants rather than tribunes and senior officers.

'My men are in disguise. It would not do to flaunt their identity in the Vortigern's capital. They rarely meet in a large group like this, so we should proceed quickly. It would be unwise if we drew attention to ourselves; large gatherings are banned in Londinium, unless approved by the Vortigern. These agents are organised in cells of three; some of them are meeting together for the first time. They have sacrificed much already, these people; and they are ready to sacrifice even more if they have to.'

Lupus's unposed question answered, the three newcomers sat down. Aureliana took the vacant seat at the head of the table; Germanus went to the other end so he could face her. Lupus sat next to his master, slightly behind him. The men looked weary, but once Aureliana started to speak, their eyes began to glisten and glow with the enthusiasm that infused her address to them. Germanus smirked as he listened. Briefly, Aureliana caught his glance and smiled back. Again, Lupus felt a pang of jealousy; he was always going to lose out to the older man.

It soon became clear that support for the Vortigern in Londinium and the south was strong. Yes, there were pockets of resistance, but they had been too weakened by betrayal, arrest, torture, and eventual death to be any serious opposition. The West British Army could only really count on Germanus's fresh infusion of soldiery, and especially the cavalry. Everyone nodded and even applauded when they heard that horsemen would be on their side.

'How many years is it since we last had cavalry fighting for us?' said one.

'What about Severianus?' Everyone stopped their conversation as Germanus spoke: the dark, deep voice; the measured tones. Lupus could see why Aureliana was in love with him.

'We have had little to do with him since he went over to the Vortigern', said one, who identified himself as Titus, though Lupus thought that he looked far more British than Roman, and his Latin was rough and ready.

'What could he do for us that he has not done already?' questioned Aureliana sarcastically.

'I understand your anger towards him, your Majesty, but if he were to be persuaded that his better interests lay with us rather than the Vortigern, he could be a powerful ally. After all, he commands the north and is a servant of the Pontifex. Perhaps he could be persuaded.'

Aureliana raised an eyebrow at the irony of Germanus talking in this way. It was now Lupus's turn to smile.

'I believe that negotiations should be opened with Severianus at the earliest possible opportunity. Think of it: forces advancing from Viroconium and forces pressing down from Eboracum. That would make the Vortigern think twice before launching any campaign, whether here or on the continent.'

'What makes you think that he would be open to such a suggestion, my Lord?' said one named Nectovilius. Titus and Aureliana both nodded in agreement.

'I believe that he can be persuaded. I have my own sources of information about Severianus. There are those in the north who would have him return to Roma in more ways than one.'

'You mean spies?'

'I mean sources of information Titus. That is all you need to know.'

Titus grunted. Nectovilius and the others said nothing. Aureliana asked for more information. Germanus gave it: strength of forces, support for the Vortigern, loyalty to the Roman way, adherence to the Catholic faith. She was impressed by the depth of intelligence. Her own *curiosi* had not had much luck in the north of Britain. The few who had managed to infiltrate had eventually been discovered and sent back to Viroconium horribly mutilated. Here was Germanus, surprising her once more.

'You make a powerful argument. Very well, we will enter negotiations with the Bishop of Eboracum', Aureliana agreed.

'Could you arrange for me to meet him on neutral territory?' Germanus asked.

'Lindum would be a good place. Near the border between Flavia Caesariensis and Maxima Caesariensis, but still just inside the Vortigern's territory', Aureliana replied.

The names of these provinces meant nothing to Lupus, but they clearly still did to Germanus and Aureliana and, indeed, the others. It seemed so odd that these men still looked to Rome for their names and their titles, their language, and their places. Would that it would always be so.

'But what of the Vortigern, Germanus? That is why we are in Londinium, is it not? I don't suppose you intend a peace summit with him, do you?'

The men all laughed at Aureliana's question.

'Not quite, your Majesty. But I do think we should try and find out more about his invasion plans, and what his weaknesses are.'

'Very well, my Lord. I will leave you to decide how best to achieve that aim. But first food and drink. Then we should sleep for a while.'

The Queen had spoken. No-one demurred.

※   ※   ※

Barita knew every nook and cranny in the palace; every street and alley, every house and shop in the capital. Viroconium was her home; it had been her parents' home, until they had died fighting the Vortigern. That seemed an age ago; another life that she could no longer believe had ever been a reality. She knew how to disappear. It was easy. Who noticed a dirty, ragged urchin? She could run in and out of crowds, lie in corners, hide in lofts. Barita was invisible. And now she worked for Germanus, even when she was working for Ambrosius, she was still working for Germanus.

'So, tell me, little girl, what have you found out about our Lord Germanus?'

'Yes, my Lord Ambrosius.'

'Well? What is there to say about him?'

Ambrosius looked her straight in the eye for as long as he could before her odour got the better of him. When she spoke, and he smelt her breath, he nearly puked. He moved off to the far side of his chamber and interrogated her from there.

'He is here at the request of the Pontifex. He is to return Britannia to Rome and the one true faith.'

Ambrosius snorted.

'And you believe that?'

'That is what I heard Germanus and his son say to each other.'

'His son? I thought he was dead or disappeared.'

'Lupus is his son now. He has adopted him.'

'Lupus is not a servant?'

'He was, but now he is a son.'

And what about Patricius. Does Germanus ever talk about him?'

'No. Every time Lupus raises the subject Germanus says that he does not want to talk about it.'

'What is Germanus doing about his missing son?'

'I do not know. Except one night I heard him crying in his room.'

'Crying?'

'Yes. It was late at night. He was sobbing and kept repeating a name: Eus–Eus-something.'

'His wife. She was called Eustachia. The man has a heart after all.'

'Can I go now?'

'Have you nothing else to tell me, my little *orba*?'

'Nothing that I can think of, except…'

'Yes?'

Barita wiped her nose on her sleeve, shifted from foot to foot, rubbing the shin of one leg with the ankle of the other as she did so.

'Except that the Queen is in love with Germanus, and Lupus is in love with the Queen.'

Barita jumped at the sound of Ambrosius's belly laugh. She became frightened at the madness in his eyes. The laughter turned to screaming.

'Get out! Get out, now!'

Barita managed to close the door behind her as Ambrosius's wine glass smashed into it.

※   ※   ※

'Germanus is alive after all? Are you sure?'

The Vortigern clamped his hands together at the news that his spy had brought him.

'Very much so, and now he is *magister militum* to the Queen of the West Britons, as well as Archbishop of Britannia, alongside all his Armorican titles.'

'Almost an emperor, you might say.'

It was Pelagius. The Vortigern nodded congratulation to a man who could slip into any room unnoticed.

'But, sadly, not an emperor on my side. How many troops does Germanus have?' The Vortigern barked, hoping that Drustans might be more fulsome in his replies.

'Well, he has the Cornovian army, and his Armorican Guard, and the troops that Aetius sent him. Ten thousand men, all told.'

'Ten thousand? That is a sizeable army!' Pelagius rubbed his chin. 'Are you sure?'

'I am sure. I have seen them all. The good news is that many of the extras are poor quality soldiers, the dregs of Aetius's armies. Germanus is even training women to fight!'

Pelagius laughed, but the Vortigern shook his head.

'And the bad news?'

'The bad news is that the Armorican Guard and the core of the Cornovian army are good: they are disciplined, fit and battle hardened. And he has cavalry with him. I have not seen horseman as good as them in a long time. They are only 80 in number, but they would make a big difference in an open battle.'

'They will be no match for my armies', declaimed Hengest. 'I have brought you three times that number. Even their cavalry will fall against my men. I remember not long ago when we overran *Augusta Trevirorum* and got into the government building, we found men so fat that they could hardly walk let alone defend themselves. Their guts split over their belts and down their legs. I bet they hadn't seen their dicks in years, not until we cut them off and held them up in front of their former owners before we garrotted them in the forum. No resistance. The empire has grown weak on complacency and overindulgence. The only real resistance came from their auxiliaries; men like me and mine. What the fuck happened to the Roman Empire?' Hengest spoke good British to say that he was a Saxon. He stood up, so tall that his head nearly touched the ceiling. The flames hissed as he threw the rest of his beer onto the *foculus*. 'There is only one advantage that our opponents have.' Hengest walked across and put his hand on the Vortigern's shoulder.

'I know.' The Vortigern nodded. 'And that is why I wanted him on our side.'

'It would have been good to fight alongside my old enemy. Now he is an archbishop as well. These bloody Christians get everywhere!'

'Hold your tongue, Hengest.' Pelagius held up his cross to the heathen Saxon. 'We will be victorious.'

'Oh, bugger off!' Hengest spat at Pelagius's feet.

'Enough! Enough!' The Vortigern made them sit down. 'We will triumph. I will take supreme command. Agricola will be my second-in-command'.

'Are you sure, my Lord?'

The Vortigern looked across at his informant.

'Of course, I am, Drustans. I have a good deal more experience than any of you could imagine. I still wish Germanus were on my side, though, especially when we invade Gallia and conquer the western empire. Perhaps there is yet time to persuade him, now I know that not only is he in Britannia, but right here in Londinium.'

CHAPTER 13

An ally is captured; a rescue mission is launched

Germanus leaned out of his bedroom window, impatient for the sun to set. Despite the season, it seemed to take an age until there was darkness. Even then, lights flickered across the city, coalescing into a glow that shimmered up towards the Vortigern's palace. Four flags, one on each corner of the central tower, blew strongly in the wind; so strongly that the Vortigern's emblem was fully unfurled. A Roman cavalry dragon: it had been many years since Germanus had seen that symbol. Fifteen? Twenty? Twenty-five? Was it so long since he had last been in Britannia? And what of Sevira? He should never have let her escape. She had been on the wrong side, and she should have been punished, like all the other rebels. Germanus had thought nothing of slitting their throats, in the case of the upper-class prisoners, or ordering his men to hang them in the case of the foot soldiers and followers of the usurper. There had been just one problem: Sevira, daughter of the renegade emperor.

'Flavius Magnus Maximus Augustus.' Germanus said the name out loud.

'Perhaps Magnus Maximus should have won. Perhaps then the western Empire would not have been in such a mess and I, Germanus, would now be *Imperator*, having taken over from my father-in-law.'

He banged his fist on the window ledge. He had been a virgin when he met Sevira. For all his military prowess and his bravado, he could not bring himself to insert himself into a woman, despite his father's early and best efforts, and later those of his fellow soldiers. In the end, he lied to get everyone off his back. Yes, he had done it; yes, it had been wonderful; yes, he regretted not getting himself laid good and proper much sooner; no, he would not waste any more time alone in the barracks instead of out on the town shagging every whore in sight. But it did not feel right. He had wanted more than the sweat and the saliva and the sperm shooting out of him. He had wanted a person to be a part of. And Sevira had been his other half.

What was he thinking? Eustachia was his *univira!* How could he even think of another woman? But Sevira had been the first. And it had been wonderful and marvellous and unforgettable and like nothing else that he had ever experienced, and ever would again experience. That was why he had let her escape. The night before she was to be executed, right in front of the same tower that still lay at the centre of Londinium, with its four dragon flags flying in the strong wind. He remembered the moistness on his lips as their mouths touched in a final goodbye kiss. He had watched as Sevira got into the boat and sailed down river to Armorica, she had said, but he had never found her there. And he had given up looking when ambition took over and success followed. Then there was Eustachia…

'Master – master!'

Lupus had opened the door as he knocked on it. Germanus could not get used to the servant as son, so he had stopped correcting him and, it seemed, Lupus was happier not to call him 'father' anyway. An unspoken agreement had been forged between the two. And they both knew that Lupus would never be another Patricius. Neither of them wanted that, in any case.

'It is Drustans!' Lupus answered the question that Germanus had raised with his eyebrows; no need for spoken word.

Aureliana followed immediately after Lupus.

'They have him', she whispered breathlessly. 'They have Drustans. One of my men saw him being taken away by two of the Vortigern's soldiers. They were heading for the citadel. My soldier returned here straight away. They will torture him. They will find out about us!'

'Wait. Not so hasty. When was this?' Germanus snapped.

'Just before sunset. They will only now be at the citadel', Aureliana replied.

'He will not yet have been interrogated?' Germanus asked.

Aureliana turned to the soldier who had brought the news. He shrugged.

'Is that all you can do? Germanus snapped.

The man stood to attention. Lupus thought he could see tears of fear in his eyes.

'He was with two of the Vortigern's men. They went off in the direction of the citadel. That is all I know sir.'

'Was Drustans being restrained? Was he tied up or in chains?'

'I could not see sir. I am not sure. They had their backs to me; I was some distance away.'

Germanus nodded for the soldier to leave. Aureliana motioned for the man to go. Once the door was closed behind the three of them, Germanus continued.

'What does Drustans know and what will he say?'

'He knows what I know Germanus. I doubt he will talk. He is a strong man. All are strong in Viroconium. He would rather die than betray us.' Aureliana nodded confidently.

'That may be the case, my queen, but I do not think we can take the chance. If he talks, you, we, all of us, are in trouble.

※　　※　　※

Germanus looked both ways down the street and then beckoned Lupus and Aureliana to follow him towards the forum. To preserve their anonymity, the three explorers covered their heads. The wind was blowing strongly from the north and drops of rain tickled Lupus's face as he looked ahead. Aureliana giggled as he sneezed. Germanus glared at the two of them. Suitably admonished without a single word being exchanged, they continued, the other two walking behind in single file, all three staying in the strongest shadows as far as they could. As they neared the forum, laughter and music could be heard coming from a side street. It sounded like soldiers playing drinking games; then a woman shrieked, and the men cheered. Some drunkards staggered towards the trio. Germanus spoke to them in British and they grunted a response. Lupus just nodded; Aureliana said and did nothing. The louts passed by, then turned down the side street from where the noise was emanating.

The forum was soon reached. Germanus gestured over to the citadel. People were going about their business; there was even a small market with shoppers milling about wondering what to buy, with stall holders imploring them to make a purchase. The Vortigern's palace was heavily guarded. There was no way that they would get in there. Germanus looked around for what seemed an interminable period while Lupus and Aureliana waited in the cold. Lupus watched Aureliana breathe in and out. He could not help but move down her body to her breasts, lightly moving. What would become of him? Of them? Aureliana looked at Lupus briefly, then turned her attention to Germanus. She nodded to Lupus to look towards the general. Lupus had not noticed that he had taken a stone from his pocket and placed it on his forehead. Then he closed his eyes. Soon, though, he put the stone back in his pocket, opened his eyes, turned, and beckoned Lupus and Aureliana to follow him. It was as if Germanus suddenly had a map in his head of every door and window, every nook and cranny, every road and street in Londinium. In a matter of moments, they were down an alley which ended in a blank wall. No chance of an entry here Aureliana thought, mouthing as much to Lupus and Germanus. Lupus nodded; Germanus shook his head, for as they approached the stonework, it became obvious that there were tiny steps cemented into the wall that led up towards a window.

Before Lupus and Aureliana could stop him, Germanus had climbed up to the window and entered. Now he was beckoning them to follow him. Aureliana went first; she had no difficulty in mounting the stony ladder. Lupus, never the nimblest person according to his master, took his time, and made sure that he did not look down. He got there in the end, thanks to a little help from his two companions, and the three of them were soon walking through the Vortigern's palace. There was laughter from a room far ahead. Lupus turned to Aureliana to ask her why the palace was so quiet, no guards, no servants, but Germanus motioned the two of them to be quiet. Lupus reassured himself that his master knew what he was doing. And certainly, if the citadel was heavily guarded on the outside, as it obviously was, then why the need for security on the inside?

Germanus seemed to know his way around the corridors remarkably well. Aureliana decided that he must have been here before. He had already told her that he had served in Britannia as a young soldier; had even met the great Magnus Maximus. She had found out a lot about this man, but not everything; more work was required. They reached a hall. It was almost impossible to see. A very few oil lamps were burning on a table in the centre of the room, while off to one side a *foculus* glowed with hot coals. As the three of them grew accustomed to the darkness, they were able to see that the room through which they were walking stretched to the full height of the building itself. Lupus wanted to ask what this place was for, but he decided that this was not the time for a lesson in architectural history. At the far side of the hall was a second courtyard, with colonnades all the way round. In the front was a large pavement area, decorated in complex geometric patterns. Beyond was a large pool. It was a long thin oval shape, with two protruding sections each of which had a fountain at its centre. The pool still had water in it, but there was a strong stench emanating from the whole area which suggested that the plumbing was not working properly. The fountains had cracks in them, and water was pouring out from all sides rather than spraying from the upper piping.

'Over there. That's where we will find their council chamber.' Germanus nodded over to a doorway at the further edge of the colonnade. 'And this way, I suspect, is the way to the cells.'

'Are you sure you want to go any further?' whispered Aureliana.

'I am sure', Germanus replied.

※   ※   ※

'Do you trust Drustans?'

'I trust him as much as I trust anyone in Britannia these days. He is from Dumnonia, the far west. They have an independent spirit; he could be loyal to anyone who gives him what he wants: Dumnonia. That and Ambrosius.'

'How do you mean, Agricola?'

'Didn't you know, my Lord Vortigern? I have it on good authority that Drustans and Ambrosius are lovers.'

'You would Pelagius. You Christians and sex! You are all fixated on it; or the lack of it!'

'Well, I thought it could be of advantage if we need to bargain with the Cornovii.'

'It could indeed Pelagius. Does Aureliana know?'

'I wouldn't be surprised if she doesn't join in. Brother-sister-commander.'

'You sound almost jealous, Agricola.' The Vortigern leered. 'Those were the days', he continued wistfully. 'It wasn't a sin then.' He glared accusingly at Pelagius. Agricola turned to the priest and then back to the Vortigern 'Little do they know', he muttered to himself.

'Anyway, who cares?' the Vortigern concluded, spitting into the *foculus* as if to underline his decision. 'Very well, Agricola, he can have Dumnonia when I am emperor. Make sure that he is kept under observation. I don't trust Aureliana as long as she is alive, and I trust Germanus even less, at least until he is pledged to me. Then I will be able to rely on his faithfulness unto death.'

'You don't think he believes any of this Christianity stuff now the Pontifex has made him an archbishop?'

The Vortigern laughed.

'You must be joking. Germanus is a die-hard pagan; always has been, always will be. I remember...'

The Vortigern stopped in mid-sentence. It would not do to reveal anything more about former relationships with the Armorican general.

CHAPTER 14

Drustans is unchained; Memor saves the day; Germanus fights on

'Enough. Enough, I beg you!'

'Then tell us where Germanus is! You will then be spared.'

'I know nothing about any Germanus.'

'Liar!'

Agricola smacked Drustans about the face then nodded to the *carnifex* to do his worst. The man took the branding iron and inspected the end carefully. Once he was satisfied that it would do what he intended, he buried the end into his makeshift *caminus*, waited until he judged the iron red hot and then applied it swiftly onto Drustans's side, whereupon he cried out to the point where he lost consciousness.

'It will be a while before he is awake. Let us go and eat. He will come round before dawn; I will make it so. But ensure that he has no water when he does.' The *carnifex* nodded as Agricola left the cell. After his master had gone, the man looked at his handiwork, checked to make sure that the Vortigern's crest could be seen clearly on the limp torso, then settled himself down by the fire. It had been a long day: time for some rest. He sat down on his *sella*, took out the *cenula* that his wife had packed for him, and started munching. It was the usual stuff, but he would have a proper meal when he got home. He stopped eating when

106

he thought he heard Drustans mutter, but the prisoner was motionless, apart from a gentle swaying in the wind as the body hung from the ceiling, the hands and arms stretched above the head. It was a wonder the shoulders were still in their sockets. But not for much longer. Not when Agricola got back.

In the meantime, Germanus had found it difficult to stop his two companions from rushing in to rescue Drustans. It would have been difficult to do so when they were three and Agricola's men were stationed around the torture chamber. Now that they were gone, and the weary *carnifex* was left to sleep off his snack, there was the possibility of cutting Drustans down and carrying him away to safety. There were not even guards at the entrance now. They were obviously eating in the mess hall on the other side of the courtyard. Perhaps Agricola himself was with them, just as Aureliana observed that Germanus regularly liked to dine with his troops. She would have to ask Agricola the next time they were in bed together; if there was a next time, that is. The cell door had been locked, but it was easy enough for Aureliana to pick it.

As they entered the room, they heard a low moan. Drustans hung there naked. Aureliana and Lupus turned away in a mixture of horror and disgust when they saw what the branding iron had done to his skin. Germanus bade them be still, but their gasps had already awakened the *carnifex*. The poor man knew little before Germanus had garrotted him; a small repayment for his labours with Drustans. Between them, Germanus and Aureliana managed to unchain their poor colleague while Lupus stood guard at the door. Drustans began to come round.

'You! Germanus…Aureliana!'

'Can you walk Drustans? We have to get you away from here before Agricola and his men come back.' Aureliana wiped Drustans's forehead with a moistened cloth while Germanus found some clothes for him to wear.

Drustans nodded, weakly. With assistance from Aureliana, he stood up, looking into her eyes apologetically. She shook her head in reply and began to dress the invalid. Footsteps could be heard. Germanus narrowed his eyes as he tried to work out how many were coming. Too many for comfort, that was for sure. But there was no way out; no way other than to stand and fight them. Germanus motioned Aureliana and Lupus to prop Drustans up against the wall by the door. Once they had done this, the general positioned himself behind the central podium where the poor victim had been hung. From there he could see anyone coming through the entrance, but they would not easily be able to see him, at least until they were well inside the *cubiculum*. The two soldiers who came in shortly afterwards never knew what hit them. Germanus had the element of surprise. Attacked from their blind side, both men were seriously wounded before they could cry for help and Aureliana finished them off with her *gladius* in their backs.

By now, Drustans was clearly regaining consciousness and seemed willing to try and escape, along with his rescuers. Germanus nodded. Aureliana nodded; Lupus decided he should nod also. They retraced their steps, hid from the few guards patrolling the courtyard, much aided by the nightfall, timed their exit to the point at which the soldiers were furthest away from them, then went through the high-sided hall and back towards the secret entrance. But their exit was no longer secret, if ever it had been. As they turned the final corner, they could see that across the passageway, ranged in front of the final opening, was a group of ten guards in full armour, marshalled by their captain: watching, waiting for the moment when Germanus and his companions would appear. The four of them stopped in their tracks, withdrawing back into the darkness of the passageway. Fortunately, as far as they could tell, their arrival had not been noticed.

'What are we going to do master?' We cannot get past them. They are so well armed, and we have so little weaponry between us?'

'We will find a way. There is always a way.' Germanus put his finger to his lips, frowning as he did so.

Aureliana wondered if he meant that, or he was just trying to convince himself as much as anybody that they could evade detection and capture. She could see Germanus wracking his brains. It seemed an eternity before he finally acted.

'This way.'

Germanus turned on his heels. Lupus assumed that they were going back to the main hall, which seemed a ridiculous way to proceed, but before they got to the centre of the complex, he led them down another corridor into what must have been the outhouses. Germanus looked behind and beyond his two followers and their wounded companion, but the guards were not in pursuit. A moment came when the cause again seemed lost: three soldiers were grouped in the doorway which they needed to pass through. What to do? Lupus looked at Aureliana, who shrugged her shoulders. After a brief moment, Germanus told the other two to stay where they were, then rushed out towards the men. He gesticulated to them: 'hurry, hurry – they are escaping. More help is needed. The Vortigern has sent for you to go and capture the intruders.' Much to Lupus's surprise, the guards gathered up their weapons and hurried off in the direction of the secret entrance. Once they were out of sight and earshot, Germanus laughed.

'Idiots. How stupid can you get?'

Aureliana laughed in reply. Lupus was too sick with worry to do anything. After all, they were still inside the Vortigern's citadel.

'Come on. This way.' Germanus exhorted the others to keep up. The double doors opened easily enough and out onto a balcony. This was a *horreum*; even Lupus recognised a grain store when he saw one. So that's what those soldiers were guarding. Germanus inspected the building. The balcony stretched all the way round the large warehouse. Beneath, there were huge sacks of grain, no doubt the provisions had been laid aside to service the large army that was assembling in Londonium. Germanus beckoned Lupus, Drustans and Aureliana to follow him to where a door opened onto a river wharf.

'We will have to jump. First, let us see if we can slow down the Vortigern's progress.' Germanus looked serious if not worried.

'How?' Aureliana's eyes were glinting with excitement and fear. Lupus could not help but notice.

Germanus saw some empty sacks near the loading bay doors. He made Aureliana and Lupus prop Drustans up against the wall and then instructed the two of them to tear the sacks into strips. Germanus lit them using the oil lamps that were burning by the entrance to the *horreum*. In order to give them more time, he bolted the double doors to the store. The three of them placed the lighted sackcloth round the balcony and into the roof rafters. It was amazing how quickly the fire took hold. Within a few moments the superstructure was alight; the flames were soon spreading up into the roof timbers.

'Come, we must escape! We will have to jump onto the wharf.' Germanus gesticulated to them all as the *horreum* doors were being battered down. The soldiers must have been inhaling the smoke since coughing could be heard. Lupus saw tears in Aureliana's eyes; his own then began to sting, as if in sympathy with her.

'You first, Aureliana. Take my hand and then climb over the balcony edge. I will lower you down as far as I can and then you will have to have faith and let go. Break your fall by letting your knees relax – don't resist, don't stiffen!'

The Queen of the West Britons said nothing. She merely obeyed, without murmur, without fear. She was soon looking up at Lupus and Germanus, beckoning them to follow swiftly.

'You next Lupus. The same way. Don't be afraid now.'

Lupus did not dare be afraid. Even a moment's hesitation would get him in trouble with his master. Germanus gasped as he took the strain of Lupus's weight once he had gone over the balcony.

'Let go now Lupus; and remember to break your fall.'

Lupus dare not do anything. He froze.

'Let go, damn it!'

'I cannot, I dare not.'

'Damn you – in the name of God – all the gods – let go!'

Lupus looked into Germanus's eyes; he could not resist. He felt as if something, or someone, had gripped him round the waist and lowered him gently to the ground as he let go of the hand that had been holding him. Aureliana then whisked him away into the shadows to avoid detection. From their hiding place they could see Germanus begin to clamber over the parapet, with Drustans on his back. The flames had reached the loading bay. As the general jumped over the bannister with his heavy load, the balustrade collapsed, and he fell to the ground, headfirst, Drustans flopping on top of him.

※　　※　　※

It had snowed heavily overnight in Armorica. Memor had not gone to the funerals but now came to the villa to collect Segovax's ashes. The muscle that had been left behind (such as it was) was busy trying to patch up the farm buildings. Germanus had given orders that priority should be given to the agriculture. People needed to be fed before palaces could and should be rebuilt. That was one thing that Memor had always liked about Germanus. He wasn't like the other overlords, making it ever harder for ordinary folk to earn a decent living, lining their own pockets, fiddling the tax returns, loyal only to themselves and not the province and certainly not the empire or its rulers. No, Greater Armorica had been lucky in Germanus; no wonder people had been fleeing from other parts of the western world and into the province. They would be safe there as long as Germanus was in charge.

Memor had a bad feeling. Something had gone wrong. Things were not as they should be. Germanus was in trouble. Memor could feel the pain; pain and fire. He decided to return to his smallholding, the one that his son had built for him when he retired from public life and began to see his visions. He bade farewell to the villa staff, then headed off, one of Germanus's servants guiding his way. The journey home on foot seemed to take forever. He was old, had lived long enough. Helping Germanus on his journey was tiring. If he could just save him this time, then the faithful Memor could go to sleep forever.

Back in his hovel he prepared a meal and made himself comfortable. He stoked the fire and felt the flames grow. He searched deep into his mind, looking for anything that would tell him what was happening to Germanus and how he could save him from danger and even death. Nothing came. He threw his special potion onto the fire to see if that would help. Still nothing. He reached for the twin stone of the one that he had given Germanus before he left for Britannia, placed it on his forehead, and closed his eyes. The sweet smell of the smoke filled his nostrils, making him lose consciousness. The scene came to him: Germanus was engulfed by fire, crying out as he fell into the flames.

Memor pressed the stone harder to his forehead. The images returned. This time Germanus was on the floor, in agony, clutching his leg. The *haruspex* concentrated on the images of his lord and master, the man who had befriended him and his son over so very many years. He opened his eyes and leaned over into his own fire, his face only inches from the flame. Then he put his hands over the top of the heat and began a waving motion, drawing the smoke towards him and past him and out of the open door. Memor closed his eyes again and focused on Germanus's face. At first the pain was excruating as he drew it out of his master and into his own body. A broken leg, possibly two broken legs from a steep fall. This would take all Memor's strength and skill.

He threw more of the potion onto the fire. The flames rose up as far as the roof of the little hut; so far that the timbers were in danger of catching fire. Not that Memor could see or care: he had to act now; this was no time for caution. He closed his eyes and pressed the stone to his forehead. The images came back, then the pain, as he drew the injuries away from Germanus and into his own body. Gradually, he could see the face in his vision begin to relax. No longer were the features grotesquely contorted. The mouth and the eyes returned to normal; the teeth were ungritted, the fists unclenched. After a final throw of potion onto the fire and one more spasm of referred pain, Memor knew that he had done his work. He could see Germanus smiling amid the flames.

'It is done', Memor groaned to himself. 'I am so tired. I will rest now.' At which point he clasped the urn in which his son's ashes had been stored, turned onto his side, and fell into a deep coma.

✳   ✳   ✳

'Where does it hurt?' Aureliana looked anxious.

'Nowhere! I am fine'. Germanus waved her away.

I don't see how you can be fine after that fall!' Lupus grimaced.

'But I am fine. I was protected. The gods were on my side. Now we must hurry.'

Germanus, Aureliana and Lupus, together with their ailing colleague, hurried back to the safe house, taking a different route from that previously used just in case they were being followed. Lupus had the unenviable task of helping Drustans. The poor man was hardly able to walk, not surprising after his torture, but it was a miracle that he could move at all. Periodically Lupus enquired if he was able to continue, but the Dumnonian merely grunted and pointed ahead, as if to say, 'keep going.' If his back was held in the wrong place, Drustans let out a cry. Lupus thought how much that branding must have hurt.

The centre of Londinium was chaos. Shouts and cries were coming from the garrison. Men were rushing from all four corners of the city to help to put the fire out. Germanus and his three companions were heading away from the citadel, though even as they reached the outskirts of Londinium, they could still hear the noise. Lupus noticed a gateway ahead; for a moment he thought that they were leaving the city altogether, but at the last instant Aureliana made them veer away to the right and into the safe house. She tapped lightly on the door, then tapped again, using the same rhythm; then tapped a third time. Eventually, the doors opened fractionally, and a head peeped out. It was a relief to the three of them (Drustans was in no state to think anything) that they were welcome in that place. The lookout hurriedly opened both doors as far as he could without making too much of a noise (though the door hinges were rusty, given the creaking sounds that they made). The escapees rushed in as quickly as possible. The door closed rapidly behind them. Once they had got their breath back, they were given food and drink. Drustans sank into a chair and fell unconscious. One of Aureliana's men nervously quizzed the group, anxious to know if there was any threat to the safe house.

'You are back? What happened?'

'Later. We will brief you later. Poor Drustans needs to be treated first. Let me look at his wounds. Fetch water and ointment.' Germanus beckoned for help in getting the invalid upstairs, now that others had rushed into the room to see what was happening.

'Space! I need space! Clear a way.' They all gasped as Germanus lifted Drustans onto his shoulder, up the stairs and into a bedroom at the back of the house. He snapped at Lupus to follow him. For the next two hours Germanus ministered to the invalid. He stripped him, bathed him, dressed his wounds, gave him medication. Eventually, Germanus came downstairs.

'He will live.' Germanus looked about to collapse. 'Now leave me! I will sit down without your aid!'

'We have paid a price for tonight, Germanus.' Aureliana was not fooled. The great man was in pain.

'A price, Aureliana?'

'Your leg. You cannot have done what you did without injury to yourself!'

'But look at the damage we have done to the Vortigern tonight. There must have been a year's worth of grain in that warehouse. The King of Kings will be very displeased!'

'Rest. Master. You are in pain.' Lupus joined in.

'I am no such thing!'

'Let him be, you two!'

'Drustans! But...' Lupus could not believe that there he was, standing in the doorway.

'I don't know what you gave me, Lord Germanus, but it has certainly done the trick. I am restored. Remarkable!'

Lupus and Aureliana looked at each other as Drustans laughed. He came forward and shook Germanus by the hand. Germanus smiled and put his hand on Drustans' shoulder.

'Well, I have had a good deal of medical experience in the field, but I have surpassed myself this time', Germanus replied quizzically.

'Come, Drustans, sit down. Let us eat. You must be hungry after your ordeal. Then tell us what happened.' Aureliana looked anxious as she spoke.

'And tell us what you told them – and what you did not.' Germanus added.

CHAPTER 15

Germanus lives; the Vortigern holds a triumph

'Well, well. *Quod mirum.* This is a turn up for the books. What shall I do now?'

Severianus put down the letter. Germanus was alive after all. It made sense given that the Bishop of Eboracum's idiot mercenaries had failed to find definitive proof of his rival's death. There must have been a double; someone made up to look like Germanus.

'Clever; very clever. I should never have trusted Hengest and his men to deliver. These *Saxoni* are all as thick as pigshit.' Severianus laughed; laughed so loudly that his servant came running in to his chamber to see what was wrong.

'My Lord, what is the matter?'

'Nothing. Nothing at all. I have just been outwitted by General Germanus, so why should anything be wrong?'

'But …'

'But nothing. Now leave me', Severianus snapped at the servant. 'Germanus – alive! Bugger! Bugger! Bugger!' That was not the plan. Now he will be Pontifex and I will not. I know it! Coelestinus would never give the throne to me. Bugger! Bugger! Bugger!'

Severianus threw the letter across the room. He lay on his bed for hours. As the evening wore on, there was a knock on the door. A servant had come to light the lamps in the chamber. Severianus let him go about his business and then leave. It was dark outside and almost as dark inside. The Bishop of Eboracum got up from his bed and searched for the letter. He found it over by his chair, picked it up, sat down and took up the oil lamp from his *scrinium*.

'What would the gods have me do? I am tired of being a Christian, or pretending to be one, more like. How many years have I spent spurning the old gods: my gods? Enough is enough. This gives me a way. While the Vortigern remains in power I will never succeed. My son has betrayed me, thanks to his master. And I will never be Pontifex as long as Germanus lives. But he need not die just yet. Not until he has served my purpose. Welcome back from the dead, Germanus, you are just the man to help me restore the true religion to this land!'

Severianus stamped his feet. A servant rushed in.

'Fetch my scribe. I have an important letter to write. Now!'

※　※　※

It had been a long time since there had been so much pageantry in Londinium. Germanus was the only one of the group who remembered when Britannia had been reconquered after the fall of Magnus Maximus and there was a special victory parade to celebrate. Not even the smoke that still rose from the granary fire could cloud the event that was now starting, judging by the cheering of the crowds that were lining the main streets all the way to the forum. Lupus felt strange in the servant's clothing that the Queen of the West Britons had made him and Germanus wear so that they could blend in. Aureliana and Drustans looked the part, even down to the dirt that they had smeared on their faces.

Germanus was keen to get as near to the centre of the celebrations as possible. Lupus and Aureliana both noticed that, despite his miraculous escape from the burning grain store, their leader walked with a limp.

The two of them looked at each other, but neither dared ask Germanus if he were in pain or needed a stick. They would not have heard the last of it if they had done so. They arrived in the forum. Every possible space was taken. All eyes were on the citadel, in front of which a wooden platform had been erected so that the Vortigern and his high command could watch the march past. The four of them were just in time to see the Vortigern emerge, in his purple robes and laurel crown, along with Agricola in full military uniform. Behind them came Pelagius in a long white robe. The three men were surrounded by a large guard of soldiers. No chances were being taken.

Germanus's heart sank when he saw Pelagius. He remembered their time together in Roma as law students. What a different world that was! Such different people they had been! Or were they? They had both set out to rule the world in their different youthful ways; Pelagius had certainly caused upset with his heretical theology. Germanus might never have 'got' Christianity, but, if the truth be known, he preferred Pelagius's free-will version to the sort that Coelestinus and that lot in the eternal city were peddling. And this was from the new Archbishop of Britannia! Germanus decided that, if there were a chance, unlikely though that might seem, he would like to meet up with Pelagius. Perhaps there could be a way forward for Christianity and the old gods in some blend that allowed people to worship in the way that they wished, whether to idols or saviours. Could some good come of an alliance between them, at least in terms of the sacred if not the secular? Germanus thought back to the days of his youth, when he and Pelagius had got drunk and pulled women together. *I wonder if Pelagius would remember me...*

The platform party was joined by a fourth figure. A huge man, far bigger than anyone else on the *rostra*. He stood there, looking all around him. Legs aggressively apart, he stamped his long spear down onto the wooden planking as if to mark his territory like some prowling wolf. His fur-lined cloak was held round his shoulders by a single brooch.

Beneath was a tunic overlaid with chain mail; a thick leather belt circled his waist. Attached to this was both a long sword and a short dagger. Unlike the other members of the platform party, this one wore trousers.

Germanus recognised this last man at once.

'Hengest, you old bugger.'

'You know him?' Aureliana looked at Germanus.

I do indeed, your…'Germanus stopped himself from adding the word 'Majesty.'

'He and I have done battle before. He has tried to invade Gallia more than once. So far, my armies have held him back. But he is a good soldier; much better than the men he commands. He is the worthiest foe I have seen so far since coming back to Britannia.'

Lupus could see that Aureliana was bristling at the thought that she was not the finest warrior in the land.

'You are not my foe, thank the gods.' Germanus had realised his tactlessness and rapidly tried to make amends. Aureliana smiled, half believing his flattery.

'Will we have a fight on our hands?' Drustans added, anxiously.

Lupus could see that, despite the miraculous treatment meted out by Germanus, the Dumnonian was still recovering from the previous day's torture. What had Drustans told his captors? He had said nothing in the safe house, and Germanus had not pushed the matter, though Lupus was certain that his master would find out soon enough.

'We will indeed have a fight on our hands, Drustans', replied Germanus. 'Look what is coming.'

The celebrations began with a *cornu* blast. This was answered from the other side of the forum by the sound of a *tuba*. The noise of the crowd died down in anticipation. The beat of *tympana* anticipated the regular footsteps of the military procession. The march past had begun. Germanus remarked to Lupus that it was almost like an old-style *triumphus*.

'Ironic, when you remember that he hasn't beaten anybody yet.'

The group laughed; Aureliana shushed them, just in case one of the Vortigern's many *curiosi* was listening in. But despite the mirth, secretly Germanus was impressed by the show of strength that was being put on that day. He counted what must have been twenty thousand troops marching through the city. Admittedly, over half of them were *Saxoni*, but even they looked well-armed and reasonably well trained. The procession must have lasted for two hours. It was tiring to be standing all that time, especially given the crowds, the pushing, and the jostling. But at least the mass of human bodies gave some warmth in the February cold. Once the last troops had passed through, it was time for prisoners to be paraded, just like an old Roman triumph. They were a sorry sight. Men, women, and children, bound together by ropes and chains and dressed in rags. Some had been whipped or beaten, judging by the welts on their bodies. One or two had lost their ears or noses, or both. The crowds jeered as these wretches were dragged past. 'Roman scum. Go back to where you came from. Britannia forever. Just wait till we take over.'

Aureliana explained that these had been families who were still loyal to Roma and wanted to be part of the empire, but one not ruled from Londinium by the Vortigern but from Roma. She did not concur with their politics, but she did not agree with what was about to happen to them either. These people were paying a high price for their opposition as they staggered to their deaths in the forum. Once assembled in front of the *rostra* they were made to listen to the Vortigern's speech before they were tied to stakes and burnt. Aureliana said that she recognised one man, his wife and two children. They had been cousins of hers who lived in the southeast; leaders of a place called Durovernum Cantiacorum before the Vortigern had pledged the land to Hengest and his troops. They had resisted eviction, and this had been the result.

The *cornu* and *tuba* players sounded their instruments in a joint fanfare and the noise of the crowd died down. The Vortigern came to the front of the *rostra* and began to speak.

'Citizens of Britannia. Your Lord Vortigern greets you.'

The crowds cheered. Germanus was intrigued by the voice's commanding resonance; what one would expect from the High King of Britannia.

'This is a momentous day for our country. Nothing can stop us now. See what armies I command. See what your leader has brought you: death to our enemies, those who would do us down and betray us; a future of plenty for all. We will rule for the people. We will conquer in your name. This place will be the centre of a new empire, a new Roma. The weaklings on the other side of the *Mare Britannicum* will be driven out. The glory days will return.'

Encouraged by the soldiers guarding the crowds to keep them in order, a chant of *Ave Imperator* went round the forum. The noise at its height must have been heard from miles away. The Vortigern nodded to the troops nearest to the *rostra*. The captives were dragged to the nearest post, tied up to it and then piles of wood were stacked around the bases. At the Vortigern's thumbs down, the piles were lit. Germanus turned to the others. 'I have seen and heard enough.'

The three nodded. They weaved their way through the crowd and back to the safe house.

※   ※   ※

Viroconium was cold and wet. At least it had stopped snowing. Still no word from Drustans or Aureliana. Ambrosius missed them both in their different ways: Aureliana as his companion and Drustans as his passion. Ambrosius smiled at the last night that Drustans and he had spent together before Germanus had taken his lover off to Londinium. There were times when he felt guilty about having Drustans in his bed, but Aureliana took it all very well. She did not seem unduly interested in sex with him, not that the full act was now possible. That had not always been the case; they had done everything together when they were younger, out in the fields on their father's estates, or in some hidden, dark corner of one of the farm buildings. At first it had been innocent fumblings; but as she became a woman, it had grown more serious. Fortunately, she had taken care of things, and they had never conceived a child together. Perhaps there should be an offspring: a son to carry on the royal line of the Cornovii. But somehow it seemed less important now that he had Drustans.

'Drustans my life; Drustans my love!' he said it out loud as if to convince himself that his *exoletus* was his and his alone. But he knew that Drustans liked women as well, possibly even Aureliana, though there was no proof the two of them had ever lain together. Ambrosius was just beginning to think about what it would be like to be with the two of them together when there was a knock at his bedroom door.

'Yes. Who is it?'

No reply.

'Yes. Who is it?'

Still no reply.

Ambrosius grew impatient. He opened the door roughly.

'You! What do you want?'

'I have information for you.' The girl wiped her nose on her sleeve. 'But if you don't want it, then I will go away again.'

'No – no. Come in. I will listen.'

Barita came through into Ambrosius's bedroom. She was scared that he might hit her like he had done before. She did not like him, but he paid her. She preferred the other man. He was gentle and kind. Now he had gone away, and she was afraid that he was not coming back. She had to keep coming to Ambrosius if she wanted to eat. She wouldn't tell him everything anymore, though, just like the man called Germanus had told her.

'So, what have you got for me?'

'I have information.' Barita croaked.

'I should hope so too. That is what I pay you for! Come on, tell me! I don't have time to waste on you.'

CHAPTER 16

Germanus brings forth a new Patricius and gains an ally

The stench from the burning captives pervaded the streets around the forum. The screams had long subsided. None of the four wanted to talk or even think about what had happened; it provided proof, if proof were needed, of the Vortigern's cruelty. Not that the empire or its Christian church were blameless. Germanus had seen enough oppression to last a lifetime. If only the old order could be re-established: the *Pax Romana*. That had to be the ultimate goal, even if he had to become a Christian to achieve it.

Germanus did not need to wait for Aureliana to show him the way to the safe house, even through the back streets. The way was almost empty; no doubt everyone was still at the celebrations in the forum. As they headed further away from the city centre, Germanus thought he saw a familiar figure in the distance. Another street and another sighting; then a third. What could Memor be doing in Londinium?

'This is not the way back to the safe house Germanus!' Aureliana shouted out louder than she should have done.

'I know, but I have seen someone that I recognise, and I need to speak with him. I want to find out why he is in Londinium. You three go ahead. I will catch you up.'

'But…'

'I will be fine.'

'No. Not since you were nearly killed. We are all coming with you', Aureliana insisted.

'Very well', Germanus sighed. 'Look, there he is.'

Aureliana looked at Lupus and Drustans as Germanus spoke. There was nobody in view; anywhere. They ran to keep up with their leader, nevertheless. Every so often he stopped, looked around, then changed direction. If they were not careful, discovery by the Vortigern's men was inevitable. They were now as far away from the safe house as they had ever been. They had to stop Germanus before it was too late, but by now he had disappeared into an alley. Which way had he gone from there? Lupus nudged Aureliana and pointed down the street towards a gateway into a town house. By the time they had caught up with Germanus, he was sitting on the floor with his head in his hands.

'What is wrong master?'

'Nothing Lupus. I was being stupid. Wishful thinking that I saw an old friend. Someone I relied on. Someone I needed and still need. It was just my imagination. We must go back to the safe house.'

'Yes, we must', Aureliana said, impatiently. 'This way.'

The four of them were about to start their return when a horrendous scream erupted.

'Someone is in trouble. We must help them.' Germanus jumped up and ran towards the source of the howling.

'It could be a trap', Aureliana said through gritted teeth, angry that yet again the return to the safe house was delayed.

'I doubt it. That was a woman in pain. I have heard that sound, not least when Eustachia was giving birth to Patricius.'

They ran into the inner courtyard. Several children played some game at the edge of a disused fountain, shrieking and giggling as they ran after another child who was obviously attempting to evade capture as part of their play. The hunted and the hunters ran towards the group of four. Not looking where he, or she, was going, the one in the lead ran straight into Germanus. He took the urchin by the elbows and hoisted him or her up so that they were face to face.

'So, my little warrior: are you winning?'

The little captive pouted his lips back at Germanus and stuck out a defiant lip. When Germanus spoke to him again, the child refused to look him in the face.

'Can you not speak? Is my little Briton deaf as well as dumb?'

No response.

'What is your name?' Aureliana interjected as she walked up close to Germanus' side.

'We are not here to harm you.'

'Leave him alone! Put him down!' A woman with blood on her tunic stormed into the courtyard to defend the child. Germanus let the urchin clamber down his chest and run away to join the others, now huddled for safety with the woman who had emerged from the townhouse. She was about to speak again when from inside the house came the most primeval shriek that any of them had ever heard. The woman ran back to the entrance to the house, crying 'Sulpicia, Sulpicia!'

Germanus went to the door. 'What is wrong with Sulpicia?' he asked.

'Why should you care, Roman?' the woman answered, spitting on the ground just in front of Germanus's feet as if to emphasise her contempt for this stranger and his companions.

'I care. Now what is the matter with her?'

'She is with child, but it goes badly. It will not come; it has been a night and a day already. Constantius, her husband, has gone to try and find a doctor, but there are few left anywhere, and it is the special celebration.'

'I will do what I can for your Sulpicia.' Germanus looked intently at the woman.

'What can you do?'

'I have knowledge and I have experience. I have done this before. I can help.'

There was another shriek from inside the house.

'It is too late,' said the woman

'No, not necessarily. Let me try.'

With those words, Germanus strode towards the house and entered. After a few moments he reappeared.

'Lupus, Aureliana, Drustans: I want you in there to keep order; and I may need your help.'

It was with great trepidation that the three of them followed Germanus into the house. It was immediately obvious that the place had seen much better days. All manner of crude farm implements, tools, and weapons such as swords, shields and spears were stacked at one side of the entrance. At the other were various sizes of cooking pot, beyond which, incongruously, stood two large *amphorae*. As they grew accustomed to the lack of light, it was possible for them to identify the source of all the noise, which had now turned to a low moan, punctuated by short shrieks and loud wailing. There were three women. Two stood on each side of the third, whom they supported with their hands under her elbows like the arms of a chair. The helpers were fully clothed; the one in the middle was entirely naked. She hung limply between her aides, her large paps drooping down to end in full, dark aureoles. Her belly was hugely swollen, the button pointing out aggressively. Black curly hair covered the place at the top of her thighs. As the unearthly sounds started again, blood and water gushed from Sulpicia's loins.

Aureliana wrapped both hands round Lupus's arm. He could see from the frozen stare and open mouth that she was as terrified and fascinated by the scene as he was. One of the women spoke, first to her companion, and then to Germanus.

'There is no hope: the child will not come.'

'There is always hope. Let me help.' Germanus walked towards where Sulpicia was trying to give birth.

'What do you know, Roman?'

'I know enough.' Germanus waved his hands. At this the two supporters stepped aside, immediately obeying his orders. Aureliana and Lupus were commanded to take their places. Before Drustans could be ordered to his station in the unfolding drama, he excused himself, ran outside, and vomited. It was a good while before he returned.

'Your name – it is Sulpicia?' Germanus took off his cloak, rolled up his tunic sleeves and knelt in front of the woman. The woman had only the strength to nod.

'Listen to me, Sulpicia. Do as I say. Can you do that?'

There was no response.

'Can you do that, Sulpicia? Your baby **will** be born.'

This time she nodded. Lupus and Aureliana looked at each other, surprised at what Germanus had just said.

'Open your legs wider, Sulpicia. Wait until you feel the movement inside and then push. Cry to the gods to release your child as you push.' Germanus placed one hand at the top of Sulpicia's stomach and massaged it. The other went down between her thighs. Gently, he widened the opening with his fingers. More blood and water spilled out.

'I feel the movement, Sulpicia. Now push; push; push.'

Sulpicia did as she was told, heaving and straining with all her might.

'Good! Now if the movement is gone, rest, breathe deeply. We will greet your child soon.'

By now Drustans had returned. He stood sheepishly in the doorway, not sure whether to look or avert their gaze. Next to him stood the children, wondering what was going on. Drustans did not stop them when they held his hand or gripped his cloak in anguish.

'The movement comes, Sulpicia – and I feel your child's head. It is not in the correct place, but I will move it as you push. It will be well Sulpicia, it will be! I promise you! Now, push, hard! Push, harder! Harder! Good; good, you are opening, Sulpicia.'

A whole shower of slimy water cascaded from the woman, over Germanus's hand and arm, splatting onto the floor. Aureliana and Lupus both felt Sulpicia's grip on their arms – like that of a strong man.

'Aureliana – bring me a stool. Don't just stand there – a stool, now!'

The Queen of the West Britons searched round for something suitable. She asked one of the two midwives, who brought one from outside. Aureliana then returned to the scene reverentially, silently, as if any other noise would break the magical bond that had now grown between Sulpicia and Germanus, who took the stool and placed it just in front of the birthing woman. He sat down on it, placing both his hands between her loins.

'Soon, Sulpicia. It will be soon now. Can you feel the child's head? Put your hand down between your legs. Aureliana, guide her hand to where the opening is. Now push hard; push hard; push harder. Now relax if the motion has gone!'

In Germanus's cupped hands could be seen the very top of a head. He turned the crown gently as more of this new life emerged.

'Again, Sulpicia, again. Push hard, hard, hard!'

More of the child appeared. Germanus held the head with the fingers of his right hand; the index finger of the left he used to draw a circle round the crown, opening the woman further. There came an enormous gushing sound, accompanied by one long cry from Sulpicia, louder and longer than all that had gone before. The head suddenly appeared, complete: eyes, ears, nose, mouth, then the rest of the slithery body dropped out into his hands. Sulpicia moaned and sighed, breathing, and panting with relief. Germanus asked Aureliana to feed hair into Sulpicia's mouth to make her sick. Moments later, she expelled the sack that was still connected to her new-born child. Sulpicia's joy turned to alarm when she saw the limp torso in Germanus's arms.

'No, no, my child, my baby. It has been too long. The gods have taken him.'

'Not yet, Sulpicia.' Germanus held the child's mouth to his and blew, gently at first, then more forcefully. He paused, then blew again. He put the still body face down over his knee; the arms and legs flopped loosely. He slapped the child's back, then turned the body over and breathed again into the baby's mouth. There was absolute silence. All around stared at Germanus. He repeated his actions, blew into the mouth one last time. The baby's hands and feet moved as if Sulpicia's child were struggling to come alive; there was a cough and a splutter; then a cry, and another cry, this time much louder, as the lungs opened fully. Seeing the child now lived, Germanus passed it to Sulpicia's open arms. Tears rolled down her cheeks as she put the newborn to her breast, rubbing the nipple to make the milk flow. All the tension fell away. Germanus turned towards the others, his own eyes moist.

'All is well. Sulpicia has a boy.' He laughed; laughed so loudly that Lupus was afraid all Londinium would hear him.

'And I have a son.'

No-one had noticed the man at the entrance or knew how long he had been standing there. The recent arrival rushed up to Sulpicia and the new-born baby, kissing the mother on the forehead as she sank to the floor in a mixture of joy, relief, and exhaustion. The man caressed her back as he looked at the infant's eyes, then turned to Germanus.

'I am Constantius, and I am in your debt.' He stood up and gripped Germanus firmly by the hand, then embraced him and burst into tears.

Lupus was surprised by how tenderly Germanus dealt with the man. He saw his master cup a hand behind Constantius's head and then embrace him to cry out all his anguish. After a few moments the man stopped his wailing and stepped back, as if suddenly embarrassed by his show of emotion in front of all these strangers.

'Who are you? Where have you come from? I could not have found such a good doctor anywhere. You must be from outside Londinium.' Constantius looked down at his fine robes, now splattered with blood and mucus. He tried to wipe the worst away, worried that he would be giving the wrong impression to his unannounced guests. He regretted asking the strangers so many questions. 'But come – this is no welcome for my guests. We can talk later.'

Germanus put a hand back on Constantius's shoulder. 'Do not worry my friend. Attend to your wife. And your son. They are your priority for now, first and foremost.'

Constantius ordered the two servants to bathe and dress Sulpicia and take her and the baby up to their bed chamber. Then he bade Germanus and the other three follow him into the living room. Another servant was waiting there. Once they were all seated, Constantius ordered food. The house was of opulent design. The walls were decorated with rich murals and the floor was covered with an elaborate mosaic depicting some theme from ancient Greek mythology. Lupus began to work out the story on the floor, but Aureliana nudged him to pay attention. Drustans stayed quiet at the back of the group.

'Welcome to my house. I am forever in your debt, strangers. You have saved my son, and my wife. But who are you? What is your name? I have not seen you in Londinium before.'

'We are from Armorica. We are here on business to see the Vortigern.'

'The Vortigern? He said nothing of any visitors from Armorica at the High council meeting yesterday.'

'High council?'

'Yes, I am a member of the Vortigern's High council.'

Lupus, Aureliana and Drustans looked at each other. Aureliana's eyes said it all: 'we are in the enemy's midst, thanks to their leader's surprising act of charity. Now what do we do?' Germanus seemed remarkably calm, given Constantius's revelation.

'And your names?'

'We will tell you in good time, no doubt. But, as I expect you will appreciate, Constantius, these are difficult times, and our mission here is secret, hence our attire, so I would be obliged if you would respect our position. We would rather remain, how shall I put it, friends in the shadows, at least for the time being.' Germanus smiled softly and bowed his head towards his host.

'Very well. I am in your debt and at your service. I will respect your wishes. But where did you get your medical training? All the good doctors have fled. I was desperate to find someone to deliver Sulpicia of her child. These are hard times in Britannia since we left the empire; or was it a case of being thrown out? Look at this house. It is years since I have been able to afford proper repairs and redecoration.'

'I had noticed that', Germanus commented. 'Perhaps that is why the Vortigern wants trade deals with places like Armorica. It can only help the British economy.'

'Indeed', Constantius replied. 'But two of your companions are familiar to me. They are surely not from Armorica but Britannia!' At this point the host pointed at Aureliana and Drustans. The two of them lowered their gaze in a vague attempt to be less recognisable. 'I am sure I have met you both before. Have you ever been to Londinium previously?'

Aureliana was about to reply when Germanus interjected. 'Yes, they have. We all have. There have been several trade missions to see the Vortigern but, as you will appreciate, these must be kept secret. I am sure the Vortigern would have told you more if he had been able to. Now let us eat.'

Fortunately, the servant's arrival with food meant that the four of them could relax from the interrogation, at least for a brief period. Germanus decided to ask some questions of his own. 'Tell me more of the high council, Constantius.'

'There is little to tell. The Vortigern rules and we support his rule.'

'How are you appointed to the Council?'

'We are the old ruling families of Britannia, or at least those in *Maxima Caesariensis*. I cannot speak for the other provinces. The Vortigern governs them through *foederati*. It is an arrangement that seems to work well enough'.

Aureliana resisted the temptation to say something at this point, largely because Germanus's eyes told her not to speak.

'You do not seem entirely happy with the Vortigern's rule, Constantius.'

'What gives you that impression, my friend?'

'Just the way you speak. You seem less than enthusiastic about the way he governs. It is not in what you say, but your tone of voice, and your eyes.'

Lupus could see Aureliana smile to herself. Yes, Germanus was good at discovering others' feelings, wasn't he?

'Well, I disagree with what happened today in the forum.' Constantius sighed and bowed his head.

'You mean the parade?' Germanus looked round the room at his colleagues.

'No, I mean the executions. There was no need for that. Some of those people I used to count as friends. But then hard times mean a strong ruler is needed. And if they were not prepared to give up their estates to help fund the war effort, then they knew what was coming to them.'

'And did you give up your estates?' Aureliana joined in the conversation with her question.

'Yes. Well, most of them. The Vortigern allowed us to keep some small amounts of land. I cannot remember the last time I saw my villa near Verulamium. I think the Vortigern uses it as a private retreat now. But I am being a poor host. Come, eat, and drink. This is the best wine that I have left; it is from southern Gallia. A great vintage.'

They began to eat. All four of the guests tucked in, not having had any food for hours.

'You must have been hungry', Constantius laughed. The wine had relaxed the five of them. 'Now we must toast my son.'

'What will you call him?' Germanus asked.

'I would like to name him after you, sir, if only you would tell me your name.'

'Call him Patricius. Name him after my son.'

CHAPTER 17

Newborn, new bond, new sign

The Pontifex paced up and down the cloister as fast as his arthritic legs would carry him. Ferox followed at a suitable distance, just in case the old man fell and needed rescuing. Despite his age and poor health, Coelestinus kept going.

'Your grace, please stop. Sit down, rest, anything. I fear for your wellbeing; we all do, every last one in your household.'

'O bugger my health. Stop fussing! I am perfectly capable of walking up and down a cloister without a nursemaid at my heels all the time! Now leave me alone. No, wait a minute. Fetch me my scribe. I will be in my study.'

'Yes, your grace. At once, your grace.'

Coelestinus positively scurried into his study. He searched across his *scrinium* for the letter that had arrived that morning.

'All this bloody stuff! Where is it?'

'What is it that you require, your grace?' The scribe had arrived.

'What, oh yes, I need to communicate with someone. Sit down; take a letter.'

The scribe had rarely seen the *Pontifex Maximus* in such a fluster. His master's strategy was obviously not going to plan. If it concerned the antics of his British friends, then what did anyone expect?

'Are you ready?'

'I am ready, your grace.'

'This is a letter to Queen Aureliana of the West Britons. Please thank her for her recent communication. Here it is, you can fill in the details from there. In reply, please tell her that I am a man of my word. She will be paid when it is clear that Germanus is going to defeat the Vortigern, and she is to become his regent in Britannia once he has triumphed. She will have to be patient for a little longer. Tell her to keep up the good work in the meantime. She will be very well rewarded in the long term. Etc, etc.'

'Have you got all that?'

'Yes, your grace.'

'Then get on with it and leave me alone.'

※   ※   ※

The wine and the euphoria of Sulpicia having been delivered safely of a son had loosened Constantius's tongue. As the evening wore on, he made his disdain for the Vortigern ever more obvious.

'Can I trust you, stranger – strangers? I will be slaughtered if the Vortigern finds out what I am saying about him. We all will. But I do not believe it is the way to govern. It was better in the old days, before this tyrant came along. He is power mad; you know that don't you? He wants to be *Imperator*. He wore the purple today, didn't he?'

Everyone nodded.

'Power has gone to his head. It wasn't so bad in the beginning, but the last few years have seen him gradually get rid of his opponents on the Council and in the country and subjugate his *foederati*. Those of us who still oppose the Vortigern do so secretly. We are silent, just like you four are, at least for now. Come, have some more wine, my friends. That is the way to stay alive, is it not? Keep quiet and drink more wine!' Constantius giggled. He continued drinking. Drustans ate or drank little; Aureliana looked bored and frustrated; Lupus just wanted to go; but Germanus remained intent on engaging with Constantius.

'I am too warm.' The host staggered up and took off his over-tunic. He threw it to the servant standing meekly in the corner of the drawing room.

'That's better. Now, where was I?'

'Just a moment. Stop. Let me see your forearm.' Germanus stood up and went over to his host and made him roll up his tunic sleeve. A gold snake amulet wound its way around the muscular arm.

'What is this? Where did you get it?'

'Why do you ask? It means nothing.'

'It may mean a good deal to me. Now where did you get it?'

Germanus held the man's arm so tightly the skin went white.

'It means nothing, I tell you. It is just our British way; just a fashion. It shows that the wearer is high born. Lots of men of my sort wear one. It did mean something once, a long time ago.'

'And what was that?'

'It meant that you were a druid priest. But they died out centuries ago.'

Lupus could see Drustans and Aureliana looking at each other anxiously.

'And that is all it means now, just a piece of jewellery? Have you been in Armorica recently?'

'No, I have not. I have never been there! Now let go of my arm!'

'Very well, I am sorry. But can you tell me who else might wear one of these?'

'As I have already said. Someone who is high born and, I suppose, long ago had Druidic ancestry. We wear them as a sign of our Britishness. It is meant to distinguish us from those who would still be Roman.'

This is all very odd, Lupus thought to himself. Here they are, saying how British they want to be, yet they flaunt their Roman ways and clothes, they speak in Latin and use our titles: tribune, patrician, forum – you name it.

'And now? Now that you are not Druids?'

'What, now we are Christian? Well, if the amulet was made of gold like this one, I suppose, I suppose it would be one of the high council members. The Vortigern made us all wear them as a sign of our loyalty to him.'

'So, it was the Vortigern's doing!'

'What was?'

Germanus began to tell Constantius what had happened while he had been away in Roma. He had hardly begun the story when Constantius interjected.

'Now I know who you are. You are the great Germanus.'

There was a sharp intake of breath from the others. Aureliana groaned.

'Do not fear, I shall not betray you; any of you. Frankly I am glad that I have met you. And I am even gladder that you have come. It is time the Vortigern was stopped. He is mad; power crazed and mad.' Constantius slammed down his drink on the table by his chair; but in his drunken excitement he missed, and the wine split over the floor. The host looked down at his handiwork and giggled again. Germanus and Aureliana nodded. Drustans and Lupus did not, albeit for different reasons. Constantius began to rise. Aureliana thought that he might have fallen over with the drink, but he remained rock solid. Germanus stood up and put a hand on each of Constantius's shoulders.

'Yes, you are right. I am Germanus, and I tell you now, that if you even think of betraying us to the Vortigern, I will not think twice about killing you in an instant. Do you understand?'

'You have nothing to fear from me, my lord. I will swear on any and every god that you care to name.' Constantius nodded vigorously.

'Then I will leave my comrades to introduce themselves to you', Germanus replied.

Lupus rose first, bowed slightly, and gave his name. For the first time in Germanus's hearing, at least, he called himself the archbishop-general's adopted son. Drustans went next. He was still weak from his ordeal and apologised for remaining seated as he explained his Dumnonian origins.

'Welcome, comrade. I used to have good friends in Dumnonia. All have now fled to Armorica, I believe. I am sorry that you have suffered so at the hands of our leader and his *magister militum*.'

Aureliana was the final member of the quartet to announce herself.

'And you know who I am, I suspect, Constantius. Aureliana, Queen of the West Britons and, for now, at least technically, a *foederata* of your Vortigern. I say "your" because I do not recognise his right to rule over this land. I am the rightful ruler of Britannia, more correctly termed Prythain, and will have my throne before long!' As if to affirm this statement, she undid her hair and let it fall down to her waist. None of the men was unaffected by this display. There was silence for a time in consequence. Eventually, Constantius opened his mouth in reply.

'I will pledge my loyalty to you, here and now. I will do whatever you command; I will help you in any way that I can. I will fight for you to the death'

'I believe you, Constantius. I really do believe you, my friend. You have no need to take an oath. I can see from your eyes that you can be trusted.'

'Thank you, Germanus. I can assure you I am speaking the truth. *In vino veritas,* except that I am sober enough to know what I am committing myself to. And my family.' Constantius nodded past Germanus and over his shoulder. Germanus turned round. Aureliana, Drustans and Lupus followed suit. Standing in the doorway was Sulpicia, with the new-born baby in her arms. She looked pale from her recent exertions, but her eyes were alive with the excitement of having a child safely delivered.

'You are right to swear to this man, my husband. He has saved me and my child; my Patricius. Now he will save us all.'

Germanus was taken aback by this affirmation. He put his hands up in the air in mock self-defence.

'I came here to do a job. Nothing more, nothing less.'

'But that job will free you – us – everybody – from the Vortigern.' It was Aureliana, now also on her feet. 'I will also accept an oath from you, Constantius. Then you will do as Germanus commands you.'

The archbishop-general nodded.

'I will call upon you when the time is ripe. In the meantime, you will carry on exactly as before, as if nothing has happened. You are more use to me right where you are, on the Vortigern's high council.'

'We will do as you ask, Germanus. Anything. But there is one small favour I would ask of you before you go.' It was Sulpicia, who now moved forward and put her baby into Germanus's arms. 'I would like you to baptise our son.'

'Baptise him?'

'Yes, baptise him as a Christian, as a follower of Jesus Christ.'

'But...'

'You are a bishop are you not? Otherwise, why would that pectoral cross be hanging round your neck? I can see it under your tunic.'

Germanus cleared his throat.

'He is an Archbishop, in fact; Archbishop of Britannia, would you believe?' It was Drustans, not entirely convinced of Germanus's conversion to the so-called one true faith. 'And he has had us all baptised', he continued angrily, 'so why should one more bother him?'

'Would you? It would mean so much to Sulpicia – and me, for that matter.' Constantius looked imploringly at Germanus.

'Yes, it would. Germanus Patricius is going to be his name.' Sulpicia had a mood of determination that no man in his right mind would counter. 'I heard you whisper to the one true God when you were delivering me of my child. That was no idle plea.'

Lupus, Drustans and above all Aureliana watched intently as their leader blushed. It was one thing to use Christianity as a way of binding his fighting forces together; quite another to make the sign of the cross over someone for real: to make them a Christian, a follower of Christ, with the archbishop as this new God's highest representative here in Britannia. Germanus took a deep breath, thought for a moment, then replied.

'Very well. Bring me a big bowl of water.'

Constantius nodded to the servant, who disappeared to fulfil his master's order. After a few moments the man returned and put the bowl on a table in the middle of the room. Germanus then pulled out the cross that Sulpicia had spotted from under his tunic. He gave the baby back to Sulpicia and asked Constantius to stand next to her. He told Lupus and Drustans to join Aureliana. After a pause that seemed to last for an infinity, Germanus spoke.

'Let us pray.'

There was a further pause while Germanus thought what to say next. Then he spoke clearly, without hesitation.

'God of heaven and earth, we bring you this child as an offering to your glory. Pray that he grows strong and wise in all things, as a follower of the one true way. This we ask of Thee, as in all things, through your Son, Jesus Christ, our Lord.'

He washed the baby's head in the water and made the sign of the cross with his thumb on its forehead.

'I baptise you in the name of the Father, and the Son, and the Holy Spirit, as Germanus Patricius.'

Germanus ordered Aureliana and Lupus and Drustans to pledge that they would be the child's guardians at all times, and to promise to keep in touch with Germanus Patricius in the future. This they agreed to do, with varying degrees of enthusiasm.

'Thank you, my Lord.' Sulpicia embraced Germanus, hugging him so tightly that he thought he would stop breathing. Constantius eventually managed to prize his wife away so that he could again shake hands with Germanus.

'We are your loyal servants.'

'Good', replied Germanus.' I expect that your loyalty will be severely tested in the days to come. Now we must take our leave of you. There is much to do before we are ready for the Vortigern.'

'Yes, there is. How will I know when you need me to act? That the call to arms really is from you, Germanus and it is not one of the Vortigern's tricks?'

'You are right, Constantius. We need some form of code. What would identify me to you, and me alone?'

Constantius thought for a moment, looked at Sulpicia then the others. He smiled, looked again at Sulpicia, and came close to Germanus so that he could whisper in his ear.

'In hoc signo vanquo.'

None of the others heard this; but they did hear Germanus's reply.

'Very well then. I shall use that as our code if, or rather when, it comes to the time that I need you.'

With that, the four of them got ready to depart. Lupus could not resist asking Germanus how he had known how to give Christian baptism to an infant.

'It was easy once I remembered the services in the house chapel that Eustachia used to make me attend. I somehow managed to bring to mind the words that her priest used when one of the estate children was baptised there.'

What Germanus did not reveal to Lupus, or anybody else, for that matter, was the warning that Constantius had whispered to him just before they left.

'Beware, Germanus. There is a traitor in your midst. I do not know who it is; but mark my words, there is one. Watch your back - at all times. Trust no-one in your camp.'

CHAPTER 18

Severianus waits; Germanus deals

'Where is he? Why has he not arrived yet?'

None of Severianus's officials dared answer. They knew to keep silent when the Bishop of Eboracum was in a bad mood. And this was an exceptionally bad one.

'I do not like to be kept waiting.'

One of the servants who had been brought along as part of the retinue tried to offer Severianus food and drink, but to no avail. The Bishop of Eboracum surveyed the city of Lindum from his seat in front of St Paul's church. The others shivered in the cold, but Severianus seemed unaffected. He had insisted that they sit outside so that they could watch for Germanus and his retinue. In addition, it gave him an opportunity to reminisce about the place that he had known as a child. He made a mental note to himself to go and visit the tombstones of his forbears. He remembered how his grandfather had told him one of his ancestors had been Gaius Valerius, a standard bearer of *Legio IX Hispana*. Oh, how he wished he could have been born 200 years sooner! In the glory days when Roma was the greatest city in the world, and not this pale bloody imitation. How long was this pretense going to be necessary?

Severianus was tired of this stupid Christian church that pretended to be all peace and love but was just another way of Rome exercising its authority over a crumbling Empire. It was better than nothing, he supposed, and it gave him a chance to get to lead the western empire. Yes, Christianity had its uses; but just wait till the old religions took over again. Thanks to his sources over there, Severianus knew that there were still lots of people in high places who would love to ditch Christianity. After all, that's why the empire was failing; weakened by people who turned the other cheek rather than stand and defend *Romanitas*. God, it made him sick! Whatever else he thought of his son working for the Vortigern, at least Agricola was a soldier, a fighting man. His forbears could be proud of that.

Even Severianus was getting cold with all the waiting, though he refused to admit defeat. He looked to the distance to see if there was any sign of visitors. The church was in a good place, atop the hill. No wonder Lindum had become a *colonia* all those years ago. You could see for miles around from the upper city. It must have been quite a place in its heyday, especially as Lindum grew and spread across and down the slopes to the river. You could still see the forum, the baths, the temples (even though the Christians had desecrated those a long time ago), other public buildings, shops, everything that a Roman city should be, and more. If you knew where to look, you could see the fountain in the centre of the forum square. Not that it worked any more since the aqueduct had fallen into disrepair and disuse. Severianus determined then and there that he would have it repaired; he would have them all repaired, from Luguvalium to Durovernum; and that was just for starters. Wait till he was Pontifex; then he would really get going.

His thoughts turned to Germanus. The great man of Gallia. They had both been law students in Rome, but Severianus had graduated before Germanus. Pelagius had told him what a brilliant student Germanus had been; top of the class. Severianus himself had never been that bothered about study: women, yes; learning, no. Then the army and promotion through the ranks and eventual command in Britannia.

It should have been the start of a glorious career: further promotion in the military, then a governorship, then preferment to the Senate, and so on and so on. Then these bloody wars had got in the way and Britannia left the empire. Had he made the right decision? Staying in the province when others had gone back? But then he was British, at least by origin. More to the point, he was an old believer, and proud of it! Think of it! A religion older than the Romans, than any of their gods; and far more fulfilling than Christianity. How ironic that he and Germanus were now both bishops! What fun!

'And oh, what a good bishop I have been! I have fooled them all! Nobody – but nobody – would ever suspect the truth!' Severianus laughed and laughed and laughed. 'And one day I will rule after all.'

At last, there seemed to be some movement on the road below: four figures in the distance, heading towards the south gate. They would be here shortly. Severianus determined that he had better prepare to meet the archbishop-general, though he decided that nothing could be said, ever, about the sacking of the villa in Armorica. Germanus could never know who had been behind the slaughter.

'Kill or co-operate? Kill or co-operate? I tried killing, but Germanus survived! Why try killing again?'

Severianus kept saying this in his head. He had developed the words into a rhythm. What should he do? Work with Germanus or have him executed, preferably in some horrible and ignominious way so that nobody else would try to replace Severianus himself as heir apparent for the pontificate? He would see what Germanus had to offer. Little had been prepared by way of hospitality for the four visitors, simply because there was little available to prepare. Lindum was not somewhere Severianus often visited, and he had therefore not spent much money on ensuring that his palace there was well stocked or served. It was no longer strategically important either for the northern provinces or the Vortigern in the south. Its main redeeming feature was where it lay midway between Eboracum and Londinium. He could meet and greet people without going all the way south. It was good that the Vortigern had to come halfway; it was an excellent way of reminding his overlord that he had to work at maintaining the support of his *foederati;* they could not and should not be taken for granted. That was the big mistake that previous emperors had made when it came to Britannia; not taken seriously enough. But it had produced rebels to upset the apple cart often enough in the past. And it would do so again.

'So, do I stay loyal to the Vortigern, wait for him to succeed, and then take over, like Allectus did with Carausius after he became *Imperator* in the west? Or do I throw my lot in with Germanus? Perhaps because *he* is the new Carausius? Kill, or co-operate?'

The four riders drew up to Severianus's quarters in the old *colonia.* A small group of the bishop's soldiers stood ready to greet the visitors. Once they had dismounted and their horses been taken away to be stabled, Severianus went to meet them at the entrance to his Lindum home. It had been a sumptuous town-house in its heyday, complete with extensive bathrooms. This latter complex had been turned into agricultural buildings long ago so that the cultivation of the spare plots of land inside the city walls could be organised easily. Severianus had made sure that this was still the case. Whatever else he was, bishop, dictator, next emperor, he wanted to ensure that his people were as well fed as possible. Especially if they were going to fight for him.

The visitors walked through the gatehouse and into the old *praetorium.* Germanus looked around. Severianus noticed a small flicker of a smile, as if he were remembering the days when he had exercised in a yard such as this. Both men could tell similar stories about their time in the army, no doubt. Severianus could not help thinking that, if the truth be told, he had more in common with Germanus than he would ever have with the Vortigern. For a moment, albeit a brief one, he regretted what had happened to Germanus's family and estates and his own part in organising the massacre.

'Not what it used to be, I am afraid, but then who knows what it may look like in the future when Roma has been rebuilt here?'

Germanus said nothing in reply. Severianus continued.

'Welcome Germanus. I know Aureliana and Drustans already, of course, but who is your other companion?'

'This is Lupus; he is my adopted son.'

'I remember your son as being called Patricius. Where is he?'

Germanus was both irritated and embarrassed. What did Severianus know about Patricius? Did he know anything? Was he trying to be clever, mischievous, or both?'

'He is ... he is missing. You may have heard that my family were ... well, they were murdered while I was away on business. But there was no sign of Patricius, so we assume that he was abducted rather than killed.' Germanus waved his arms at Severianus. 'But we are not here to discuss my family; we are here to discuss a possible alliance between Queen Aureliana, me, and you. That way we would have enough to counterbalance the Vortigern's forces, even with all the troops that Hengest has brought over.'

'Come, food and drink first. There is much to talk about over your proposal. But not on an empty stomach.'

The two bishops spent the next two hours assessing each other. Lupus and Drustans had little to say or do in the meeting. Aureliana, on the other hand, was keen to ensure that she was an equal partner in the agreement that was being forged that evening in Lindum. They argued and argued and argued. Severianus was a tough negotiatior. He wanted concessions from Germanus: promises of land and privilege after the Vortigern had been defeated; clemency for his son Agricola, and a chance at being Pontifex, supported by Germanus. If Severianus succeeds Coelestinus, then Severianus will see that Germanus succeeds him. Aureliana does not like the terms: where does it leave her and the Cornovii? Will she not just be substituting one Vortigern for another, if Severianus retains control of Britannia? She is offered the governorship of Britannia under a western empire led from Roma by Pope Severianus, with Germanus as Archbishop of Gallia, Hispania, and Britannia. To guarantee her position, she will divorce Ambrosius and marry Agricola, providing he is spared and allowed to retain his military role in the new regime.

'I need time to think about what is now on offer. I would imagine that you need to do the same. I propose that we adjourn for the night. We can continue in the morning.' Severianus gave nothing away as he spoke.

Lupus thought that Germanus looked tired. He felt sorry for him, his one-time master and now his adopted father. It had been a challenging three months: such a short time since he and Germanus were in Roma being asked by the Pontifex to go to Britannia. Look what had happened since then! They were living in a different world. Germanus must be in constant pain, as evinced by the fact that he now walked with a limp. But there was never any gasp or sigh; no complaint nor expletive; just passive acceptance.

'Very well. I agree that we need to consider what we have discussed today. Show us to our quarters.' Germanus nodded and stood up.

'You must forgive me for the rooms. I do not often stay here and there is little in the way of comfort. But I have asked my servants to ensure that you are warm.' Severianus clapped his hands and motioned to his acolytes to attend to his guests.

Germanus looked long and hard at Severianus. Was this a man he could trust? Unlikely. Was this someone he could rely on for now? Probably, while ever Germanus was a better bet than the Vortigern. But then could he trust Aureliana or Drustans? Could he trust any of them?

'We will begin again when the sun rises.'

'Indeed, my Lord Germanus.' It was as Severianus put his hand onto Germanus's shoulder that his sleeve fell down his arm and the amulet on his forearm was revealed. Germanus visibly tensed. He clenched his fists and was about to challenge his host when he thought better of it. There would be a more opportune time and place to investigate his likely new ally's background. For now, it was more important to seek allies, and Severianus would have the capability to turn the coming war against the Vortigern.

'Till the morning, then', Germanus said.

CHAPTER 19

Aureliana seduces; Lupus is lost

Lupus knocked; then knocked again, louder, whispering her name; no answer and again no answer. He pressed gently on the door handle and leaned his body against the wood. There was a slight sound as Lupus moved into her room. Aureliana was humming gently to herself as she sat at a table on which was a mirror propped up against the back wall. The Queen of the West Britons was combing her hair. It hung far down her back, right to her waist. No, it did not hang, it cascaded, like thick flames, enveloping her body. Lupus could not stop himself looking at her, thinking things that no man should think. It was wrong! He just stood there watching her; the long movements of the brush, the sound of her voice, singing quietly; some British song, presumably. She stopped her music, but continued the stroking, hair hanging all the way down her naked back. The movements slowed, became more deliberate, then stopped. She put the brush down on the table and smiled at her reflection.

'Well, Lupus, are you not going to come in? Or are you set to stand there and gawp all evening?'

'How...?'

'The mirror, Lupus. I can see you in my mirror: look!' Aureliana giggled and turned round, holding the glass to Lupus so that he could see himself. He was more interested in looking at the thing of eternal beauty that was in front of him.

'So, my handsome young man, what are you doing in my bedroom?' Aureliana shook her hair. She knew that Lupus could tell she was naked from the waist up. 'Shall I put the mirror down now, Lupus? Have you finished admiring yourself? I hope so because you should be admiring me!' At which point she flung the mirror onto the nearby bed and stretched her arms out wide.

'Do you love me, Lupus? Do you like the way that I look? Don't turn away now. I know that you like me. You liked me in Dubris. You liked me a lot, did you not? Would you like to love me, Lupus? You could love me tonight if you wanted to. I want you to: do you know that Lupus? Look at me Lupus, now!' Aureliana stood up and walked slowly towards him. He could not resist gazing at her, at those wonderful breasts, surrounded by her divine hair. She fingered the ends of her locks, curling some of the threads round her left nipple. Lupus imagined he would die with embarrassment; but he could not stop himself.

'Germanus wishes to see you, me, us, in his quarters. I must go to help him prepare for the meeting.'

'What a pity Lupus. Does he need us right away? Surely, he would not expect us immediately. We have a little time, I imagine.'

By this time, she was facing him, her mouth a breath away from his mouth. He had to look at her eyes. She giggled as she stroked his ever-fuller beard.

'Quite the grown man, aren't we, Lupus? And I can feel that you have grown somewhere else as well...'

'No! I must go!'

'Wait a while. Come. I need you, now.'

Lupus knew that he should not be there, that he should be back with Germanus, planning for the further negotiations with Severianus the following morning. After all, that was why he had come knocking on Aureliana's door. Or that was what he persuaded himself was the case.

But Germanus was not calling the meeting for another hour. Lupus knew that, and Aureliana knew that. And he really did hope that she wanted him.

'Are you sure you need me and not my master?'

'What makes you say that my dear little wolf?' Aureliana seemed genuinely surprised by the question.

'Well, I thought that you preferred older men, or at least one particular man. I could not help noticing the way you look at him, and, if I am not mistaken, the way he looks at you.'

Aureliana waved her hands in denial, but her blushing cheeks told Lupus how she really felt. 'You are wrong Lupus. Yes, I admire your father, your master, whatever he is to you, very much, but it is you I want. Come, stop talking. Come.' Aureliana moved her tresses behind her back so that Lupus could see her breasts. He smiled as he saw the freckles on her neck and shoulders. She smiled back, then undid the belt on her lower garments and let them fall to the floor. He revelled, just as she did, in her nakedness. She walked into his arms and let him bury his head in her breasts, then suck each nipple in turn. She clamped her legs around him as he carried her to the bed. He threw her down, then undid his tunic and fell on top of her.

Drustans could hear the moaning from his next-door room. He began to pen a letter to Ambrosius, then thought better of it. He did not want to upset his lover, who had endured enough traumas of late. In any case, with Aureliana otherwise occupied it meant that she was less likely to trouble her husband-brother. Drustans put down his *stylus*. *'Quieta non movere'* he whispered to himself. Then he took up his *stylus* once again. While he did not wish to trouble his lover, he decided that he should trouble his master, the Vortigern.

※   ※   ※

'So how did you manage it?'

Germanus remained silent. He looked at Aureliana and smiled.

'Well – how did you do it?' The Queen of the West Britons giggled as she looked at him; then squeezed his arm to press her question. Lupus and Drustans looked on as they followed. Both men, in their different ways, were now angry; were they angrier with Germanus or Aureliana? Lupus sneaked a look at Drustans and Drustans sneaked a look at Lupus as if to see who was the maddest. There was little emotion on either face; neither dared let their guard down against the other, or their leaders riding in front of them, for that matter. Would she be flirting with Germanus all the way back to Viroconium? Would he be letting her flirt with him?

Aureliana had protested her feelings for Lupus and that her marriage was not really a marriage. She was more interested in someone her own age; a proper man, not somebody who preferred other men to women, especially women like her. If that were the case, why did she spend so much time with his master? Why her girlish giggles; the admiring looks; the long gazes; the hanging on his every word. Or so it seemed...

Drustans had less and less time for Aureliana. How dare she treat Ambrosius like that! He understood why she had married her brother; that was the old Prythonic way that he also fought to protect and restore. But to cuckold him like this, with the father as well as the son. What was her purpose? What was her intention? What did she hope to achieve? Drustans tightened his horse's reins and kicked his heels into its sides to make the beast catch up with Germanus and Aureliana.

Lupus did not follow, at least not straightaway. He looked at the three of them riding side by side along the wide road. It was not in the best of condition, but it was a testament to the excellence of Roman engineering that it was passable at all. There was little other traffic that met them in either direction. It seemed strange, though, that they were able to travel so easily through the countryside. True, they were in the northern part of Britannia, following the border between the two old Roman provinces and true also that they had been given a right of passage by Severianus now that Germanus had struck a deal with him.

Lupus, like Aureliana and Drustans, was intrigued to know what the details of the agreement were and, even more so, how Germanus had managed to persuade the curmudgeonly old man to support his cause and abandon the Vortigern. This all assumed, of course, that Severianus really had changed sides. What would Agricola, his son, think about his father's betrayal?

'I know all about betrayal', muttered Lupus, safe in the knowledge that he was far enough behind the others not to be heard. He should catch up before he was too far behind and got lost. Just as he was going to kick his horse into action, he heard a high-pitched whistling sound. Something told him that he needed to get going; he kicked his horse again, but not soon enough. Lupus felt a searing pain in his right leg. He looked down and saw that an arrow had gone right through it and into the side of the horse. It yelped, and he cried out. He looked around, trying to see the source of the attack. This time he had warning; the whistle and then the arrow. He ducked out of the way. The horse neighed and bucked; they were off. Lupus could not control the animal, despite keeping it on a tight rein. It reared and stomped, then set off down a track away from the main road. He cried out, calling for his companions. There was no sign of them. There were shouts and cries behind him. Lupus could not tell what they were saying, but it did not sound at all friendly. He tried to turn the horse back in the direction of the road and the place where he had last seen his companions, but his attackers were running behind him. Despite his speed advantage, they were advancing on him.

'Shit!' Shit, shit, shit! Now what am I supposed to do?'

The horse was steaming with sweat. Still his pursuers gained on him. This was Lupus's worst nightmare, but for real. He was well away from the main road, and the scene could have been from an entirely different world, unaffected and untouched by anything from his, or Aureliana's, or even that of the *Saxoni*. The horse suddenly pulled up at the edge of a clearing. Whatever he did by way of goading or admonishment, the animal resolutely refused to move. The attackers were closing; in front there was a large round hut in the middle of the clearing, with a great pointed roof, from which came heavy smoke. Around the hut were various pens to keep in livestock: goats, sheep, pigs. At the entrance to the building, chickens scratted or huddled in the dirt. Several children played some game at the far side of the clearing, shrieking, and giggling as they ran after another child who was obviously attempting to evade capture as part of their play. It was Lupus's turn to be captured. A group of men dragged him from his horse and over to the hut. He heard the shouts of women, men, and children; they must have been jeering at him. More than one spat in his face. He was vaguely aware of four of them carrying him; then he was hit over the head with something very hard and all went black.

CHAPTER 20

Lupus is saved; Coelestinus shares a secret

Lupus could see a thousand images: his father and mother, his brother, his dear little sister; Ambrosius came came into view, with Drustans behind him, but this time he had both eyes, whole and bright. Then Aureliana, smiling, walking towards him, laughing, beaming, letting her dress fall from her shoulders, beckoning Lupus into an embrace. Her hair blew in the wind; then Lupus saw that it was not hair, but snakes, their heads bulging, tongues stretching out towards him, their prongs attacking his flesh, digging into him, sucking his blood, draining all his breath, his life, his soul...

Lupus did not know what to do or where to turn. He looked down at his legs as they started to burn up: feet, ankles, shins, knees, thighs. The flames got as far as his genitalia. He experienced pain like he had never felt before. Looking down, he could see his penis shrivel to ash. A great hole opened up between his legs and out of it spewed the bloodied head of Patricius which rose up and spat him in the face. There was no way out; no way out at all. The head spoke to him.

'Ah! Dear Lupus! Dear, sweet, obedient, lapdog Lupus! What a *cunnus* you are! Yet my father has taken you in as his son, as my brother! If I ever see you again, I will make sure that you do not steal my inheritance. I am the rightful heir to the governorship of Armorica. Not you, not anyone. I thought my father knew that. But now…'

Lupus woke up, drenched in sweat and vomit. Where was he? He spoke words he had never spoken before.

'*My God, my God, why hast thou forsaken me?* For the love of Christ help me! I need you to protect me from her, from me, from my lust. I do not want this. I do not want this; but I do want it, I want it so much, so very much. I have longed for her since I first saw her. I have had her, want to have her. But she does not really love me! She loves him! What am I to do?'

Why this crying out to this new God; this Jesus? Where had Lupus heard those words before? Where? Yes, he remembered! It was in the chapel at home. A reading from the book that they called the Bible! But what came next? Was it a puzzle that he had to solve? What happened in the story? What happened to this Jesus Christ? He had heard Eustachia talk so much about him. Could he, Lupus, be saved? Saved from all that he did not wish in his life? Could he be someone else? Someone new? Someone that Germanus would be proud of? Another Patricius even?

Lupus felt all the blood draining from his body. He looked down at his leg. He collapsed back onto the bed. He could see the arrow worm its way up his thigh and into his groin. It sowed its way through his testicles and his penis and then shot up into his abdomen. He sensed the arrow tip piercing one lung, then the other. It ascended his throat and out through his mouth. It then turned back to face him. The arrow tip swelled and turned into a serpent that opened its jaws and breathed fire into his face. He smelt the burning flesh.

All went dark.

'Am I dead? Is this all there is? No heaven; no hell? Nothing?'

At least in this oblivion the torment was over. No more lust, no more love, no more tenderness, and no more jealousy.

※　　※　　※

'I wish you would tell me how you persuaded Severianus to come over to our side.' Aureliana looked at Germanus, willing him to answer.

'I have told you all that I am going to tell you, for now, at least. We will see when the time comes whether or not the bargaining has worked.'

'Bargaining?' Aureliana began to worry.

'What have you given him?'

'Enough. A man like him will support whichever side he believes will give him what he wants.'

'But he cannot have what he wants. That is mine, and mine alone! I am to rule Britannia after the Vortigern, not him.'

'Easy, easy, calm down: who says that he will get it?'

'But you made a promise and I know that you are a man of your word.' Aureliana smiled and looked down, averting his gaze.

'Maybe I will never have to keep it.' Germanus nodded and smiled. Aureliana turned round to what the other two members of their group had been doing while she and Germanus had been arguing.

'Drustans?'

'Yes, my lady?'

'Where is Lupus?'

Germanus turned his horse around. 'What happened? Why did you not keep an eye on him?'

'I am not his bodyguard.' Drustans spat out the stalk of grass that he had been chewing lazily.

'Drustans! You will answer my Lord Germanus!'

'Very well, your majesty.' Drustans explained that he and Lupus had been talking and then Lupus had fallen back. That was all. There was nothing more to it.

'We must find him, and quickly', Germanus said hurriedly. 'It will soon be night and these country roads are not safe. There are many *bagaudae* round here, or so I have been told. They answer to no-one.'

Germanus ordered the others to follow him as he turned back and kicked his horse into a gallop. It was not long before they had retraced their steps and found the last place where they were certain that Lupus had been with them. Aureliana and Drustans took a keen interest in Germanus's next actions. He rode up and down the path, searching the road and the undergrowth to the sides to see what clues as to Lupus's whereabouts could be found. The trail seemed to have gone cold; until something jumped out to the intrepid tracker. Germanus beckoned the two others to follow him down a pathway that led away from the old Roman road and into dense forestry. Aureliana looked at Drustans and Drustans returned her gaze. The Queen of the West Britons had never been attracted to her Dumnonian commander in any shape or form; she had tolerated him because of his good grasp of strategy and tactics and the way in which the army respected him; that and the fact that Ambrosius loved him like the brother that he, and she, had lost. It felt such a long time (it was only two years) since Aurelianus had been snatched by raiders from across the *Mare Hibernicum* acting on the Vortigern's orders? Neither she nor Ambrosius had been the same again; but she felt it more deeply. How could you not when your twin was taken from you? Perhaps that was why she had turned to Ambrosius for more than brotherly comfort. It was the British way; always had been and always would be. The bloodline had to be kept pure; and if that meant marrying and sleeping with your own brother, so be it. But that did not mean there could, and should, not be others, especially after Ambrosius lost his manhood. She knew how to keep other men's sperm out of her; her mother had taught her the old ways well, though even so, she took the Roman precautions also when necessary. Drustans wouldn't have that problem of course when he buggered Ambrosius. Or was it the other way round? Aureliana resolved that if she were not carrying a child of the royal line within the next few months then, after that, when she made love with a certain one of the two other men in her life, she would not bother with either sponge or wild carrot.

The Queen of the West Britons was brought back from her thoughts by Germanus; he whispered to her and Drustans as he pointed towards an encampment in the forest. It was a curious mixture of Roman ruins and British huts. Big round houses like those in the countryside around Viroconium; these ones were surrounded by the remains of villa walls, living accommodation and farm buildings. Only one of the stone and brick constructions looked well maintained, or even maintained at all. A temple; and even more strangely, a temple with a cross on the top.

※   ※   ※

Ferox assumed the Pontifex was asleep. Coelestinus rarely snored, unlike some of the old men who had slept in the pontifical bedchamber over the years, so nobody could be fully sure when and if it was possible to leave him to his slumbers or whether they needed to remain on call. The Pontifex had a wonderful knack of sensing when they were about to go, then the high-pitched whine would start, and an order would be issued; day or night, morning, and evening, they had to be ready, and woe betide any of them if they were caught napping. Privileges would be revoked, and allowances cut; the more serious misdemeanours resulted, without fail, in beatings, which the Pontifex was at pains to watch, especially if the miscreant servants were female.

This time, Ferox thought that he was safe to put out the lamps and close the doors on his master. To make sure, the trusty servant waited once he had left the bedroom to see if he really was clear. Then he went off duty and enjoyed a glass or two at the tavern around the corner from the palace. On the other side of the door, the Pontifex was also waiting. Once he heard Ferox's steps fade into nothing, he opened his eyes and sat up in bed as best as his arthritis would allow.

'You may come out now.'

There was movement behind the curtains surrounding the pontifical bed. Coelestinus thought that the young man who emerged from the other side of the *velamentum* could have been the angel that Mary Magdalene had discovered in the tomb of Christ, with his long blond hair and flowing white robes. He did not so much walk as glide forward until he stood by the Pontifex's left-hand side. Coelestinus smiled at his son. 'Just like his mother', the old man thought, remembering the day his one and only boy had been born. He beckoned his young guest over to him.

'Give me your hand Palladius; hold it firmly.'

'Yes father.'

'It is good to see you again, my son. I am not sure how long I have left. I grow weak. All this business with Britannia and the Vortigern and Germanus. I am too old for it; too old. It needs a younger man.'

The angel gave a smile. 'Yes Papa. I came as soon as I received your message.

Coelestinus made Palladius lean over him. The old man stroked the youth's cheek. 'You look just like your mother, my son. You always did, with that golden Saxon hair of yours'

Palladius saw his father's jaw muscles flex; watched the single tear stream down his desiccated cheek. Coelestinus had never spoken about the love of his life to him before; never.

'I wish I had known her, father', Palladius said quietly, bowing his head as he spoke.

'So do I Palladius, so do I.' Coelestinus sighed as he eased himself onto the *lectus*. He groaned as he lifted his legs. The Pontifex patted the *stratum*; Palladius hesitated for a moment and then decided to walk over to where his father now lay. He sat down next to the *Pontifex Maximus* and took the old man's hand. His palm grazed the pontifical rings as he squeezed the bony fingers. Coelestinus was surprised at the tenderness in his son's eyes.

'I should tell you about your mother, before it is too late.' The Pontifex smiled gently. 'She was a slave, taken from her family when she was young. I was a rich merchant, living in Augusta Trevirorum. Given that it was near the border with Germania, a lot of slaves in that city were *Saxoni*. My wife chose her from amongst a whole number at sales in the market. I was attracted to her at first sight, and she to me. I erred and strayed within days of her coming into our house. My wife never found out, for she died very suddenly within a few weeks. One morning she just never woke up. But I wasn't sorry, because I never really loved her; I loved her money, but not her! I married my slave girl as soon as seemed decent. Then you were born. She died giving you life. Thusnelda, dear, wonderful, beautiful Thusnelda, my love, my life, my all. There were no others after that; it seemed the right thing to do: to go into the church. Celibacy is easy when you have had enough of sex. And look at me now! What I would not give to have her back here with me: to listen to her to laugh; to watch that wonderful smile; to look at her while she shook her head and let that heavenly blonde hair of hers fall down her back; to hold her in my arms just one more time. Who knows? Perhaps we will meet again. This Christianity stuff might actually be true!' Coelestinus let go of Palladius's hand. He bowed his head as if in silent prayer.

'Father?'

'Yes, my son. I know there is much to talk about.' The Pontifex grabbed the angel's hands in his. 'You have been a good boy; she would have been so proud of you! So good at your studies. You could be, you will be, a future Pontifex!'

'Yes father, but we need to talk about Britannia. I cannot stay long. There is much to do back there if we are to succeed.'

Coelestinus took his son's hand. Palladius was surprised at the strength of the grip. 'I may not live much longer. I should tell you everything while there is still time. It will be our secret. Nobody else will know; and nobody else must know. You hear me!'

CHAPTER 21

Lupus restored; Severianus appeased; Visinius silenced

Lupus felt sick: very sick. It was as if all the blood had flowed out of his veins. Every part of his body hurt; his muscles convulsed, tightening, tensing, and pulsing uncontrollably. He looked around, trying to work out where he might be. The walls were a curious mixture of plastered brick and the kind of wattle fencing that he had seen around some of the hovels where the poorer Britons lived. In a few places, where the plaster had not fallen away, it was possible to see the decorations – a headless nymph played with an evil-looking satyr. A nude goddess was about to shoot an arrow into nothingness. A naked woman; that made Lupus think of Aureliana. Well, at least if he were going to die, he would not now die a virgin. Despite his predicament, he smiled at the thought of being a real man. Lupus gasped as he realised that he was awake. This was reality; the *insomnium* had gone. He tried to get up.

'Ow!'

Every bone in his body seemed to be broken. The pain was unbearable. Was he still dreaming after all? He felt nauseous once more; the pain was real, almost as excruciating as the torture he had undergone in his fevered dreams. Having failed to get out of the crude bed in which he lay, Lupus closed his eyes. He was so tired. Soon he was asleep again. He could see a thousand images: father and mother, brother, dear little sister. Then Aureliana, smiling, walking towards him, laughing, beaming, beckoning Lupus into an embrace. Her hair blew in the wind, but then Lupus saw that it was not hair, but snakes, vipers, their heads with tongues stretching out towards him, their prongs attacking his flesh, digging into him, sucking his blood, draining all of it; his breath, his life, his soul...

Cool, balmy water, lightly scented, fell on his face. The drops ran into his mouth and sweetened his breath. Lupus's tongue reached out for more. A small saucer was being placed to his lips. He drank, slowly at first, then greedily, now choking to the point where the saucer was removed. Lupus opened his eyes. The sunlight blinded him; he turned his face away. His name was being called. He turned back, re-opened his eyes. This time the sun was merely a backdrop for a figure standing just in front of the door frame. Lupus now focussed on this person. For an instant, he thought he had gone to meet his God as the shadow floated towards him.

'It is over Lupus. All is well. The fever has gone. You are whole again.'

'Germanus? Master? Father?'

'Stay calm Lupus. You have been far away. A dreadful sickness overcame you. We all feared for your life. But you will recover.'

'My Lord...'

'Not now; when you are stronger. Here, drink this, it will help you to regain your strength.'

Lupus coughed and spluttered as he sipped the foulest-tasting medicine that he had ever downed. He hated to think what it contained, but he comforted himself with the fact that Germanus would only be giving him something that would be of benefit. 'How are you feeling?'

Lupus nodded gently after some thought.

'Nothing is broken, and nothing permanently damaged. Your wounds were not too serious; they have now been treated – and treated well. You will just feel very sore for a little while.' Germanus squeezed Lupus's hand as he spoke.

'Where am I?' Lupus sat bolt upright. 'Where am I? What happened?'

'Calm down Lupus.' He smiled as he heard her voice.

'Aureliana!' She seemed genuinely pleased to see him. Unlike Drustans, who now appeared in the doorway, behind the other two.

'Are you well enough to get out of bed Lupus? We cannot stay long here.' Germanus looked out of the window as he spoke.

Lupus pushed himself up on his elbows. But it was not his master's words but the sight of the strange people standing in the doorway that made him so alert; and afraid.

'Who are these people, Germanus?'

'They are friends; they are on our side. But hurry, the Vortigern knows we are here. Agricola is on his way to capture us.'

Lupus still ached everywhere. He grunted and groaned as he rose from the bed.

'Come Lupus. I will explain.' Aureliana took hold of him as he rose and stood, tentatively putting one foot in front of the other; Lupus was glad of that, for all sorts of reasons, though even he could not think of what he loved doing to her just now, as he limped his way to the door and out into the fresh air. He shivered. It was not the cold but all the eyes staring at him. Men, women, and children; all in rags; all staring at him. Lupus shivered again. The smallest child came up to Germanus and whispered to him. Germanus smiled and nodded. Then the urchin came over to Lupus and gave him a flower. She said something that Lupus did not understand, smiled, then ran back to the rest of the group.

'She hoped that you were better. She said that she would pray for you.'

'Pray for me, master?'

'Yes, Lupus.'

'To the Gods? Which one?'

'To the Lord Jesus.'

'My Lord, what…who…'

'Look around you Lupus. They are Christians. They saved you from the Vortigern's men.'

'Come, my son. You must eat something before you and your companions leave us.' An old man smiled at Lupus as he walked towards him. His dark brown eyes looked straight ahead. Lupus tried to turn his head towards Germanus, but he could not. The man put his hand on Lupus's shoulder.

'The peace of the Lord be always with you.'

All of them said this, then they applauded.

'Am I dreaming this my Lord Germanus? Is it a fever?'

'No Lupus, this is real. They are good people. But let us be quick; something to eat and then we really must go. We cannot stay long. They will be back, and I fear for our safety, and that of these good people.' Germanus looked at Aureliana as he spoke. She nodded, then helped Lupus to follow the others. They were in a large villa complex, what must have been a fine house in former times. No longer. In the middle of the ruined bath house there was a thatched wooden building with smoke rising from a hole in one end. Germanus, Aureliana, Lupus and Drustans filed inside, followed by the old man and a woman. They all sat down on the floor, while two others served them some hot liquid in wooden bowls.

'Gratia. The Lord be with you. Let us break this bread in the name of our Saviour. Please, brothers and sisters, eat. We are pleased that you are well, Lupus. The Lord has answered our prayers.'

Lupus looked at Germanus.

'These people saved your life, Lupus. We are all grateful to them. This is Visinius, the leader of these good people. I leave him to tell his story – and what happened to you.'

Visinius laughed. 'There is little to tell, brothers and sisters in Christ. We are followers of the one true faith. We have been since my father built that house chapel over there. But it has not been easy being Christians, real Christians that is; not the stuff that Pelagius peddles and the Vortigern supports. No, it has not been at all easy; not for a long time now.'

Lupus drank the gruel that had been put before him. The others watched as he downed it in three gulps.

'You must have been hungry, Lupus.' Aureliana laughed. 'But then it must be at least three days since you had anything to eat.'

'Three days? Is that how long I have been here?'

Germanus nodded.

'Continue brother Visinius.'

'Of course, my Lord Germanus. Well, look around this place. It was not always like this. We were one of the richest families in the whole of Britannia. Our lands stretched for miles in every direction. My father was on the high council. We practically ran this province. But the place is not what it was. It has been downhill ever since the Vortigern took over. Everything and everyone is focussed on his needs. He started out well enough; involved others, brought the province together after the legions left; gave us stability, a degree of prosperity, peace even. But then it started: the confiscations, the assassinations, the desecrations. It did not take him long to pillage our country and accrue all power to himself. There were no good men left in government by the time he had finished.'

Aureliana and Drustans nodded as they looked at each other in agreement. Germanus thought of Constantius.

'And that is nothing compared to what he has done to our beloved church.'

'How do you mean?' Germanus leaned closer to Visinius as if to hear the answer better.

'He has turned it into a money-making venture. All the funds are syphoned off, just like everything else, into his war machine. The British Church has lost its way, thanks to him and his so-called spiritual advisor.'

'But there are some true Christians left; a few of us, anyway.'

'Who are you?' Lupus started as a woman entered the room.

'This is my wife Nigra', Visinius replied.

'Welcome to our home Lupus – such as it is. Are you better?'

Lupus nodded, unable to take his eyes off the blackest woman that he had ever seen.

'What? Who?'

'Stop staring Lupus. Have you never seen a black woman before?' Germanus snapped. Aureliana laughed; Drustans looked shifty.

'Yes, but…'

'I am from Africa. My family has served Visinius and his forbears for many generations. But I am no longer a slave; I am free, thanks to the Lord Jesus Christ, and my husband.' She smiled across at Visinius. He took her hand.

'But I still do not know how I got here.'

'These good people rescued you, Lupus.'

Lupus laughed. 'I thought they were the ones who captured me!'

'Quite the opposite Lupus. You would have been dead if Visinius and his sons hadn't got you out of that village over on the other side of the valley.' Germanus nodded in the direction of the window. Lupus limped across to the open, broken window.

'Over there, you mean?' Lupus pointed at the smoke curling up from a group of huts in the far distance.

'We had some help from our Lord Archbishop', Visinius replied. 'He masterminded our raid. Very clever. But they will be searching for you. I am surprised that they have not been here already.'

'The main thing, Lupus, is that you are safe from those *Saxoni* over there. But it was a close-run thing. If you hadn't been discovered when you were, you would be dog meat by now.'

'Dog meat, my Lord Germanus?'

'That's what these pagans do to Christians like us.' Nigra sighed.

'*Saxoni*, here?'

'They are gradually taking over. The Vortigern gives them land, our land, in return for loyalty to him. They are sworn to serve in his army when he calls them up. Fortunately, they have yet to try it in my province, eh, Drustans?' It was Aureliana. She took Drustans' hand, squeezed it, looked into his eyes. Drustans was not sure how to respond, so did and said nothing.

Lupus cleared his throat. Aureliana and the others turned back to him.

'So why have they not taken over here?'

'Because they are supposed to live peacefully alongside us. Laughable, isn't it?' Except Nigra was not laughing.

'They come over here now and again. Raid us for what they can find and take. They threaten us; kidnap and ransom us; beat us and rape us. One day they will come back and finish us off.' Nigra continued. Visinius put his hand on his wife's shoulder.

'The Lord will protect us, my love.'

'I sincerely hope so, Visinius. I sincerely hope so.'

'Lupus?'

'Yes, master?'

'Are you well enough to travel?'

Lupus thought for a long time, knowing what the answer had to be. 'I believe so.'

'Then we must leave. Those *Saxoni* will have got a message to the Vortigern somehow. We must not tarry.'

'Will you not stay the night, Germanus? It will soon be nightfall.'

'No thank you, Visinius. The going down of the sun is all the more reason to go; we will be able to get away more easily without detection.'

'Then at least celebrate the Lord's Supper with us.'

Much to everyone's surprise, the Archbishop of Britannia agreed.

※　　※　　※

'Well?'

'Well, what?'

'What happened?'

Severianus sat down in his favourite chair while an *ancula* took off his *caligae*.

'Ow! Careful woman! Mind my feet.'

The assembled men coughed and shuffled.

'Very well, you may sit.'

'What are your orders, my Lord?'

Severianus pushed the serving girl away with his foot.

'We are to fight alongside the new Archbishop of Britannia, if required, and for as long as it suits us.' Severianus raised his voice to quell the muttering.

'I said if required, my brothers in Christ. But I will make sure that we are late to the battle.'

'To what end, your grace?'

'To my end, *follis*! That way we can see who is winning and join the victors. Sometimes...'

'When and where will the battle take place?' said one of the brothers

'Does Agricola know what you have agreed?' said another.

The *ancula* brought Severianus wine. He took one mouthful and then spat it out.

'Not this muck, for God's sake! Bring me something better, you useless *serva!*'

'Do not be so hard on her, your grace. That is all we have left in the *vinariam*.'

Severianus looked at the priesthood, then into his cup. Slowly, he poured the remains of the wine all over the kneeling servant girl.

'We shall just have to hope that the wine tastes better after I am Vortigern and *Imperator*.'

❋　❋　❋

'We did the right thing Nigra. We could not tell the Vortigern's men where Germanus was, or what he was planning.'

'The archbishop is a good man. He is troubled, that is true, but he is a good man; a godly and Christian one, Visinius.'

'We will be together in heaven soon, my love.'

'It hurts, Visinius. It hurts so much.'

'Just pray harder, my love. Think of it: we are enduring what our Lord Jesus Christ endured. We will be in Heaven today.' Visinius held out his hand to his wife. If only he could have touched her. They were too far away from each other as they hung there, nailed to their crosses. The other villagers, men, women, and children, had been made to come and watch while the two of them were crucified. Nigra prayed that her husband would die first. He was by far the older of the two of them and was in poor health. She was surprised that he was not already dead from the beatings that the Vortigern's men had given him. But Visinius was not dying. The soldiers were giving him just enough support to keep him from expiring through lack of air. When it looked as though he could no longer pull himself up to draw breath, one of the Vortigern's men would put a ladder up against the cross, climb up it and lift the naked, sweaty body for long enough for the victim to breath back into life.

Agricola was growing impatient. He had tried everything to get this man to say where Germanus was and what he was planning. Surely, watching his wife being beaten within an inch of her life would make the husband talk. Not even that worked. Killing every tenth villager had yielded nothing either. Agricola had left himself no option but to carry out his ultimate threat. Now they were definitely going to talk. Their children, their families and friends, their brothers and sisters in Christ were all begging Visinius to tell Agricola where Germanus was.

Time was running out. Germanus would soon be beyond reach back in friendly territory. Then Agricola heard wailing. He looked back up at the crosses. Nigra's body hung limply from the wood. Visinius was mouthing something: a prayer no doubt.

'Fuck you, Agricola; you and your Vortigern. Germanus is out of your clutches. He will take his revenge on you all!' With these words, Visinius died.

CHAPTER 22

Barita reports back

'I thought as much.' The diminutive *exploratorem* looked up at the archbishop; the archbishop looked down at his *exploratorem*.

'You are sure?'

Barita nodded.

'They were good people, Visinius and Nigra. Not only did they save Lupus, but they harboured us until he was well enough to travel and then gave us enough time to get back into safe territory so that Agricola and his men could not capture us. *Vixere fortes ante Agamemnona.* They and their kin were unsung heroes. Coelestinus was right; these people will do anything, even give up their lives, for their Christ. And they did it for me as God's servant. Do you know what the word "bravery" means, Barita?'

Barita shook her head and wiped her nose.

'Never mind.' Germanus snorted.

Someone must have got news back to the Vortigern about their whereabouts after leaving Lindum and that they would be sitting ducks while they waited for Lupus to get better. Should they have left him and got back to Viroconium sooner? Perhaps, but it seemed the right thing to do at the time, especially after Drustans's capture and liberation. Germanus could not cope with a second member of his core team falling to the Vortigern. They had not been caught, thanks to those two Christians.

'I owe those two people a real debt of gratitude Barita. Do you understand that?'

The *exploratorem* nodded, unknowingly, preferring to watch her adoptive father sit down at the table where his food lay untouched. It was more than she had eaten all week. Realising she was looking at his meal, he pushed the plate over to her.

'Here: eat it; it is yours. But use a fork, for Heaven's sake!'

Germanus wondered how he could have missed the spy in their midst; and someone who seemed so loyal to the cause – or at least Aureliana's cause. But then could any of these Britons be trusted? What had Constantius said? Was even the Queen of the Cornovii untrustworthy? Or perhaps especially the Queen of the Cornovii! Having shared a bed with her made it harder to detect her deceit, if there was any. There had to be at least some; she was a woman, after all!

Germanus's assumptions were based on Barita's intelligence being correct. It was all plausible enough; it would have been naïve to think that the Vortigern did not have sympathisers this far west, just as Aureliana had spies in Londinium and probably elsewhere. They had found it easy enough to meet Severianus in Lindum without detection, unless the Vortigern wanted them to meet up, or Severianus was still acting on the Vortigern's behalf. Germanus grew tired of all this intrigue; and the bloody church was just as bad – oh for being back in Armorica talking to Segovax about what to do with the vineyards. That was the best problem to have!

Germanus heard slurping. Barita was licking the plate clean.

'Finished? Did you enjoy that?'

The *exploratem* nodded, wiping the sauce away from her mouth with her sleeve.

'Is that everything?'

Barita thought for a moment and then shook her head.

'There is more?'

She nodded.

'Go on then. Spill it out.'

Barita remained motionless.

'Well?'

Still no movement.

Germanus smiled, rose, and moved to the chair over which he had thrown his overcoat as soon as he arrived back in his room in Viroconium. He rummaged around until he found his *sacculus*. He took out a coin and held it up to Barita. She tried to snatch it from him, but he was too quick for her. The game continued until at last he relented and held the coin steady; inches from her face.

'So, what is the other thing that you have to tell me?'

'I know who the traitor in your camp is. I have proof, and lots of it.'

CHAPTER 23

Germanus learns of Eustachia and appoints a chaplain

'Come in.'

No reply.

'Who is it?'

Germanus grunted as he put the tablet down on his bed and walked over to the door. *Not Barita again!*

'Hello?'

He could hear breathing and the creaking of floorboards. Germanus sighed as he went to the door, one hand on his *gladius*. With the other he gripped the latch, ready to open it suddenly as necessary.

'Who are you?'

'Someone who wishes to speak with you privately. May I come in?'

'First tell me who you are and what your business is, and then I will consider letting you in.' Germanus grimaced. 'But be quick about it! I have much to do!'

'Thank you. I am grateful to you, my Lord.'

'Get on with it then!'

'I would rather speak behind closed doors. There is much that I would prefer not to say when others may be listening.'

Germanus looked out down the corridor and smiled as he saw

Barita hiding in the shadows. The urchin smiled at him, waved, and then departed, as instructed by Germanus, to see what else she could discover.

'Very well, in you come.'

Now that the man was inside the bedroom and the door closed, Germanus could get a good look at him. Another bloody Christian! And a well-dressed one, too!

'My Lord', the visitor exclaimed as he sank down on one knee.'

'Yes, yes. Get up!'

'Yes, my Lord.'

'Enough of this title stuff! What do you want!'

'I am Elafius, my Lord, your brother in Christ. My father knew your mother. He knew her well.'

'How did he know her?'

'He brought her to the one true faith. He baptised her.'

Germanus put his sword down on the table, beckoned the man to come in and sit. As he closed the door, Germanus noticed that Barita was sneaking up the corridor. He nodded at her; she waved back. The *exploratorem* obviously thought it more important to listen in to the conversation about to take place than to be spying on Aureliana and her high command. Germanus did not disagree. *That urchin thinks like I do. She could have been my daughter!*

'So, your father converted my wife. When was this?'

'Eustachia needed little persuasion, or so I am told.'

'What does that mean?'

'She came to him asking to be baptised. He did not need to convert her to Christianity.'

'And when did all this happen?'

'It was many years ago. My father was a priest in Armorica. One day after the service this young girl stayed behind and said that she wanted him to baptise her, but in secret.'

'In secret?'

'Eustachia said that she did not want anyone to know that she was becoming a Christian. She would have been ostracised by her family and friends. And she did not know how the man she was in love with would have felt about her being a follower of Christ when he was not.'

'You have a very clear memory of all this. Yet you could not have even been alive when all this happened, if what you say is true, that is.'

Elafius laughed. 'Oh, it is true alright.'

'Because?'

'Because my father never stopped talking about the love of his life.'

'And who was that?' Germanus almost whispered as he spoke.

'Eustachia. Your wife! He always loved her from the moment he first met her. He told me so on his deathbed.'

'On his deathbed?'

'He died from his wounds.'

'From battle?'

'From torture; by the Vortigern's men.'

'He would not agree to follow Pelagius. He said that he would never betray the one true faith. At least the Vortigern let him come home to die; not that there was much left of him. It was then that he told me about Eustachia.'

'What happened between them?'

'My father wanted to marry her. But she refused. Even though her man was an unbeliever, she would be with none other than her beloved Germanus. What was it my father said? She was his *univira*.'

Germanus sank his head in his hands. 'My *univira*.' Germanus repeated these words over and over. He turned away from Elafius to make sure that his guest could not see the tears.

'Are you alright? Shall I come back later?'

Germanus stopped his chanting and straightened his tunic.

'No I am; I am fine. They never…'

Elafius shook his head.

'You are sure?'

'I am sure. They wrote to each other until my father's death, but no, there was never anything more, much as my father would have wished it.'

'I never knew anything of this! I must have been away in Roma. What was your father's name?'

'Restitutus; that was the name he took when he became a Christian. I do not know what he was called before that. I have only ever known my father as a priest. I never knew my mother. She died giving birth to me. She was from these isles-a local woman. That is why my father and I ended up staying here. She is buried just outside the city walls.'

'And what does Queen Aureliana say about your Christian church?'

'She tolerates us. I assume you are aware that she is an unbeliever; worse than that, she is of the ancient Prythonic religion and would reintroduce her ways if she had her way. At least, unlike some, she has not put us to the torch or the cross – not yet anyway. There are too many of us in her army, especially now that you have had them all baptised!' Elafius laughed before continuing his introduction. 'She hates you for that. But it was a masterstroke! Even I realise that to make God's kingdom here on earth we have to use wile and guile sometimes.'

Germanus nodded and raised an eyebrow. He thought how Eustachia used to tell him off for using his 'dark eye', as she would say. She would then stare at him before breaking the moment by laughing and putting her arms round her 'little bear of a husband.'

'I still have the letters – here they are.' Elafius pulled out a pile of writing tablets from his long-sleeved over-garment. 'I thought you should have them.'

Elafius held the correspondence out to Germanus. For a long time, there was no response; finally, the letters were taken and put on the bed.

'But you have not come here just to reminisce.'

'No. There is something else. I wanted to come and see you to pledge my support for your mission to Britannia.'

'What do you know of my mission?'

Elafius looked puzzled. 'It has been difficult for us true Christians in Britannia for many years now. You will learn something of our tribulations from that correspondence.'

Germanus rubbed his eyes. His wife had been carrying on correspondence with this man's father all these years? This Restitutus?

Elafius coughed; the young priest was waiting for an answer. Germanus decided he had better give him one.

'I have very specific orders from the *Pontifex Maximus*; from Father Coelestinus.'

'No, you have been sent by the Lord to help us; you are here from the One True God, not that lonely, pathetic old man!'

'I would hardly call the effective leader of the Western Empire pathetic!'

'He is not a Christian. My father never thought so and neither do I!'

'How would I know whether he is a Christian or not? Anyway, I care not for all these theological disputes. I really am not bothered; not one iota. I am a man of arms; I want action. I fight to save the empire. If that means propping up Christianity, then so be it. I've even had this silly tonsure, not that I had much hair on top anyway. If I thought for one minute that it was not best to embrace your Jesus Christ as the way of saving all that I believe in and hold dear, then I would be offering sacrifices to Mithras before you could say "Our Lord and Saviour!"'

'Then you yourself really did not mean it when you poured water over all those people in our *amphitheatrum*?'

'It bound them to a common cause, as you yourself have recognised; needs must, Elafius. That is enough. I cannot do with all these warring factions if I am to defeat the Vortigern. Apart from that, they can believe what they want.'

Germanus looked up at his visitor and then down at the letters that Elafius had brought. He picked up the correspondence and began to trace his finger round the edges of the tightly-bound writing tablets. The young man must have been about the same age as Patricius, perhaps a little older. His clothes could do with a good wash and mend, despite their opulence, though. He needed a woman to look after him; or at least a slave.

'Where do you live? Who looks after you?'

'I live across the far side of the city. I have a room next to our church. Other members of our flock look after me. But I do not worry about earthly things. The Lord will provide.'

'Well, it is about time he provided you with some new clothes! What you are wearing now has definitely seen better days!'

Elafius looked away in embarrassment.

'Your wife must have been a good woman. My father certainly thought so.'

Germanus nodded.

'I see that you are a priest as well, Elafius. How long have you been ordained?'

'Since just before my father died. He ordained me. He had a vision the night before he passed away; he said that one day a strong man from across the seas would come among us and save us from the evil ones.'

'And you think that is me?'

'I know that is you, whatever you might say about your beliefs. What you say with your mouth is not what is in your heart. Not any longer. You just have not realised the truth yet. But it is there, deep down inside you.'

Germanus gave no answer. Elafius fumbled in his pockets and eventually pulled out a small bag. 'Here. This is for you.'

'What is it?'

'You will see.'

Germanus opened the little pouch and looked inside. He pulled out a ring, finely wrought, made of gold, with a *chi-rho* symbol around the circular band that formed the base.

'A Christian ring?'

'Yes, a Christian ring. It was my father's. He told me to give it to the man who came to save us. That is you, my Lord Germanus. I have prayed for it, my father prayed for it, everyone in Viroconium who is a true Christian prayed for it. And I am sure that it is you. I do not care what you say or think or feel. Take it; and wear it!'

Germanus bit his lip. He looked at the ring already on his finger, then slowly slid this second one over his knuckle next to it.

'Thank you. You will not be sorry. I promise.' Elafius seized Germanus's hands and squeezed them to the point where the knuckles were white. The archbishop-general prised his brother-in-Christ's arms off him.

'Thank you Elafius. That will be all.'

Elafius was slow to get up until Germanus seized him by the shoulders and made him move. He marched the young priest to the door, one arm firmly round his shoulder. 'You are a good man Elafius. I am sorry if I have been sharp with you. Hearing about my late wife and – well, those letters – you know how it is.' Germanus patted Elafius on the back then, much to the latter's surprise, embraced him. 'Your father would have been proud of you, by the sound of it!'

Germanus paused for a moment before continuing. 'Tell me Elafius, can you hold a *gladius*?'

'I am a man of peace, your grace. I do not carry weapons.'

'Very unwise in these turbulent times if I may say so.'

'The Lord will protect me – you – all of us.'

'I thought the Lord helped those who helped themselves?' Germanus laughed. Elafius relaxed and joined in the mirth.

'You have never fought in battle?'

'No, but, but I was taught how to defend myself.'

'Then you would fight if you had to?'

'If I had to defend myself, or those that I love, then yes, I suppose that I would fight in such circumstances.'

'Will you join my forces?'

'As a soldier?'

'As a priest, Elafius?' Germanus smiled.

'Why?'

'You said it, Elafius. Your religion binds people together. I need you to make sure that they remain bound, and especially the ones I am going to have to lead into battle during the difficult times ahead.'

Elafius frowned. Germanus continued.

'You would be doing your people-and your God- our God if I must put it like that-a great service if you were to come alongside me and my commanders. I am sure that many would receive great comfort from you and your cross: before, during and after our battles.'

'Very well. I will! Praise the Lord!'

'Praise the Lord indeed!' Germanus replied, then closed the door on his newly-appointed chaplain, lay down on his bed and cried until he fell asleep.

CHAPTER 24

Coelestinus finds secret papers; Germanus sees a ghost; Severianus receives a letter

'The old man has been grumpier than ever since his son went back to Britannia. God, he is an awkward sod!'

'Watch out, here he comes!'

The two guards stood to attention. They could hear the Pontifex's shoes squeaking as he came down the long corridor to his private apartments. The old man sniffed at the soldiers.

'Have you been drinking?'

'No, your holiness.' The guards spoke in tandem

'Are you sure?'

'Yes, sire.'

'Absolutely, 100 per cent sure?'

'As we would swear on the Bible, your grace.'

'Very well. Now open the door for me.'

The guards made short work of pushing back the heavy doors into the basilica. Even after all this time they marvelled at the sight of the high altar in the far distance, with its large golden cross hanging down from the ceiling. As the Pontifex scuttled away, the soldiers looked at the pictures of the saints watching them, and anyone else who entered that church, from their alcoves high up in the roof.

'Goodness!' Coelestinus thought to himself. 'I am not even out of breath. There is life in the old bugger yet!' He chuckled. The steps up to the high altar were more of a challenge. The pain in his leg bones was getting worse by the day. How long did the doctors say he had left before the cancer finally got him? Time was of the essence. 'Grit your teeth old boy and carry on! You have endured far worse on the battlefield!' The Pontifex turned back to the west end of the basilica to see if the guards were watching but, as ordered, they had closed the doors behind them. It was cold and dark. Was there a presence with him? Was there a God? One god above all gods even?

'Oh, fuck it! I don't have time to think about bloody theology now!'

Coelestinus pulled himself up by the altar rails and then walked round to the back of the podium. It was hard to see where he was going with only a few oil lamps to provide any illumination. For a moment he thought about getting the guards to fetch more light, but then reminded himself of how secret his secret was. He finally found it; found the button on the under side of the high altar. He pressed: once, twice, thrice. For a moment nothing happened. Then the trap door creaked open. For the first time in a long while the Pontifex felt fear as the cold air rushed up from the burial chamber below. He steadied himself and held the oil lamp tightly as he gathered up his robes and walked down the steps into St Peter's crypt. Coelestinus smiled to himself as he wondered how the great saint would react if he knew what his bones were hiding.'

'Riches beyond compare.'

The cackle echoed all around the crypt.

※　　※　　※

Cracks of early morning light pushed through the shutters. The oil lamp still flickered in the breeze. Germanus shivered, much to his surprise: he never felt the cold, not ever. How long had he been asleep? His cheeks were sticky. A final tear ran from his eye and onto the still-moist pillow. It was the first time he had cried since the butchery at the villa. He shook his head; that place would never be home again. Where was home now? Roma? Londinium? Viroconium? The Church? None of it mattered any more; none of it.

Roma: think of it. *Imperator*; *Pontifex Maximus*. What would Eustachia have thought? Not much, probably. Would she have sat next to him on the throne? Unlikely? What about Pope Germanus? Possibly. But then she would have been his sister in Christ and not his wife. Something she had talked about; no more sex, heavenly rather than earthly love. That was hard to accept; making love was so much a part of him! Always would be! There had been other women, even after he and Eustachia had exchanged vows; there had to be, to satisfy his urges, but nobody had been like her. Eustachia was the only woman who had ever given herself fully to him; and he had never had anybody else who came remotely close to his wife, his *univira*.

Then Germanus realised that he was deluding himself. If Eustachia was so important to him, the only one, how was it that he had jumped at the chance of being in Aureliana's bed and relished the thought of staying there? Then another face came into his mind. Every time he tried to think of Eustachia or Aureliana, it was Sevira that he saw. Queen Sevira she would have been now; just Princess Sevira when he had known her all those years ago. She was so different from Eustachia: passionate, not tender; dominant, not passive; sensuous not placid. Perhaps that was why he was so attracted to Aureliana; she and Sevira had so much in common! What would have happened if he and Sevira had been married; if she had not been deposed along with her father after the great rebellion? He had been right to betray them. They would have overrun Britannia and made it their own.

What was he saying? It had been overrun anyway! The battle for Britannia had been in vain. Perhaps he had backed the wrong side. If he had not betrayed Sevira and her father, he would have been King to her Queen; western emperor in succession to the great Magnus Maximus. He laughed: but everything comes to he who waits; I am now to be *Imperator* and *Pontifex* all in one, if Coelestinus is to be believed!

Germanus felt so tired. His leg ached. He reached out for the wine jug. How he wished for Memor's potions! It was the *haruspex* who had saved him from the fire and the fall in London; he knew that it could not have been otherwise. Would he be able to rely on the old man's magic again? Germanus felt humbled that his mentor had used his powers to save him rather than Segovax. But the loyal servant would not have wanted it any other way; nor would Memor.

The wine tasted awful. None of the drink he had imbibed since he landed in Britannia had been any good, not even the stuff that Severianus had served up. But then times were hard; only the Vortigern could summon up a good vintage; and that was from wine laid down before the time of the troubles. Germanus put his glass back down on the table next to his bed. He hoped for sleep. As his eyelids finally began to close, he thought he saw someone else in the corner of the room: a shadow, nothing more. Germanus was not taking any chances, now more than ever. He reached to the side of the bed for his *gladius*. The shadow took form; had a shape. Germanus screwed up his eyes and opened them wide alternately, then finally narrowed them to focus on the other occupant in the room. The figure grew larger as it approached him, all veiled in black.

'Is it you? Is it really you?'

The figure stood before him.

'I so want it to be you. I miss you. You know I miss you.'

The figure bowed its head.

'I wish to be free of this. I wish to die to be with you, my love. Will you help me? I will pray to the gods to let me die – as I have always wanted to die – on the battlefield.'

The figure dissembled as the dawn broke. Germanus was alone. It must have been the drink that made him believe his dead wife was in the room. There was silence for what seemed an eternity, then singing in the distance. Germanus arose and walked over to the window, gasping as he did so at the pain in his leg. Over the far side of the courtyard stood Elafius at his bedroom window, thrown wide open, despite the cold. The frost hung on his breath as the young priest sang a hymn. Germanus recognised it: it was one that Eustachia had sung so often that he could remember it and joined in quietly, singing under his breath. For a moment he wondered about going to join his newly-appointed chaplain in his worship, then thought better of it and closed the shutters quietly before Elafius realised he was beng observed. Germanus was about to return to his bed when there was a knock at the door. He ignored the tapping. The visitor would not go away. Germanus could see the latch move. He sighed, stood up, wiped away his tears and opened the door.

'You!'

※   ※   ※

'Do you really mean to side with Germanus?'

Severianus belched. He continued to chomp on his apple, then wiped the surplus juice from his mouth as he replied to his second in command. 'Perhaps; perhaps not. Pass me some more fruit, grapes, I think, and then leave me. I have an important letter to reply to.'

Severianus picked bits of apple and grape skin from his teeth until he was confident that there was no-one anywhere near his private chamber. To make sure, he got up, tiptoed over to the door, put his ear to it and then wrenched the door open as rapidly as he could to surprise anyone who might have been listening at the other side of it. There was no one there as he looked up and down the corridor. He closed the door quietly, locked it and put the key in his pocket, then went over to the couch on which he liked to rest. He reclined, pushing his rear end down then up as if to test the comfort level of the piece of furniture before deciding whether or not to buy it. Then he gripped the couch frame on either side of his thighs and pushed. A compartment sprang open between his legs. He pulled up his ecclesiastical robes and took out a writing tablet from the drawer that had appeared. He reached for his glasses and began to read.

My dear Severianus,

I hope this missive finds you well. How long is it since we last met? I hope that I will see you at least one more time before the end of my tenure of office. I trust that you are leading the faithful ever more fully into the light of Christ. How do you find Archbishop General Germanus? He should be very useful to us from now on.

I give you my word that, if you support Germanus in the upcoming war in Britannia, that once victory is secured and the Vortigern is deposed, I will abdicate in your favour. The world is yours!

In Christ's holy name,

Coelestinus, Pontifex Maximus

Severianus lay the letter tablet back down on his lap. Could he trust his old sparring partner? They had served in the army together long enough; saved each others' lives more than once. But Coelestinus had changed; changed into a completely different person. Not that he had been converted to Christianity or, if he had, not that he had been changed by it. No, it was the thought of power, ultimate power. He didn't want to be emperor, but he did wish to be Pontifex, and that was far more worthy a prize than taking the purple ever would be again. Severianus laughed to himself.

'Of course, that is why I became a priest!'

CHAPTER 25

Germanus gains a daughter

Germanus tried to ignore the tapping at his door, but the noise persisted.

'Go away' he murmured.

More tapping.

'Go away, please!' This time he shouted.

'No, I won't. I won't, I won't, I won't!' It was Barita. She rattled the door so hard that the latch broke and she fell into the room.

'Go away!'

'No. I want to know what is wrong with you!'

'Nothing! Nothing is wrong with me!'

'Then why have you been crying?'

'I haven't.'

'Yes, you have!'

'No, I haven't!'

'Yes, you have!'

'Haven't!'

'Have!'

'Haven't!

'Have!'

'Ha –'

Germanus looked up at his little spy, then burst out laughing. Barita joined in. She crawled onto the bed, nuzzling up to him. He put his arm round her; she relaxed into his chest. He squeezed her close.

'I know why you are so sad.'

'Do you?'

'You have lost your wife, and you miss your son.'

Germanus stayed silent for a long while. Then he answered.

'Yes, that is true. My whole world fell apart when Eustachia died.'

'Eustachia – that is a beautiful name.' Barita snuggled closer to him; Germanus made no attempt to push her away.

'She was a very beautiful woman. There will never be anyone else like her, even though one or two have close...'

'Was she as beautiful as Queen Aureliana?'

Germanus hid his blushes from Barita.

'No-one could be as beautiful as my wife. I could never love anyone like I loved her.'

'What about your son?'

'I don't know where he is. I fear that he is dead, but we never found his body.'

'And Lupus, he is your son also?'

'He is my adopted son. My good old friend asked me to look after Lupus if anything happened to him and his wife, and it did. They were murdered by *barbari*.'

'You do not feel the same about Lupus, do you? I have watched you talk to him. He calls you master.'

Germanus laughed.

'You are very perceptive for an *uricia*!'

'What is an *uricia*?'

'Never mind.'

'So why are you here?'

Barita shrugged. Germanus looked down at his little spy. Her hair could do with a good wash, just like her face. He stroked her head, trying to straighten out the matted locks.

'Will you adopt me?'

'What!'

'I have nobody. You have nobody.'

'Yes, but…'

'You adopted Lupus. Why can't you adopt me?'

'But he is a man.'

'Don't I count? I thought you Christians loved everybody.' Barita gripped his tunic as she spoke.

'But I am not a…' Germanus stopped himself. What if his little spy was still spying for Ambrosius?

'Please. I have nothing; I have nobody.'

At that moment, Germanus had an image of Eustachia come into his head. He wondered what she would have done. He pursed his lips. What he was about to say went against every instinct inside him; he still said it though.

'Very well. I will adopt you.'

Barita jumped up and danced around the room.

'But on one condition', Germanus shouted.

'What is that?'

'You have a bath!'

They both laughed.

'I have something else to say.'

'You can tell me later. Just get cleaned up before I change my mind!'

Barita ran to the door. Germanus called her back.

'But first fetch Lupus. I have decided that it is time.'

CHAPTER 26

Viroconium is attacked;
Severianus watches and waits

Germanus looked out across the amphitheatre. 10,000 troops ready and waiting for his order; the command to march on Londinium. It felt good; like the old days. They even had a good supply of weapons, thanks to Aureliana's well-stocked armoury and the extra supplies that Aetius had squeezed out from his western armies and delivered to the Armorican Guard before they set sail for Britannia. There was a good number of heavy weapons such as *ballistae,* and an ample supply of hand-held weaponry. The West Britons had proved to be quick learners when it came to the latest tactics in warfare. Germanus had said to Lupus more than once how pleasantly surprised he had been as to their fighting spirit. It would have helped if the combined forces had been able to call on more cavalry units, but that was the state of affairs across the empire. At least they were now a unified fighting unit. What a pity that he had been forced to use Christianity and baptise them all to bind everyone together! In the good old days, it would have been allegiance to the empire; an allegiance that could have been taken for granted. Now…

Aureliana, Ambrosius and Drustans were waiting; waiting for Germanus to raise his *gladius* and give the battle cry. He turned to the three of them. Could they be trusted? What had Drustans given away when he had been tortured? The Dumnonian swore before Germanus that he had revealed nothing, but it was hard to believe he could have survived the torture that he had endured. Drustans had recovered remarkably quickly. Either he had a strong constitution or the hardships that he had suffered had not been as terrible as one might have expected. Germanus knew what it was like to be tortured, branded even; but he did not know what it was like to give in, to tell the truth, to betray his own. Perhaps Drustans had done the same; perhaps not. There was as yet no way of proving what had happened, either way.

The rain had stopped. The army and the cavalry were assembled. It was time. Just as the archbishop-general was raising his hand, a *nuntius* ran up the steps to the podium where the high command were standing. The man stumbled twice in his haste to reach Germanus. Two guards tried to stop the *nuntius* in case it was an attempt to kill the West Britons' new *magister militum*. Germanus told the men to release the messenger, confident that he could fend off a frontal assassination attempt if he had to.

'What is it boy?'

The *nuntius* fell at the master's feet. His lungs were bursting; he could not speak.

'They – they – they are coming. Soon – now.'

'Who is?' Aureliana strode over to the prostrate *nuntius* and helped him up, more anxious to hear his message than ask about his welfare.

'They…'the boy pointed east.

Germanus and the others turned to the road to Londinium. In the far distance, there was movement.

'Everybody inside! Close the gates!' The murmur of a large army could be heard in the distance as Germanus issued his orders, quietly at first, then louder- ever louder-until everyone realised what was happening and needed to be done.

Aureliana looked at Ambrosius and Drustans and then at Germanus.

'How did they know? How did they know we were planning our attack?' Germanus got no answer then decided to stop his questioning. 'Later- we will find out who betrayed us later. Take your places. You know what you have to do!'

Aureliana nodded to Germanus as she turned away from him to run down the steps and get into her armour. Germanus smiled back at her, acknowledging her unspoken compliment to him. She had argued that there was no need to strengthen the city's defences or prepare to be attacked. After all, they were meant to be marching on Londinium, not the other way round. But they had been beaten to it. Her country was being invaded.

'By the Gods of my ancestors, the traitors will pay for this!' The Queen of the West Britons shouted to her *magister militum* as she went to get ready.

Between them, Aureliana, Ambrosius, Drustans and Lupus had command of the city walls. Germanus had argued that, in the event of an attack, it was better to draw the opposition forces as near as possible to the city walls, to let them through the outer defences and then to attack them once they were encircled on all sides.

The scouts sent out to gauge the size of the Vortigern's army had returned; all but one of them, that is. Germanus was saddened to hear that Nonus had gotten too close to the enemy. He had been encircled, speared, pulled off his horse and, unwilling to give anything up about the forces in Viroconium or Germanus's tactics, had been butchered and his headless body sent back on horseback as a warning. After their initial encounter on the way to Roma, the *bagauda* had been turned into a loyal servant and a good soldier. Germanus looked on as Lucius took his brother's body down from the horse and cradled it in his arms, swearing to fight for the two of them, until his final breath.

Hengest's forces were beginning to encircle Viroconium. The Saxon commander was surprised that Germanus had not yet fired one arrow nor let a single *ballista* loose. There were signs of hasty abandonment of work in the fields that fed the city; but not so hasty that the animals giving food and drink to the West Britons had not been corralled behind the defensive walls. There were still fires burning where the farm workers had been clearing the ground for future crops. Carts and baskets lay upturned and untidied.

Hengest raised his hand to tell his troops to stop. There was something not quite right. The long lines of soldiers took time to come to a halt. Hengest looked around. He knew Germanus of old. Knew how the devious bugger worked. Something must have been set as a trap. The Saxon commander sighed, then gave the signal for his troops to advance. Then the barrage started. Hidden in the derelict barns on either side of the road, a series of *ballistae* had been wheeled into position and were being let loose on the unsuspecting invaders. Large rocks and burning bales of wood were but two of the sorts of trajectile that rained down on Hengest's forces. Before he could countermand his initial orders, many of his men had set off towards the city walls. Having broken ranks, they were easy targets for the archers in the turrets all around Viroconium. Many *Saxoni* fell in those next moments.

Aureliana watched from the outer ramparts. The last time she had looked out on a battle like this, she had lost; lost to the Vortigern. Ambrosius had already been a captive and Drustans was no match for the Vortigern and Bishop Severianus. Severianus. That was a name to conjure up! She had been less than impressed when they had met in Lindum but understood why Germanus was keen to have an alliance. If it meant getting rid of the Vortigern once and for all, then she was willing to countenance it. Was the Bishop of Eboracum really prepared to be an ally and not a foe? Times had changed. They certainly had for the Vortigern. Last time it had been Romano-British soldiers from the east of the country who had marched into Viroconium. Now it was mostly *Saxoni*. How could that man have sold out to those foreigners? Better Roman than Saxon! British best of all!

Aureliana could see that there were still some Britons in the

Vortigern's army: she recognised their uniforms and their bearing. How could they kill their own? Even if they were Christians. That would all stop when she was Queen of Britannia. Britannia for the British. That is if Germanus could deliver her the prize of conquest and the Vortigern's demise. Then she could deliver Germanus.

❊   ❊   ❊

'How goes the battle?'

'I would say that the two sides are evenly matched, my Lord Bishop. The Vortigern, or rather Hengest, has more men; but Germanus has more…'

'More cunning. He always did have.'

Severianus thought back to the time when he and Germanus had been in the army together. How the two men had risen rapidly through the ranks as they made their names in the service of Roma, when Theodosius quashed the rebellion of Magnus Maximus.

'I expect he has lured the opposition forces into the outer defensive area and then ambushed them, bolting the doors behind the *Saxoni* and then butchering the enemy ten to the dozen where they stood.'

'But…'

'But nothing, my friend. And that will have been after he pushed them towards those defences with *ballistae* fire. Assuming the West Britons still have weaponry like that.'

Severianus laughed at his fellow commanders. He was getting cold out here. What a dump Mediolanum was! But at least it was in striking distance of Viroconium and also within his diocese. He reminded himself to have the central buildings repaired, or even rebuilt, after he had become Vortigern. A statue of the great Severianus would sit well in the reconstructed forum.

'So, what do you wish me to do with the troops, your grace? Shall we move them up to the front line?'

Severianus pulled his beard. Time to have it trimmed, he thought.

'More wine first.' He gesticulated to the old servant in the corner of the room that was his temporary headquarters. 'Don't I know you?'

'No, I don't think so sir.' The old man shuffled over, pouring wine from his flask, as requested.

'Yes, I do. I remember you now! You're the old man in my congregation at Eboracum! The old *equite,* or so you say!'

Severianus laughed. 'If you were an *equite* then I must be Jesus Christ himself! What's your name, old man?'

'Augustus, your grace. A loyal follower. I always enjoy your sermons.'

'Ha! An admirer! What do you think I should do, Augustus? Join the forces of Germanus or Hengest? Or do nothing? Come on now. An *equite* like you must have some idea what I should do'

Augustus put down the *ampulla.* 'I say bide your time, your grace. It is too soon to know whether Germanus will succeed in his quest. But I would not trust the *Saxoni;* I would not trust them one inch. The archbishop-general will prevail in the end; he is by far the greater tactician.'

'So that's what he is being called now, is it? Augustus smiled; Severianus stroked his beard. 'Augustus, tell my barber to come in. You can tell me more about tactics and your cavalry past while I have my hair and beard trimmed. We have time on our hands...'

※　　※　　※

Lupus could see that Germanus was worried. He had made it one of his tasks to know what the various almost-imperceptible expressions on his lord and master's face meant. That was usually the only way of finding out what was going on inside that complex brain of his. And Lupus, despite his novice status in military strategy, had worked out why. The initial phases of the battle had gone in the West Britons' favour, not least because of Germanus's tricks. Many *Saxoni* had been slaughtered in the *vicus* surrounding the outer defences of the city. Even more had perished as they stormed through the city wall and into the enclosures that had been prepared for the attackers. Once inside, the gates had been closed on the *Saxoni*; they were then easy pickings. Hundred after hundred must have been slaughtered in that enclosure: from behind, around, and above.

Lupus turned back to the fighting. He was surprised how quickly he had become used to the sight of blood and the smell of death. He urged his men to fire down on the Saxon soldiers below, whenever and wherever it was safe to do so, without injuring any of the defenders. He took up his own *manuballista* and started firing again, taking great pride in having turned into a good shot. Time and again he hit his target. The more successful he was the more his insides raged. He wanted to kill every one of those bloody *Saxoni*. As the enemy crowded together, tripped up by their own over-enthusiasm, he shouted out to his troops to fire at will. In between taking aim himself, he spied out where his people should fire. They really were doing well, he smiled to himself.

Aureliana had stripped off to the waist. The body paint glistened as the sweat ran down between her breasts. She undid the clasp that held her hair in place and let it furl down as she shook her head. No-one, except Lupus, that is, noticed her half-nakedness in the furore of battle. Some of the other men and women in her contingent had done the same. They all had a blue pigment smeared on their bodies. They fought fearlessly. Woe betide the *Saxoni* who fell foul of them.

Drustans's troops engaged in battle like Romans rather than Britons: more disciplined, more calculating; but with less fire and passion. They were counterattacking what was a rough approximation of three or four centuries, at least in terms of numbers if not discipline and ability. Germanus shouted encouragement to Drustans, warning him of the ever-present dangers from the *Saxoni*, and especially those who, like the men of these centuries, had previously served in the Roman Army. Drustans could even hear their commanders barking orders in Latin.

Ambrosius led the troops who had been stationed in the outer part of the city, ready for when the first wave of *Saxoni* rushed through the deliberately opened gates. Despite wounds in the arm and shoulder, he rallied his men and women, shouting out encouragements and instructions as he deployed his army to best effect. Germanus was impressed with Ambrosius for his bravery, energy, and tactical skill. He could feel the determination in the Briton's fighting: an opportunity to give the Vortigern a taste of his own medicine as reparation for the loss of his eye, and his manhood.

Germanus did a tour of the walls, assessing the situation from every angle; encouraging the troops, telling them where to focus their energies, giving instructions to the officers in charge. Under his command, Aureliana, Ambrosius and Drustans did the same. Extra *manuballistae* were handed out to compensate for the imbalance in the numbers. Aureliana signalled across to Germanus that it must have been three-to-one or more. Lupus observed her gesticulations. As she turned back to the ramparts, she caught sight of him looking at her: there was a brief nod and a smile. Then she raised her sword and shouted something in British to her troops. Lupus wondered what would happen to him, and her, if they got out of this alive.

Germanus knew that the trick of enticing the enemy into the city and then shutting the doors would only work the once. As the captive audience was being killed, a second wave of *Saxoni* were attacking the city walls. Distracted by the opportunity to get rid of so many of the enemy at one fell swoop, the Vortigern's men had an opportunity to take advantage of the reduction in British and Roman troops on the city walls. Lupus remembered how many men they had seen march through Londinium on that *triumphus* (as Germanus had sarcastically labelled it). Had the Vortigern sent all of them? They were surrounding the inner walls as some of the outer gates collapsed. The *ballistae* had finally given out and the men that operated them captured or killed. Germanus's army began to look beaten.

Not all the West British forces were in Viroconium. An advance party had been sent out by Germanus to scout, clear, and guard the road to Londinium. They were crack troops as well, a large part of the Armorican Guard. Lupus saw Germanus instructing messengers to reach out to them to return and help fight the battle. Having these extra men on side would certainly turn the tide, but could they get back to Viroconium in time?

Germanus gave the pre-ordained signal to all the contingents to fall back and re-group in the amphitheatre, where more traps lay in store for the invaders. The General was pleased with the way the combined Armorican, British and Roman forces fell into line and enticed the Vortigern's Saxon *foederati* to follow. He could not help smiling to himself at the way his army had come together in such a short space of time. He laughed as he shepherded the troops, battling the *Saxoni* as they went. Then he suddenly felt a hot, searing pain. He reached round to feel the bolt. He quickly gave up trying to pull it out.

'No matter. If I am to die today, then so be it.' Germanus gritted his teeth, straightened himself and carried on with his command. Lucius, who had rarely left his commanding officer's side since his brother Nonus had died and the battle began, noticed the blood stain on the general's back gradually increase in size.

'If he dies, we are doomed', Lucius said to himself, 'and I will be with Nonus and the gods by the end of the day.'

CHAPTER 27

Germanus conquers in that sign

'Let me be, I tell you! Let me be!'

Lucius and Lupus had no option but to let Germanus alone. They watched as he pulled the arrow from his back, threw it on the floor and spat on it.

'No Saxon can defeat General Germanus! Come, this way.'

Whereupon the troops were ordered to fall back and head into the forum. There, they were instructed to line up on three sides of the town square and leave the way they had come clear for the *Saxoni* to rush in. Germanus commanded the troops from a vantage point on the top step of the temple at the far side of the forum. There, he was in the perfect position to see both his own armies and those of the Vortigern. Aureliana had positioned herself next to her *magister militum*. Drustans was on the left side of the forum; Lupus on the right. Aureliana could not believe how stupid the *Saxoni* were, but, as anticipated by Germanus, they followed her forces into the forum. In their eagerness to go for the kill, as they saw it, they had not realised that the way into the town square was a dead end. Once in the forum, more British troops closed any possible escape route behind the invaders.

Arrows, hot coals and worse rained down on the Vortigern's troops. Many fell where they stood, for they did not have the armour to protect themselves in the way their opponents did. Nevertheless, the battle was still evenly matched; there were so many more of the *Saxoni* than British, Armorican and Roman put together. Worse; the Britons who had cut off the Saxon escape route back out of the forum were themselves now forced onto the defensive by a further wave of enemy troops pouring into the outer city as the British had retreated.

'Will these *Saxoni* never stop coming? By all the gods, is there no end to their number?' Aureliana looked at Germanus, hoping for an answer. From their different vantage points, Drustans and Lupus could see that the West British forces were growing weary. Ambrosius, leading the centuries that had trapped the *Saxoni* in the forum and were now themselves trapped, began to feel that the battle was lost. For every soldier on the British side, there must still have been three or four on the Vortigern's, despite the enemy's losses.

Germanus was finding it difficult to control the pain. He could feel blood trickling down his lower back from the arrow wound. Several of the braver, tougher *Saxoni* reached the temple steps, but between them, Aureliana and Germanus killed them all. The more they slaughtered, the more the fire in their bellies raged. Then a moment came where the General had to rest. He signalled to the Queen of the West Britons that he was going inside the temple to catch his breath. It took Germanus some little time to acclimatise to the low light inside the building. When his eyes had adjusted to the darkness, he could see the statues at the far end of the hall: Mithras, Bacchus, Mercury, Serapis, Minerva; just like the army temples he had known in his youth.

'This is more like it.' Germanus smiled, then grimaced. The pain returned, sharper and fiercer than before. He suspected that part of the arrow tip was still buried in his back; it may even have been a poisoned one. He touched the wound but could feel nothing. The pain was unbearable. 'I must do something. Help me, gods of my forebears! My gods! Help me!' Germanus moved to the altars, asking each of the gods in turn for their help. Then he remembered the stone that Memor had given him. He took it from the pouch that hung from his *balteus*. He checked to make sure that his *pugio* was still in its place. He would be able to kill one last Saxon with it, and then himself, if he had to.

Germanus undid his tunic and placed the stone over the wound. He pressed hard. He could hear the fighting getting louder. The *Saxoni* must be winning. The pain was just as bad as before. He pressed harder. Still nothing. Then a third time. A warmth began to emanate from the stone and into his back. Germanus could feel Memor's spirit burrowing into his flesh and eating away at the poison. He saw the old man's face, with his long white hair and his even longer beard in front of him, looming large out of the dark shadows in between the statues of the gods. Then the pain was gone. Germanus felt for the wound, but there was nothing there. He smiled, knowing that the old *haruspex* had worked his magic one more time.

Germanus exhaled as if to blow the temple doors open. There was still a battle to be won, and the fight did not go well. At its base were the words, *In hoc signo vinces*.

'Conquer in this sign.' Germanus smiled, as he had an idea.

CHAPTER 28

Severianus gloats; Germanus triumphs, then falls

'So?'

'The battle goes badly for Germanus. His people are being forced into the citadel. They are outnumbered at least three-to-one.'

'Thank you. Your information has been most valuable. I wil see to it that you are rewarded in due course. I always remember the people who have been good to me. You might even have a medal pinned on your chest before we have finished this war.' Bishop Severianus smiled, wondering how long it would be before he donned the sacred robes of the *Pontifex Maximus*. Perhaps he might take the purple as well, having got rid of the boy-emperor and her meddling mother. That problem was for another day.

'Where are the General's other troops? The scouts and forward army that he sent off to Londinium?'

'They are racing back to Viroconium, my Lord. Germanus has summoned them as reinforcements. They include at least some of his cavalry.'

'Do they now...' Severianus walked around his *contubernium*. As befitted his status, the Bishop of Eboracum's tent was twice the size of those set aside for his senior officers, while at least eight soldiers slept in each of the remaining *contubernia*. Though keen to show his rank and determined to exert his power over his troops, Severianus knew how to treat his men properly. They were all well fed, their armour and weapons were in good condition, and the chain of command structured to best effect. Everybody knew their place and the orders were clear and logically set out. The army might be small by the standards of former years, but the force remained powerful, especially in a province where much of the old hierarchy and the respect for the rule of law and strong military discipline had collapsed. This was just like the old days, out on a campaign north of the wall, or down in Isca or over in Augusta Trevirorum, or even, as once had happened, in the east. *One day I will be in Roma, and then on to Constantinopolis!*

'Tell the troops to prepare to march. I think we should greet Germanus's men and help them with all our might to return to Viroconium as swiftly as they, and we, can.' Severianus clasped his hands and laughed. 'It might take a while for the General's reinforcements to arrive, of course. God will be with them, no doubt.' Severianus guffawed. His high command followed, laughing uncontrollably.

※　　※　　※

Germanus reappeared from the temple. He squeezed Memor's stone and put it back in his pocket. To be on the safe side, he also took a small cross that had stood in the temple. Once back in the thick of the fighting, he assembled those of his commanders who were nearest him and explained what he had in mind. They in turn instructed their troops to pass the order around the centuries. To work, the plan would have to be implemented immediately; there was no time to lose.

Much to the surprise of the *Saxoni*, Viroconium's defenders started a full scale retreat. Not like the measured withdrawal into the inner city that had so fooled the enemy. They just started to run, abandoning any pretence of defence. The Saxon attackers were so taken aback that they did not immediately set off in pursuit but stood and stared for some considerable time. This had to be another trick. Within a few moments, the Vortigern's army had the forum to themselves. Not a Briton, an Armorican or a Roman in sight.

The Saxon high command were agreed: this was simply too good to be true. A large contingent of Hengest's men (led by son Oeric) walked toward the temple at the far end of the forum; the place where Germanus had last been seen, instructing his high command. The temple, and all the surrounding buildings, including Aureliana's palace, were empty.

'How can you claim victory if your enemy has simply disappeared?' Oeric reported back to his father. Hengest turned to his senior officers and asked for suggestions. After much consultation the order was given to advance, slowly and carefully, sure in the knowledge that this was another of Germanus's ruses. Every building was searched; every alleyway inspected; every road checked for Britons. Not a single person was found. The most that could be captured was a few chickens. Eventually, there was little of the city left to search. The only remaining area was the amphitheatre, off to the northeast.

Hengest knew it was a trap. What else could he do? He had but two options: either proceed or abandon the attack. If he did the latter, he could at least raze Viroconium to the ground and destroy what munitions were still in the city and had not been taken as people fled. If he did the former, well, he could finish off his old enemy once and for all. Hengest could see Germanus mocking him. Goading him into giving the order to attack. *I'll get you, you bastard. You and your filthy Armoricans!* Hengest and Oeric shouted the battle cry in tandem. The *Saxoni* charged ahead. There were so many of them that they fell over each other as they forced themselves headlong through the narrow streets towards the amphitheatre. The gates were open wide. Hengest and his high command held back while the foot soldiers streamed into the *harena*.

Germanus had been waiting all the while for the *Saxoni* to arrive.

He knew that Hengest would not be able to resist following the British troops and their allies: any opportunity to settle old scores would be taken, almost irrespective of the tactical validity or the cost of such a move. The amphitheatre was quickly full to overflowing with Hengest's men. Germanus gave the signal. The seats all around the *harena* were filled with his troops. As if with one voice they all shouted 'Allelulia, Alleluia!' And they kept on shouting, so that the walls echoed with the sound. The chant multiplied in volume; the reverberation was deafening in the ears of the enemy. The *Alleluias* became so loud that the *Saxoni* dropped their weapons so that they could shield their ears. At which point, the British and their allies attacked.

Germanus ordered his forces to show no mercy. Within minutes, the amphitheatre was piled high with bodies. This was not simply the rage of the day's battle, but a release of the pent-up anger of years of living under the Vortigern's oppressive rule and in his dark shadow. Aureliana and Ambrosius took especial pleasure in savaging any British turncoats that they spotted in Hengest's army. Traitors to the cause, every one of them! Hengest soon saw that the battle was lost. Germanus had tricked him again! He ordered the remainder of his forces, such as they were, to retreat. Meanwhile, on the highest vantage point over the *harena,* Germanus was thinking how useful this Christian God was becoming. Then he could see only blackness as he fell to the ground below.

CHAPTER 29

Severianus advances; Germanus dreams; Ambrosius triumphs

'We had better advance.' Severianus kicked his horse into movement and the troops began their march to Viroconium. Germanus's men had taken some convincing to join forces with the Bishop of Eboracum. Only when he quoted from the agreement between the two bishops about fighting the Vortigern as a common enemy did the combined British, Armorican and Roman soldiery submit to the command of Severianus. It turned out that the two armies had men who were related: Briton with Briton, Armorican with Briton, Roman with Briton. Some of the older soldiers had served together in the final days of the Roman Army in Britannia.

Severianus ordered everyone to speak in Latin, to ensure clarity of communication; no use of British or Armorican. The bishop smiled at the enlargement of his army: he now had twice as many soldiers as had left Eboracum; there was even a *cohors equitata*. Why had Germanus sent these men out on the road? With hindsight, they should have been in Viroconium, should they not? But then Germanus could not have imagined that the Vortigern would have seized the initiative and attacked, especially when Viroconium was so far from Londinium, and the support and supply lines were not what they once were.

Severianus ordered the joint forces to speed up. Whatever the fate of the West British forces, he would be the winner. For a moment, the Bishop of Eboracum thought about turning on Londinium, given that Hengest and much of his army was in West Britannia. But then, who knew what reserves were still in the capital? First west, then east, decided Severianus. Whichever side was victorious in Viroconium, he could take command, especially now he had a fresh army at his disposal. Any escape route back to Londinium could be blocked and Aureliana's army would be in no state to put up an effective resistance, especially if Severianus came as a saviour.

They would be in Viroconium before darkness.

⁂ ⁂ ⁂

Eustachia stood in front of him. How lovely she looked as he floated towards her. *I must have gone to Elysium. I have fought hard; I have stayed the course; the battle is won. Now I am with my love, and all is calm.* Eustachia welcomed him with open arms. But as Germanus took his wife's hands, someone was grabbing him by the neck and pulling him away. He turned to face his assailant so that he could be with Eustachia, now and forever. It was Sevira. His Sevira! She laughed at him, told him to look at his beloved wife, now turned into a *senex mulier,* with shrivelled skin and whispy hair and yellow teeth. While Germanus was so distracted, Sevira took out a *gladius* and plunged it into his neck. She watched the blood spurt out; then began to drink it. *No! No! No! Not this! Not this!*

Feet; all Germanus could see were feet. Feet wrapped up in crude leather shoes. Saxon shoes. Every bone ached; he tried to get up, but his body would not respond to his brain. The shoes were all round him, kicking him over onto his back. As his vision cleared, Germanus could see legs, then bodies then heads. Heads of Saxon soldiers. Fingers pointed down at him; swords and spears were aimed at his heart, his head, his groin. Was this the end? After all this, to die in a decaying outpost of a once-great empire, having failed in what was supposed to have been the most glorious mission of his life. What had it all been about? Why this? Why now?

'Look! Hurry! Please! Hurry!'

A little girl's voice. Germanus knew that voice.

'Barita!'

Another voice. 'Saxon scum. You will be with your gods today!' It was Ambrosius.

The first two *Saxoni* fell where they stood, the sword having pierced their hearts from the back. Two more had their throats cut. The final three put up more of a fight against the Queen's husband-brother, but they were no match for him. Germanus had never thought that a one-eyed man could be so effective. But here Ambrosius was, taking on three of them at once. He used his arms, his elbows, his legs, his head. Every part of him was used to distract, disarm, and then kill the enemy. It was a long time since Germanus had seen such savagery. This was a man out for revenge; against anything and anybody. By now Ambrosius was hacking into the dying bodies of the men. Shocked and scared by the butchery, the Saxon soldiers turned tail and ran. Hengest had already ordered the retreat and the first wave of troops were on the road to Londinium.

'Enough Ambrosius. Enough now. Stop!' Aureliana drew her sword and pointed. 'We have won!'

Germanus managed to stand, pushing himself up on top of the dead Saxons.

'We have; for now. This is only the beginning.'

CHAPTER 30

Coelestinus thinks quickly; Germanus investigates; Severianus arrives

'Bugger! Bugger, bugger, bugger! And double bugger!'

'Yes, Holy Father.' Ferox bowed, wearily; he was used to hearing the *Pontifex Maximus* swear.

Coelestinus wondered what he was to do. All was not well in Britannia. The West British were on the verge of defeat, and Severianus was still playing Germanus and the Vortigern off against each other. It looked as though the Vortigern was going to live to fight another day, with or without the Bishop of Eboracum, but especially with, and all those bloody *Saxoni* on top.

'This was not what I planned; not what I planned at all. Germanus should have won; neutralised the Vortigern; brought Severianus into the fold; eradicated Pelagius; helped me to secure the succession; and got rid of that awful Aureliana woman and her disgusting tribe.'

By now Coelestinus was shouting out of his bedroom window and across the courtyard. Priests and other clerics in meditation turned to see what the matter was. The Pontifex stopped suddenly, turned round, motioned to Ferox to close the window as quickly as possible, and went back to his *scrinium*. He sat there sheepishly, realising what a fool he had just made of himself.

'What am I to do now? If my plans for Germanus have all gone awry?' Coelestinus looked up at the cross hanging above his bed. 'Hmmm. I have an idea...'

※　　※　　※

'Who betrayed us? And who pushed me off the city walls?' Germanus looked around the high council. No-one spoke. 'It has to to be someone in this room. No-one but you, all you sitting here, knew of our plans: to send an advance force to mop up local resistance and rally more to our cause in between here and Londinium; that we were less than fully defended as a result; and we were not ready for a surprise attack!'

'Except we were ready, thanks to my *magister militum*!' Aureliana looked at Germanus. He was sitting next to her in his full uniform. He looked battleworn and should have been resting after his latest injuries, but he had insisted on rooting out the traitor before further damage could be done. The Queen of the West Britons had agreed to hold an emergency meeting of the Council as the combined armies mopped up after the battle of Viroconium. The fatalities and the casualties had been remarkably light, given the onslaught and the Vortigern's significantly larger army. The enemy had reckoned without the genius of General Germanus. Aureliana smiled as she remembered the tactics that had given them victory. Whatever else this man was to her, and would be in the future, he was her saviour and her rock, at least for now. And he was right; somebody had betrayed them to the Vortigern. It must have been one of her tribe. She felt ashamed that she, and her people, had been let down so badly like this.

Germanus rose and walked round the table. Lupus, from his vantage point in the corner of the room, noticed the limp. As he stood there, watching Germanus stand behind each member of the council in turn before moving on to the next suspect, Lupus realised that his adopted father had made a man of him; had trusted him to lead soldiery in real and bloody battle. He had done so; and done it well. Perhaps now Aureliana would treat him like a man; just as he treated her like a real woman. *Lupus the wolf!*

Germanus inspected every member of the high council, including Ambrosius, Drustans and Aureliana. He then returned to his seat and was about to speak when a *nuntius* burst in.

'Sir! Your Lordship! They are here!'

All eyes were on the boy.

'They?' Aureliana stood up quickly.

'Yes, your Majesty. Our troops. They are back from the east. And there is a man I do not know leading them'

Germanus laughed and turned to Aureliana. 'Well, well. Severianus arrives at last, and just in time for the victory celebrations.'

CHAPTER 31

The Vortigern's plan; Germanus and Aureliana are one, for now

Pelagius had never seen the Vortigern like this: not in all the time they had been together. The two men did not like each other, especially; but that was of no consequence. As long as this earthly ruler held power in Britannia, then Pelagius could spread the word, and not just to the four corners of the old province, but beyond it, once they had taken Roma and the Vortigern wore the purple: him as *Imperator*; Pelagius as Pontifex. *Pontifex Maximus!* With the whole ecclesiastical apparatus at his beck and call.

What if the Vortigern lost? Could Pelagius make a pact with Germanus? They had been good friends and even occasional drinking partners in their days as youthful law students. Then religion got in the way. Germanus had not been persuaded by Christianity. Pelagius had been so persuaded, in fact, that he had formed his own branch, where human beings still had free will and where God did not command them to do the impossible. Germanus should have agreed with that. Pelagius had lived an unimpeachable life and asked his followers to do the same: and been excommunicated for his pains. Germanus would understand.

Pelagius wanted more than anything to see his views prevail. He had lost the theological argument, but he could still win the ecclesiastical war. Would Germanus be willing to negotiate now that he was a cleric himself? The thought of his old drinking partner as an archbishop! Would it have changed him? Was he really a convert to the Christian faith? Germanus was a clever man. He would have determined what was the best thing to do and then done it, even if it meant abandoning old beliefs and embracing new ones. Whatever flavour of the one true faith that Coelestinus had served up would be a mild version by comparison with some of the extreme forms that were now being peddled in parts of the empire. Perhaps the two of them could forge an alliance.

Pelagius looked back at the Vortigern. The supreme leader had regained some of his composure. He was not beaten yet, not by a long way.

'What have you decided to do my Lord?'

'What have I decided, Pelagius?' The Vortigern rose, walked round the room and back to where he had been seated. 'I am going to continue with my plans – or rather my revised plans: now that I know where we stand with our brother in Christ from the north.'

'And what about Agricola? He has not covered himself in glory on the campaign to date. Nor, for that matter, did your Saxon friends.'

The Vortigern grimaced as Pelagius reminded him of the ignominy of their recent defeat at the hands of the *Cornovii*, the Armoricans, and the Romans. How could such a disparate group of fighters have beaten back his troops? Especially when they had a traitor in their midst? Someone who had been feeding information about Germanus and his movements, his plans and his alliances since the great general had arrived in Britannia at the beginning of the year. How could he not have seen Severianus's treachery? How could he have ever trusted that man? Could he trust Agricola or Hengest? Even if he could, were they up to the job of leading the army in battle against the West Britons and their allies, let alone sweeping across the continent and conquering Roma? Drastic action had to be taken; and taken quickly.

'Pelagius, I am going to summon the high council. We have to act now.'

Pelagius bowed and left the Vortigern to plan his speech to the Council. The high priest was still going to keep his options open though.

※　　※　　※

'So, who is it?'

'I know now. It became obvious as I looked at everyone in your council chamber. I had my suspicions, but I suddenly realised the identity of the traitor.'

'So, who is it? I must know!'

'No, you must not. I have decided not to reveal their identity to anyone.'

'But I am not anyone.'

'No, that is true. But you will behave differently if you know; everyone will. And for now, we need to be sure that our traitor remains unaware of my discovery.'

'To what end?'

'To play the Vortigern at his own game, which is why I am telling no-one else for now.'

'Not even me?'

'Not even you, my Queen.'

Germanus arose from Aureliana's bed and dressed. He looked back at her. It had been a long time coming, this relationship, but he had regretted nothing when they had finally come together and consummated their feelings for each other. She could have been his daughter, and for much of the time since his arrival he had treated her as such, while she seemed to enjoy having a father figure in her life. But there was more to their relationship than that. From their first encounter when she had sobered him up, he had desired her, and she had desired him. They had fought like lovers; not enemies; companions; not rivals; but lovers. It was not about being paternal; despite their age differences, this was a primeval bond: he wanted to bed her, and she wanted him in her bed. Yet the child inside her was not his. Nor did Germanus realise who his adopted son was and why Lupus had to be the father of Aureliana's child. Aureliana knew. She had always known.

CHAPTER 32

Agricola plans revenge;
Lupus greets his destiny

The sun shone over Londinium. Smoke still rose from the warehouses that Germanus and his crew had set on fire. In the old forum the troops were regrouping, while their commanders assessed the losses. Most of the larger equipment had been left behind at Viroconium in order to speed the retreat, though after a few miles, it had become clear that the West Britons were not going to give chase. Despite their victory, Aureliana's combined forces were too exhausted. Severianus had no intention of having his troops exert themselves upon arrival in Viroconium, and Germanus was not going to let the Bishop of Eboracum have command of the expeditionary force for a moment longer, now that those men were back on home ground. Agricola watched the rays of light pierce the window shutters as he let the woman treat his wounds. The battle had been going so well; right to the very end, when the Saxon troops ran amok in the amphitheatre and Germanus delivered his master stroke. 'That is why the Vortigern wanted Germanus as his *magister militum* and not me.'

The nurse did not answer.

'I did not expect it. Nor did Hengest, even though my Saxon thug had served with Germanus at one point if I understand what that *barbarus* has been droning on about correctly.'

The woman continued her work in silence.

'You, what's your name?'

Agricola might be sore, but he still had enough life left in him to notice the woman's breasts as she leaned over his body to wash his chest.

'Aedesia, sir. That is my name.'

'And where are you from?'

'I was born in Gallia, but I came here with my family when I was a baby.'

'You are a slave?'

Aedesia nodded.

'Who owns you?'

'I am the Vortigern's.'

'Would you like to be mine?'

Aedesia stopped her work and looked at Agricola. Eventually, she spoke.

'I could be his, I could be yours, I could be anybody's. I do not care who owns me. Will you feed and clothe me? Will you be kind to me? Will you want to touch me?'

Agricola thought of Aureliana and then of his father.

'Let me tell you a story Aedesia. I was in love with this girl; a beautiful girl, with long ginger hair. She was called Aureliana; she was, still is, a queen.'

The nurse said nothing, never looking at Agricola, washing his body all the while that he spoke.

'And I thought she and I had an understanding. That one day she and I would rule this country. Ow! That hurts!'

'I am sorry sir, but your wounds are very deep. I will take more care.'

'Very well, Aedesia. Are you a Christian, by any chance?'

'No, sir. I was brought up in the old ways. I have little knowledge of this Jesus Christ. Now I need you to stay still while I bandage the wound on your shoulder.'

'Good. Can I trust you to keep a secret? If I tell you more, will you promise me that you will tell no-one else?'

Aedesia nodded and smiled.

'I should have known I could not believe in Aureliana. Now I see that her promises were all a ploy to get our forces to West Prythain. She knew that Germanus would never give in; would somehow score a victory, even though her troops were massively outnumbered. And the intelligence that our *exploratorem* in her high command was either wrong or deliberately falsified. Great! Just what you want as your military campaign gets started! The enemy were far better armed than we had been led to believe. They even had fully working *ballistae*, for God's sake!'

Aedesia asked Agricola to lie on his side so she could clean the sword slice on his back. He told her how even his own father had betrayed him, not that there was much love lost between the two of them; there never had been.

'Why do you not love your father, sir?' Why does he not love you?'

'That is a good question, Aedesia, to which I do not have a good answer. My mother died giving birth to me, and I believe that he blamed me for her death. That is the only reason that I can think of.'

'That is no reason. But why has he been disloyal to the Vortigern?'

Agricola sat up.

'How did you know about that?'

Aedesia stopped her work.

'Well, I, well, everyone knows, don't they? It is common knowledge that Bishop Severianus has changed sides. I heard people talking in the market this morning when I went to buy food. Some of the soldiers you took to Viroconium were talking about it all. About how your father arrived as the battle had finished, along with the extra troops.'

Agricola relaxed and lay back down on his bed. He decided not to say any more to this woman, other than to ask her to come to his rooms that evening. He pondered the message from Coelestinus. It had come by special courier as the troops were nearing Londinium. Agricola had realised the significant of the Pontifex's words as soon as the writing tablet had been delivered. *Could I really be Imperator? Would Coelestinus support me?*

Aedesia woke Agricola gently.

'Sir, you fell asleep. But you must wake now. Your master needs you. The Vortigern commands you to attend him.'

Aedesia helped Agricola get dressed. He told her when and where to come to him, tipped her, then left for the citadel. As he grew near, he wondered what his fate would be, and if it was time for him to forge new alliances before it was too late. In the meantime, Aedesia ran to the safe house where Aureliana's people were waiting to hear her latest information.

※　　※　　※

Lupus was exhausted, but happy. Yet despite his tiredness, he was unable to sleep. Too much had happened in the last few days for his mind to rest. He tried to order his memories of the previous week; to make sense of everything. There was only one thing on which to focus: his surprise at how effective he had been as a commander at the Battle of Viroconium. Germanus had taught him well and he had not let his master down. Quite the opposite, and there had been a special mention of him at the high council meeting after hostilities had ceased and the mopping-up operation was completed. Lupus had watched as the others had looked towards him and nodded in agreement at the deservedness of the accolade that Germanus was giving him. One thing above all had pleased Lupus: the look in Aureliana's eyes. That told him all he needed to know; she was proud of him. Lupus felt sad as he remembered his parents. They would have been proud of him too! His father had always said that he would achieve greatness, and now he began to believe that might be possible. Whereas before coming to Britannia with Germanus, Lupus had grown pale at the thought of soldiery and battle, he now relished the thought of armed conflict. Having seen how Germanus had marshalled his forces, Lupus himself began to contemplate the next campaign: the capture of Londinium and the deposing of the Vortigern.

He decided that sleep was going to elude him, so he might as well get up and do something useful. He took the *cistula* in which he kept his person effects down from the *vestium*. He lit an oil lamp by his bed so that he could see its contents more clearly. There was not much to show for his life; but then much had been destroyed when the *barbari* overran his homeland. He could not immediately find what he was looking for inside the little box. Then he saw it, right at the bottom. He had read the letter once before, as his father lay dying, and he had ordered his son to look at it while he explained what it meant. The words had signified nothing; he had not been listening and could not understand as he sat there crying as his father drew his last breath. Now, after all his adventures, he understood.

CHAPTER 33

Nulla dies sine linea: Coelestinus resolves to keep going

'You got it wrong again! Didn't you? How am I supposed to plan when you keep buggering it all up?'

There was no reply.

'What are you playing at? What the hell are you playing at?'

Still no reply.

The Pontifex sighed, looked up at the cross above the high altar, then signalled to his acolytes to help him up from his knees. He looked at his aides, who immediately averted their gaze. But Coelestinus knew what they were thinking. *That incontinent fool is losing it; has lost it, in fact.* Senex bis puer: *the old man is in his second childhood. How long before we are serving a new Pontifex Maximus? Perhaps we had better start preparing for his successor. Who will it be? Germanus? Severianus? Pelagius? Palladius? Take your pick!*

It had all gone so horribly wrong. Germanus was on the verge of defeat and death, along with the Queen of the West Britons and her army. Then he was not, and the Vortigern's troops had been sent packing, by which time Coelestinus had switched his patronage to Agricola, on the assumption that Aureliana must have been killed, or had committed suicide to avoid being taken prisoner by the enemy.

The post was not like it was in the old days; and the couriers that the Pontifex had at his personal disposal were not much better. Thick *barbari* to a man, as far as Coelestinus could make out. So, when his agents in Britannia had said that the messages were *urgens*, which bit of the word urgent had not been understood by the boneheads who had been responsible for getting the reports of the goings-on in Viroconium back to Roma? What part of *instans* or *necessarius* had not been comprehended?

To make it worse, bloody Severianus had swapped sides; or was it swapped back? Whose side was the Bishop of Eboracum on? Silly question! Nobody's side; but his own, that is! It had been clever of Germanus to persuade him to support the West Britons and their armies, but not surprising that he had so hedged his bets. *Ubi mel ibi apes*: 'where there is honey, there are bees', Coelestinus mumbled to himself. 'More to the point, where is the hive? Is it with Germanus or the Vortigern? Or do I keep faith with Severianus, given that he is the only one of them of the mainstream faith, allegedly?'

Coelestinus thought back to his early meetings with the Bishop of Eboracum. He had never trusted Severianus, even then, when he had professed the one true faith and sworn to be the Pontifex's main man in Britannia, combatting Pelagius and his semi-pagan filth. That had been the real threat; someone who was challenging the one *true* faith. *My faith, the faith that will see me and my line as Imperator for evermore: world without end, Amen!* Coelestinus looked up angrily at the high altar again as he pondered the issues with Germanus and Aureliana and Severianus and Agricola and Pelagius, not to mention the bloody Vortigern.

'Bugger me! You could not have made it up! *A fronte praecipitium a tergo lupi*: a precipice in front, wolves behind. The Pontifex narrowed his eyes, still pretending to be deep in prayer. Wolves behind: or at least one wolf: Lupus; Germanus's new son. Where does he fit? There is a lot more to him than meets the eye. Now that I know something of his past and his heritage, he could be useful to me; very useful, in fact.'

Coelestinus pulled himself together, reminding himself that he was still in charge. The acolytes helped him down the altar steps and out of the church. The supreme leader of the Christian church smiled as he walked through the secret passageway to his private apartments.

'*Dabit deus his quoque finem.* God will grant an end even to these troubles.' The Pontifex whispered to himself as he opened the door to his *cubiculum.* He was about to shut the door on the acolytes when he turned round and shouted at them as they disappeared back down the corridor and back to their altar duties.

'*Dabit deus his quoque finem!'*

The two acolytes pretended not to hear him.

'I'm not done yet! I am still *Pontifex: Pontifex MAXIMUS!*

CHAPTER 34

Germanus and the Vortigern
make far-reaching decisions

Londinium was cold that evening. The Vortigern had already ordered the slaves to light several *foculi* in the council chamber when Agricola arrived for the *consilium*. All the others, including Pelagius and Hengest, were already there, lined up on either side of the table, the Vortigern at its head. There was only one member absent: Constantius. Agricola and Pelagius had both noticed a change in that man of late. The two of them had exchanged glances whenever Constantius spoke; or did not speak. The man had a strange look about him all the time. His wife had nearly died in childbirth, but she had survived and Constantius now had a son and heir. He should have been happy, but he was not; rather, he was preoccupied. Agricola was about to ask if the meeting should start without everyone present when Constantius arrived.

'I am sorry my Lord. I should not have kept you waiting, but my wife is still not fully recovered. I needed to tend to her.'

'Welcome, my Lord Constantius. Thank you for gracing us with your presence, especially when you obviously have so many domestic duties to perform. I thought one had slaves to perform such duties, but that is clearly not the case in your household.'

'Yes, my Lord Vortigern. I am sorry. But it is difficult to...'

The other council members laughed. Constantius decided it was best not to lecture the Vortigern on the difficulty of getting good quality slaves for an affordable rate in present-day Londinium.

'*Nemo sine vitio est.*' The Vortigern looked round the room as he admitted that no one was without fault. They discussed what had gone wrong and how they put it right. The Vortigern asked for suggestions as he planned his next moves. Hengest blustered; Agricola advised caution; Constantius said nothing. Pelagius castigated everybody, except his Lord and Master. No-one else spoke. The conversation petered out.

'So that's the best you lot can do? How am I to conquer the empire if I cannot even defeat those *rustici* in the west of my kingdom?'

Constantius winced inwardly: the Vortigern saw himself as *rex*. This was not a man who wanted to bring back the glory of Roma; to create a new republic based on the best of the old ways and the glory of the risen Jesus. He had known it all along, but, now that he had seen a real leader, Constantius could no longer keep persuading himself that what the Vortigern was doing was best for the people and best for *Britannia*.

'Why don't we sue for peace, my Lord?'

Silence.

'It is the last thing Germanus would be expecting us – I mean you – to do.'

Pelagius snorted; Hengest guffawed. Agricola raised an eyebrow. The Vortigern stroked his chin. Constantius clasped his hands together and looked down at his feet, fearful that his proposal would result in his immediate expulsion from the Vortigern's High council.

'Agricola, can you get a message to Drustans?'

The *magister militum* nodded hesitantly.

'I expect so, my Lord, but what do you wish to say to him?'

'Ask him to invite Germanus to peace talks.'

※　　※　　※

'You should rest. After all that has happened to you over the last few weeks.'

'No, we attack now! The Vortigern will be anxious, wondering what to do. His forces are depleted, and morale low, if our intelligence is to be believed. We have the advantage, but it will not last long. He will soon regroup.'

Aureliana and Lupus knew that arguing with Germanus was pointless. A lesser man would be in bed recuperating. Despite having broken ribs and lost much blood, the General was still on his feet, re-organising the army now that Severianus had joined them. Elafius and Barita had previously tried to get Germanus to rest, but their pleas had also fallen on stone deaf ears, hence the request to Aureliana and Lupus to get the man to stop, even for a few days.

'I am fine. Stop fussing! All of you!' Germanus would not be told.

'You have yet to find the traitor. Do you really think we should advance on Londinium while we have yet to identify him?' Lupus turned away in frustration.

'Or her, Lupus, or her.'

'Do you think it is me?' Aureliana looked at Germanus angrily.

'No one can be trusted, Aureliana.'

'But we have just…' The Queen of the West Britons blushed. Lupus gasped. 'I mean, we have just had a meeting where we agreed what we were going to do next.'

Germanus looked stone faced. Lupus was not amused. *What the hell is going on between those two?*

'Do not fear. I will rest when we are in Londinium and the Vortigern is no more. If we act now, we will be victorious and sooner than you think. Now I want to be alone for a short while. I will address the troops in the amphitheatre at sunrise.'

Aureliana and Lupus stood where they were.

'Now leave me! Let me be!' Germanus turned away from his companions and went over to the window. He tried his best not to limp, but Aureliana and Lupus were not taken in by his attempts to walk normally. The two of them looked at each other briefly. Aureliana tried to smile at Lupus, but he refused to react to her mild advance. She nodded and left. He followed her. Germanus took his mind off the pain by focussing on the bustle of troops in the street below. They were laughing and joking; some were singing. It was good that morale was high. Beyond, the city's defences were being repaired. They had held up well, but they would not survive another onslaught.

'May God, the Gods, give me strength. How much longer do I have to ensure this pain?' Tears ran down the General's cheeks. *If only I could have this all taken away from me!*

There was a knock at the door. Germanus tidied himself up and wiped his tears away.

'Come in.'

The door opened slowly, and a dirty face gradually appeared.

'You asked for me?'

'I did indeed, my little *orba*. Now tell me what my Lord Drustans has been up to since he got back to Viroconium.'

CHAPTER 35

Two bishops consider their options

Severianus was less than impressed with his quarters. The roof leaked, the floorboards creaked, wind whistled through the window, the bed was hard and lumpy. And as for going to the toilet, there seemed to be no end to the privations that would have to be endured. Had it been a mistake to throw his lot in with Germanus and Aureliana? It was so difficult to judge who would win this war. Germanus had been the victor this time round, but the Vortigern still had significantly more resources at his disposal: not just men and munitions, but a better supply chain. There was a difference between supporting an army in Viroconium and one based around Londinium and the southeast of Britannia. The capital had all that was needed to feed, clothe, and arm soldiery, despite the loss of the grain store, and the transport and communications infrastructure was robust right to Durovernum, Rutupiae and Dubris in the southeast, Venta Belgarum and Calleva in the west and Camulodunum and Verulamium to the north of Londinium. All that was obvious from the earlier reconnaissance mission when Drustans had been captured and then rescued. That was in the Vortigern's favour, and always would be.

Against that, what did the Queen of the West Britons have? Viroconium; and not much else, apart from the rind of the country, all the way down to what was left of Isca in the south and Deva in the north; Dumnonia was beyond the pale; always had been. Aureliana had one advantage: Segontium. Had she evoked help from her Druidic ancestors yet? And if so, what was the price they had demanded in return for help? They would have driven a hard bargain; they always did. But having their power could make a difference; a big difference.

Severianus turned in his bed, trying to find a spot, any spot, where he could get comfortable. The repairs to the city's defences never stopped. Germanus had ordered that the damage from the battle be made good as quickly as possible. As a result, teams of men and women (there was little differentiation between the sexes amongst the Cornovii, it seemed) were labouring day and night to complete the work. The noise never stopped; sleep was impossible. Then it occurred to him. Aureliana had a *second* advantage: the one and only Germanus. That was the single biggest difference between the two sides. How he had laughed when he had heard what Germanus had done; baptised the lot of them as Christians! What genius! And how Aureliana would have hated it all! But it would have done the trick: it was the ultimate oath of loyalty. And how brilliantly, by all accounts, Germanus had turned ignominious defeat into glorious victory. *Una salus victis nullam sperare salute:* knowing there is no hope can give one the courage to fight and win. There was hope now, even though there were more battles to be fought before Britannia and the empire could be united under a single leader: Severianus of Eboracum. He finally fell asleep, not waking until dawn had long broken and old Augustus brought him his breakfast.

※   ※   ※

The man had never seen so many freckles; it would take him a lifetime to count them. The downy triangle at the base of the stomach was the same ginger as the hair on the head. He stroked the hair, then twined the wisps around his finger. As the man arranged the down carefully into neat strands, he watched the breasts rise and fall in time to the shallow breathing. This was the second time they had been together in as many days. The man had vowed not to make love to her again; but she had insisted, and he had not resisted. The first time had felt strange; what they had just done was much more accomplished and eminently satisfying for them both. She had shouted his name out so loudly that he had to put his hand over her mouth; they could not afford to be discovered under any circumstances.

He was not at all sleepy despite the exhausting trials and tribulations of the battle; quite the opposite. He had more energy than ever and felt ten or even twenty years younger. That was not so bad; twenty years younger would make him thirty, only a few older than the woman he had just bedded. Germanus lay back down and looked up. Thin strands of light danced across the ceiling. The patterns which they made were also being cast across Aureliana's body. It suddenly occurred to him that in all the frenzy of the fighting, the intrigue, the plotting, the passion and now the seduction, not once had he thought about Patricius. The call of leadership and the excitement of warfare had made him stop thinking about his flesh and blood. Not only that, but as Lupus had grown to be a man and distinguished himself as a soldier and a leader, his adopted son had taken over from Patricius in his affections.

'What is it? What's wrong?'

She looked more beautiful than ever in the half light.

Germanus sighed. He did not want to end the magic of the evening but knew that he must.

'Where is Patricius? Where is my son? Where is he, Aureliana?'

'You have a son, Germanus. He is called Lupus.'

CHAPTER 36

The march to Londinium begins; the Vortigern counterattacks

There was little resistance at first. Quite the opposite, for now that 'the army from the west', as people started to call it, began to advance on Londinium and to liberate towns and villages from the Vortigern's rule, numbers grew. Between leaving Letocetum, the last of Aureliana's strongholds, and reaching Lactodurum, the combined forces must have added over two thousand men and women to the army. As word had spread of the march, people from all over the old province of Flavia Caesariensis were flocking to the cause. Germanus told his commanders to select those volunteers who had most fighting potential and to see that they were given basic training whenever the army stopped at the end of the day's travel. It turned out that many of the older men had been soldiers in the legions stationed in the province. They had not left when the recall came from Roma; Britannia was their home now. Germanus could see the excitement in their eyes at the thought of being in uniform once again. Some still had their original kit; a few even brought out and wore the medals they had earned in the last campaigns before Honorius cut the province loose from his imperial rule. Germanus spoke to these veterans separately, swearing them into his army as *evocati*. Old Augustus tried to sneak into the ceremony and join up with these men, until Severianus told his servant to get back to his domestic duties. The younger recruits had no memories or experience of military life on which to draw; reports back to Germanus confirmed that most were unused to combat. It was as if the Vortigern had made sure that, apart from his private army and the *Saxoni*, no town or village would have arms or men trained in soldiery: it would therefore be difficult for a renegade leader to form a competent militia to challenge the supreme ruler's overlordship.

After discussion with Severianus, Lupus, Aureliana, Drustans and Ambrosius, Germanus commanded that only the most able and experienced should be allowed to join the forward armies. The less fit and healthy were given non-combatant roles, ensuring the supply chain from Viroconium and the west remained robust so that communications were good and the fighting force well fed. Some of these people were to be stationed not only on the routes back to the heart of Cornovian lands but also delegated to form and maintain (with a small detail of soldiers to defend them in the event of counterattack) forward supply dumps once territory had been captured, secured, pacified and, eventually, if all went well, assimilated. This would mean that Germanus's forces were never far away from necessary munitions as they pushed further into the Vortigern's heartlands, where it might be more difficult to persuade the locals to change sides. The more able and athletic of the remaining civilians were then sworn in as *munifex*. Germanus summoned Lucius to the private quarters that had been hastily arranged for him and the rest of his high command in Lactodurum and put him in charge of turning these new recruits into a reserve fighting force.

'I must protest! I want to go with you, my lord; to fight by your side; to avenge Nonus.' The former *bagauda* had tears in his eyes. 'And above all, I want to repay my debt to you.'

Germanus laughed. 'Your debt to me? You owe me nothing, Lucius.'

'I owe you everything, master. When you captured me and my brother, we had lost everything: our families, our homes, our worth, our integrity. Then you gave us a purpose, a reason for living, and more than anything, a new belief. We have seen the way, the truth and the light.'

'Excuse me?'

'Yes, you have truly saved us. We became Christians like all the rest that day in the amphitheatre at Viroconium. We believe in the one true God, through his Son, Jesus Christ.'

'Oh, my goodness! Do you really?' For a moment, Germanus did not know what else to say. Then he remembered why he had summoned Lucius into his presence.

'If you can't do it for me, Lucius, do it for Jesus. Have faith!' Germanus was surprised at the transformation in the servant's demeanour as he heard these words. The man's face shone; he seemed to have grown taller; his eyes glistened.

'I will do it! And I will prevail!'

'Good man Lucius. Now get to it!'

Once the new training officer had left, Germanus thought for a moment, then summoned Severianus and the other members of the high command and instructed that all those who had not yet been baptised were to be initiated into the faith at dawn the following morning before the advance on Londinium recommenced. No-one demurred from this order.

※   ※   ※

'*De pilo pendet!*'

'Nonsense, Pelagius, we are nowhere near the critical point of this war.'

Agricola and Hengest looked at each other wearily and knowingly as the Vortigern and his spiritual adviser argued about the next stage in the fight with Germanus and the West Britons. The *magister militum* and the leader of the *Saxoni* were in as much disagreement as were their two leaders.

'*Quod homines, tot sententiae*: so many men, so many options.'

The Vortigern's laugh irritated Agricola. *The fool! I'm getting fed up with this man. I want this war to be over so we can get on with the real job in hand: getting Coelestinus to make me Imperator!*

The Vortigern stood up and walked round the council chamber before returning to his seat. He then clasped his hands, cleared his throat, and began to speak, softly, but clearly.

'I have decided, gentlemen. It is time to act. You were right to withdraw from Viroconium, Agricola and Hengest. *Quidquid fugiebat rursus proeliabitur*: or, for Hengest's benefit, he who fights and runs away may live to fight another day. And you, we, have lived to engage Germanus again and, this next time, to beat him. My agents have informed me that he is already on the march. That is good. At least our attack on Viroconium has stung him into action. The nearer he gets to us, the further away he is from home, and he does not have our command and control of men, munitions, or supplies. We will draw him into our net one way or the other. This is what we are going to do. Listen carefully, gentlemen.'

CHAPTER 37

Memor and Coelestinus reflect on the battle to come

It was the first meal he had eaten in days. One of the servants from the villa had brought it for him. As she warmed up the *juscellum*, the girl told Memor how Germanus had sent word to go and make sure that he was being looked after.

'It was kind of you, and so thoughtful of your master. What have you heard from over the water?'

'That the armies are soon to engage in combat.'

'And is your master optimistic of victory?'

'Nothing was said in the message, sir. Only that we were to make sure that you were looked after and that the Lord Germanus was well.'

'Thank you. What is your name?'

'I am called Samianta.'

'A good old name. Well, thank you Samianta. Please leave me now.'

Memor listened as the servant's footsteps grew fainter. Once he could hear nothing, the old *haruspex* cried out.

'By all the gods, take this pain away from me! I cannot go on!' Shouting at the top of his voice eased Memor's anguish somewhat. The broth in his belly had started to take effect. He kept eating. It was good to have a full stomach at last. 'Perhaps I can keep going after all', he sighed.

Memor ate the last of the bread and then belched. The meal had tasted good. The cooks at the villa were the best. Germanus was the best. And he had to stay alive long enough for his master to prevail. He had grown weak: saving Germanus more times than he could remember was hard from so far away. The old man could cope with all that. It was taking away the pain from the broken leg that was the hardest thing for the *haruspex* to bear. Germanus was starting to heal and would soon not need Memor's help, but not yet.

'It will all be over in two weeks. Germanus will prevail. His struggles will only just be starting when he finds out who the Vortigern really is. At least Lupus will come good in all of this. I just wish I could connect with Patricius. But I feel nothing; if he lives, then he must be somewhere very far away.' Memor determined that there was a limit to what he could do, and he had to stay within it. Having made that resolution, he felt that he could now sleep. He lay on his bed and dozed, hoping that he would dream about his dead son. Segovax did not appear to him; instead came Patricius, writhing in agony and shouting to the *haruspex* for aid. Alas, the old man was unable to help.

✳   ✳   ✳

The *Pontifex Maximus* pored over the map. Though out of date, Coelestinus decided that it would still be accurate enough for him to work out what was happening and how the war might play out.

'It is time for the service, my lord.'

'What service?' The old man croaked.

'The communion service, your grace.'

'Bugger the service! I am busy!'

'But your flock…'

'Tell them…tell them…tell them to go and fuck themselves!'

The deacon scuttled away, shutting the door just before the *cultellus* hit it.

'Bugger them all!'

The *Pontifex Maximus* muttered, once more inspecting the map of Britannia. First of all he found Dubris, where Hengest's forces must have landed, then traced his finger up to Londinium. Who was the Vortigern? This was a title, not a name, so who was it who held the role? Roman gentry, Prythonic nobility, or what? They must be Christian, with Pelagius as their spiritual adviser, just the wrong sort. Are they any good at military matters? The Vortigern would have had the best in the business if he had got Germanus as *magister militum*. Agricola could give a good account of himself as a commander on the battlefield despite being the son of Severianus, though, to be fair, the Bishop of Eboracum had seen service in his time and had, by all accounts, distinguished himself in battle. Coelestinus moved his finger around Londinium in ever larger circles, estimating the extent of the Vortigern's direct power. Hengest's forces gave the Vortigern an advantage, and a big one at that. It had not helped in the battle of Viroconium, though.

With his other hand, the *Pontifex* drew the extent of Germanus's territories, from Deva in the north to Glevum in the south. Was the Bishop of Eboracum's change of sides going to make much difference? It still did not even out the numbers between the two protagonists. Did Severianus's allegiance give Germanus an advantage? There was no way that Eboracum could be trusted further than you could throw him. If he had changed sides so easily, he could change back to support the Vortigern again. He was supposed to be loyal to Rome: where did Severianus stand on that now? Was he really a Roman, or a Christian?

Time to move on, thought Coelestinus. The battle would not take place in the north, given that Severianus's army was now encamped in Aureliana's kingdom. The old lands of the Iceni in the east were of no use to anybody, so it had to be somewhere between Viroconium and Londinium. The Vortigern was staying put for the time being, drawing the opposition towards the capital. All the reports that the *Pontifex Maximus* had received suggested that Germanus was taking the straight route down the main road from Viroconium. Coelestinus wondered how Agricola would respond to that.

'If I were Agricola, I would split my forces in two and have one group guarding London and the second based in Verulamium. Germanus then attacks the capital and Agricola's secondary force sweeps in from behind once the Archbishop of Britannia has been well and truly drawn in.'

Coelestinus put his head in his hands and groaned. Then he laughed to himself, then out loud. 'Germanus will never fall for that. Not in a million years! All my options will still be open to me!' He poured himself some wine and sat down, happier than he had been for days if not weeks. The *Pontifex Maximus* called for his deacon.

CHAPTER 38

Hengest ponders; Germanus dreams

'I remain unconvinced. Germanus is too clever to fall for this old trick. Does the Vortigern not have anything better up his sleeve? I would have thought that Agricola would have had better advice for his commander-in-chief. And wasn't Pelagius once a senior army officer?' Hengest looked over at his son. Oeric snored, belched, and farted. 'That boy never could take his ale.' The leader of the *Saxoni* refilled his glass and downed the contents in one gulp. Having wiped his mouth with his sleeve, he proceeded to look again at the battle plan that he had been given at the Vortigern's high council meeting. It was difficult for him to stand since he had been wounded at the battle of Viroconium, but he had little option if he was going to study the map properly.

Instead of looking at how the forthcoming contest might play out, Hengest thought back to an earlier skirmish, when he and his men had attacked Germanus's villa, as ordered by that scumbag-cum-turncoat Severianus. It was not meant to happen like it did. Germanus, Patricius and Eustachia were to be captured and held hostage; nothing more, nothing less. The general would be neutralised and Hengest could increase the price for his services: the Vortigern, Severianus, Aureliana, even the *Pontifex Maximus,* had all been interested. Better if Hengest could have offered Germanus as the commander-in-chief: what a combination that would have been! Instead, the two of them were on opposite sides, and Hengest already knew whose army he would rather be in. But the Vortigern was paying handsomely for *foederati*, even without Germanus at the head, and there was more to come if the recent conversation with Agricola had any truth in it.

The Germanus they had found at the Armorican villa turned out not to be the real thing, and there was no Patricius either. All his men got for their trouble was serious resistance from farm workers. The plan to call the Armorican Guard away had worked, but Germanus's estate had been stoutly defended nonetheless and Hengest had lost good men in the battle.

'An eye for an eye! That's what they say, isn't it?'

Oeric had no answer.

Eustachia had to die. Hengest has lost a son in that battle thanks to that woman. She had fought like a man and killed like a man; killed his best son and left him with Oeric. The wife was no use if the husband were not there to beg and bargain for her life. Yet the woman's death had troubled him. The look on her face as he pushed the sword into her abdomen was one that he had never seen before; not in all the time that he had raped and maimed and murdered had he looked into someone's eyes and seen her *sawol*. For a second, he saw the paradise that she was going to. She said that she forgave him and blessed him in the name of her Jesus Christ. It had stopped Hengest from pushing the sword all the way into her innards and made him carry her to the chapel where she said she wished to be taken. He had lain her on the altar where she could pray for her Lord to take her. And that look had haunted Hengest ever since. What would he see when he stared into Germanus's eyes as he thrust the same sword into his enemy's abdomen? Would he even dare to do it?

❀   ❀   ❀

It was the largest force that he had ever commanded. Everyone had been baptised and every shield, every weapon, every piece of armour had been painted with the *chi-ro* symbol. Aureliana, Ambrosius and Drustans looked aghast and disgusted; Lupus did not react; Severianus greatly approved. He told Germanus over the dinner that they shared in Lactodurum how useful he had found Christianity; how it had enabled him to unify all the disparate groups in the north. It was almost like the old days of the empire at its best, when there was a loyalty to Roma that transcended local and tribal loyalties. Now, it was this new religion that bound people together in a way that the Bishop of Eboracum had found surprising and even heart-warming. 'I even sort of believe it, you know, Germanus. The idea that we are forgiven; that there is an afterlife, though I am still of the old order in my heart.'

The General had just smiled, more concerned with his memory of a previous visit to this place when he was a young man and he had been with Sevira. The rebel forces under her father, Magnus Maximus, had used the old garrison town as their headquarters at one point. That was where he had met her. He had infiltrated the rebel forces, fed information back to the true emperor's agents and helped to make sure that Magnus would eventually be defeated. He had fallen in love with Sevira in the process and, for a time, had seriously contemplated going over to the other side. That was a different world, and he was a different man. After he had let her escape, he had never seen or heard from her again. She was probably dead; killed as she tried to get back to Hispania via Armorica. That was where she said she was going to go; but it might have been a ruse designed to put him and his fellow officers off the scent. After all, she had found out that he was a double agent when her father had been arrested and Germanus had testified at his trial.

This was no time for reminiscence. Here he was, leading this great force brought together to defeat the Vortigern. Not only that, but success would bring even greater glory: everything that he had ever dreamt of since that time with Sevira and her father; when Magnus Maximus had shown him the glory that could once again be the Roman

Empire. Germanus had regretted betraying the usurper; perhaps the west would not be in the mess it was in now if Sevira's father had been left to succeed. There was still time, though; time to make the Empire great again. Germanus nodded to his commanders to put the plan into action.

CHAPTER 39

The troops advance; the strategy is formed; Lupus takes sides

Much to his surprise, Severianus was enjoying himself. He had never liked the Vortigern, and only really tolerated the man because, for all his faults, he was Agricola's commanding officer, and Agricola was still both his son and the right sort of Christian, in as far as the one true faith had anything to do with it. The Bishop of Eboracum grimaced to himself as he thought of the Vortigern as 'commander-in-chief'. How had a bureaucrat like that got to the top? Yes, he could hold a *gladius* and a *scutum* when he had to, but it seemed to Severianus that the Vortigern was far more at home holding a *stilus* in his hand. Come to think of it, had there been a single battle where the Vortigern had been on the front line? It was Hengest who had led the combined forces' attack on Viroconium: fair enough, given that the troops constituted a surprise expeditionary force, rather like the advance party that Germanus had sent out to Londinium; but who would be in charge when the West British, the Armorican Guard, the Roman Army, and the Bishop of Eboracum's own forces engaged with the Vortigern's men? Not the Vortigern, thought Severianus, as he turned to look at Germanus. There was hardly likely to be a hand-to-hand, to-the-death combat between Germanus and the Vortigern, was there?

Germanus was at the head of his combined forces. It was impressive, both in number and discipline. Even the equipment was looking good. Severianus had shared all (well, almost all) his intelligence with Germanus and his high command upon arrival (the Bishop of Eboracum had lamented how unfortunate it was that he had not seen active service at the battle) in Viroconium. There were one or two things that Severianus decided not to impart to Germanus, at least for now, just in case events took a different turn...

Severianus kicked his horse into life and caught up with Germanus and the others at the head of the *processio*. Old Augustus, the self-styled cavalry officer, tried to run after him, without much success. Aureliana, Ambrosius and Lupus were riding alongside Germanus. There was just enough room on the road for a fifth horse and its rider.

'No Drustans, Germanus?'

'No, Severianus. I have sent him on ahead with a small advance party to see how the land lies. There may be more who could be persuaded to join our forces rather than fight us. We have done well so far in that respect.'

'And you approve of such a move Aureliana?' Severianus turned to the Queen of the West Britons.

'Indeed, I do. But then Germanus is *magister militum*. I defer to him in such matters as this.' The Queen of the West Britons stared straight ahead as she spoke. Severianus decided not to pursue the conversation. It was obvious that she did not wish to talk to him. He could see that Ambrosius was cursing under his breath, but the Bishop of Eboracum also realised that the Queen's husband-brother had a grudging respect for Germanus. Lupus only had eyes for Germanus and Aureliana.

'We reach Magiovinium tonight, Severianus. Calleva Atrebatum is ours; a messenger arrived this morning saying that the city fathers have acceded to my request to join and that means our southern flank is better protected.'

'Are you sure Germanus? Can they be trusted? I always thought that the Atrebates were loyal to the Vortigern.'

'Indeed, they were, but they have seen the light and are now fighting for us. I trust them as much as I trust anybody, just as I trust you, Severianus.' Germanus smiled. Severianus remained silent. Why had he heard nothing of any treaty with these people? It meant that the Vortigern was encircled if Calleva had gone over to Germanus and Aureliana. There could only be a retreat to the coast and the continent if he were defeated in Londinium. And he could not easily enter Gallia, given that Germanus held sway, at least in the north, so he would be forced to take refuge with the *Saxoni* and continue the fight from there, assuming he had survived and had any fight left. Hengest would certainly not be one to continue backing a loser in all of this. He might even side with Germanus if he thought it was in his best interests to do so, and the price was right!

'The Vortigern believes that we will aim straight for the capital. And that is what I want him to think.' Germanus pointed ahead. Severianus gasped slightly. Germanus had read his mind. Aureliana smirked, amused at the Bishop of Eboracum's disquiet. 'Except that he will then think that we are bluffing; we can't possibly be so stupid as to march into a trap, with his men in Verulamium and Londinium ready to close in behind us once we have been drawn into the city.'

'So, what do you expect to do then Germanus? Is this bluff, double-bluff, triple-bluff, or no bluff at all?'

Wait and see, my Lord Severianus; wait and see!'

＊　　※　　※

So, she was to bear a child. Inside the woman riding next to him was the beginnings of a life, formed from his seed and her womb. He was not old enough to be a father, he said to himself; or was he? If he could kill and command; if he could survive hunger, and deprivation; if he could prevail over fear and anguish and win; then he could do this. And what better person to be the mother of his offspring than Aureliana, a Queen and a warrior? She had led him on to the point where he wanted nothing more and nothing else than to be inside her. Again and again, he had thought of her and her alone: awake, asleep, in battle, at rest; at no point was she anywhere but inside his head. He ached inside whenever he saw her; even now, when he had been in her bed on numerous occasions; he just wanted more.

Deep down, he knew that she did not want him, at least not in the same way as he did. She wanted Germanus. And he had come to realise that Germanus wanted her too. But Lupus would be the father of her child; she had chosen him not because he was the adopted son of the governor of Armorica; not because he was from Dalmatia; but because he was a Druid. His parents were not his parents at all; Lupus had been delivered to them for safe keeping until it was time for him to return to Britannia to take his place alongside the rest of his kind. The letter from the man he thought had been his father now made perfect sense. It had been written for him to read and understand in a way that Lupus would not have comprehended until Aureliana had explained it all. Lupus also realised now that Germanus was making sure that he was being prepared, and well, for command and leadership. Did Germanus also know what was supposed to happen in Britannia, now that Aureliana was pregnant?

CHAPTER 40

Drustans is fearful

'I am sure he is on to me. He must know I am the guilty party.'

'Nonsense Drustans, I am quite sure that you are safe. Nobody would ever suspect that a man tortured in the way that you were whipped and branded would really be an agent for the Vortigern. That would be taking things too far; it would be unheard of, in fact. The perfect cover, especially when Germanus, Lupus and Aureliana were witnesses to your extreme distress.'

'Don't be so sure, Agricola. Germanus was the one who treated me after my rescue. He must have realised that my wounds were not as great as they should have been. If I had really been tortured like that in the citadel then I would have been in a far worse condition than I was when they got me back to the safe house.'

Agricola raised his eyebrow. 'So Aureliana still has a safe house in Londinium, does she?'

'Well...'

'Never mind. I knew that anyway Drustans. Do you think we are stupid?' We have been keeping an eye on that place since the peace was signed with the West Britons and Aureliana became a *foederata*. It was in our interests to let it be. More importantly, why did he say nothing when he inspected your wounds and treated them?'

'I do not know. He was silent for a long time; then he just nodded and smiled when he had finished.'

Agricola laughed. 'Well, it's obvious now you say that Drustans, isn't it? The "Holy Spirit" had come down on him and, as God's servant here on earth, he was able to make you whole again.'

'Its not funny, Agricola. Just because your bloody father is a bishop! Germanus knows! I know he knows! After the battle of Viroconium was over, I could have sworn that he had worked out that I was the traitor. He ordered the senior officers to assemble in Aureliana's council chamber. Germanus then walked all the way round the table as we stood at our places, looking deep into our eyes, one by one. Nobody was spared, not Lupus, not Ambrosius, not Aureliana. I was the last one to receive the treatment. He looked at me for a long time before he moved on. I feel sure that he suspects; that he knows I am the one who told you and the Vortigern about the advance party and that Germanus's troops were still preparing for battle and were not fully ready.'

'Then why did he not name you, then and there, Drustans?'

'I do not know, Agricola. Perhaps he is waiting for me to make a false move so that he has clear evidence of my guilt.'

'Nonsense, Drustans. He did not name you because there is no evidence that you are a traitor. You have been a loyal servant to the West Britons since before Aurelianus was killed; you are from Dumnonia and what do people say about men from there?'

'Loyal to Dumnonia above all.'

'Exactly, Drustans. And the last tribe who would end up in league with the Vortigern.'

'We are not "in league", as you put it, with the Vortigern. I simply see your leader as the best chance of independence from the Cornovii. We have been their vassals for too long.'

'Indeed, Drustans. So now, you must deliver Germanus to us a different way.'

'There is no way I can deliver Germanus, to you, or anybody else for that matter.'

'Oh yes there is. Now listen to me.'

CHAPTER 41

The battle ebbs and flows; dream turns into nightmare

The battle for Britannia began slowly and quietly. Germanus commanded that small groups of *bucellarii* (in the pay of the few rich landowners still left in the west of Britannia) position themselves in the small townships surrounding Verulamium and Londinium. This was easier said than done. Not only were these places loyal to the Vortigern, but they also put up fierce resistance. People eventually retreated from these outposts and headed towards one or other of the two cities, depending upon which was the easiest to reach. Given that Germanus had stationed soldiers along the roads into Londinium, most headed for Verulamium.

Coordinated by Constantius (who had also been feeding Germanus vital information about the Vortigern's battle plans), Aureliana's agents in Londinium caused disturbances. They lit fires, damaged equipment, captured and murdered as many soldiers as they could find without, as far as possible, being detected. Some had infiltrated the Vortigern's forces spreading misinformation about troop movements and countermanding Agricola's orders, sowing doubt, and dissension, in the ranks.

As the main West British forces grew closer to the Vortigern's strongholds, the southern flank was attacked from the rear by a large band of *Saxoni* stationed in Pontes, to the southeast of Londinium.

Lupus led the counterattack with a group of *limitanei,* including *milites, numeri, pedes* and *auxilia,* supported by a small number of *equites* who rallied the troops and cut pathways through the enemy's attempts at *testudines.* The Vortigern's men were eventually driven back to their base camp, but not before they had inflicted sufficient casualties to pause the advance on Londinium from the west.

To the north, Ambrosius encountered fierce resistance around Sulloniacis. The Vortigern had ordered that this vital staging post on the road between Londinium and Verulamium should be defended at all costs. Only when Germanus ordered reinforcements to support the attack did the Vortigern's forces fall back. Then more *Saxoni* came down from Verulamium, resulting in a standoff between the two sides. Sulloniacis became a no-man's land. The local population fled, some heading up to Verulamium under the protection of the Vortigern's *foederati*; others decided to take a chance and surrender to the West British army, where they were interrogated and assessed as to any security risks. Those who were able to prove their 'Christian faith' were immediately assimilated into the supply chain (in the case of the women) and sworn in as *pedes* or *auxilia,* depending on their demonstrable ability in combat and previous military experience. Those who could not demonstrate their credentials had to listen to Elafius preach the Word and convince them of the need to convert. Once they had agreed to do so, these people were baptised and sworn in.

Germanus ordered Ambrosius to hold the line against the Vortigern's forces while he and Aureliana took their troops south and then east of Londinium, capturing Noviomagus and effectively cutting off the chance of further *Saxoni* arriving from across the *Mare Britannicum,* landing in Dubris, marching up through Durovernum and reinforcing the Vortigern's army in the capital. Severianus led his forces around the north of Verulamium towards Caesaromagus, where he encountered a large if ill-disciplined force of *Saxoni,* intermixed with the remnants of the Roman forces formerly stationed at Camulodunum. The conflict went badly in the east, for though the opposition was unruly, it was well commanded according to traditional Roman ways (there were even some *equites* overseeing the foot soldiers and occasionally engaging in combat with the West British horsemen). These men were led by a few old professional soldiers experienced enough not only to remember the traditions of the imperial forces but also how best to deploy the appropriate battle tactics. Severianus was wrong-footed, underestimating the Vortigern's forces in every regard. The veterans were able to use the sheer numbers of their *Saxoni* to force the enemy into retreat. Hearing of the setback, Germanus ordered Severianus to fall back towards Londinium. The Bishop of Eboracum was reluctant to obey this command but did as he was told once he realised (and much appreciated, despite the continuing underlying enmity between the two men) how Germanus intended to turn possible defeat into definite victory.

With Severianus's forces on the run, the *Saxoni* broke ranks, despite their commanders' entreaties, and followed, expecting to ram home their victory. The trap worked. Germanus moved his army up to meet Severianus's; the combined forces then lay in wait for the opposition on either side of a narrow, steep, valley. When the pursuing soldiers appeared, the West British forces attacked from all directions. As they charged, and as directed by Germanus, they shouted what was rapidly becoming the familiar battle cry of 'Alleluia', just as they had done at the battle of Viroconium. It was no contest. Taken by surprise, the Vortigern's *foederati*, despite their numbers and the reasonable quality of their leadership, could not regroup in time to defend themselves. Panic ensued and many were slaughtered; some fled back to Camulodunum or as far north-east as Venta Icenorum where they could escape to the continent if they so wished; others retreated and regrouped as they headed to Londinium to join the Vortigern's main army. The remainder (mainly British men) stood their ground and fought. Eventually, they surrendered. Severianus and Aureliana wanted to show no mercy, but

Germanus ordered that the remains of this East British army be offered the opportunity to swap sides. The general spoke passionately about the need for unity; about how the only way to save Britannia was to accept a new overlord and fight for a new empire in the west, under the Christian banner that had served the Emperor Constantine so well; a banner that would in future be the symbol of a new Roma and a new beginning. Seeing that they had little alternative and, in some cases at least, welcoming liberation from the Vortigern's tyranny (as Aureliana described it) all but a very few (who were then put to death) acceded. Having accepted the Archbishop of Britannia's demand, the new converts were baptised into the faith by Elafius.

※   ※   ※

Coelestinus dozed. He was back in Augusta Trevirorum, in the good old days before the troubles started. There were his wife, his slave girl, his riches, and his status. He was one of the leading citizens in the province. Coelestinus had it all. *Non semper erit aestas.* 'Be prepared for hard times', a voice had told him. Then came doubt, dissension, disease. The old ways were no longer the good ways. The state had turned away from its founding principles; Christianity was throwing out past beliefs and replacing them with a new morality. These changes were not to everyone's liking. Coelestinus would have to decide where his future lay.

The gods made the decision for him. Both the women in his life were soon dead and all he had to remember them by was the baby boy that his slave girl had borne him. Worse than that was the fact that his livelihood was threatened by the increasingly bold and vicious attacks from Germania. Trade was slumping; people were leaving; law and order were breaking down. In the battle that then went on inside Coelestinus, Christianity eventually won. The rich merchant had never done anything by halves. If he was to be a follower of Christ, then he was going to be His number one disciple; to make something of this religion; and make even more of himself in the process.

The *servus* standing guard noticed how the Pontifex was smiling as he slept. He wondered what the old man was dreaming. Sometimes he cried out a woman's name in between his groans and his snores. He thought how even a cantankerous *senex* like Coelestinus must have been a young man once; must have loved and lost; must have laughed and cried. The Pontifex became more agitated as he dreamt. The smiles gave way to cries of anguish. The Vortigern appeared, laughing and jeering, calling him a weak old man who could do nothing to stop the great overlord of Britannia. Behind the Vortigern stood Germanus, robed as *Imperator* and *Pontifex* at the same time, holding the imperial eagle aloft. Germanus and the Vortigern embraced, turned their backs on Coelestinus and walked towards a large *arca*. They opened its lid and tipped the contents out before Coelestinus's eyes. But instead of gold and silver and jewels, there came nothing but snakes that crawled towards the Pontifex, entwining, and devouring him, sucking away all his life blood. Coelestinus cried so loudly that he woke himself up, startling the *servus* in the process.

'My God! I know what is going to happen in Britannia! It will be the worst of all worlds, and I must stop it before it is too late for me!'

CHAPTER 42

Two enemies assess their positions;
Germanus receives an invitation

'He is willing to negotiate.' Drustans looked at the other members of the high command.

'Is he now?' Germanus rubbed his chin.

'Yes. Or at least that is what Agricola says', came the reply

'And does Agricola speak for the Vortigern?' Ambrosius challenged Drustans

'As far as I am aware.'

'You do not sound certain.' Germanus took over the interrogation. The Dumnonian shrugged in response.

'You will have to do better than that Drustans. What does "willing to negotiate" mean?' Aureliana snorted. 'And over what? Do you mean negotiate a surrender?'

'I do not know Aureliana. Agricola merely said that the Vortigern was willing to negotiate.' Drustans looked at his comrades as they responded to his news. Aureliana paced up and down the room; Ambrosius remained immobile; Severianus spat out of the open window and grunted.

'We have been brought here under false pretences.' Lupus threw his *gladius* down on the table and shook his head. The Queen of the

West Britons looked at the father of her child and smiled; the man who had just spoken was so different from the shy, stuttering boy she had seduced, and kept on seducing. She smoothed the cloth down over her swelling belly and pondered what Lupus had just said. Aureliana had to agree with him; Drustans had hardly any new information to give up after his expeditionary force had returned from its tour round the outskirts of Londinium. She was surprised that Agricola had offered so little to attract Germanus to the negotiating table. Earlier in the year, the Vortigern's *magister militum* was offering her much more, even as Germanus was taking control of her armies in Viroconium. She had let Agricola into her bed in order to find out what he intended. He told her much and proposed an alliance once he deposed his master. He let her set up and maintain the safe houses in Londinium. He even fed her information through his network of agents in the west; Barita had been the final link in the chain, delivering the messages to Aureliana early in the morning, before the rest of her court was awake, returning late in the evening to see if there was any reply that needed sending on its way to Londinium. Then the messages had stopped. No reason had been given, despite Aureliana's attempts to contact Agricola through the safe houses in the capital. She reflected on the point at which the change happened. Then it came to her: it had been the point where Drustans was captured by the Vortigern's forces, taken back to the citadel, and tortured, before being freed by Germanus and the others.

The commanders of the West British forces had gathered on the makeshift border with the Vortigern's armies outside Sulloniacis. The no man's land between the opposing forces was so narrow that, as Ambrosius had put it, you could almost smell the *Saxoni* across the other side of the valley that framed the main road from Londinium to Verulamium. The West British high command had assembled there in order to learn what Drustans had discovered. The information about troop deployments and numbers within and around the capital had been useful enough, but it was the approach from Agricola that had made them keen to meet up and learn what the Vortigern had to offer. Germanus had remained silent all the while Drustans had been relaying the news of his encounter with Agricola's agents. The archbishop-General did nothing but stare out of the window towards the enemy encampment. After the others had finished their interrogation of the Dumnonian, Germanus called for wine and bread before any further discussion. Ambrosius remained in a sullen mood, despite having his thirst and his hunger quenched; he had cautioned against the summit meeting with Drustans, even though the two men had been staunch allies on previous campaigns against the Vortigern. Lupus was weary and longed for a bed, with or without Aureliana in it, while the Queen of the West Britons longed for her son to have grown inside her to the point where she could give him life and fulfil her destiny.

Germanus had gone ahead with the summit meeting regardless, and now, because of his decision, the contingents of the West British forces were all without their commanders; what if they were attacked while they were leaderless? Even worse, if the Vortigern's forces moved on their position in Sulloniacis before they had dispersed, the whole of the West British high command could be captured and killed in one fell swoop. But here they were, wondering if the Vortigern's offer to negotiate was worth taking seriously. Germanus drank deeply from his *poculum*, looked around the room at each of his commanders and then let his eyes rest on Drustans. 'What are his terms?'

'I told you, my lord, he has not said. Agricola merely instructed me to say that the Vortigern is willing to negotiate. You are to come alone to a spot just outside Londinium. And as an incentive to attend, Agricola's agents told me to give you this. The message from the Vortigern himself was that you would understand the significance of what I am to give you.' With that, Drustans handed over a pouch. Germanus opened it slowly. Inside was an ornate gold amulet pendant to which was affixed a long chain. The pendant swung gently; the links glinted in the evening firelight. Germanus looked closer at the inscription in the pendant's centre. Lupus could see that it was in Greek but could not make out the words, apart from one: Bacchus. Germanus grew pale as he mouthed the motto to himself. He clasped the pendant and, much to everyone's surprise, put it round his neck. Standing up, he addressed the assembled officers.

'Say that I will go. Tell him that I will meet the Vortigern. When and where? I need to know, and soon!'

※   ※   ※

The Vortigern had expected Hengest to be reporting victory, or at least major advances. Instead, as he looked at his *magister militum* and his Saxon *foederatus*, he sensed defeat. It was not a feeling that he enjoyed. He looked at the members of his high council, trying to determine whether they too were wondering if the game might be up. Hengest went first, reeling off the gains and losses. The outtownships situated on the main roads into Londinium and Verulamium had slowed down the West British advance considerably, and many casualities had been inflicted. The initiative had given the Vortigern's armies time to regroup and to glean information on which to base future defence and further attack. The regiments based in Pontes had been successful in their quest to disrupt the West Britons, and Hengest estimated that honours were reasonably even at the end of that round of fighting, though heavy rain had hampered the push to force the opposition into retreat.

The Vortigern then briefed Agricola and Hengest on what had been happening in Londinium and to a lesser extent in Verulamium as a result of the enemy within. There had to be a traitor high up within the ranks for the sabotage to be so well targeted and effected. The resistance movement had known just where to strike to best effect. But they would not survive long. The high council members shuddered as the Vortigern told the assembly in great detail what would happen when those who had betrayed him were discovered and captured. Agricola followed up with his report on the war to date. Sulloniacis itself had fallen, but the route from the capital to Verulamium was still perfectly passable because the road was defended. The *magister militum* then paused his report. Slowly, he turned and pointed to Hengest. 'As to what happened in the east, I leave my Lord Hengest to describe the shit show that happened at the battle of Noviomagus.'

CHAPTER 43

Memor pleads in vain; Germanus and Agricola meet

'Don't do it.'

'I have to.'

'No, you don't. You're just pursuing a silly dream; no, not even a dream; a memory of something that never was.'

'That's not true! It happened!'

'I thought Eustachia was the only woman for you?'

'She was, but...'

'But nothing. You were her *univira, remember?*'

'I know.'

'But she wasn't your only one, was she?'

'She was while she was alive!'

'But since she died you have moved on to others!'

'No, I have not!'

'What about the Queen of the West Britons, then?'

'That was, that is different.'

Memor laughed. 'What was different about it? It was still sex! Good in bed, was she? A younger woman? Knew what she was doing, did she? You're the Archbishop of Britannia now, in addition to everything else, General Germanus, sir!'

'O shut up Memor!' But the voice inside Germanus's head would not stop talking. The *haruspex* was as present before him as if the general were back in Armorica visiting the old man's cave. He tried to get that long white beard and the vacant, staring eyes out of his mind, but the images would not go. Ever since Germanus had left the main camp on his journey to meet Agricola for the peace talks with the Vortigern, Memor had been there, trying to persuade him not to go. How could he fall for what was obviously a trap? There was no way the opposition would want to negotiate a truce so early in the conflict. It was true that the West British forces had made gains, with standoffs at two major points along the battle fronts, but the Vortigern still had the larger army and had yet to go on full attack. There was no way in which the opposing forces were anywhere near ready to surrender. This was about drawing Germanus away from his command and into an ambush. And what better way to make the General throw caution to the wind than to tempt him with a remembrance of a long-lost love? That pendant had been hers. Germanus thought of the last time they had been together. They had kissed and then parted. As she buried her head in his chest, he had felt the pendant press against his stomach. She never took it off, not even when she was naked. Now he was wearing that chain round his neck; the amulet rubbed gently against the hair on his chest as he rode into Londinium. Could she still be alive? Was Memor right? Was this one of the Vortigern's tricks? Sevira's execution years had probably happened years ago. Germanus's attempt to let her go free after her father's capture would have been in vain.

'You will regret this, my Lord.'

'I know I will Memor. But I have to find out what happened. You know that as well as I do.'

At which point the image of Memor vanished.

※　　※　　※

Drustans greeted Germanus and his small cohort. Lupus was the only one of the high command who had come with him, at the General's request. Aureliana had protested but her *magister militum* had ordered her in no uncertain terms to stay behind. She did have a point, as Ambrosius tried to comment to Germanus. He was the supreme war leader; why take the risk of being captured by the enemy, when other envoys could go on his behalf? They would be expendable where the general was not. But he would have none of it; they were now to the east of Londinium, a good day's ride from Noviomagus. At least the battle lines were holding firm.

Drustans whispered something to Germanus, who nodded in reply. Members of the cohort quickly set up a makeshift camp which gave the party some rudimentary shelter. It was a cold evening; the wind blew across the wide estuary where they were now waiting for the opposition to arrive. The *Tamesis* was flowing rapidly after heavy rainfall; the ground was muddy. Germanus had selected the place for the meeting with Agricola and Lupus could see why. It was open; there was nowhere for attackers to hide and then spring out; there were plenty of ways of escaping if the discussions turned sour; even by boat if all else failed. Sailing upstream would be difficult because of the cross currents, as Drustans pointed out, but Germanus decided that in the event of an escape by water they would go downstream and aim for Regulbium. That was a final resort, however, and the general was confident that it would not be needed.

Lupus was not so sure. The words of the remaining members of the high command kept coming back to him. Though he trusted his master's judgement, he could not help but agree with Aureliana's comment that this was a foolhardy mission if ever there was one. Lupus had never trusted Drustans from that day five months ago when the Dumnonian had greeted Germanus's party after their voyage across from Armorica. What did Aureliana think of him? The Queen of the West Britons could be warm hearted to some and just as cold hearted to others. Drustans fell into the latter camp, he felt sure, especially now that she was going to be a mother and had no need of men.

Germanus was the first to hear the sound of horses' hooves on the road. To his surprise, the riders were approaching from the east and not, as he expected, from Londinium to the west. Was this a ploy to throw them off guard? Had the Vortigern's delegation come from the west then circled round the West British cohort so as to gain some idea of their numbers? Or, as Germanus surmised, had they come in fact from Durovernum Cantiacorum near the eastern seaboard, where Aureliana's spy network had reported that there was a contingent of *Saxoni* waiting in reserve. Lupus smiled at the thought that these troops would have a hard time getting through to Londinium given the way Germanus had deployed his troops around the capital and between the Vortigern's strongholds and the coast.

'We are unarmed.'

'And you are?'

'Gnaeus Severianus Agricola, *magister militum* to the Vortigern, high king of Britannia. You must be the great Germanus. I have heard so much about you. And seen you in battle. We thought we had you beaten at the battle of Viroconium, but no such thing! I hate to admit it, but you deserved to win there. Which is why we are here now; to negotiate a peace.'

'And I have heard much of you, Gnaeus Severianus Agricola, not least from your father.' Germanus walked up to his opposite number and saluted him in the Roman way.

Agricola grimaced as he saluted in return but decided not to comment on the Bishop of Eboracum and his decision to switch sides. Though the Vortigern would never admit it, that change of heart had hurt and done much damage to his credibility as well as the morale of his forces, even though they must still outnumber the combined West British armies two to one.

'Let's leave my father out of this, shall we? I am the Vortigern's representative here. I answer to nobody else.'

Germanus smiled, and then reached down inside his tunic to pull out the pendant that he now wore around his neck. 'What is the meaning of this?'

Agricola smiled back. 'I believe you already know the answer to that question, Germanus. Which is the real reason why you are here, is it not? Whatever else we must discuss, you need to know what happened to the original owner of that jewellery.'

Drustans intervened and suggested that the two groups go inside the hastily erected tent before the weather worsened. A light meal had been prepared and would set them up ready for the discussions that were to ensue. Everyone willingly agreed, just in time to evade the storm that blew in from the estuary mouth. On a rise to the west of the encampment, Aureliana, Ambrosius and their cohort watched and waited, ready to attack and reveal Drustans as the traitor that they now knew him to be. Meanwhile, to the east, the owner of the pendant watched and waited also.

CHAPTER 44

Memor, Coelestinus, Germanus, and Drustans become unlikely partners

Memo tossed and turned. He had always been such a good sleeper but had not rested for more than a few hours at a time since the butchery at Germanus's villa. Deep down, he knew that he could have stopped it; could have warned of the impending attack; could have told Segovax, his own son, what was going to happen. He chose not to: rather, he let the raping and burning and looting and killing proceed because all that horror *had* to take place; and it had to occur for one simple reason, and one reason alone: the redemption of Germanus.

Memor rose from his bed and went to pee. Upon his return, he decided there was no point in going back to bed; better to get up and do something rather than worrying about his charge. He laughed out loud as he realised how he was thinking about Germanus. 'He is still a young man to me!' The laughter turned to tears as he felt the pain of loss; not of his own son, but of Germanus. The new Archbishop of Britannia did not realise it yet, at least not in his waking hours, but he was turning to the new faith. Memor sensed it and recoiled from the sinking feeling, the growing knowledge, that once Germanus followed the one they called Christ, then there would no longer be any need for a *haruspex*. At which point, Memor could take his leave of this world and return to whence he had come. He sighed and tears formed in his eyes at the thought of being reunited with Segovax in the afterlife. Just as Memor's influence over Germanus might be waning, so someone else's aura had been ever more present: an old man, high born, of great wealth and power, often came into the mind of the *haruspex*. At first, it was not clear what this person wanted, but over time, Memor had begun to understand that the one called Coelestinus had also much to lose or much to gain depending on what happened to Germanus.

Memor now communicated regularly with this man. Did this correspondent know he was talking to a white haired, long bearded, sightless old *haruspex* in northern Gallia? Probably not: Coelestinus must surely be thinking he was talking to his God. There they were: two dying men, both anxious to leave their mark; each wanting to see Germanus prevail in Britannia and beyond to Roma itself.

Coelestinus was worried to death about what might now happen on the other side of the *Mare Britannicum*. Memor had sensed that the Pontifex knew more than he was letting on, even to his God, about the Vortigern's past. There was something about the over-king of the Britons that did not ring true. Germanus had said that he was nothing more that a jumped-up bureaucrat, reliant on others to fight his battles for him. Coelestinus, however, regarded the Vortigern as a serious military tactician, well capable of leading his troops in battle. Which was correct? Whatever the answer, the Pontifex was deeply afraid that if Germanus and the Vortigern met, they would sue for peace rather than pursue the war that was now paused. Memor feared for Germanus's safety in any such encounter and subsequent possible alliance. The two of them decided to work together to prevent this happening.

❈   ❈   ❈

Germanus looked at Lupus and Lupus looked at Drustans. Agricola had not offered anything like the terms that would be needed to consider a truce. Quite the opposite. What had been laid on the table were demands: to withdraw back to Viroconium; to release the cohorts of Aetius and send them back to the continent; to disband the Armorican guard; and to agree not to interfere in the Vortigern's plans for the future domination of the empire.

'You are not in a position to offer those terms, Agricola; not that they are terms!'

'That is the Vortigern's best, and only, offer, Germanus!'

'Then tell your master and commander that we remain at war. And that my armies are winning on all fronts. Surely as the Vortigern's *magister militum* you can see that?'

Lupus saw the doubt in Agricola's eyes. He sensed that Germanus and Drustans could see it as well. Germanus nodded to the *servus* to pour more wine. The assembled group was about to drink and ponder on what to do next to break the stalemate. Just as Agricola was going to say something, the guards outside the tent sounded the alarm. The skirmish was brief but bloody. Agricola's men defended stoutly and bravely, but they were no match for Aureliana's crack troops. Germanus ordered Aureliana to desist from the attack and told his own guard to protect Agricola at all costs, especially when Ambrosius was hell bent on killing the Vortigern's *magister militum* on the spot.

The Queen of the West Britons had a different target in mind, and, because Germanus was wholly taken up, ironic though it must have seemed, with protecting his opposite number, it was easy enough for her to run Drustans through. Once the *gladius* had entered his stomach, Aureliana made sure that there was no chance of recovery by gutting the Dumnonian's insides.

'Stop, stop at once!' Germanus barked his order and the Queen ceased immediately. But it was too late. Drustans was dead. 'What have you done?'

'I have done what you should have done a long time ago, Germanus!' Aureliana held up her bloodied sword in triumph.

Germanus looked at Agricola and told him to leave, promising him safe passage back to the outskirts of London. Once the Vortigern's *magister militum* had departed, he rounded on Aureliana.

'What was the meaning of this, you fool, you idiot, you stupid woman?'

'Drustans was a traitor, Germanus. He was in the service of the Vortigern. He betrayed us. His torture and branding was all a fiction, to make us believe that he was loyal to my cause. And all the time he was feeding information back to his master in Londinium.'

Germanus fell into a cold, silent rage. Then he spoke. 'I know, Aureliana, And I have known for some time. He was a double agent. Why do you think we have done so well in the campaign so far? I had already discovered his treachery. Drustans then had two choices: to be killed on the spot, or to work for me, not only sharing the Vortigern's plans and Agricola's troop movements but feeding his supposed master false information on our strategies and tactics. We have lost a great advantage, thanks to your rash actions!

CHAPTER 45

Nil desperandum: all but one live to fight another day

The owner of the gold amulet pendant regretted that the Vortigern's scheduled meeting with Germanus had not taken place. It would have been an interesting encounter, with the possibility of an alliance, if Agricola's plans had been given a proper airing. Would the Governor of Armorica, now the Archbishop of Britannia, have been interested in the terms that would eventually have been offered? Without a doubt!

The initial proposal had been of little interest. Germanus had rejected it out of hand, knowing that he was never expected to do anything else. That was only the start of what the Vortigern, through Agricola as his *magister militum* and chief negotiator, had intended to be a series of staged discussions, gradually tempting Germanus into an agreement, with the promise of the final session being conducted with the Vortigern in person. Surely the Governor of Armorica would have seen the benefit of an alliance? The cessation of hostilities would have been followed by Germanus's installation as co-Vortigern and the beginnings of a well-organised and well-resourced campaign to take the western empire, conquer the *barbari* beyond the *Rhenus* and then take Roma and oust the Pontifex.

That opportunity had passed; what might have been agreed

could only be irrelevant speculation. The arrival of Aureliana and the assassination of Drustans had made the continuance of the negotiations impossible. The Vortigern was never going to come anywhere near the encampment after the intervention of the Queen of the West Britons, even though Germanus had made sure Agricola and his personal guard came to no harm and, when negotiations had broken up, had personally arranged safe passage back to Londinium, much to the annoyance of the Viroconians.

The Queen of the West Britons was not so naïve as to think that Drustans was not acting in his own interests rather than hers. She feigned shock at Germanus's revelation that her Dumnonian colleague had turned on the Vortigern, but inside she was smiling at her *magister militum's* cunning. Aureliana was also aware that he was genuinely angry at her arrival and the way in which she had frightened Agricola off and scuppered any chance of a face-to-face meeting with the Vortigern, let alone the killing of his recently-acquired and very valuable double agent. But then she did not want the two of them to meet. There was too much at stake to let Germanus and the Vortigern do a deal. Where would she fit into their new world order? What price her dream of a Prythonic kingdom ruled over by her and her alone, with the Germanus duly sacrificed as a thank offering to the old and true gods? She would be sad at her *magister militum's* eventual death, but it had to be achieved if her ultimate goal was to be realised. Not that she was going to forego his companionship, or that of his adopted son, until the time came to deliver Germanus to the high priest for ritual slaughter.

In the meantime, Aureliana could hardly contain her delight at the thought that all chances of a deal with the Vortigern were now over. Germanus now knew not only that she was aware of the possibility of a grand alliance was pure fantasy, but also that she had deliberately planned it that way. The two of them had shared the most intimate moments possible in his bed, or occasionally hers, and they could often tell what the other was thinking without any hint being given or taken;

this was one of those occasions. As Germanus had long recognised and accepted, they had always been like that, right from the first encounter when she helped Lupus to sober him up after Eustachia's funeral.

Nevertheless, that was no reason for her to behave in the way she had done that night. Germanus had persuaded himself to think that negotiations with Agricola and an opportunity to meet face-to-face with the Vortigern were worth the risk of capture, especially given the tight security arrangements that had been put in place. He had seen it as a case of *est modus in rebus,* a way of choosing the middle ground (if there was middle ground to be had), instead of the all-out warfare that Aureliana had favoured. In any event, he was not going to pass up the opportunity to find out where the gold amulet pendant had come from, and whether or not its original owner was still alive.

Conversely, Aureliana had seized on the knowledge of Drustans's treachery to 'save' Germanus from betrayal at the hands of both Agricola and her erstwhile Dumnonian military leader. Not unreasonably, Germanus's security detachment had let the Queen of the West Britons and her entourage into the encampment where the negotiations were taking place without question. Why would they do otherwise, even though she appeared unannounced? It had pained her to kill Drustans, despite everything, though Aureliana could not help thinking that this left Dumnonia open to full integration into West Britain once her other military aims had been achieved. Whatever the merits of the various arguments for and against the abandoned talks might have been, the deed was done: Aureliana was still waging war on the Vortigern and vice versa, and Germanus and Agricola remained on opposite sides.

Back in Londinium behind the safety of the citadel's thick walls, the Vortigern and his *magister militum* reflected on the fact that they had not lost much of an asset as a result of the Dumnonian's departure to the next world. Though originally a valuable agent and a likely client-king in the southwest after the war with Aureliana had been won, Drustans had outlived his usefulness. Germanus had been very clever in the way that he had manipulated the Vortigern's agent into supplying vital information back to the West Britons, but it had gradually dawned on the Vortigern's high command that Germanus was acting on inside information; and Drustans had been supplying it.

Agricola and Germanus each (in their own different ways) believed that their forces were evenly matched in terms of military and tactical intelligence, though Agricola and his master (not that they would ever admit it) felt that Germanus still had the upper hand because of his military genius and, much to everyone's surprise, the way in which he was harnessing Christianity through his archbishopric to forge an almost fanatical commitment to his cause. Germanus would have agreed with this assessment if he had known of it. Severianus, waiting to be involved in the next round of discussions with Aureliana, Ambrosius and the Archbishop of Britannia (as he now preferred to call Germanus, albeit with a smirk on his face) thought otherwise, not least because of the information that he was regularly being fed by his own agents in both camps. In the meantime, the owner of the gold amulet pendant wondered when there would be another opportunity to meet Germanus. They had waited all these years; another few days or weeks would do no harm.

CHAPTER 46

Coelestinus has an unwelcome guest; a visitor to Britannia arrives

'The *Imperatrix* wishes to see you, your Grace.'

'O God! Do I have to?'

'She is insistent, my lord. In fact, she is in your antechamber at this very moment. Her son, the *Imperator*, is with her.'

Coelestinus sat up in bed.

'My God, it must be important if she has brought the little brat with her!'

The *Pontifex Maximus* levered his worn body out of the *lectus* and snapped at his servants to wash and dress him post-haste. He ordered Ferox not to pluck his face hairs out; that would take too long, and he did not want to keep the *mulier* waiting.

'What is his name again?'

'Who, your grace?'

'You know, him, the pimply youth, our beloved *Imperator*.'

'He is called Placidus Valentinianus, your grace.'

'Ah right, yes, of course, how could I forget?' Coelestinus snatched his stick from Ferox and hobbled his way down to the atrium, where Gallia Placidia and her son were waiting.

The *Pontifex Maximus* held out his hand. She shook her head.

After a short standoff, Coelestinus gave in, bowed his head and kissed Galla Placidia's ring. The two of them were ushered to thrones that had been hastily brought in from the *basilica*. The effective head of the western empire and its spiritual leader faced each other. Placidus Valentinianus climbed on to his mother's lap and pawed at her *mammae*. The *Imperatrix* pushed her son's hands away and whispered to him.

'To what do I owe this honour, your majesty?' Coelestinus looked and smiled.

'Your grace. It is always a pleasure to see you.'

Coelestinus said nothing. The two of them looked at each other, then around the walls and up at the ceiling. Coelestinus tried to look at his Empress without making it obvious that he was inspecting her outfit, and what was inside it. *She is wearing well; I will grant her that. Any man would be captivated by those eyes, that mouth, those lips, that hair, as I once was, among many others…*

'How can I assist you, your majesty?'

'Tell me what you know of the war in Britannia.'

'War? In Britannia? Is there a war?'

'You know perfectly well there is a war, Coelestinus.'

'I have heard … heard some rumours.'

'Rumours? And what about the rumour that you made Germanus an *archiepiscopus,* sent him on a mission to Britannia to overthrow the Vortigern and establish *your* rule?'

The *Imperatrix* found the *Pontifex's* cackle irksome in the extreme and grimaced appropriately. Coelestinus cleared his throat.

'I may have had some dealings with Germanus. But I did not wish to trouble your majesty with such a minor matter. What is Britannia but a worthless renegade province; what are the teachings of Pelagius but a trifling theological issue?' The *Pontifex Maximus* waved his arms in the air as if to demonstrate the meaningless immateriality of a minor Pelagian land far from the eternal city.

'Trifling issue? I believed Pelagius until you persuaded me otherwise!'

The *imperatrix* raised one of her immaculately manicured eyebrows as she twiddled with her pearl necklace. She adjusted herself on her throne, making sure that the sleeping *imperator* was not disturbed from his nap.

'He is a dangerous man, that Pelagius. No wonder he was banished from Roma. We must maintain the one true faith above everything'

'And what about the one true Vortigern? How is your strategy working there, your grace?'

Coelestinus cleared his throat as a way of re-starting the conversation with Galla Placidia.

'So, you know about my campaign, then?'

The *imperatrix* nodded. Coelestinus wondered who her informant was. He would carry out a full investigation of his palace staff later.

'And Germanus's role?'

Galla Placidia nodded once more. Then added some words to her affirmation.

'Except that I am unclear as to what he really intends to achieve and where this Queen Aureliana fits in to his plans.'

Coelestinus sighed.

'I will be frank with you, your majesty. Neither am I. Germanus was meant to conquer Britannia, depose the Vortigern and rid me of that awful Pelagian heresy. Then, and only then, I would hand the province back to you, along with its populace and its wealth. As you well know, your majesty, it provides the most effective base from which to launch any and every campaign to re-capture the empire. I know that Aetius approves.'

'General Aetius no longer counts for anything in my court.'

'Your majesty?'

'I have sacked him.'

What? You stu-'Coelestinus suffered a terrible coughing fit, from which he only recovered after Ferox poured him a *calix* of red wine. 'You were saying, your grace: you have got rid of Aetius?'

The *Imperatrix* nodded. The *Imperator* moved his head between her breasts. The *Pontifex* raised both his eyebrows.

'He would take the purple himself given half a chance. And I could not take any chance. I can no longer tolerate his manouevrings; not one second more.'

'So where is he now?'

'Aetius? I heard that he was on his way to Britannia.'

The *Pontifex Maximus* had another coughing fit.

※   ※   ※

'More wine!'

Litorius ordered one of the foot soldiers to bring him and his commander-in-chief some drink. It was not easy for the boy to pour from the *amphora* at the far end of the boat and then navigate the rowers and reach the vessel's bow. But he did so, and the two senior military men were duly grateful.

'We will soon be in Britannia. Have you decided yet?'

Aetius turned to his second-in-command.

'That is a difficult question to answer Litorius; a very difficult question, to which there is no easy answer.'

'Have you been in touch with Germanus yet, sir?'

Aetius shook his head.

'But you have communicated with the Vortigern.'

Aetius nodded, then raised his index finger.

'Well, in truth, the Vortigern has been in touch with me.'

Now it was time for Litorius to raise his hand.

'You are a wanted man in more ways than one, Aetius.'

The general laughed.

'I never thought to be banned from Roma, and especially not by a woman!'

Litorius snorted.

'That woman has a lot to answer for. I just do not understand why she would get rid of her most successful *magister militum* at a time when the empire is fighting for its very existence. The stakes are too high to play political intrigue now!'

'Galla Placidia survives and thrives on game playing, Litorius, and you know it. My sacking will be all part of some complex strategy that she will have spent hours, days even, working on. All to further her position.'

'But she is already *Imperatrix*. What more could she want or need?'

'She is a woman, Litorius. Gallia Placidia is not content with being the power behind the throne; she wants to be on it! While the *Imperator* is just a lad, there is a danger that he will be got rid of and then she is nothing; if he survives to adulthood, then he will have no further use for her; she will end up in a temple sisterhood somewhere remote. No, she has to grab power soon, if she wants to keep it.'

'But why get rid of you?'

'I am a rival *Imperator*. Many of my cohorts are already pressing me to take the purple. And believe me, I have thought of it more than once.'

'So why go to Britannia, especially if you are not going to support Germanus and his cause?'

Aetius shrugged.

'Why do you think, Litorius? Why do you think?'

CHAPTER 47

Constantius says a last goodbye; Aetius waits for his host

Sulpicia smiled at her son as he drank from her breast. The boy was growing well, and she was now fully recovered from the trauma of the birth of Germanus Patricius. It seemed like only yesterday that Germanus the elder had delivered her baby, against all odds. She looked around the *tablinum* and thought back to when she was a little girl and the house had been full of laughter and chatter and comings-and-goings. Those were the days, she said to herself. *When we were a part of something bigger and my family had a position in society.* Sulpicia and her brothers and sisters had wanted for nothing: clothes, food, toys, education. Each of them had their own slave to fulfil their every need. When they were not at the town house in Londinium, they would be down at the coast, enjoying life at their villa near Venta Belgarum.

Even when Sulpicia met and married Constantius, things were good; not as they had been, but she and her husband still enjoyed a fine lifestyle, especially when Constantius was made *rationalis*, treasurer for the province, the richest in the whole of Britannia. Then came the fateful day. What was left of the imperial civil service left, taking as much of their wealth as they could with them. Some of the more optimistic buried their bulkier valuables in the hope that one day Britannia would rejoin the Roman Empire and they could return to claim their riches, their possessions, their homes, and their estates. The Vortigern had other ideas. It began slowly: a gradual, almost imperceptible erosion of freedoms and democratic government. The man had portrayed himself as a liberator, throwing off the Roman yoke. At first, he had consulted; set up a high council representing all the Britannic provinces, the key families, and the major tribes; promised reform and a return to the good old days.

After the initial attacks from the *Picti* and the *Scotti* and the raids and skirmishes perpetrated by the *Saxoni*, all that had changed. The Vortigern imposed martial law; seized land and other assets; made the tribes swear allegiance to him and him alone. It was all supposed to be in the interests of national security; liberties would be restored once the threat from the *barbari* was over. The return to riches had not happened and was not going to happen-ever. There had been neither opportunity nor motivation, at least on the new ruler's part, to restore civil liberties. Indeed, there were those who said that the Vortigern was deliberately keeping Britannia in a war state so that he could continue to justify his seizure of power and his appointment as *dictator*. One rumour went as far as implying that he was paying for the periodic invasions to justify his tyrannical rule. As a result, some British tribes, notably the Cornovii and the Dumnonii, had rebelled, but they had regretted their actions after a bloody civil war, and nothing had come of their attempts at secession from Londinium. Now, after years of the Vortigern's rule, there was no going back to the glory days.

Sulpicia stopped feeding Germanus Patricius, burped him, wiped his mouth, and put him down in his *stabulatio*. Her son fell asleep straight away. Once upon a time she would have had a *nutrix* to do all this for her, a high-born woman. Constantius and Sulpicia had to be grateful for small mercies. It could have been a good deal worse, given what they had heard of life in other parts of Britannia; and what they saw in Londinium itself: the oppression, the poverty, the hunger, the immigrants. Perhaps it was all a punishment from God for turning away from the one true way. Sulpicia heard the back door of their town house creak open, then slam shut; the noise was followed by the sound of rapid footsteps up the stairs. She grabbed the *gladius* that she always kept close by, but soon breathed a sigh of relief. It was Constantius, so out of breath that she could not understand him when he tried to speak. Sulpicia calmed him down, hoping that he would not disturb the baby with his noise.

'They are on to us! You must escape!'

'Who, what, where to?'

'The Vortigern. I will be denounced at the high council today. I was on my way to the citadel when I was warned off by one of Aureliana's agents. I turned back to let you know what is happening. It is only a matter of time before I am found. Hurry! Pack some things for you and the baby.'

'And what about you?'

'I will stay behind. They will not come after you if they are chasing me, that is for sure.'

'No! You must come with me! I cannot live without you! And what about your son? He needs his father!'

'I will come on later, I promise!'

'But you won't! I know you!'

'There is no time to argue – do as I say!'

'I want to stay here with you, Constantius!'

'Then we will all die. At least if you leave now then you, and our son, have a chance!'

Sulpicia gathered some clothes and other belongings that could easily be carried. Then she took the sleeping Germanus Patricius and wrapped him in a sling that fitted around her middle. Constantius escorted her to the back door of the townhouse and walked her to the end of the side street. There, they were met by one of Aureliana's men who led Sulpicia away to the only remaining safe house in Londinium, from where she and her son would be guided out of the capital and away to lands occupied by Germanus's armies. The *rationalis* watched his wife and child disappear into the dusk. It was the last time he would ever see them.

※ ※ ※

Aetius and his troops landed in Gariannonum. It was late and the fort was no longer occupied, but the lead boatman knew the area well from when he had been stationed on the east coast of Britannia. As a result, the *portitor* was able to navigate the fleet up to the landing stage at the head of the river. Though the defences were part ruinated, the soldiers' quarters were still habitable, and the men encamped with ease. Aetius, Litorius and their personal guard occupied the remains of the *praetorium*. It was dank and dusty, but easily defendable. There were signs that *Saxoni* had used the fort as a stronghold at some point in the recent past, but a thorough search of the quarters confirmed that the buildings were completely empty. Litorius surmised that Gariannonum was one of the places where Hengest's men had landed and been briefly stationed before marching to Londinium to join forces with the Vortigern's army.

The commandant's house could still be warmed using the original heating system, and the officers' private chef was able to cook a passable dinner. Once the meal was finished, Aetius insisted on calling a strategy meeting, much to his colleagues' annoyance, given the long days and nights they had endured on their journey from Augusta Trevirorum, where they had been stationed when the fall from power had been announced. Aetius waited until all were comfortably seated and their *poculi* had been refilled. Then he opened the meeting. The former *magister militum* thanked the assembled company for their presence, and their willingness to support him in his quest to regain control of the empire. He was saddened by recent events and felt that the time had come to take control of the situation before it worsened to the

281

point where there would no longer be anything to rule over. An offer had come from Britannia that gave Aetius, all of them, in fact, the ideal base on which to launch an attack on Roma, on the Dowager Empress, Galla Placidia.

'What of Germanus and his campaign?' one of the officers asked.

'That is still to be determined, depending how he chooses to react to our presence in Britannia. But first we need to meet with the one who invited us here. He is on his way as we speak.'

'And his name? the officer queried.

Aetius looked around his high command.

'His name? Severianus, Bishop of Eboracum.'

CHAPTER 48

Germanus and Coelestinus wonder if anyone can be trusted

The *Pontifex Maximus* was tired: of prayer, of the church, of his friends, of his enemies, of Galla Placidia, of the intrigue and the conflict and the not-knowing where you stood or who your friends and who your enemies were. Coelestinus threw down his writing tablet and eased himself out of his seat. The searing pain in his legs as he stood up made him gasp and groan.

'I cannot be for this life much longer: *nascentes morimur.*'

He used his sticks to get himself over to the *lectulo,* but instead of getting into it, he ended up kneeling, his face buried in the *stratum.* He was not expecting to pray, but his frail arms gave way, his sticks fell out of his pathetic grasp, and he stumbled forward. Now that he was in this prone position, Coelestinus resolved to prepare himself for the worst: *ad utrumque paratus.* But what was 'the worst'? It was not death, for the *Pontifex* half welcomed the idea of leaving this life: if there was no love, no companionship, no sex; what was left? Power; that was what was left. And Coelestinus worried that he was losing control. If he did not have power, then he had nothing. Instead of crowning his career with the ultimate success of creating a new Roman Empire, he feared that he was now in danger of losing it all: power, authority, control, riches, status; everything.

The *Pontifex Maximus* let his head remain buried in the *stratum*. As he breathed in the musky smell of the bedclothes, a face appeared before him, as it had done before and as it was doing ever more frequently.

'What will happen? What should I do?'

The face smiled back at the *Pontifex Maximus*.

'Well? Talk to me!'

Nothing. Coelestinus could only look at the image before him and study its features: misty eyes; long white hair; long white beard. *Was this a joke? Was this what God looked like? No, of course not! There **was** no God; at least not the one that these Christians prayed to. O for the old gods! O for the glory days!*

The face continued to stare at him.

'What do you want?'

The face smiled.

'Well, tell me what you want!'

'Germanus.'

'Germanus? What about him?'

'He is your best hope.'

'Of what?'

'Of saving yourself.'

The *Pontifex* snorted.

'I don't *need* saving.'

'O yes you do. Or rather you will if Aetius and Severianus get together.'

'But Severianus is fighting with Germanus!'

The face laughed.

'He is for now.'

'But?'

'But what about when he, or rather they, align with the Vortigern?'

Coelestinus looked up and over at the cross in the corner of his room. 'Germanus will be finished. Even he will not be able to withstand superior forces on that scale, especially if Aetius is in charge.'

The face smiled again.

'So now you know what you must do, your grace.'

Coelestinus sighed. He stared at the cross then looked down at the bed.

The face had gone.

The *Pontifex* pulled himself up by his elbows, hobbled over to the *scrinium* and began to write.

※   ※   ※

Germanus fingered the gold amulet pendant. *What a cruel trick it was! Just to get me to go and talk to the Vortigern. Why did I take it seriously? After all these years, there is no way that she would still have that pendant. There is no way that she would still be alive.*

'What are you doing? Come back to bed.'

Germanus shook his head slowly.

'Give me a few moments.'

'I will make it worth your while.'

'I just need to think.'

Germanus squeezed the pendant so hard that it made his clenched hand bleed.

'I am waiting, your grace.'

The archbishop-general heard her giggle. He looked at the woman lying on his bed. She looked more beautiful than ever now that she was pregnant. Her belly had started to swell. He looked her up and down. He had wanted her from the very first moment he had set eyes on her. Even in his drunken, grief-laden stupor, he had fallen in love with this woman. And here she was, the Queen of the West Britons, naked. Germanus remembered the first time that she had unbuckled her belt, dropped it on the floor, then slowly taken off her outer and then her inner garments. Aureliana had smiled at him as she walked over and put her arms and then her legs round his body, taking his mouth to her mouth, his body to her body,grinding into him. The Queen of the West Britons beckoned Germanus to join her.

'Is it mine?'

'Is what yours?'

'The child, of course. What else?'

Aureliana smiled. 'A woman knows.'

'Are you sure?'

'I swear by your Jesus, I am sure! Who else could be the father?'

Germanus snorted at the name of the Christ. He hesitated, then spoke again.

'Well, what about Lupus? Were you not intimate with him?'

Aureliana raised herself up on on one elbow. Her breasts drooped to one side. *How full they are! How I want to bury my head there! How I want her like I have never wanted!*

'Intimate with him? That sounds very formal! You mean had sex with him?'

Germanus nodded.

'What if I did? That was before you, my *cicaro*. Now come to bed. That's an order!' Aureliana giggled. Germanus unbuckled his belt. In the next room, Lupus tossed and turned, wondering if the Queen of the West Britons would join him, like she did some nights.

CHAPTER 49

Lupus and the Vortigern: two minds made up

The Vortigern looked around his high council. Each and every one of them started back at their leader, not daring to say a word. Agricola stroked his beard; Pelagius fiddled with his cross; Constantius adjusted the snake amulet on his forearm. The others cleared their throats or adjusted their over garments.

'So, what now, my Lord?' Only Hengest dared speak.

The Vortigern looked long and hard at his Saxon *foederatus*. 'We continue as before, as we planned. There is no need to change our strategy – no need at all.'

Hengest raised an eyebrow, less than convinced.

'You may be sceptical: Hengest, Pelagius, Constantius, even you Agricola, but believe me, the war is about to turn in our favour.'

'We still have more troops than Germanus, but he is pushing us back on every front. It is a pity that Aureliana spoilt the peace negotiations!'

Agricola snorted. 'Don't be so naïve, Constantius! You may be a great *rationalis,* but you wouldn't last five minutes as a *magister militum.* There was no way that Germanus was ever going to agree to consider negotiations let alone sign a treaty.'

'Don't be so sure, Agricola. He is a pragmatic man, and he would want to avoid bloodshed, if he could.'

'How do you know that Constantius? Have you met the great man?'

Constantius looked down at his hands, clasped tightly on the *mensa*. 'No, I merely meant that, from what I have heard, he is not going to send his troops into battle if he can avoid a conflict. He comes with that reputation and, as you all know, he is an *episcopus* now.'

Agricola snorted again. 'That doesn't mean anything: look at Pelagius here; and look at my bloody father.'

'And you can add *proditor* in the case of Bishop Severianus.' It was the Vortigern, stroking his favourite dog and feeding it *dapis*.

The other members of the high council nodded in agreement; Hengest picked his teeth and belched. 'But it is not as you think. Nothing is as you think, *iudices*.'

※ ※ ※

Much to his surprise, Lupus found that he enjoyed killing people. The change had come at the battle of Viroconium, when Germanus had put him in charge of a whole section of the army. Yes, they were seasoned troops, and knew what they were doing, but he had marshalled and led his forces well. He had seen how people fought, and how they died. Sometimes, the death was quick; sometimes it was slow. Germanus had instructed the high command to make sure their forces knew how best to kill someone in battle. There was no time to be wasted; once a fight was over, then get the life ended as soon as the assailant was able. It was important to move on to the next person as quickly as possible. Sometimes, as he became more confident, Lupus had killed two at once. There had been times when he had been a different person when he was fighting: the rage inside him spilled over and he felt that he could do anything; especially kill and kill again. He had lost count of the numbers who had perished at his hands. When the fighting was over, he could often not remember what had happened. When his compatriots and his subordinates told Lupus what he had said and done, he had no recollection of the events. Germanus had warned him about this blackness; told him that he needed to guard against it; that he should be in control all the time. Lupus felt like asking his master, his father, if he was 'in control' when he made love to Aureliana, even though she bore the child that Lupus had given her. He thought better of it, knowing why the Queen of the West Britons had seduced him, and why she got into bed with Germanus as well. He would have to live with it, for now. The anger and the jealousy served him well: each and every person who died at his hands looked just like Germanus.

The 'no man's land' had been breached in several places along the road from Londinium to Verulamium. Germanus had commanded Lupus to seal the breaches before what had been a trickle of troops and a series of skirmishes turned to a deluge and a full-scale attack when the West British forces had not fully regrouped. Lupus obeyed the order and said he would do as commanded, but he determined to do far more than that. He would take Verulamium; he would show the world, and his Queen, that he was the man for the job, for every job from now on. What better way to prove it than to strike at the holiest place within the Vortigern's lands? Capturing the city, the shrine, beating the elite army that was deployed in and around Verulamium, securing the route north, then forcing the enemy back to Londinium. It could all be done in two days, and Lupus had worked out how best to do it. His plan was fool proof. One third of his forces went south of the opposition, encamped on the far side of the road, mid-way between Verulamium and Londinium. A second third attacked head-on, while the final third circled to the north. The battle went well. Taken by surprise, the central attack enabled a quick and easy victory to be scored. Within two hours the Vortigern's forces had retreated east, their only way out of the conflict, but not before Lupus's men had cut many of them off from both north and south. His master's battle cry of 'Alleluia' had been so effective in previous conflicts during this war that all the troops now adopted it without even being told to do so.

Having cleared the main and subsidiary roads in the area and secured the few remaining villas and villages, Lupus had his forces regroup and march north towards Verulamium. As night was falling, he decided that the army should rest until dawn before the final assault on the city. The hills around provided plenty of opportunities for safe encampment and it was not long before Lupus was surveying the lights of the city appear as the sun finally went down.

CHAPTER 50

Old rivalries surface as the battle for Britannia begins

'What do you think of this place, my lord?'

'Not much, to be honest, Litorius. No wonder the armies kept wanting to invade Gallia and Italia. That meant they could get away from Britannia!' Aetius took another swig of wine, swilled it round his mouth and then spat the liquid out of the window of his quarters. 'Where did this *urina* come from? I would get more pleasure out of drinking pig's piss!'

'I am sorry, sir. It is all we could find. There is not much civilization left round these parts.'

Aetius looked around the ruins of the town where they were now stationed. *With some patching up, those walls could last a bit longer. Not sure there is much point, though. I hope we have done our business before the month is out. I need to be back in Roma to stop Galla Placidia and Coelestinus forming an alliance. The Pontifex does not know the meaning of the word* fiducia. *He would sell his own mother into slavery if he thought it was in his best interests.* Aetius toyed with his *secundae mensae* as he worked out the best way of defending the encampment from a surprise attack.

'What did you say this place was called, Litorius?'

'*Venta Icenorum.*'

'*Venta Icenorum:* the place of the Iceni. If I remember my history correctly, a foe worthy of our steel came from here, did she not?'

'She did indeed. The local tribes still talk of her with reverence.'

'What was her name? Boo, Bo, Ba…'

'I think she was called Boudicca, General.'

'That's right, Boudicca, Queen of the Iceni. I would like to have met her; my kind of woman.'

'By all accounts there is a latter-day Boudicca for you to meet shortly.'

'Ah, yes, the fair Aureliana, Queen of the West Britons. I am told she is quite something.'

'Who told you that?'

'Who do you think, Litorius? My old sparring partner, Germanus, now the high and mightly Archbishop of Britannia.'

At which point the two men belched and laughed loudly before retiring to bed.

※　※　※

'The fool! The bloody fool! Why on earth has he done that? I gave him his orders, and he has disobeyed me!' Aureliana smiled at Germanus. She squeezed his forearm as they sat at the dining table next to each other. The other members of the dinner party looked away.

'He is a young man, my lord. He wants to prove himself to you – and me, for that matter.'

Germanus got up and paced around the room. Aureliana could see how much he cared for Lupus, even though the two of them had to share her and Germanus was not the father of her child. Her *magister militum* had obviously abandoned Patricius once and for all and was now investing everything in his adopted son. The Queen of the West Britons smiled to herself. *Lupus was a boy when I first met him. But he is a man now. He is the warrior that he needs to be; the father of my son must be a great soldier. I knew that Lupus had it in him to be a worthy descendant of our great tribe. The blood line will continue!*

Ambrosius looked at the Queen and her General. His empty eye socket pained him; the sight from his good eye pained him even more. *I will have that man. I will have my sister-wife. I will have my revenge on both once Britannia is ours. When we are again Prythons, like our forefathers!*

Germanus looked at Aureliana and Ambrosius. 'There is nothing for it. We will have to bring forward the plan. Assemble the forces for a dawn attack on Verulamium.'

CHAPTER 51

Lupus is in trouble; Aetius must decide; a traitor is outed

If only my so-called brother could see me now! He would not believe it! He would not be able to stomach the fact that I have made it to where I am now! He was the albae gallinae filius; *the lucky devil born with the silver spoon in his mouth. And where is he now? Who knows? And who cares? Because I have become the first of the house of Germanus and more! I will be King of Prythain and leader of the Celts, alongside my Queen.* Lupus looked at the birds flying overhead and smiled. The sun was rising fast. It was time to go and conquer.

Initially the battle went well. The outer wall was soon breached, and the forward troops were able to open the south-eastern entrance to the city and the remainder of the forces under the command of Lupus poured in. The Vortigern's troops were no match for the brutality and the skill of the British forces. Within an hour of sunrise, the battle was won. Or so it seemed. As Lupus was about to stand in front of the temple of Albanus and proclaim victory, a large army of *Saxoni* entered Viroconium from the southwest and the northeast, let in through the city gates by forces loyal to the Vortigern. Within minutes, the troops under Lupus's command had been forced into the forum, where the slaughter began. The men tried to surrender, but the Vortigern's army would have none of it. They had been given strict orders to kill all Germanus's men. Nobody was to be spared. Lupus did not know how to respond.

What would Germanus do? How would my master save the day? Lupus looked around the forum. His men were in the centre, backed up all the way to the temple steps where Lupus had thought to give his victory speech. *How stupid could I have been! What possessed me to rush in like this? We are doomed!* Lupus ordered two of his men to break loose from the battle and aim to escape back to the battle line where the main forces were stationed. They were to inform Germanus and ask for help, and urgently. Then Lupus turned to the temple entrance. He decided to move the remainder of his forces inside the building defending it until the requested reinforcements arrived. He ordered the men to fall back and enter the temple as quickly as they were able. The building was deserted. Candles burned and incense wafted through the huge space. Lupus looked up at the high ceiling. Not since he had been in Roma had he seen such a lofty structure. The absolute stillness of this holy site contrasted with the grotesque and squalid noise of battle outside. Lupus walked up to the statue at the far end of the basilica. The mouth spewed smoke; the eyes glowed red. It was Albanus, the martyr of Verulamium.

❊   ❊   ❊

Aureliana was worried; sick to the bottom of her stomach. Lupus was the father of her yet-unborn child. She would miss him: the youthful enthusiasm; the boyish delight; the naivete. Ultimately, however, Lupus was expendable. He had served his purpose. He might have been a possible contender for the post of *magister militum,* but Aureliana had already decided that Lupus was going to be surplus to requirements on the field of battle as much as between her sheets.

The Queen of the West Britons turned to Germanus as they rode hard along the road to Verulamium. The archbishop-general seemed to be his usual self: jaw tightly set, eyes glistening, armour shining, reins tightly held. Aureliana was comforted by the large cohort of *celeres* that made up the forward contingent, followed by a much larger band of *equites* and at least a third of the combined force of *miles* and *pedites* that had been assembled for the war with the Vortigern. Messengers had reached their encampment only a few hours before, but the news of Lupus was then already so grim that both she and Germanus feared that the rescue attempt would be in vain.

Why am I so nervous? It will be sad if I lose the dear boy, especially if he does not see his son and heir before he is no more. But my child is the important thing and I carry him safely. What if Germanus is killed? I will mourn his loss if he dies on the battlefield and not on the sacrificial altar at my hand. No, I am nervous because this conflict cannot be lost. The war must be won at all costs!

※ ※ ※

Aetius thought he would never stop pissing. *God, I drank so much last night! Why did I bother to down that pigswill?* As he dried himself off and remounted his horse, the General looked backward then forward along the rows of men and equipment lined up along the road from Venta Icenorum to Verulamium. 'We are a goodly number, Litorius. Not as big a force as I would have liked, but enough to do the job!'

'And you know what the job is, my Lord?'

Aetius snorted. 'The trouble with our empire, my friend, is that there is no true leadership. There has not been for at least thirty years or more, at least not in the west, and the east has troubles enough of its own. Now, we have a little boy for an *Imperator*, told what to do by an overbearing and ambitious mother. Then, there is the Almighty and most merciful, his Holiness the Lord High *Pontifex Maximus*, God bless the devious old bastard, and his network of ex-soldiers turned bishops. Not to mention the pretenders here, there, and everywhere. Take here, for example: the Vortigern, whoever he is, sees himself as not just the king of all Britannia but fancies himself as yet another bloody usurper from this miserable island. Not to mention the amorous Aureliana, conquests in the bedroom as much as the battlefield have seen her get on top, by all accounts.'

'So where do your loyalties lie, my Lord?'

Aetius looked across at his companion. 'That's a very good question Litorius. A very good question. And one that reminds me that I have still not made my mind up as to whether to obey Galla Placidia or Coelestinus.' Aetius took out two letters from his over-tunic. 'One from the dowager empress and one from the pope. If I follow the instructions of the first, Germanus and Aureliana die; if I do as the second commands, then the Vortigern will be yet another failed, deceased, usurper. So, Litorius, what would you do?'

⁂　⁂　⁂

'We have an opportunity to beat Germanus and Aureliana once and for all, your majesty.'

'I agree, Agricola. What do the rest of you say?'

'Get the bastards now, that's what I say.'

The high council were taken aback by the vehemence of Pelagius and his response to the Vortigern.

'Well, I agree with our *magister militum*! We have a once-in-a-generation opportunity to get rid of all opposition on this island and move our cause forward. Without any challengers to contend with here, we can invade Gallia and then march on Roma. I will be *Pontifex Maximus* and the Vortigern will be hailed *Imperator* before you can say 'alleluia!'''

All the other council members nodded vigorously; all except one. The Vortigern looked down the table, bowing his head to each member in turn until he reached the last governor. 'And what about you Constantius? What do you say about Agricola's proposal? You are very silent these days. What is wrong with my *rationalis*?'

'Nothing wrong, sire, nothing at all.'

'O yes there is, my friend. There is something very wrong. And it has been wrong for a very long time, has it not?'

'My Lord Vortigern, I have absolutely no idea what you are talking about.'

'I think you know exactly what I am talking about, Constantius.'

'Guards: seize this man!'

'But what are you doing, your majesty?' Constantius tried to resist as the soldiers on duty at the entrance to the Council Chamber manhandled the Vortigern's treasurer out of his seat and dragged him towards the King of Kings's throne.

The Vortigern stood up, looked around the room at his high council, then looked down at Constantius, now flat on the floor by the throne.

'Now tell me, dear Constantius, my beloved in Christ. How long have you been passing information to Germanus?'

CHAPTER 52

Constantius meets his fate; new alliances are forged; Lupus promises

'So, Bishop Severianus, we meet at last.'

The head of the Christian church for North Britannia smiled and saluted his guest.

'Ex army, I see. Like most of your lot!'

'And what is my lot, Flavius Aetius?'

There was laughter in response before the General responded.

'Oh, military men gone soft through Christianity. If people like you had not deserted the cause, the empire would not be in this great big bloody mess!'

'Not true, sir. The Christian church is one of the few things that is holding the west together these days; you mark my words. Even the great Germanus has turned to Christ! In any case, who says I have gone soft? I could still give you and your high command a run for their money any day!'

For a moment, the two men looked po-faced at each other. Aetius was the first to crack and burst out laughing. 'I imagine you could Severianus; I imagine you could. Once a Roman soldier, always a Roman soldier!'

'Come, join me for food and drink, Aetius. We have much to discuss.'

To his great surprise (and his better judgement), Aetius found himself liking Severianus. The Bishop of Eboracum had ensured that his guest was well looked after at his makeshift headquarters in Durovigutum. Aetius was tired after his journey from Venta Icenorum, and the warm welcome made him feel relaxed and accommodated. The two men could talk tactics, strategy, politics and much more. Once sated on food and drink (including the best wine that Aetius had tasted since he landed in Britannia), they got down to business.

'How far are we from Verulamium?' Aetius scratched his ear and looked at Litorius, who raised an eyebrow in response.

'A day-and-a-half's march at most. Your *equites* could be there by nightfall.' Severianus could tell what Aetius was thinking.

'And the present situation there? *Periculum in mora*, as Germanus would say: there is danger in delay.' Aetius thought back to when he and the archbishop-general of Britannia were comrades-in-arms.

'That is very interesting.'

'Go on then Severianus. Stop beating about the bush! I want to know how things stand before I make my decision, *per fas et nefas!*'

'It is a mess, Aetius, my friend. The war was going well for Germanus. He had managed to repel the *Saxoni* when they attacked Viroconium. Then their advance on Londinium was going to plan, with some setbacks, but nothing insurmountable, until his hot-headed adopted son Lupus decided to break ranks and attack Verulamium, even though the orders had been to hold the line, making sure that the Vortigern's forces were split between the two cities. Now, thanks to that young idiot, we have troops hemmed inside Verulamium and holed up in the temple to Albanus and no obvious means of escape: local forces on one side and a sizeable cohort of the Vortigern's men on the outside. The last I heard, Germanus was hot-footing it to Verulamium to rescue Lupus and what was left of his forces.'

'And that leaves Germanus and Aureliana exposed to the south?'

'It does Aetius. I have it on good authority that the Vortigern's main forces have now left Londinium. The British forces will be squeezed on all sides, and all because Lupus wanted to show his adopted father what a man he had become. As you can imagine, I am wondering where my loyalties should now lie.'

'People warned me about you, Severianus. That you are loyal to no-one but yourself.'

The Bishop of Eboracum snorted, then swilled down the last of his wine, looked at his empty glass and bade a servant refill it. 'And what about you, Aetius. Where does your loyalty lie?'

'Now that is an interesting question; a very interesting question. And one to which there is an obvious answer.'

The two men laughed heartily. Meanwhile, old Augustus noted every word they spoke as he cleared away the dishes, ready to send a message to Germanus about what was being discussed and planned.

※　　※　　※

Constantius looked down from the north gate as the army left Londinium on its forced march to Verulamium. Alongside the Vortigern rode Agricola, Hengest and Pelagius. The four men turned towards the city and smiled as the body of their former colleague swung from the turret top. Blood still ran down his face from the holes where his eyes had been.

'See the traitor Constantius and be afraid: *acheruntis pabulum*; food for the gallows. All who betray me will suffer the same fate.' With these words, the Vortigern commanded the army to set forth. 'We can be assured of victory. Severianus is wavering and an even greater general than Germanus has landed on these shores and is set to join us by this time tomorrow at the latest.'

'A greater commander than the Archbishop of Britannia?'

'He means Aetius, Agricola. The one and only; recently sacked *magister militum* to your tiny-tot *Imperator.* Pelagius belched as he spoke.

'You mean his mother, more like! I would not trust that bitch an *uncia*. I know all about Galla Placidia and her power struggle with Coelestinus. She has ordered Aetius to thwart the pope's plans for Britannia. And that suits me down to the ground, now that Germanus and I are on opposite sides.' The Vortigern looked pleased with himself for once.

'Do not underestimate the *Pontifex Maximus,* my Lord Vortigern. If the dowager empress is devious, then the pope is doubly so. Remember, I studied with him in Roma many years ago. And that, of course, is where I met the great wonder-boy of the time.'

'And who was that Pelagius?'

Germanus of Gallia, your majesty. I know more about that man than I have ever told anyone.'

'Then start talking Pelagius. You can entertain us before our great victory in Verulamium tomorrow'

CHAPTER 53

Renewal on every front

'I do not believe I can continue. I could go on so long as my mind stayed fresh, even though my body was but a walking skeleton. But now, I fear I am no longer the man I once was, even in my head.' Coelestinus took off his spectacles and lay down his *stylus*. The Pontifex looked at Ferox. Answer came there none. 'You know not what to say to me, do you? That is because I speak the truth. I have heard you talking about me in the corridors. *The old bugger's past it; he's losing his marbles; he wets himself at night; he talks nonsense most of the time.*' The Pontifex buried his head in his hands and wept. 'Leave me! Leave this old man.'

Ferox bowed and withdrew from his grace's presence. Coelestinus tried to gather his thoughts. A large glass of wine helped him to focus. *Think, man! You must keep going! You are not the kind of man to give up; you never have been, remember? You owe it to Roma and all our wonderful heritage and traditions to see this through. You can still make your plan work! You must make it work! If Aetius supports Germanus and Severianus stays loyal to him also, then the Vortigern can be defeated, and the threat of invasion is neutralised. We then have time to regroup and refresh our resources! I will make Roma great again!*

The Pontifex poured himself more wine.

You must keep going. The church has come too far to be ransacked by

Pelagius and the others. He will destroy all that I have worked for; everything that my predecessors planned and built; our strategies for preserving the empire through Christianity.

Coelestinus burst out laughing and looked up at the cross above his writing desk. 'You know, there are times when I almost believe in you! If I believed in you now, would you help me? Would you aid me in preserving a way of life that I hold dear, and which means the survival of *your* church?' The *Pontifex Maximus* drank a third large glass of wine as he waited for an answer. He determined that he should visit his estates in the north from whence this vintage had originated. He swilled the liquid round in his mouth, appreciating the fulness of flavour and the aftertaste that lingered across his palette as he downed each gulp. He looked up at the cross once more. Answer came there none. *Someone up there just does not love me!* Optat supremo collocare Sisyphus in monte saxo! Coelestinus shrugged his shoulders and looked down at his half-finished diary entry then back up at the cross. *Perhaps I have been looked at this from the wrong perspective!* Cui bono? *Who stands to gain? That is what I must remember! Enlightened self-interest, Coelestinus; enlightened self-interest!*

The Pontifex rang his little bell and Ferox reappeared. 'Have my carriage prepared. I must go to see the dowager *Imperatrix*. But hurry, there is little time! And before you chunter on about how the old bugger has lost it, no he has not, he is still very much in charge! I have worked out what I must do to save the day. *Praestat sero quam nunquam:* better late than never!'

※   ※   ※

Aureliana's forces had arrived near Verulamium more quickly than she had imagined was possible. Germanus had driven the troops hard, but they had responded well to his leadership and were only too willing to follow, given the prospect of an early engagement with the opposition and the possible capture of one of the Vortigern's main strongholds. Not only that, but it was also the case that possession of the shrine of Albanus was an especial incentive for those of faith, whether Christian or pagan, given the saint's significance to both parties. This man represented Albion: all that was the best of the Prythonic way; and at the same time, his adoption by the Church had given Albanus a cult following among those who favoured either a continuation of *Romanitas,* a furtherance of the Gospel of the one called Jesus; or both. Whoever controlled Verulamium and its holy temple controlled the hearts if not the minds of those who sought to rebuild the province of Britannia and the Prythonic kingdom.

Aureliana had all these thoughts going through her mind as the troops pitched camp to the southwest of the city. As she dismounted from her horse, she felt the first stirring inside her belly. Germanus noticed how his queen was stroking her stomach.

'*Auspicium melioris aevi.* An omen of a better time.' She smiled.

CHAPTER 54

All roads lead to Verulamium

The Vortigern's army arrived to the southest of Verulamium in the late afternoon. Rather than pitch the troops into battle immediately, Agricola and Hengest agreed between them that it was wisest to rest the men so that they could pitch into the fray afresh. The Vortigern acceded to this idea, on condition that scouts were sent into the city to determine the state of play between the two sides. Once this was done, Hengest urged the Vortigern to send the whole of his forces into Verulamium to finish off the job. Agricola, to the others' surprise, advised caution, proposing that only half the army be deployed at this stage, arguing that, because the forces commanded by Lupus were so outnumbered and nearing defeat, it was pointless to use all the available resources on what would, in effect, be a mop-up operation.

'*Festina lente*, Hengest; *festina lente!*'

'Do stop buggering me about with your poncy Latin, Agricola. What does that mean in plain English?'

'It means *make haste slowly*, Hengest.'

'Thank you for the "clarification", my Lord Vortigern. So why did your *magister militum* not say that in the first place?'

'Now, now, you two. No falling out when we are on the edge of victory.' The Vortigern laughed at the look of complete surprise on the faces of his two commanders.

'*De nihilo nihil.*'

'O for fuck's sake! Can't you stop the bugger, my Lord Vortigern? I know that I don't have Agricola's airs and graces and all his learning and knowledge, but what good is all that when it comes to a war? You need me, you two. You would be nowhere without your *foederati*; men like me. Nu hit ys on swines dome, cwæð se ceorl sæt on eoferes hricge.'[1]

Agricola and the Vortigern looked at Hengest. The Saxon leader grimaced and shifted his weight from foot to foot.

'Very well. I may have had something to do with the ransack of Germanus's villa.'

'What? You! When I got there the place had been completely devasted. Why did you do what you did?'

'Why do you think, Agricola. Why do you think my forces are here now? *Weregild* – that's why the Saxons are here: money. If the other lot pay me a higher fee than you are offering me, then I am off: *ádrogen.*[2]

'And who paid you?'

Hengest laughed. 'That would be telling. But, as his lordship the high and mightly Lord Agricola would say, *aureo hamo piscari;* "money talks".'

※   ※   ※

By this time, the West British forces had arrived to the southwest of the holy place of Albanus. Germanus commanded Ambrosius to take a cohort and skirt round to the north of the city walls and attempt to gain entrance. This move proved unsuccessful, and the expeditionary force returned within the hour to report that it would be difficult to scale the walls or batter down the gates without specialist equipment or a significant body of men (and much loss of life), or both.

---

[1] It's up to the pig now, said the peasant sitting on the boar's back.

[2] Done; finished

'What of Lupus?'

'As far as we can make out, he is holed up in the temple of Albanus with what is left of his forces. But that is not our biggest problem, Germanus.'

'No. Then what is Ambrosius?'

'The Vortigern.'

'The great man and his forces have arrived in Verulamium, then?'

'They have! How did you know?'

Germanus grimaced. 'I have, or rather had, a source close to the Vortigern, who managed to get a final message out to me before he was discovered, tortured and then executed.'

Aureliana gasped. 'I know who you mean Germanus. The man whose child you saved. Constantius! I remember him.'

'*Bella detesta matribus:* "war, the horror of mothers". We have executed traitors as well, Aureliana. Remember Drustans?'

'I remember him only too well, Germanus. I can never forgive him for what he did. I expected better of the Cornovii.'

'What are we to do now? I doubt Lupus can hold out much longer.'

'Very true, Ambrosius. And I expect that, by now, the Vortigern will be aware of our arrival.'

'What are you going to do, then, Germanus? Ambrosius and I grown impatient to know your orders!'

The General smiled. 'There is a way. But it may surprise you what I have in mind.'

CHAPTER 55

Battle lines are drawn; Lupus is shocked; Aetius and Severianus ally

Germanus awoke early. He left Aureliana to sleep. They had been late going to bed. There had been much to talk about, and the Queen of the West Britons had been keen to hear what tactics her *magister militum* intended to employ now that the war was coming to a climax. Germanus smiled as he remembered the way she had pored over the plans and asked so many pertinent questions. But it was the way she ruffled her hair; the way she pursed and pouted her lips in concentration; the way she looked at him. *The way she looks at me! Just like Sevira all those years ago…*

Germanus put on his remaining armour, ate the last of his *jentaculum* and went out to give final orders to his high command. He was impressed at the sight of the armies as they stood to attention and saluted him. As he looked across the squares of men and machinery, he was aware of a hand take his. He turned to look at Aureliana.

'We have come a long way in such a short space of time, have we not, my Queen?'

'*Tempus edax rerum*, Germanus.'

'You know your literature! "Time, the devourer of all things". I am impressed!'

'You should be!'

Germanus turned back to the assembled troops. He made Ambrosius raise his shield, on which had been painted a cross. The General pointed to the symbol.

'In hoc signo vinces. "In this sign shalt thou conquer!"

'Alleluia, alleluia, alleluia', came the reply.

※   ※   ※

'What was that fearful noise?'

'Goodness knows, Pelagius. Perhaps it was the enemy shitting themselves!'

'Hengest, I do wish you would refrain from such crudities.'

'Well, we all have to shit! Better that they empty their bowels now so that we can get stuck into them more easily on the battlefield!'

'Shut up you two! You can have a go at each other after our victory!'

'Thank you, Agricola. Is all ready?'

Agricola and Hengest nodded.

'The battle will be ours; then on to Gallia, Italia and Roma!' The Vortigern raised his shield.

'The troops await your command, my Lord.'

The Vortigern, followed by Pelagius, Hengest and Agricola, emerged from their tent. The troops stood to attention as they saw the high command.

'Shall I bless the men?'

'You will do no such thing with my men, Pelagius! We will pray to Woden and Tiw, for sure; but not your god of peace!'

'Enough! No more arguing. We will pray to nobody. Each to their own beliefs. I thought that was what you proposed Pelagius. Everybody will pray silently to whatever gods they choose!' The Vortigern allowed the assembly a moment of silent reflection. *And who do I pray to?*

What do I pray for? Today Vortigern, tomorrow, Imperator! Victory over Germanus, but not death to him! I want him; I need him; I will have him!

※　　※　　※

We cannot hold out much longer. The men are on the verge of surrendering. What a fool I was! Now I will never see my child. I have let Germanus down. I have let Aureliana down. What will they think of me? Did the messengers get through to them? Is there any hope or should I give the order to commit suicide? Our position is no longer tenable. What would my master do? Lupus ordered his remaining men to retreat into the inner sanctum of the Temple of Albanus and bar the doors. They managed to do so, but only with considerable difficulty. The bodies of dead soldiers were used to add weight to the barricade that was hastily erected. Having secured the entrance, the cohort regrouped around the high altar.

'Comrades. You have fought bravely. I do not deserve to have led such fine warriors. We have been outnumbered ten to one, but still we have not been captured. You have been the victors today, whatever happens. I – and I alone - am responsible for this situation. And it weighs heavily on my heart that you will not be reaping the true reward of your bravery, your courage, and your strength.'

Lupus paused. Nobody spoke, whether in support, or protest.

'We know what we must do. Let it be so!'

Lupus drew his sword and held it aloft.'

※　　※　　※

'Have you decided?'

'Yes. I think so. Have you?'

Severianus smiled at Aetius.

'I have if you have!'

Aetius laughed.

'*De bono et malo?* Come what may?'

Severianus nodded. 'Yes. I believe so. That latest missive from Coelestinus was the deciding factor for me.'

'For me as well. If the pope's plan works, then we all stand to gain. Provided, that is…'

'Provided?'

'Provided, Bishop Severianus, that you stick to this agreement!'

'How could you doubt me, Aetius?'

The General snorted. 'Very easily, given your past betrayals: first you were for the Vortigern, then Germanus, then … well who knows?'

'I am totally loyal to you and your decision.'

'Let us hope so, Severianus. But mark my words: *cave quid dicis, quando, et cui*: "beware what you say, when and to whom". One false move, one message to the opposition, one sign of changing sides again and I will have you crucified – literally.'

'*Experto credite, Aetius!*'

'I sincerely hope so, Severianus. I really do want to trust you.'

'Then let us ride forward with confidence, Aetius. We have to save the day, you and I.'

CHAPTER 56

The fight to end all fights,
for two men at least

The two armies engaged straight away. Germanus led the West British forces from the front. Though depleted thanks to Lupus's rush of blood to the head, the archbishop-general was still able to command an impressive fighting force. Ambrosius and Aureliana had both expressed concern at the disparity between their army and the Vortigern's significantly greater numbers, but as Germanus kept reminding his colleagues, the *Saxoni* did not have any cavalry and this gave the West British a distinct advantage, even though the Vortigern did have a small number of *equites* who had previously served in the Roman Army. Aureliana had easily accepted the assurances of her *magister militum* (she had nothing but disdain for Saxon soldiers and not much respect for the Vortigern's so-called 'crack' troops). The Queen of the West Britons was less easily reassured when it came to the non-appearance of Severianus and his men. The Bishop of Eboracum was meant to sweep around from the east of Britannia, cutting off the Vortigern's escape route into old Iceni territory. Germanus told Aureliana and Ambrosius that their fellow commander must have encountered stiffer resistance than had been envisaged. Privately, however, he was beginning to worry that his fellow cleric was up to something, and whatever it was, it would not suit the West British cause.

Agricola, Hengest and Pelagius led the opposition. The Vortigern remained on the hills overlooking the main battlefield at the back of his armies though, as Germanus remarked to Aureliana, their enemy's communications line was an effective one, despite their leader's position relative to the conflict. The archbishop-general of Britannia had the bolder plan, which meant fighting on two fronts at the same time. Aureliana (much to her annoyance, given her wish to engage the Vortigern in hand-to-hand combat to the death before the end of the day) had been ordered to attack and overcome the troops holding Verulamium and, at the earliest possible opportunity, to free Lupus and his men. Though motivated to rescue the father of her unborn child, she would have much preferred to see off her arch-rival, settling several scores in the process, not least the emasculation of her husband-brother. Germanus told her in no uncertain terms that was not to be; Ambrosius would have to wreak his own revenge for the loss of one of his eyes and the whole of his manhood.

Commanding Aureliana and her forces to attack Verulamium made sense for several reasons, not least the fact that this made best use of the limited West British heavy weaponry. The *ballistae* were put to particularly good use, thanks to the intensive training that Germanus had given the soldiers put in charge of this equipment. Every stone hit home; continuous careful aiming meant that the city walls had been breached within twenty shots. Once the soldiery on the other side of the three gaps that had been created by this assault had begun to retreat, Aureliana led the charge. Germanus was equally successful in the first round of fighting and the greater number of expert horseman under his overall command made a big difference to the West British attack. The Vortigern's troops fought bravely, however, and there was a limit to how far the opposing *equites* could fully compensate for the endless rows of *Saxoni* now pouring onto the battlefield from the southeast. Germanus noticed how these *foederati* had been taught at least some of the Roman ways of fighting and were starting to put their learning to good effect.

The Vortigern continued to hold back from the fighting. Agricola, Hengest and Pelagius seemed well able to cope without the immediate presence of their commander-in-chief and the three senior leaders had no difficulty with communicating backwards and forwards up and down the hill. The Vortigern's view of Verulamium in the distance was not so rosy. Seeing that the whole of Aureliana's forces were now inside the city's outer walls, the Vortigern commanded that a cohort of expert troops (the remains of the once mighty legions of Londinium) be detached under the leadership of Pelagius to slow if not arrest the Queen's advance towards the Temple of Albanus. In response, Germanus ordered a band of *equites* to chase after the group led by Pelagius. He then took advantage of the ensuing gap in the Vortigern's forces to prize the two halves of the opposing army apart. The move brought Ambrosius and Agricola face to face. The two men dismounted, each eager to finish the other off in hand-to-hand combat. Germanus and the Vortigern could only look on from their respective command positions. The opposing troops, somehow sensing that this was a serious one-on-one contest, cleared a space for Agricola and Ambrosius to fight to the death. Only one of them would see the end of the day.

CHAPTER 57

Elafius makes a surprise discovery

Elafius had always been afraid of the dark, but now was not the time to tell anyone. Certainly, there was no way that he would ever let Germanus know of his phobia. He greatly respected the man (even though the new Archbishop of Britannia had said he did not follow the Lord Jesus Christ) and hoped that there would be an opportunity to bring Germanus to the one true faith in the light of the Vortigern's defeat. Elafius determined to persuade the General to renounce his old pagan ways. The young priest had several good reasons (or so he had determined) for optimism in this regard: Germanus had insisted that all his troops paint a cross on their shields before they went into battle; the General himself always shouted *in hoc signo vinces* before any engagement, however minor; the 'Alleluia' acclamation had become the standard battle cry; and, most importantly of all, Germanus had insisted that all his followers, men, women, children, *even* his high command, should be baptised.

It had come as no surprise when Germanus requested that Elafius act as chaplain to the combined forces. Sermons to the army were allowed on occasion, once the archbishop-general had vetted the proposed texts and made alterations designed, it would seem, to emphasise the congregation's patriotic duty to rid Britannia of the

Vortigern. Germanus had also accepted that Elafius would be a non-combatant member of the West British alliance. Neither man had any issue with such a role, given that all, or almost all, the combined forces were spoiling for a fight with the Vortigern's troops and especially the hated *Saxoni*. In retrospect, the young priest should have spent more time clarifying what his duties as chaplain were to be, once hostilities began in earnest. He did not expect the role to include leading a small detachment of men through underground tunnels that led from a small ruinated *templum* on the northern outskirts of Verulamium all the way to the Shrine of Albanus.

Elafius found himself on hands and knees crawling through a narrow opening with nothing but an oil lamp and the wind in his face to guide him. The tunnel opening had been easy enough to find, thanks to Germanus's instructions, and the first few hundred yards of the secret passageway into the city had been easy enough to negotiate. Then, thanks to subsidence, the ceiling and walls had collapsed in some places (Elafius surmised that the increased weight of the recently-reinforced defences had also played a part) and the tunnel had been reduced to small openings in what were otherwise piles of rubble. At one point, the tunnel was blocked and Elafius and his comrades had no option but to remove the obstruction and shore up the weakened roof as best they could. The young priest had never had good lungs, and the dust and dirt in the underground passageways were playing havoc with his breathing. He persevered, not wanting to show himself up too much in the eyes of the battle-hardened soldiers that Germanus had assigned to his reconnaissance team. Once the rubble had been cleared, Elafius went first (knowing that Germanus would approve of his chaplain's leading from the front) and managed to navigate the tiny opening that had been created. When the members of the expedition had all passed through the hole, the going became relatively easy. Elafius surmised that they were not many feet below ground, for he could hear the noise of the battle raging above. This must mean that they were beneath the city forum and not far from the catacombs beneath the Shrine of Albanus.

The passageway opened out into a high-ceilinged chamber with at least four exits (including the one through which the party had entered). At some point, the place had been used as a prison and a torture chamber, judging by the many implements hanging from the walls and the skeletons strewn about the floor. Some of the bodies were headless; others had limbs missing. Elafius looked at his comrades and wept. He thought of the horrific deaths that these people had endured, in some cases recently, given that several of the corpses had flesh on them still. For a moment, the chaplain wondered about saying a few prayers over the dead (there must have been at least thirty of them) committing them into God's care. He decided that he would have to do that later when his present mission was complete. One of the men nudged the chaplain as he stood meditating. A light flickered in the distance; footsteps could be heard; a figure appeared.

'Good Lord', Elafius cried. 'What are you doing here?'

'I could say the same of you', came the reply. 'But I assume you are here for Lupus.'

CHAPTER 58

One man's fight ends; another's begins

Ambrosius kept telling himself that he must keep going. The effect on the troops if he fell now would be incalculable. It was hard. The loss of an eye had made him less of a fighter, just as castration had taken away his manhood. Here was the perfect opportunity for him to avenge all the wrongs that the Vortigern had done to him, his brother, his sister, and his people. Once again, he could be a man in the eyes of his kinsmen and women and, above all, his Queen. He would be able to hold his head up now and forever as the King of the West Britons. He looked at his opponent. Agricola stood facing him in full battle gear, *gladius* already drawn. The Vortigern's *magister militum* had been the first to dismount. Ambrosius had resisted, thinking that the initial combat would be on horseback, but, if that was the way Agricola wanted it, then they would engage in hand-to-hand fighting from the start. Ambrosius made sure that he positioned himself in relation to the enemy so that he could make the most of his vision. He had learned how to compensate for the narrower spectrum, but he was also aware that Agricola would play on the handicap that he had personally inflicted. Ambrosius could still remember the pain of having his eye gouged out.

Both men had fended off the initial arrow attack and used their shields to protect themselves from the other's *pilum*. Agricola was the first to approach, but Ambrosius was too fast for him (he had learned much from his encounter with Germanus in the amphitheatre back in Viroconium all those months ago), anticipating his enemy's every move. After the first round of parrying, honours were even, with both men having grazed the other. Though the bigger battle was raging round them, the two combatants' followers were still able to shout and cheer when their man scored an advantage over the other. Ambrosius thought he could see Aurelianus, his dead brother, in front of him, willing his younger brother on as he attacked Agricola more fiercely than before. This round, both gladiators struck home: Agricola managed to shove his *gladius* up inside Ambrosius's body armour. At the same time, Ambrosius struck his opponent a heavy blow in the thigh. Each realised that the other was seriously wounded. The two men continued the fight regardless. Both refused assistance. It was only a matter of time before one of them became so weak that they would lose their concentration and drop their guard to the point where the other could go in for the kill. Sweat ran into Ambrosius's good eye, momentarily blinding him. Agricola sensed that his opponent could not see properly and took the opportunity to thrust his sword once more into the much weakened body. As he sank to the floor, Ambrosius saw Aurelianus holding out his arms to welcome his brother home to the Prythonic afterworld.

※　　※　　※

Aetius and Severianus were both quick to appreciate the state of play in the battle of Verulamium. The two men determined that, though the troops had been marched hard all the way from Venta Icenorum, it was essential to deploy them immediately.

'Are we agreed, Severianus. No turning back now?'

'What do you think, my Lord and Master? I have determined to follow you and my word is my bond. How could you ever think otherwise, Aetius? I do this *ex propriu motu*; I am a man of free will, as my faith dictates. *Auro quaeque ianua panditur*, my dear comrade; "a golden key opens any door".' The Bishop of Eboracum laughed and saluted.

'Very well, Severianus. You know what you must do. Have all your men painted the symbol on their shields?'

'They have. Just like yours have done. And what a pretty pattern they all make. I feel quite emotional about it all! Now Germanus will know whose side we are on!'

Aetius snorted. 'You and your bloody religion. Give me the old gods any day.'

'Then let us engage in battle. Your troops to the southeast; mine to the southwest.'

And so it was that Aetius and Severianus added their significant resources to the armies already on the field. Both men had been swayed by the letters that had arrived from the *Pontifex Maximus* while they were meeting in Venta Icenorum. The offer that Coelestinus had made to them, both individually and collectively, was too considerable to resist. They would be rich men, able to buy the western empire several times over; and probably the eastern empire as well. They could do what they wanted; no more scrimping around to muster enough forces to keep the *barbari* at bay for a while longer.

CHAPTER 59

Comrades reunited: but can anyone be trusted?

Aureliana relished every moment of the battle that was now in full swing. She had longed for the day when she could engage with the Vortigern's forces head on. Her troops watched as she carved her way through the enemy ranks. *I feel so alive. More so than I have done for years! This is my day! I will have my victory! Britannia, Prythain, will be mine!* The Queen of the West Britons had grown tired of waiting and talking and plans and tactics. She wanted action. She had wondered at times if Germanus was up to the job of leading her troops. Every time she had been keen to attack, he had advised caution. They had argued many times, in her bed as much as her council chamber. *Si sic omnes.* A part of her wished that their relationship could have lasted this way forever. But it was not to be; it could never be. *Summa sedes non capit duos:* 'the highest seat does not hold two'. *And the Prythonic Crown is mine; and mine alone!* Nevertheless, the Queen smiled as she remembered the disputes that she had experienced with her *magister militum* and the way some of their more intimate disagreements had climaxed. All this made her more rampant in her struggle with the *Saxoni*.

She scythed through the scum. Aureliana's outrage got the better of her in the end. Despite Germanus ordering her to retire, she could not resist chasing a whole group of the enemy back from whence they came. But she had been noticed and they were ready for her. First, they speared her horse, which fell from under its rider. Then, they dragged Aureliana out from under the carcass. Rather than kill her on the spot, she was transported up the hill to the Vortigern's encampment, despite her vigorous attempts to break free. Aureliana never made it to the enemy's headquarters. As if from nowhere, a detachment of men in full Roman military dress butchered her Saxon captors on the spot. Then their leader appeared from behind the group and lifted her onto his horse. '*Aut vincere aut mori*', the man said, as he gripped Aureliana round the waist.

'Otherwise translated as "victory or death". Thanks to you, I choose victory today.'

'Germanus warned me from the start that you could be a hothead. Now I have seen it with my own eyes.'

Aureliana laughed at her rescuer.

'Good to have you back Severianus. And to know that you are on our side.'

The Bishop of Eboracum snorted.

'Who says I am, your majesty?'

※   ※   ※

'This is so easy, Aetius; a complete piece of piss.'

'I agree Litorius. It is too good to be true. Why are the Vortigern's men so lacklustre? And why have so few troops been deployed on this side of the city? It is such an obvious place to strike.'

'Or is it a double bluff, my Lord?'

'Nah, the *Saxoni* aren't bright enough for that!'

'But what about Agricola, or the Vortigern?'

'True. Agricola is Roman-trained. Who knows about the Vortigern? A shady character if ever there was one.'

Aetius's men were now pressing hard against the northwest gates.

Their *ballistae* had hit home to the point where the city walls either side of the entrance were starting to crumble. Aetius himself had regretted not having the time or the resources to burrow under the foundations, but that was a technique requiring time and effort, neither of which was in great supply in Britannia, nor anywhere else for that matter. The gates finally gave way, collapsing inwards. At the same time, the city wall to the south of the entrance collapsed. Aetius gave the order to stand back in case there was a trap immediately inside. But he need not have worried. Out of the dust and the clamour a figure rode to greet them.

'*Salve!*' came the cry.

'Hail, my old friend. I wondered when I would see you again!'

'And I you, Aetius. It is good to have you here, in person, with more troops. Now that you are on my side, we are invincible.'

'I am glad that you think so, Germanus.'

※　　※　　※

'We are back on track! Absolutely back on track!'

The *Pontifex Maximus* clapped his hands and cackled.

'I have got her! I have got that bloody woman! I will have the last laugh! That bitch Galla Placidia will regret having crossed me. What is a dowager empress compared to a pope?'

The two acolytes looked at each other and then smiled at Coelestinus.

The Pontifex caught sight of the young men. 'I saw you looking at me! Any more insolence like that and I will have you scourged, and worse. The problem is you might enjoy it!' The Pontifex cackled and clapped his hands once again. 'Now leave me. I have business to do and letters to write.'

Once the door was closed, Coelestinus took out his writing tablet and started scribbling.

My dear Germanus. I am so relieved that all is well with you. I am glad that I acted when I did. If I had not done so and promised Aetius and Severianus a share of the empire and the riches of the church, it would have been curtains for you and me in all this: no pope; no Archbishop of Britannia – or anywhere, for that matter.

*Anyway, by the time you receive this letter, you will no doubt have triumphed, and the empire is ours. I cannot wait to see you crowned as Imperator **and** Pontifex, with Aetius and Severianus as your two Caesars!*

CHAPTER 60

Albanus is the goal; Lupus descends into oblivion

Aureliana remarked to her high command that the Vortigern seemed to be pouring ever more troops into the fray. The Queen's remaining spies had been able to inform her that so many reinforcements were being brought up from Londinium to Verulamium that there was now but a handful of men defending the capital. Having received this intelligence, Aureliana had persuaded Germanus, Severianus, and Aetius (who had now sworn loyalty to the archbishop-general of Britannia) to take advantage of the fact that the Vortigern was focusing almost all his resources on the present battle. Germanus got word to Lucius back in Lactodurum ordering them to set off forthwith for Londinium with the reserve forces (on the assumption that they had been well enough trained to succeed in their mission) to secure the city now that it was defended by a much depleted army.

Aureliana learnt of the death of her husband-brother. She was able to see from a distance how his body had been strung up on the temporary defences that the Vortigern's forces had erected around their encampment. *So, I am the last of my family. No Aurelianus, and now no Ambrosius. Only me! For now. But my child will rule one day, when I have done away with the Saxoni and the Romani and above all those bloody Christians! I will call him Ambrosius Aurelianus in memory of my brothers; in our native Prythonic he will be named* Artur Airell, *the strong noble one.* Having made this decision about naming her unborn child, the Queen of the West Britons surveyed the battlefield. Since her 'rescue' by Severianus, she had been more cautious about attacking the Vortigern's forces with such abandon, especially now that she had reminded herself of her destiny as the mother of the future King of all Prythain. She had therefore withdrawn to the south of the warzone and met up with Germanus, who had introduced her to Aetius. The sight of the latter's additional forces had much cheered her, especially as she remained concerned at the ever increasing numbers of *Saxoni* who were encircling both the battle area and the outer regions of Verulamium itself. Germanus agreed, but felt that, despite the commanders of the Vortigern's troops, not least Agricola, and Pelagius, being trained in the Roman way, the numbers were of little concern when the West British forces were so much better led, trained, and disciplined, especially now that the numbers had been increased once more by soldiers from the continent. Germanus estimated that, to date, for every one of Aureliana's soldiers that had been killed, at least four of the Vortigern's men had fallen. With Severianus holding his own to the east of the city, and the Vortigern himself still not having directly engaged in the battle, Germanus commanded Aetius (who was more than happy to accept orders from his old comrade, given the Pontifex's promise of wealth and a future share of the empire) to push all remaining resistance in Verulamium itself while he and Aureliana took a small group of elite troops to aid the rescue of Lupus from the temple from where, up until now, he had been unable to break free.

※　　※　　※

Lupus was down to his last ten men. The troops had fought bravely (to the death in most cases) but they could hold out no longer. *There is no way that I will surrender! Germanus would not do so, and neither will*

I. Pushed back right up to the shrine of Saint Albanus, Lupus thought it both ironic and fitting that he should die on an altar, just like Eustachia had done. He looked up at the giant statue above and behind him. It was as if the martyr was smiling down on him, ready to accept his soul. *Do I believe in this God? In this Jesus Christ? Or the old Gods? Or the Gods that Aureliana has taught me about?* Lupus thought how he would never be in his Queen's arms ever again. How he would never see his child, the descendant of the ancient race of which he knew himself to be a part. He was now one of only three men left, pushed right back against the statue of Albanus. Oeric, Hengest's son, was advancing towards him, ready for the kill. As he leaned back against the marble slab, it gave way. Lupus felt into darkness; oblivion; the underworld.

CHAPTER 61

Surprises all round

Aureliana was surprised at the effectiveness of Severianus's command. She had never rated any of these Christian leaders. Too soft for her liking: 'all this love thy neighbour stuff.' But the Queen of the West Britons was glad that the Bishop of Eboracum was on her side. If only he and his army had been with the Cornovii sooner, then Prythain might have been in Aureliana's hands already. *Except then there would have been a rival for the throne when Severianus and I had got rid of the Vortigern. At least I now know that he is not really one of those 'followers of Jesus.' You could have knocked me down with a feather when I found out that he is of the old order. And he wants Germanus killed just as much as I do, albeit for very different reasons.* The other big surprise for the Queen of the West Britons was what seemed to be the total absence of the Vortigern. All the leadership on the other side had come from Agricola and Pelagius. *Pelagius! Another Christian who turns out to be a good fighter! Perhaps this new religion is not so bad after all. I still would not trust them when it comes to ruling Britannia when this war is over, and victory is mine. Pelagius is certainly for the chop. But Severianus; well, the council of druida can decide.*

Having sorted these post-war issues in her mind, the Queen of the West Britons surveyed the battlefield once more. The Vortigern's forces were completely split in two, at least to the east of Verulamium. Aureliana's armies had pushed the opposition right inside the city walls, where Germanus and his cohorts had crushed all but a few small pockets of resistance and had joined forces with Aetius on the west of the city. That was the good news. There remained the question of the large force on the hills to the east of Verulamium. Why had the Vortigern not yet deployed these troops? *And what has happened to Lupus? The father of my child. Does he still live?*

※   ※   ※

Is this death? Am I dead? I feel nothing; but I still feel. I have a pulse; I hear my breathing; I can touch my belt. Where am I? What am I? If I am no more, why does my leg hurt? Lupus decided that the pain in his thigh was real and that he was not dead, despite appearances to the contrary and especially his recent fall. He could hear nothing, and he could see nothing: total darkness. He reached out his arms and felt cold; not the cold of death, but the cold of brick and stone, as built by humans, not gods or devils. *I am still alive! This is life, not death!*

Lupus tried to stand; the pain was excruciating. He laughed. *Dead people do not break their legs!* Lupus found that if he stood on his right leg only and bent his left slightly at the knee, the pain was bearable. He leaned on the wall of his man-made Hades. Sweat rolled down his forehead; the liquid stung his eyes. He thought of Ambrosius and what it would be like to lose an eye; just to have the socket left; not to be able to see properly; to be blind. Lupus shuddered. A blast of cold air assailed him. Was hell as cold as this? Light blinded him as his prison door opened. The last few moments had been full of surprises, but the sight that greeted him now was the biggest surprise of all.

'Thank God! It's you. I thought I had breathed my last! You two are the prettiest sight that I have ever seen. You really are!'

※   ※   ※

Germanus and Aetius could not understand how any of the Vortigern's troops could still be defending the temple of Albanus.

'Men seem to spring up from nowhere. No sooner have we cut one lot down than more appear.'

'Indeed, my Lord Aetius. But there is a good reason for that. They must be using the underground tunnels.'

'Tunnels, Germanus?'

'Don't look surprised, Aetius. You are well aware of all the underground networks in Roma, Constantinopolis and all our major cities. Why not in places like Londinium and Verulamium?'

Aetius shrugged.

'This province is not as backward as you might believe. Why do you think it is proving such an attractive battle ground?'

'I know, my old friend. Who controls Britannia controls the western empire, and more.'

'And more? What does that mean?'

'Nothing, Germanus.'

'I know you too well Aetius. When you say "nothing", that means everything. So, tell me.'

'When we have captured and killed the Vortigern.'

'Uh-oh, Aetius. Captured yes, killed no.'

CHAPTER 62

The Vortigern's final attack is launched

'Well?'

'Well, what?'

'How is the battle going?'

'What do you think, my Lord?'

'Are we lost?'

'Not yet, but at the present rate, we soon will be.'

The Vortigern could hear the noise of battle getting ever closer to the encampment on the top of the hills to the east of Verulamium.

'Why are we in this position Agricola? We were supposed to be invincible, with our superior numbers!'

'We bargained without Germanus. Now I understand why you wanted him on your side all those months ago. Having his military genius makes a big difference.' The Vortigern's *magister militum* swigged down a glass of wine in one go before turning to Pelagius.

'And what is your take on all this, priest?'

'Well, if Agricola's turncoat father had not betrayed us and buggered off to the other side, we might not have been so badly off as we now seem to be. That and the fact that Aetius was supposed to be fighting for us too.'

'My father and I do not see eye to eye, as you will be aware, but I did not think that he would do this to us. There must be something motivating him other than his dislike for me, and you two, for that matter.'

The Vortigern beckoned a *servus* to refill his glass. He looked at Agricola and Pelagius. *God, they look worn out! Hengest should be here by now; we need a council of war and need it quickly!*

'You know what is motivating Severianus and Aetius?'

Agricola and Pelagius shook their heads in tandem.

'Not power, not glory, not religion; *aureo hamo piscari.'*

Agricola and Pelagius nodded in time with each other.

'Money talks. It does indeed. But, my Lord, what have they been offered beyond what you have been intending to pay them?'

'If I knew that, Agricola, they would be fighting for us now, because whatever that double-crossing rat Coelestinus has offered them, I would have doubled it!'

'Then why don't you, my Lord? It is not too late. I, we, have never seen you so indecisive or so low. You can still win this battle and go on to win the war!'

Do I want to win the battle; do I want to be Imperator any longer? I grow tired of all this. I have ruled this land for ten years. I thought to make it the centre of a new world order; Londinium *as the new* Roma. *But I cannot do it on my own, and my high command are failing. They know it, and I know it. Coelestinus has gained the upper hand. He has outwitted and outmanouevred Galla Placidia and made it well nigh impossible for me to persuade Aetius and Severianus into my fold ever again.*

So, my Lord Vortigern, what are your orders now?'

'Welcome, my Lord Hengest. We have been waiting for you. Wine?'

'No thanks. Ale, if there is any left.'

The Vortigern snapped his fingers and the *servus* went to find some beer for the *foederatus.* 'It does not go well, does it, Hengest?'

Hengest looked at the Vortigern, then at his *magister militum* and his high priest. 'No, my Lord, it does not. The last of my men have gone through the tunnels and up into the temple of Albanus. I have no more troops to throw into the fray inside the city walls and the rest of our armies are hard pressed on every side now. The reserve troops in the east are unable to break out from their camps and join us. Aetius and Severianus are great commanders, and they are being led by someone who is even greater.'

'You mean Germanus?'

'I do. He has turned all those men and women into a real fighting force. He did that from the start when we attacked them in Viroconium and were repelled. What do you Romans say? *Unguibus et rostro*; with all their might?'

Pelagius snorted. 'Very good Hengest. We will make a Roman of you yet!'

'Not if I have anything to do with it, you won't! Once a Saxon, always a Saxon. And if you lot do not turn this battle round to our advantage soon, then I am buggering off home. You know what is really impressive about Germanus and what he has done?'

Hengest's three comrades shook their heads.

'He has used this Christianity very cleverly. The cross on the shields, the marrying of the faith with pagan beliefs, and the Roman and Prythonic patriotism. They are a fighting force because they have a common enemy; you three! We do not have the same binding agent. We never will have!'

The Vortigern took one last swig of his wine, put the glass down on the table and clasped his hands. 'Very well. You want me to retreat, I can tell. To withdraw and regroup. I will not do that: never! *Tu ne cede malis sed contra audentior ito!*' Do you know what that means, Hengest?'

Hengest shook his head.

'I thought not. Your Roman education will be continued later. Tell him Pelagius.'

'Yes, your Majesty. It means "Yield not to misfortunes but advance all the more boldly against them".'

'Agricola, have my horse readied. I am going to lead the final attack. I have a plan, and it will work beyond your, and my, wildest dreams.'

CHAPTER 63

A wanderer returns

Patricius was home: the villa looked lovelier than ever. Germanus was barking orders to senior members of the Armorican Guard, while Eustachia was entertaining ladies from the neighbouring villas. Segovax was playing with him and Aello, who barked and scampered round the courtyard while man and boy played gladiators. Segovax always let him win, or so Patricius used to think, though not without a fight. Thanks to Segovax, Patricius had become a fine swordsman, even as a boy. He was proud that his father Germanus was proud of him. And his father had started to talk to him about his future; about how one day he would govern, just as Germanus had governed. 'Who knows?' Germanus had said, 'one day, my son, yous might become a great Roman general; even greater things might happen. *Imperator*, perhaps?' The two of them had laughed at the thought; but deep down, Patricius warmed to the idea of ruling the western empire; he liked that idea very much.

Dream turned to nightmare. He saw his father leaving for Roma. Patricius had asked Lupus why they were going. His adopted brother had no answer; just that the Pontifex had summoned Germanus for talks and Lupus was to go as his personal assistant. Even in his troubled sleep, Patricius could feel the sadness of his father's goodbye. His mother's face showed the grief of parting. She had gone to pray in the private chapel as soon as Germanus and Lupus had left the villa. Eustachia's face appeared before Patricius. At first, she was smiling, then the face grew pale and grey, the hair unkempt. Her hands hid her eyes; he heard her crying in long low moans. The sky grew dark. Patricius felt as if he were being drawn into a long dark tunnel. Strange men were on either side of him, with knives and spears in their hands. They attacked him, causing him to bleed. Ahead, he could see Segovax, beckoning him to follow down the tunnel. Patricius could not move. They managed to touch fingertips and then Segovax, dear old Segovax, was dragged away. He saw his father's foreman being executed, over, and over again.

'We are here. You should wake now.'

Patricius was relieved to have escaped from his dream-cum-nightmare. 'Where are we?'

'Just off the coast of Armorica', the *navicularius* answered. 'You had better get ready. I do not want to stay long. Is there anyone on shore to greet you?'

Patricius shook his head. It would be a long way back to the villa. He would have to find a route that took him past friends' houses or towns that he knew from the many times when he had travelled round the diocese with his father. That all seemed such a long time ago! *It will be so good to get back home; to see mother and father and Segovax and Aello.* Patricius smiled at the thought of throwing sticks for his dog and seeing the silly thing scamper after them like a mad thing, running back to its master, ever so pleased that the projectile had been retrieved safely and efficiently.

The ship's captain nudged Patricius and helped him to his feet. The heave of the vessel caught him off balance and it took three attempts before he was fully upright. Ahead lay the Gallic coast. The harbour looked deserted. As they drew into dock, Patricius could see but a single figure. The long white hair and beard blew wildly in the breeze. That could only be one person!

'Memor! Memor! It's me!' Patricius began to wave, forgetting that the old *haruspex* was blind. Even so, Memor put his hands up in reply. Before the ship had moored, Patricius had jumped off and run to greet the old man.

'Memor! It is so good to see you. You are a sight for sore eyes!'

'So are you, Patricius; or at least you would be if I were not blind!' The two of them laughed.

'Where have you been, my son? We had no idea what had happened to you. I could not find you. You were lost to us all. You must have been to far away for my powers to find you.'

'I have been a long way away, Memor. But I am still alive, thanks to Segovax. He spirited me away before the *Saxoni* came. I wanted to stay and fight but he insisted that I leave.'

'So where did you go?'

Patricius could see that there were tears in Memor's eyes as he spoke.

'I was taken to Hibernia. Do you know of it?'

Memor nodded, slowly.

'I do. It is across the waters to the west. What happened to you there?'

'That is a long story and there are things I wish had never happened. I would much rather know about my parents and Segovax, and Aello, of course! Tell me. How are they all? And what of Lupus? How did he and my father fare in Roma? Is all well at the villa?'

The *haruspex* put his arms on Patricius's shoulders. 'There is much that you need to know, my son. Come, let us eat before we set out home and I will tell you the story of Germanus the Gaul, and his adventures in Britannia.'

Patricius was shocked. Memor put a finger to his mouth to silence the young man.

'Do not be afraid of what you are about to hear. There is much more in this story that has yet to happen; the adventures are far from finished and you will play a big part from now on.'

CHAPTER 64

A disappearance and an appearance

'Where is he?'

The Temple of Albanus was empty. Not a single soul was left alive. There were plenty of dead bodies strewn about the shrine, but no-one still breathed apart, that is, from the men and women who had fought their way on Aureliana's behalf into the holy place of Albion. Many had marvelled at what they saw inside the building: the high ceiling, the ornate decorations, the rich and varied statues all around the outer walls and the massive pillars that held the structure in place. Above all, the huge effigy of Albanus himself at the far end of the basilica made the invading army stop in its tracks and look up at the holy martyr's face. The glowing eyes stared down as if to admonish those who sought to defile this holy place. Smoke spewed forth from Alban's mouth. Germanus roused the troops from their torpor, ordering them to check all the carcasses to locate Lupus. But he was nowhere to be seen.

'He must have escaped, Germanus.'

'Or been captured.'

'Will he talk?'

Germanus shrugged his shoulders. 'Not if he has learnt everything that I have taught him. But he is still only a boy inside, and a timid one at that, if the truth be known.'

Aureliana was about to speak when Lucius rushed into the temple and alerted them to the fact that a new attack was now taking place immediately to the east of Verulamium. Germanus and Aureliana rushed out of the shrine, mounted out and rode to the eastern city gates. They were so taken aback by the Vortigern's onslaught that for a good while they thought that the battle, a conflict that they expected to have won within the hour, was now turning against them once more, and their enemy might yet score a great victory. Aureliana was the one to point out how the Vortigern was at last leading his troops from the front and, in so doing, had given them a fresh energy and fight that was remarkable. Germanus responded by noticing how the opposition was, for the first time, being led in classic Roman style in a way that he had not seen since the time of Magnus Maximus. *Magnus Maximus! My hero! Perhaps I should tell Aureliana what nearly happened back then. What might have been. How different my life would be now if I had gone over to his side!*

'Come, Aureliana, at last we have a worthy foe!'

'How so, Germanus? I thought we had far superior forces to theirs!'

'*Una salus victis nullam sperare salutem.*'

'Indeed. "Knowing there is no hope can give one the courage to fight and win".'

'Yes, my Queen. That makes the Vortigern more dangerous than ever.' Germanus regrouped his troops and horsemen and rode out to meet the Vortigern. The focus of the conflict returned to the fields immediately to the east of the city walls. Germanus and Aureliana responded to the enemy's three-pronged attack with a five-pronged response. The Vortigern's army was no pushover; quite the opposite, in fact, for it soon became obvious that the crack troops had been held back to the last and these were men who were trained to the highest Roman standards and been battle hardened in the process.

Germanus thought the battle would never end. The forces were evenly matched in both size and skill. Moves were countered and matched;

advances repelled and met with opposing surges. He decided eventually that there was only one way to break the deadlock. *Occasionem cognosce* he shouted to Aureliana as he rode headlong towards the Vortigern. He recognised the opportunity as his enemy came into the very centre of the fighting.

Germanus and the Vortigern engaged each other, thrusting, and parrying, while still on horseback. Germanus was the first to draw blood with a blow to the Vortigern's arm. A spear hit home in the General's mount, which fell from under him. The Vortigern jumped off his horse immediately, though Germanus had lept to his feet and was ready to continue the struggle, *gladius* and *scutum* in his hands. He thought back to the glory days when he had presided over gladiatorial contests in the amphitheatres of Armorica. They were long gone, but here he now was in the fight to end all fights.

Germanus felt the years fall off him as he and the Vortigern circled each other, waiting for their opponent to make the next move. No longer was he a senior commander but a young soldier ready to make his mark. He had not been so close to the Vortigern before. The General thought his opponent too slight to be a serious threat to his superiority in the fight, but what the Vortigern lacked in sheer strength he gained in nimble footwork and was too quick for Germanus's sword-strikes to yield blood.

Germanus thought back to that night when he and Aureliana had bonded after their fight. She had proved a worthy opponent, and now here he was struggling against another one. Every tactic that the General tried was countered. It was as if they had attended the same military school. Had they been? Germanus began to wonder if they had been comrades, just as he and Aetius had attended the same establishment as young soldiers.

Then there came a point when Germanus felt that the Vortigern was tiring. The General went for the oldest trick in the book: he entwined his right leg round that of his opponent, catching him off balance and throwing him to the ground. Before the Vortigern could get up, Germanus was on top of him, with his *gladius* at his enemy's throat.

'At last, I have you, my Lord Vortigern. Surrender, before I cut your throat with this sword!'

Germanus gasped as he saw that his opponent was crying. The tears rolled down the Vortigern's cheeks and onto Germanus's hands.

'What did you do with the pendant that I sent to you? Do you remember that pendant; you know, the one that you gave my mother all those years ago?'

Germanus pulled off the Vortigern's headgear as he kneeled on his opponent's arms. 'Your mother? God, who are you?'

'Your son, Germanus. Sevira was my mother, and you are my father!'

To be continued

Printed in the United States
by Baker & Taylor Publisher Services